WITCHES & WHISKY

Wendy Hewlett

This book is a work of fiction. All names, characters, places, and events are a result of the author's imagination or are used in a fictitious manner and any similarities to real life names, places, and events are strictly coincidental.

This book may not be reproduced in whole or in part without permission. Making or distributing electronic copies of this book infringes upon copyright laws and could subject the infringer to criminal or civil liability.

To Andrew, who I miss so much.
I love you to infibity & beyond.

Prologue

Edinburgh 2004

Mairie sat on the edge of Magaidh's bed, curling her daughter's long dark hair between her fingers. 'It's time to sleep, Magaidh darling.'

'Can I have one more story, mummy?'

Mairie gave Magaidh the brightest smile she could manage. 'Aye, one more, my darling. But, you must listen carefully.'

Magaidh bounced her head up and down, eyes wide in anticipation and her stuffed dog, Rufus, cuddled close.

'There once was an order of men. Distinguished men, they were. Leaders in their fields or destined to become them.'

'Were they royalty, mummy?'

'No, *mo ghràdh.*' Only in their own minds, Mairie thought. 'Just men who thought they were above others. Men who took offence to women stepping out of line.'

Magaidh's brows drew together. 'Why did they step out of the queue?'

'Out of the mouths of babes,' Mairie said as she laughed then tapped her finger on the tip of her daughter's pert nose. 'They didn't step out of the queue, my wee darling. They dared to excel in fields traditionally held by men. They

1

refused to submit to the will of the men of the order. These men felt threatened by strong women, do you ken?'

'Because they were better at their jobs than the men?'

Mairie laughed again. 'Not necessarily. But, they were successful, aye? These men felt this made them look inferior and they couldn't have that.'

Magaidh screwed up her wee nose as if she smelled an offensive scent. 'But, you're a successful woman, mummy. Does that make men look bad?'

'It shouldn't. But, these men are insecure. They want to control women, to keep them barefoot and pregnant in the kitchen.'

'No man will ever keep me in the kitchen.' Magaidh crossed her long arms over her chest and pouted. 'I'm going to be as successful as any man.'

'Aye, that you are, Magaidh Ealasaid Ghlais. That you are.' Goddess, she would miss these sweet moments with her precocious wee lass. 'The order of men were so afraid of these women outdoing them that they decided to take matters into their own hands and rid themselves of the threats.'

Magaidh's nose screwed up again as she scowled up at her mother. 'They have no right.'

'No, they don't. And these men got away with their evil doings for many years until a clever young woman and her friends began to pick away at the layers of their deceptions and coverups.'

'The polis?'

'Aye, the young woman and her friends are the polis.'

'And they put the men in gaol?'

Goddess, she hoped so, for there were two endings Mairie foresaw. 'Aye, my wee darling. Justice was served. Now, listen carefully, because this is the important part.'

'Aye, I'm listening,' Magaidh said with a bob of her head.

Mairie whispered, 'The key to justice is through a woman

2

named Allan.'

'I don't understand,' Magaidh said, her face pinched.

Mairie leaned over and kissed her daughter's forehead. 'You will when the time is right, my wee warrior.' She scooped her daughter into her arms. 'And now it's time to sleep. I love you, *mo ghràdh* Magaidh.'

'I love you too, mummy.' Magaidh wrapped her arms around Mairie's neck and pressed her nose into her hair. Then she turned on her side, buried her nose in Rufus's fur, and closed her eyes. The stories mummy told her tonight were strange, but mummy never told stories without meaning. Magaidh just had to figure out what it was.

Mairie waited until her daughter was fast asleep before she cast the spell. Come tomorrow, Magaidh's memories would be lost. She wouldn't remember the horrific events that would come to pass this night, nor the love Malcolm and Mairie had for their wee darling. That part hurt more than anything, but it couldn't be avoided. Wiping her daughter's memories was the only way Mairie could save her life.

That done, Mairie laid down next to Magaidh and snuggled into her daughter, holding her and inhaling the sweet smell of her child one last time.

Then, wiping the tears from her eyes, she went to her husband, holding him, loving him, one last time. Long after they made love and Malcolm slipped into the dream world, Mairie whispered, 'They're coming for us now.'

Malcolm stirred and turned to his wife, mumbling, 'Who's coming, love?'

'Witch hunters.'

Chapter 1

Edinburgh 2022

The bumpy drive up the cobblestones of the Royal Mile was made difficult by the darkness and the haar – the thick Scottish fog that drifted in from the North Sea. Detective Constable Maggie Glass could barely see the bonnet of her steel blue Range Rover, never mind the road ahead. Only the multitude of flashing blue lights through the haar guided her up Castlehill to the Esplanade of Edinburgh Castle.

After showing her warrant card to the constables guarding the barricades at the entrance to the Esplanade, Maggie was presented with a package containing crime scene PPE. She pulled the Range Rover between a Police Scotland marked Peugeot 308 and a red and yellow fire engine. It wasn't unheard of for the fire brigade to attend a crime scene, but it gave Maggie pause to wonder why several fire engines were present. The only thing she'd been told by dispatch was that a body had been discovered on the Esplanade. She preferred it that way. The less she was told, the more open-minded she entered a crime scene. A quick peek in the rearview mirror showed the sleep crease in her left cheek remained. *Ah well, maybe no one would notice in the haar.*

Two uniformed constables awaited her as she emerged

from the vehicle. The slim female with a lock of blonde hair escaping from the hood of her white crime scene coveralls took a step forward. 'DC Glass.'

'PC Dunn,' Maggie said with a quick nod, her eyes on the similarly clad male constable at Dunn's shoulder.

'Should have known they'd send you,' he said.

'How's that, PC Murray?' Maggie asked, her pale hazel eyes as cold as the misty fog.

'Well, it's yer speciality, aye?'

Maggie forced her eyes from Murray, addressing Dunn. 'Perhaps you'd show me the body.' She didn't want to hear another word from Murray. His comments told her everything she needed to know. This was no ordinary death. Maggie glanced over to where she knew the entrance to Edinburgh Castle stood at the far end of the Esplanade and saw only a faint glow of lights. She began to don her protective equipment over her crisp, tailored suit – face mask, gloves, crime scene coveralls, overshoes, and a second pair of gloves.

'Right,' Dunn said as Maggie dressed. 'The Procurator Fiscal has been notified and forensic services are en route.'

Maggie followed Dunn's path to the body, stepping over two fire hoses. She stopped in her tracks as a heap of charred wood came into view near the entrance to the Esplanade. She'd driven right past it and hadn't seen it for the fog. Tendrils of smoke oozed up out of the black remnants to mingle with the mist. The smell of burnt wood and charred flesh permeated the damp air. And something else. Maggie lifted her head and sniffed. Petrol.

A cold shiver ran up Maggie's spine and an image of leaping flames flashed through her brain. That particular combination of scents was familiar in some far recess of her mind.

Dunn turned to find Maggie had stopped several feet

behind her, standing stiffly and staring off into space. 'DC Glass?'

The sound of Dunn's voice jolted Maggie back to the present. She focused on the dark spire rising from the centre of the mass of burnt wood and the roasted remains attached to it, mouth gaping as if in mid-scream. 'Fuck sake. She's been burned at the stake.'

'She?' The body was so severely burned, Dunn hadn't been able to determine the sex.

Ignoring Dunn's question, Maggie surveyed the area as far as the fog allowed. She couldn't see it, but on a wall only feet away from this atrocity was the Witches' Well – a cast-iron fountain and plaque honouring the hundreds of women accused of witchery and burned at the stake on this very spot between the sixteenth and seventeenth centuries. Firemen and police officers lingered in the periphery, drifting in and out of the fog like ghosts. It was eerily silent, as if everyone was too shocked at the grisly display for words. The fire brigade significantly contaminated the crime scene extinguishing the flames. Still, there was nothing they could have done to prevent it.

'Start knocking on doors,' Maggie said to Dunn. 'Take PC Murray with you.'

'No one will have seen anything with the haar.'

Did they pick this night for that very reason? Maggie wondered. Had they waited for the haar to roll in to give them cover to commit this heinous act in such an open and populated space? 'No,' she answered Dunn. 'But they may have heard something or seen the glow of the flames.'

Dunn motioned for Murray to join her as she walked away.

Maggie stepped closer to the body, the acrid odours continuing to tug at the threads of memories long repressed – furious flames, burning flesh, primal screams. She shook her head and forced her gaze upon the ruined face on the stake.

'May the Goddess Hekate light your path to the other side,' she whispered.

* * *

The rumble of Detective Inspector Will MacLeod's beat-up yellow Fiat preceded its presence on the Esplanade by minutes. In contrast to Maggie's crisp and pressed suit, MacLeod's appeared as though he'd been wearing it since his promotion out of uniform. It took another few minutes for him to struggle into his PPE next to his sad wee car. He lit a fag as he stepped to Maggie's side and surveyed the heinous sight.

'Mhac na galla,' he said on an exhale of smoke. When it came to expletives, MacLeod preferred Gaelic, this particular one translating to *son of a bitch*. 'What evil is this?' As Maggie turned her head, MacLeod met her gaze, noting her watery eyes, her dark lashes wet with unshed tears.

'The worst kind, I suppose,' she answered in a quiet voice. 'The worst kind.'

He would have offered her comfort if he thought she'd accept it. 'Catch me up then, Glass.'

She told him the little she knew and that Dunn reported finding two witnesses to a woman's horrific screams at approximately 3:20 am. Two vehicles were heard driving away, only the glow of head and tail lights seen through the haar. 'The 999 caller saw the glow of the flames from her bedroom window after hearing the screams.' She pointed to the building on their left, whose entrance stood behind a wrought iron fence with a gate next to the Witches' Well.

'The haar provided the perfect cover. Convenient or planned?'

'Hard to say,' Maggie answered. 'But my gut says planned.'

MacLeod raised an eyebrow as he drew on his cigarette. 'What else does your gut tell you?'

'With two vehicles leaving the scene, we know that more than one suspect is involved. Whoever they are, they're misogynists.'

'How so?'

Maggie's blood began to boil, a fury she couldn't explain bubbling to the surface. 'An estimated four thousand women were murdered in this country on the premise of being witches. Only a misogynistic society could be responsible for that. But, imitating the barbaric act nearly three hundred years later? It's a reprehensible act of misogyny.'

MacLeod almost wished he hadn't asked. Maggie's answer was disturbing, to say the least. What concerned him most was the insinuation there would be more murders. He left unspoken the similarities between this case and the one years ago that fuelled his determination to make detective and the Major Investigations Team. 'You presume the victim is female.'

'A presumption I'm willing to risk.'

'Careful, Glass. *My* gut tells me we need to dot every i on this one.'

As he walked back to his car, Maggie called out, 'I thought you were going to take that sorry excuse for a motor to the garage.'

MacLeod raised his hands in the air without turning back. 'We don't all have deep bank accounts to provide us with a shiny new hundred and twenty thousand quid Range Rover, DC.'

Ow, that one hurt. Maggie glanced around to see how many ears picked up on that little nugget. Not that it was a secret. Maggie's background and finances were fodder for the water cooler gossip. Several heads turned as she glanced around. Few dared say it to her face, but many resented her wealth. She doubted they would feel the same if they understood the price she paid for it.

She would have offered to pay to have MacLeod's muffler replaced if she thought he would accept it.

* * *

Maggie arrived at the St. Leonard's Police Station with two coffees in hand. She set one on DI MacLeod's desk before settling into her seat across from him.

MacLeod peeled the lid back on the coffee and took a long sip. 'Bless you. You've discovered the way to my heart.'

Maggie scoffed. 'Keep dreaming, darling. What have you got?'

'No similar cases. Recently, at least. We'll have to rely on dental records to identify our victim.'

'Our female victim,' Maggie cut in. 'Confirmed by the pathologist. The victim's fists were clenched. If there's evidence under her fingernails, it may have been preserved.'

'Don't get your hopes up. The body curls up when it's burned like that.'

Maggie knew it, but it seemed like the only sliver of hope. She needed something to cling to. 'Forensics are working the scene.'

MacLeod nodded, tapping a pencil on his desktop. 'I thought maybe you could reach out to the witch community. Ask if anyone's unaccounted for.'

Maggie raised her eyebrows, gawking at him over their desks. 'The witch community?'

'Well, you know what they say about you?'

'*They* say a lot about me.' Maggie knew it was petty, but she enjoyed watching MacLeod squirm in his seat.

'Aye, I suppose.' He cleared his throat. 'They say you're a witch.'

Maggie's dark fringe feathered down over one eye as she leaned over the desk. 'And what do you say?'

The edge of MacLeod's mouth twitched before a wide grin spread across his face. 'You know me well enough to know

I'm not the judgemental sort.'

'So you think I'm a witch?'

'Aren't you?'

'No.' Not a practising one anyway. 'You can't believe everything you hear, MacLeod.'

'Apparently not. I apologise. I didn't mean to offend you.'

'You didn't.' Being labelled a witch was not at all offensive, in Maggie's opinion. 'I know someone I can ask. I'll look into it.'

* * *

Maggie drove to Clermiston in northwest Edinburgh, to the quaint little house that had been her childhood home from the age of eight. All memories before that time remained locked away. Until this morning. The flames. The screams. Her heart raced as she parked the car. She was well aware her memories had been seized by traumatic events and the death of her parents. Any details beyond that she didn't have. She could have asked Iona. She could have looked for the investigative files on her parents' murders. She hadn't been ready.

Iona Bryars opened the front door before Maggie was out of her car. Despite her fifty-odd years, she maintained a youthful beauty with pale, delicate skin accentuating a flowing mane of flaming red hair. She bussed Maggie's cheeks when she arrived on the doorstep. 'To what do I owe this pleasure? It's not like you to visit during a workday.' Iona smiled brightly as she drew a finger lightly across Maggie's brow, righting her unruly fringe.

Maggie grinned back at her godmother. 'Sorry, I should have visited before now. It just seems like every day is a workday.'

'Then you're working too hard, hen. Come in. The kettle's on.'

Maggie removed her overcoat as she entered the house,

depositing it on a peg next to the door before following Iona through the lounge to the kitchen. 'I actually came to ask a favour.'

'Ask away.'

'You're so easy,' Maggie said with a chuckle. She crossed to the hob, turned off the gas, and filled the teapot with boiling water as Iona prepared the cups, milk, and sugar.

They brought the tea into the lounge and Maggie made herself comfortable on the settee before posing her question. 'I wondered if you could check in with the local covens. Ask if anyone is missing.'

Iona looked up sharply from stirring her tea. 'Missing? What's happened?'

'You know I can't say much, but a woman's body was discovered this morning and we need to identify her.'

'You believe she's a witch?'

'She may be.'

'Can you describe her?'

The image of the torched body crystallised in Maggie's mind, followed quickly by roaring flames. It took a moment before she could offer an answer. 'I'm afraid she was unrecognisable.'

Iona leaned over, placing her hand over Maggie's. 'I'm sorry. I don't know why you picked such a morbid career.'

Maggie turned her palm up, wrapping her fingers around Iona's hand. 'Aye, you do.'

Chapter 2

Maggie arrived back at her desk to find MacLeod in the same position as when she left. She knew better than to assume he'd done nothing. He preferred to investigate from his desk when he could, but it didn't mean he hadn't been working the case. 'Anything new?' she asked.

MacLeod got to his feet, pulling his Columbo style overcoat from the back of his chair. 'Come on then. I'm away out for a fag.'

Maggie didn't smoke, but followed MacLeod out to the back of the building, where they often discussed cases. She waited patiently with her hands in her coat pockets while he lit up, getting his hit of nicotine before he would divulge any information.

'This one's going to be a baw breaker, Glass. I talked to Missing Persons, but there's not much they can do without a description until the poor lass is identified. We're hoping to get reports from forensics and the pathologist tomorrow. The only other thing I can suggest is canvasing.'

Maggie nodded. He'd confirmed her own thoughts. 'I don't even have a clue on the motive. Why burn a woman like that? Are they sending a message?' Just thinking about it made her want to punch something. As far as women's rights had come, there was still a long way to go. 'I'll head back up to the Esplanade and knock on some doors.' She also wanted another look at the scene in the daylight with the fog beginning to lift.

'Ring me if you need anything.' MacLeod watched Maggie disappear back into the building, taking a long haul on his cigarette. He was only twelve years older than his new partner, but felt a deep paternal connection to her. A link that went back years to a shared moment in the past which Maggie had no memory of. Before this investigation was over, he feared that may no longer be the case.

* * *

The body had been removed from the scene before Maggie left that morning, but forensics techs in their protective white coveralls continued to sift through the charcoaled remains of the fire. Maggie approached slowly, surveying the heap of burnt wood and the blackened tarmac. She could still smell the sickening mixture of burnt flesh and wood. The roaring flames and primal screams flashed through her mind again. She wasn't sure if the wind had picked up or the heinous vision had turned her cold. She tugged her coat tighter, crossing her arms over her abdomen.

'Magaidh Ghlais?'

Maggie turned despite the use of her Gaelic name. She'd changed it years ago to distance herself from her parents' company – Ghlais Whisky. The bullying of the child who owned one of the most successful whisky businesses in the UK had been relentless. Maggie changed schools and her name, not that it helped much. People still seemed to know who she was.

She scrutinised the woman before her, taking in the slick business suit, expensive wool coat, perfectly coiffed blond hair, and carefully applied makeup. If Maggie hadn't recognised Kaleigh Logan, she still would have pegged her for a reporter. *Shite.* 'No comment. You shouldn't be here.'

She glanced around, looking for a uniformed officer to escort Logan off the Esplanade.

Kaleigh took a step forward, determined to get her question in and this young woman's reaction before being ejected from the crime scene. She wondered if Magaidh Ghlais realised how closely she resembled her mother. 'Is this case connected to your parents' murder?'

Maggie couldn't help herself. Logan's question definitely piqued her interest. 'How so?'

To say she was disappointed with Ghlais's reaction would be an understatement. Her face didn't give anything away. It remained cold and her pale hazel eyes were like lasers, holding Kaleigh in place. 'It's obvious, isn't it? The burning at the stake?'

The flames lashed furiously as primal screams pierced the air over the roar of the fire. Maggie couldn't move her head, couldn't turn away from the sight of the skin melting away from her mother's face.

'Ms. Ghlais, I'm so sorry.' Kaleigh grabbed onto Maggie's arms to steady her. The colour had drained from her face and her eyes went from laser-sharp to unfocused in a split second. Clearly, Magaidh Ghlais hadn't known how her parents died.

Maggie snapped out of the memory and pulled her arms from Kaleigh's grasp. Gripping Kaleigh's bicep, she marched her around the mobile forensics unit, which blocked the view of the crime scene from the tourists on the Royal Mile, and over to the constables guarding access to the Esplanade.

As Maggie released her, Kaleigh turned back. 'I really am sorry I upset you, but I can help. I covered your parents' murders.' It wasn't often she felt remorse for her actions, but it pained her to see Ghlais so hurt for some reason. She handed Maggie her card. 'Contact me when you're ready.'

Maggie watched until Kaleigh disappeared around the corner at the Castle Wynd stairs next to the Cannonball, confident that she wouldn't be contacting Kaleigh Logan. She didn't know whether she wanted to scream or throw up. Maggie spun around to the constables guarding the entrance to the Esplanade. 'How the devil did she get by you?'

The two constables looked at each other, then back at Maggie. 'She didnae come in this way, DC.'

Maggie threw her hands up in the air. 'It's the only way in.'

'Well, there has to be another as she didnae come through here.'

Maggie walked back onto the Esplanade, searching every direction before quickly stepping over to the wall on the south side. She looked down the grassy hill to the street below. There's no way Logan could have climbed up that steep hill in heels and Maggie couldn't see a path trampled in the grass. Even if she'd managed the climb, Logan wouldn't have been able to scale the wall without a grappling hook or something. She turned around, eyeing the building with its door next to the Witches' Well. It had to have another entrance.

Maggie marched over to the cream coloured building with brown trim and went through the wrought iron gate. The door leading into the flats stood to her left. To the right was an archway with a sign on the wall next to it stating *Private Garden*. She went through the archway and down a pathway and steps. Not only did she discover another entrance to the building, but the steps led directly down to a small cobblestone street – Ramsay Gardens. Logan wouldn't have even needed to go through the building to access the Esplanade.

Maggie sat in her car after posting another uniformed officer at the gate between the building and the Esplanade. Now that the memory of her mother's face melting crawled from the recesses of her mind, she'd never be rid of it. She wished she could go back to yesterday when she was blissfully unaware of the method in which her parents were murdered. Was it possible those responsible for this murder were also responsible for her parents' murders nearly twenty years ago? *Shite*. She would have to look at the investigative files from her parents' murders. She pulled her mobile from her pocket and rang MacLeod.

* * *

Maggie didn't go back to the office. MacLeod wasn't going to let her near the files from her parents' case. She'd be lucky if the Inspector didn't pull her from the investigation altogether, given her possible connection to it. It was too early to tell.

She found herself sitting at the bar in The Regent, sipping a glass of eighteen-year-old single malt Ghlais whisky. She may not have anything to do with running the company she owned, but she was still loyal to the brand. Besides, it was damn good whisky.

'Rough day?' PC Nichola Dunn asked as she took the stool next to Maggie, dressed in faded jeans, a grey Edinburgh hoodie, and a black puffer jacket. Her blonde hair was loose and hung down past her shoulders in waves.

'It's not over yet,' Maggie answered without looking up from her drink. 'Did you get some sleep?'

'Not much. I kept seeing that woman. It's going to be a while before I get over that one.' Nichola never slept well when she worked night shifts, but she'd tossed and turned most of the day. It was going to be a long night.

'Yeah, I ken what you mean.' Maggie took a slow sip of her whisky before turning to Nichola. 'MacLeod call you?'

'No. Should he have?'

Before Maggie could answer, Ainsley, the pixie-haired barkeep, placed a cup of coffee on the bar in front of Nichola and the truth hit her. 'Ainsley, you called Nichola?'

Ainsley fisted her hands on her hips as if affronted by the accusation. 'I most certainly did not.' She winked at Nichola and added, 'I texted her.'

Maggie rolled her eyes, but she couldn't be angry at her friends for caring about her. 'I'm okay. I just needed a wee dram and a think.'

As Ainsley busied herself with another customer, Nichola asked, 'What's upset you then? This case?'

'Aye, I suppose.' Maggie wasn't ready to talk about the memory this case triggered and when she was, it was Iona she needed to speak to first.

'Any leads?'

'Maybe. A related case from years ago. MacLeod's looking into it.'

Maggie's mobile rang and MacLeod's name displayed on her screen. As much as she dreaded answering, she had no choice. 'Glass.'

'We may have a lead on the identity of our victim. Jamie Kenmore didn't show up for work this morning. Her PA went to her house to check on her. There are signs of a struggle and Kenmore isn't there.'

'Why does that name sound familiar?'

'She's the CEO of the most successful media relations firm in the country.'

Gold Star. Ghlais Whisky used their services. In fact, Gold Star was partly responsible for the considerable success of Ghlais. 'Give me an address. I'm on my way.'

* * *

Several police vehicles were parked outside Jamie Kenmore's four-storey Georgian home on Charlotte Square in the New Town, just a few doors away from Bute House, the First Minister's official residence. Maggie had considered a house across the Square from Kenmore's when she was in the market for a place. She ruled it out simply because there was far too much space for her alone. She climbed the stairs to Kenmore's front door, donning the paper booties provided by the constable documenting entrance to the crime scene before signing in.

She noted the damage to the door jamb before stepping into the foyer. That was sloppy, she thought. The house's layout was similar to the one Maggie had viewed, but it differed significantly in the decor. The one Maggie toured was modern and comfortable, while Kenmore clearly preferred the stiff Georgian style.

MacLeod stood in the centre of the lounge to her left, waving her over.

Maggie took her time taking a mental inventory of the room before making her way to MacLeod. The pale yellow walls were lined with old portrait paintings, except for the massive one hanging over the fireplace – a recent portrait seemingly of Kenmore herself. *How did she live with all of these people staring down at her? Creepy.* Two antique settees faced each other in front of the fireplace, separated by a Queen Anne coffee table with curved legs resembling a cat. A crystal vase lay smashed a few feet from the table. The chair at an antique mahogany writing desk was overturned. Otherwise, the room appeared pristine.

'You're quite sure she's our victim?' Maggie asked MacLeod as she stepped to his side.

'Just a gut thing,' he said. 'It's too much of a coincidence that Kenmore disappeared within hours of our victim's demise. We've requested her dental records.'

'Next of kin?'

MacLeod patted his overcoat, checking for his cigarettes. 'Husband. David Campbell. He's on his way from their estate in the Highlands.'

'Convenient.' His alibi would be that he was in the Highlands, not in Edinburgh. It didn't mean he couldn't hire someone to off his wife. 'What does he do?'

'He's an artist, apparently. Wood carvings.' He patted his coat again. 'Let's go out for a fag.'

Maggie surveyed the room again before following MacLeod out to the street. She found him leaning against a lamppost, blowing out a stream of smoke. Maggie stood next to him, looking across the square, wondering if someone looked out their bedroom window last night and witnessed the suspected kidnapping. 'Do we have a timeline for when she went missing?'

'The PA says she spoke to Kenmore just after eleven. Could have been any time after that.'

'The fog wasn't as dense down here. I'll look into CCTV footage and knock on some doors.'

'Let the uniforms handle the canvassing. The PA needs to be interviewed.' MacLeod pointed to a house several doors down. 'We may get something from the First Minister's cameras.'

Maggie scanned the house in question. Several cameras faced the square. Sloppy, she thought again. 'I'll see to it.' Then, turning back to MacLeod, she asked the question she wasn't sure she wanted to be answered. 'Did you get a chance to look at my parents' case?'

MacLeod shifted and sighed, staring out over the green space in the middle of the square. 'You really don't remember anything?'

Maggie's gaze joined MacLeod's, focused on that awful memory instead of the denuded trees and green grass. 'Just what I told you earlier.'

'Do you know the details?'

'No. Iona would have told me if I'd asked, but I never did. I suppose I figured if it was so horrific that my brain buried it, I was better off not knowing.'

'I haven't taken it to the chief inspector yet, but when I do, you may be pulled from the case.'

'You think the cases are related?'

MacLeod took a long haul off his cigarette, dropped it, and stomped it out. 'Maybe it's time you had that talk with Iona.' He turned and walked off towards his beater of a car.

Maggie stood on the pavement, absorbed in the image of her mother's melting face for a long time. You would think remembering something like that would trigger nausea, horror, and shock, but she felt nothing. Perhaps that was a safety mechanism of her brain as well, protecting her as it had done for nearly twenty years.

It was only when the cold seeped into her bones that she stirred and pulled her mobile from her pocket. She called the First Minister's office to request the CCTV footage from her house system.

* * *

Crouching over the broken vase, Maggie noted the blood on pieces of the crystal and spatter on the wall and carpet. Whether it belonged to the victim or suspect remained to be seen. She hoped like hell Jamie Kenmore fought the bastards.

The overturned chair appeared to be a result of Kenmore standing quickly. Beside her laptop on the desk was a notepad where she'd been writing her to-do list for today. All seemed to relate to her business. She had more planned before 08:00 than Maggie usually did in a day. This was one organised, motivated woman.

Sarah Graham, Kenmore's PA, sat in the kitchen with one of the constables, her face pale and her hands shaking as she lifted a teacup to her lips. She still wore a grey wool coat despite the warmth inside the house. Maggie's own coat lay draped over her forearm. Maggie observed the PA for a moment before crossing the room and taking a seat across the table. 'Ms Graham?'

Graham carefully set her cup in its saucer before raising

her eyes to Maggie. 'Yes.'

'I'm Detective Constable Glass. I have a few questions for you.'

'I don't know what more I can tell you. I don't know what's happened to Jamie.'

Jamie, Maggie noted. Informal. 'You were close to your boss?'

'We worked long hours together, Detective Glass. You get to know a person quite well.'

Maggie supposed that was true enough. She knew MacLeod quite well, but wouldn't call their relationship a friendship. Colleagues. Acquaintances. They may have a pint after work now and then, but usually with other colleagues. Still, she only addressed him as DI or MacLeod. 'Can you think of anyone who may want to harm Ms Kenmore?'

Graham's eyes widened. 'Harm her? No. Do you think someone has harmed her?'

'I can't say. I assume Ms Kenmore had a mobile phone.'

'Yes, of course. It's always with her. She may be needed at any time, especially if a deadline was approaching or an issue arose with one of our clients.'

Kenmore's handbag and briefcase were on the floor next to the writing desk, but Maggie hadn't found her mobile.

'I've tried calling it all day,' Graham continued. 'It just goes to voicemail.'

'What time did you arrive here to check on Ms Kenmore?'

'I don't know. Just past half three?'

'You didn't think to check on her earlier?'

Graham swallowed. 'I … I saw on the news that a woman's body was discovered near the castle and … and I started to worry.'

'Is it usual for Ms Kenmore to go off the grid?'

'No, it's quite unusual. I just wasn't sure what to do about it. I mentioned it to the other executives and their admins.

21

Everyone seemed puzzled, but no one thought to come here and check on her. Until …' Graham's eyes pooled and her lower lip trembled. 'Is the body Jamie's?'

Maggie couldn't afford to lose her yet. She still had questions she needed answers to. 'This appears to be a kidnapping. Do you know of anyone who would do this? Anyone who resented Jamie's success?'

'No, no. Jamie is ambitious, determined. She works very hard and expects the same from those she employs, but she treats her people well. She's well respected.'

'What can you tell me about her husband?'

Graham's eyes widened and she blinked several times. 'Her husband? David wouldn't be involved. He stays at their home in the Highlands.'

'Why is that?'

'Um…' Graham pursed her lips as if she was trying to prevent herself from blurting something out.

'I'm going to find out anyway. You may as well just say it.' She waited patiently while Graham's blue eyes betrayed her internal struggle.

Graham blew out a breath and shut her eyes. When she opened them, she stared directly into Maggie's. 'Their marriage was an arrangement. They lived separate lives. A woman in Jamie's position sometimes benefits from having a husband by her side and, at those times, David fulfils his agreement with her.'

'A woman in Jamie's position?'

'Exactly,' Graham said forcefully. 'A woman. A successful woman. A woman with power. A woman in the business world still very much the domain of men.'

'A gay woman?'

Graham narrowed her eyes, venom spewing from them.

Maggie raised her hand. 'I'm asking, not judging.' If Kenmore needed a man at her side for appearance's sake, she didn't need to marry one to fill the role. It seemed extreme to Maggie. Unless perhaps she was trying to hide her homosexuality. 'What about someone in the office? Any disgruntled employees? Anyone with ambitions to take over the company?'

'No, as I said, Jamie treats her people well. Jamie started Gold Star with her best friends when they graduated from uni. It's one of the few all-female companies on the planet. They're a united team and the women who work there are loyal.'

The edge of Maggie's mouth curled up. 'How does she get away with that without being called out for discrimination?'

She almost got a smile out of Graham. 'I think you may find there aren't many men who apply to work in an all-female organisation.'

Maggie's smile widened. 'I imagine not. Does Jamie have a partner? A lover?'

'No,' Graham said with a short shake of her head. 'Not at the moment. At least, not that I'm aware of.'

'Walk me through what happened when you arrived here.'

'I've already explained it to Constable Maguire. Shouldn't you be out looking for her instead of asking the same questions again?'

'I'm sorry. I know it's tedious, but I need to hear it from you. Let's start with the door. Did you knock? Did you have a key?'

'I started to knock, but the door was open. I mean, it looked closed, but when my fist hit the door, it pushed open. The door jamb was splintered. I took out my mobile and called 999.'

'You didn't enter the house? Call out for Jamie?'

'I did. I went into the foyer, calling her name. All I heard was my own echo. I glanced into the lounge and saw the broken vase and the upended chair. I was scared, Detective.'

She dropped her head. 'I went back outside to wait for the police.'

And in doing so, preserved the crime scene. Had the perpetrators still been inside, she also could have saved her own life. 'You did the right thing.'

Graham raised her head and gave a short nod.

'Does Jamie own a car?'

'Yes. It should be parked out back.'

'Did she typically drive to work?'

'No. The office is just a few minutes walk away. On George Street.'

A few minutes walk away and no one thought to check on Kenmore until the news hit with the story of a murder on the Esplanade? Something about that didn't sit right with Maggie.

Chapter 3

Kenmore's car was indeed parked out back – a sleek Jaguar XJ Autobiography in Loire blue. Maggie would have loved to take it out for a spin, but even if it was a possibility, there was still too much on her to-do list. At least she'd confirmed Kenmore hadn't driven off somewhere.

It took her less than five minutes to walk to the offices of Gold Star on George Street. At nearly 17:30, she was taking a chance that everyone hadn't gone home for the night.

It was Sarah Graham who answered the door. She escorted Maggie up to the executive offices, where she met the two women who'd worked closely with Jamie Kenmore since university. With short dark hair greying at the temples, Sharon Dunbar held the position of Chief Financial Officer. Kelsey Gray, her hair long and blonde, was a VP. They were both the same age as Kenmore, forty-eight. They both wore expensive business suits similar to Maggie's own.

They went into a glassed-in conference room and took seats around a beautiful mahogany table that looked as Georgian as the furniture in Kenmore's home. Dunbar sent Graham for coffee then turned her blue eyes on Maggie. 'Is it Jamie? The murder victim at the castle?'

'I'm sorry,' Maggie responded. 'I can't answer that.' She needed to take back control already. She needed to ask the questions, not answer them. 'Can you tell me if there's anyone who threatened Ms Kenmore?'

Dunbar and Gray shared a quick look, then Dunbar said, 'Threatened? No.'

Interesting answer, Maggie thought. 'Is there anyone you think may have been a threat?'

The two women looked at each other again as if they were communicating telepathically. Gray gave Dunbar a slight nod.

'Thomas Campbell,' Dunbar said. 'He's been offering to buy the company for years. Jamie grew tired of the harassment and advised him, even if she decided to sell, she would never consider selling to him.'

'And was she?' Maggie asked. 'Thinking about selling?'

'No. Of course not. The three of us have been running this company together for over twenty-five years. And quite successfully. We have no intention of selling.'

'Do all three of you own the company?'

Dunbar nodded. 'Kelsey and I each own twenty per cent. Jamie owns sixty. Her money, her vision started the company, but she insisted Kelsey and I own at least twenty per cent. She felt it would give us more incentive and keep us loyal.'

'Were you happy with –'

'Let me stop you there, Detective.' Dunbar raised a hand. 'Jamie didn't need to give us that twenty per cent. We would have been loyal and motivated without it. We appreciate it and it has certainly been rewarding over the years, but it wasn't necessary. We're a strong team, work well together, and are loyal to a fault.'

'What about her husband?'

Dunbar snorted out a laugh. 'David is a sweetheart and despite their marriage being for show, he loves her dearly.'

'Who gets Kenmore's share of the company if she dies?'

Dunbar and Gray looked at each other again with sombre expressions. 'Her shares would be split between Kelsey and me,' Dunbar said.

'Why didn't either of you go to check on Ms Kenmore when she didn't show up for work this morning?'

Dunbar closed her eyes and sighed. 'We tried calling her. Several times. I guess we supposed she needed a break.'

'You weren't worried?' Maggie asked.

'Aye, we were, Detective. We were trying not to assume the worst.'

Maggie didn't get much more out of the pair. As she walked back to her car on Charlotte Square, she Googled Thomas Campbell, a successful media relations mogul in his own right. But from what she could get online, he wasn't nearly as successful as Gold Star. That would eat at a man, wouldn't it? That three women were much more successful than him? Good on them, Maggie thought. Succeeding in a man's world wasn't easy, and she had no doubt it was still very much a man's world. And yet, these three had done it with an all-female staff. That had to burn.

* * *

The exterior lights were on when Maggie pulled to the curb in front of Iona's house. She took a moment to settle her nerves before getting out of the car. This conversation was probably long overdue, but still one she wasn't looking forward to.

She tapped on the door before entering. 'Iona?'

'In the kitchen, Mags.'

Maggie hung her coat and wandered through to the back of the house. Iona stood at the counter pouring tea as if she knew Maggie would be arriving at this moment. She handed Maggie a teacup and saucer then led her to the lounge.

Maggie set her tea on the coffee table and took a deep breath. She may as well jump right in. 'I think my memories are beginning to return.'

Iona lifted her cup to her lips, then drew it away at Maggie's statement and set it in its saucer. With sympathy in her eyes, she asked, 'What have you remembered?'

Maggie described her gory vision, bringing tears to Iona's eyes.

'I'm so sorry, Mags. Are you okay?'

With a shrug, Maggie said, 'I don't know. I feel numb. I don't know how I'm supposed to react to something that horrific.'

'You've remembered the worst of it. I can't imagine.' She reached over and took Maggie's hand. 'What can I do?'

Although she was going to fight for it, there were no guarantees that MacLeod and the chief inspector would allow Maggie to view the files from her parents' case. And even if they did, Iona may give her something that wasn't in the files. 'I need you to fill in the rest. I want you to tell me everything you know.'

'This is about the woman murdered this morning,' Iona said. 'She was burned at the stake?'

Maggie nodded and Iona dropped her head with a sigh. When she lifted it again, there were tears in her eyes.

'I contacted the High Priestesses of the covens in the area. They don't gather until the full moon, but they're checking with their sisters and brothers. So far, no one is missing.'

After speaking to Kenmore's PA and colleagues, it was what Maggie expected, even though it wasn't confirmed that Kenmore was their victim. 'It's looking like our victim wasn't a witch.'

'Someone like your mother then?' Iona continued to hold Maggie's hand, her sympathetic eyes locked on Maggie's. 'A woman successful in business. A woman with political friends and power.'

It took a moment for Iona's words to sink in, confusing as

they were. All this time, Maggie thought Ghlais was her father's company. 'My mother ran Ghlais?'

'Technically, they both owned the business, but Mairie's passion and her brilliant management of the company made it so successful. Malcolm was hands-on in the distilling of the whisky while Mairie stood at the helm on the management side.'

'She hired Gold Star to build the brand?'

'Yes. Jamie Kenmore was a personal friend and a genius in media relations.'

Not only was Kenmore tied to her parents' death by method, but in business and in friendship. 'Do you know if someone was trying to buy them out?'

'I wouldn't know. Your mother was like a sister to me, Maggie. But we rarely discussed the business. It wasn't that I wasn't interested. I just found it all so boring.' Iona smiled at a private memory and squeezed Maggie's hand. 'But I do know that neither Mairie nor Malcolm would have considered selling.'

It was time Maggie paid a visit to the company she owned but knew very little about. She'd left the running of it to her uncle, Alastaire Ghlais, and he'd given her no reason to interfere. Maggie received quarterly financial reports, but found them mind-numbing. Still, she knew the bottom line and it continued to grow. Ghlais, however, could wait until tomorrow. Tonight, she needed to learn the details her mind held hostage. 'Tell me about the murder of my parents. Everything you know.'

Iona released Maggie's hand and sat back in her seat, closing her eyes for a moment. 'I knew this day would come no matter how many times I prayed it wouldn't. Forcing you to relive the horrors of that night is not something I relish, hen.'

Maggie placed her hand on Iona's knee, meeting her gaze.

'I know and I'm sorry to put you through this, but it's time.'

Iona placed her hand over Maggie's on her knee and nodded. She didn't look at Maggie as she spoke. Instead, her eyes seemed to be focused on the past. 'I wasn't there, you ken? I can only tell you what I learned from Detective Sergeant Claymore, one of the detectives on the case.'

'Yes, I understand.'

'You were taken from your home in the middle of the night. A witness saw a white van driving away from your house at half one despite the heavy fog. There were signs of a struggle in your parents' room. They believe it was Malcolm who fought back, but Mairie would have fought them as well, especially if it meant protecting you.'

The one thing Maggie did know about her mother and father was that they loved her very much. Iona reminded Maggie of that at every opportunity over the years.

'At half six, the police were called to the Esplanade of Edinburgh Castle, where two bodies were found amongst the charred remains of a large fire. About an hour later, you were found huddled in a wee ball in Lady Stair's Close, wearing nothing but your Winnie the Pooh pyjamas. You were soaking wet from the rain and hypothermic, so you were taken to hospital where you remained for several days. The police questioned you, but you didn't speak a word.' Iona met Maggie's gaze with a slight smile on her lips. 'It was nearly a year before you would utter a word. Do you remember what you said?'

'I do. You'd just patched up my skint knee and pressed a kiss to it. So I said, 'Thank you, Mummy."

Iona's smile grew, although the sadness in her eyes remained. 'It was a moment I'll never forget. That you accepted me as your mother meant the world to me.'

'You're the only mother I remember.'

'That will change,' Iona said as she patted Maggie's hand

on her knee. 'You will remember them and the love they had for you.'

'Perhaps, but I will never forget you and your love for me.'

* * *

Macleod was where Maggie expected him to be – at his desk. She laid her coat over the back of her chair and flopped down opposite him, throwing her feet up on her desk before updating him since their last meeting.

'Your sense that the people responsible for this grisly murder are misogynists fits then.'

'You've been through the file on my parents' murders. What do you think?'

'If this murder is related to your parents', and it certainly appears to be, the chief inspector will pull you from the case.'

Maggie scoffed. 'So, you're not even going to share your thoughts with me until you know whether or not I'll be tossed off the case?' She pulled her feet from the desk and stood as MacLeod shrugged. 'Fine. I'll go up and speak to the chief inspector now.' She turned and marched across the room.

'Maggie?'

It was rare for MacLeod to use her first name. It was for that reason Maggie slowed to a stop and waited. When he said nothing further, she turned.

MacLeod waited for Maggie's eyes to meet his before he spoke. 'Good luck.' He needed her to know he meant it.

Maggie nodded and turned again, her steps still determined but not as forceful. It was MacLeod who usually dealt with the chief inspector. Chain of command and all that. Maggie's experience with him was limited to a pat on the back and a quick word of welcome when she joined the team. She was confident she could convince him to keep her on the case though.

A tiny woman with short ginger hair and bright green eyes

sat at the desk guarding Detective Chief Inspector Kenneth McTavish's office entrance. Maggie stepped right up to the desk. 'I need to speak with DCI McTavish.'

The woman raised a brow and smiled. 'Can I tell him what it's about?'

'The Esplanade case.'

'Right.' The woman picked up her phone and dialed an extension. 'DC Glass would like a word regarding the Esplanade case.'

Maggie wasn't sure how she knew her name, but let it go. The woman hung up the phone and waved her over to the thick wooden door with a brass plate declaring 'DCI McTavish'.

Maggie knocked and entered, closing the door behind her. 'DCI McTavish,' she said with a nod and walked over to stand in front of his desk.

McTavish looked like a relic from days gone by, a Highland Chieftain reigning strong and proud over his tenants. He was big and rugged with rosy cheeks and rusty ginger hair. He peered at Maggie over half reading glasses. 'What can I do for you, DC Glass?'

'I assume DI MacLeod has kept you updated on the Esplanade case.'

'Aye, he has.'

'So you know that it bears a striking similarity to the murders of my parents eighteen years ago.'

'Aye.'

He wasn't making it easy on her. He was going to make her spell it all out. 'Sir, I'm requesting to remain on the case. I have no memory of my parents' murders and I assure you I can objectively investigate this case.'

McTavish raised a hand to stop Maggie from speaking. 'You're new to the Major Investigations Team, DC, so I'll clarify how things work here.'

Maggie nodded.

'You scratch my back and I'll scratch yours. You want something from me, Glass. What are you prepared to pay for it?'

Good lord! Did he just ask her for a bribe? 'Uh … a bottle of Ghlais Whisky?'

'A bottle? Just how much do you want to remain on this case, DC? It can't be that important to you.' He scoffed with a quick shake of his head and picked up the pen sitting atop a notepad. 'If you'll excuse me, I've work to do.'

'A case?'

McTavish set the pen down and peered at Maggie over his specs again. 'That would be the eighteen-year-old, of course.'

Shite. McTavish wasn't cheap. 'Of course.'

'Very well. You can drop it off with my admin tomorrow.' He took up the pen again and began writing on his notepad.

* * *

MacLeod waited for Maggie out the back of the building, taking a long draw on his cigarette.

'You could have warned me,' she said with a scowl as she burst out the door.

'Are you still on the case or not?'

'Yes, I'm on it.'

MacLeod smirked, one bushy eyebrow raised. 'What did it cost you then?'

Bastard! He was enjoying this. She exhaled loudly, like a bull ready to charge. 'A case of Ghlais. Not a bottle, a fricking case.'

'Oh, aye,' he said and laughed. 'The eighteen-year-old, no doubt.'

'Shut up. Why didn't you warn me?'

'And take all the fun out of it?'

Maggie couldn't stay angry at MacLeod with that big grin on his face. He had a great smile, one she didn't see often. She shook her head as a smile broke over her own face. 'Ah well. I'm stopping at Ghlais tomorrow morning anyway to ask my uncle what was going on at Ghlais before my parents' murders. Thomas Campbell, a media relations mogul, was apparently harassing Jamie Kenmore to sell Gold Star to him. I want to know if my parents were experiencing anything similar.'

'While you're doing that, I'll check on forensics and the pathologist. I spoke to the husband, by the way. He came in when he arrived in Edinburgh. Nothing there. Their marriage was a mutual agreement, a contract. He had nothing to do with her murder.'

'The PA and her partners told me about the marriage. I don't get why a guy would agree to that. What was in it for him?'

'He was a starving artist and a good friend of Kenmore's since childhood. In exchange for marrying her and fulfilling certain duties, he got an estate in the Highlands and a sizeable income which continues despite her death.'

'But what if he'd met someone he wanted to marry?'

'He wasn't worried about that in the least. He says he's asexual.' MacLeod took one last drag from his cigarette and stubbed it out. 'Go home, Glass. It's been a long day for both of us.'

He didn't have to tell her twice.

Chapter 4

It wasn't until she woke with a grumbling stomach that Maggie realised she hadn't stopped to eat yesterday. She made herself an omelette and toast and dined by the window, gazing out at her spectacular view of Arthur's Seat and wishing she had time for a run in the hills. With any luck, she'd be home in time to take that run before dark.

When she finished breakfast, Maggie washed her dishes and took a quick shower. She turned on the telly in the bedroom to listen to the news as she dressed. Maggie hadn't been to the Ghlais offices in years and intended to make an impression, choosing a dark charcoal suit with light grey pinstripes. As she buttoned a grey shirt, Maggie's eyes fell on the photograph in a silver frame sitting on her dresser. The picture was of eight-year-old Maggie and her parents on holiday in the south of France just weeks before their death. A holiday she couldn't remember. She had no memories of her parents except that one disturbing memory of her mother's face melting. She could hear awful screams, but she couldn't see or hear her father. If she had seen him burning that night, she hoped she never remembered it. She'd much rather remember them as they were in this photograph – suntanned, laughing, with their arms wrapped around their daughter.

At the mention of the Edinburgh Castle Esplanade, Maggie turned to the wall-mounted telly. Kaleigh Logan stood at the top of the Royal Mile, the view of the Esplanade still blocked by a forensics vehicle.

'A still unidentified woman was burned to death here on the site of the burning at the stake of over three hundred women accused of being witches in the fifteen and sixteen hundreds. Police are divulging little this morning, but we can tell you the details of this murder closely match the murder of Mairie and Malcolm Ghlais eighteen years ago. The Ghlais's owned Ghlais Whisky, a popular brand around the globe. Their murders have never been solved.

'While we wait for the identity of the murdered woman, one can't help but wonder if the disappearance of Gold Star Media Relations mogul Jamie Kenmore is related. Police sources tell me there are signs of a break-in and struggle at her home on Charlotte Square, matching the scene of the Ghlais home on the night they disappeared.'

'Shite.' Maggie picked her mobile up from the dresser and dialed MacLeod. 'Are you watching the local news?' she asked as soon as he answered.

'Yeah. Fucking Logan. This is going to turn into a media shite show. They'll be hounding us from start to finish.'

In her six years with Police Scotland, Maggie had managed to stay clear of contact with the media until Logan approached her yesterday. Since Logan hadn't identified her as one of the investigators, Maggie may get away with staying on the case. She picked up Logan's business card from the dresser, wondering if Kaleigh Logan would take a bribe as easily as the chief inspector.

* * *

Ghlais Whisky was housed in an old stone building outside Edinburgh. Maggie walked along the front of the building, trailing her fingers over the ancient stone as if she could tease out the scenes it witnessed over the years. The stone was cold, smoother than she expected after being battered by North Sea winds for centuries. In the foyer, she stood for a moment, the scents of yeast and a smokey whisky flavour tweaking a memory she couldn't quite grasp.

Maggie took the stairs to the first floor, crossing the slate floor to reception – a long, curving oak counter with a woman in her sixties sitting behind it. She looked up through red-framed glasses with a smile on her face. The smile grew when she recognised her visitor.

'Maggie. So good to see you.'

'You as well, Mrs Brown. Is my uncle available?'

'Aye, he's in his office.'

'Thank you.' She walked to her right and turned left down a hallway to the double oak doors of Alastaire Ghlais's office. Her mother's office, she realised for the first time. She gave the door a quick tap. Alastaire must have redecorated after her parents' death as it was decidedly masculine now, dark woods and paint that brought to mind an old gentleman's club. If not for the floor to ceiling windows presenting a view of open fields and sizeable forest behind his regal desk, the room would have been oppressive. A fire had been lit in the hearth of the black marble encased fireplace to the left of Alastaire's massive mahogany desk. Maggie wondered what this space looked like when her mother occupied it. She couldn't imagine her mother in it as it was today.

'Maggie,' Alastaire said as he rose from his seat behind the desk. He'd recently turned fifty, but appeared younger. His dark hair showed no signs of thinning or greying and the only visible wrinkles were at the corners of his blue eyes. He looked as fit as he'd always been with a trim body and broad shoulders.

The man sitting in one of the chairs facing the desk stood. Alexander, Alastaire's son, greeted Maggie with a nod. He resembled his father, right down to the light grey suit and stiff white shirt.

'Uncle Alastaire. Alex. I hope I'm not disturbing you.'

'Not at all, pet. We're just having a coffee. Can I pour you one?'

'Yes, please.'

'Alex, be a lad and get your cousin a cup,' Alastaire said as he retook his seat.

Alex scowled at his father, but did as he was told. He went to a sideboard, retrieved a plain white china cup, and set it on the desk in front of Maggie.

Maggie took the seat next to Alex as he poured coffee into her cup.

'Cream and sugar?' Alex asked with a sneer.

'Yes, but I can get it myself, thanks.' She added a spoonful of sugar and cream then stirred, taking her time while she figured out how to start the conversation. 'I have a few questions I'm hoping you'll be able to answer for me, uncle Alastaire.'

'Ask away then, lass.'

'Do you know if anyone was enquiring about purchasing Ghlais before my mother and father were murdered?'

Alastaire leaned back in his chair, steepling his hands and tapping his forefingers against his lips. 'It was a long time ago now, but I don't believe so. Mairie never would have sold anyway.'

'Anyone seem resentful of my mother's success?'

Alastaire leaned forward now, his forearms on the desk. 'Resentful of your mother? Malcolm was as much a part of the success of Ghlais as your mother.'

'Of course, but I'm considering a theory that involves targeting successful women.'

Alastaire gave her a tight-lipped smile. 'I don't remember anyone resenting Mairie.'

The room seemed cold all of a sudden despite the roaring fire. Maggie took a sip of her coffee, her gaze locked on her uncle's. 'Is there anyone you can think of who may have wanted my parents out of the way?'

'Like I said, pet, it was a long time ago.'

Maggie couldn't feel the cold now because her blood was beginning to boil. She took a long swig of her coffee, so she didn't waste it – it was a damn good blend – and stood. 'Okay then, thanks for the coffee.' She walked halfway to the door before an idea struck and turned back to the two men. 'You know, perhaps it's time I started to learn more about the business.'

Alastaire smiled while Alex paled, his lips tightening to a fine line.

'Whenever you're ready, I'm quite happy to show you the ropes, pet.'

Maggie gave him her best smile. 'Thanks, Uncle Alastaire. I'll let you know. Oh, and I need a few cases of the eighteen.'

'Drive around to the loading dock. I'll have someone bring them out.'

'Cheers.'

Alex glared at his father as soon as Maggie left the room. 'Show her the ropes? Are you insane?'

'Relax, son. She's never been interested in the business. It was a bluff.' He leaned back in his chair, tapping his lips with his forefingers again. 'Give Robbie a ring. Have him keep an eye on your dear cousin.'

* * *

Maggie walked out to the reception desk and turned to Mrs Brown. 'You were here when my parents were alive, weren't you?'

'Oh, aye. It broke my heart when they were murdered. Your Mum was very dear to me. You used to spend a lot of time here back then, do you remember?'

'No, I'm afraid I remember very little.' Maggie leaned on the counter and lowered her voice. 'Do you remember if anyone was enquiring about purchasing Ghlais back then?'

Mrs Brown answered, 'I don't think so. Of course, we have had offers over the years, but I don't remember anything specific at that time.'

'Do you remember if anyone was resentful of my mother or if anyone wanted rid of them?'

'Your mother was well respected, lass. She was very good at her job.' Mrs Brown looked over her shoulder then whispered, 'The only person I know of who may have resented her was your uncle.'

A tall, striking woman with short platinum blonde hair rounded the corner with an armful of papers, preventing Maggie from asking another question.

'Mrs Brown, do you happen to know –' The blonde looked up, spotted Maggie, and grinned. 'Oh, I'm sorry. I didn't realise you had company.' She held out her hand, giving Maggie a firm handshake. 'Sylvan MacKenzie.'

Maggie kept her grip on Sylvan's hand, staring into her aqua blue eyes, like the waters of an Isle of Harris beach. 'Maggie Glass.'

The grin dropped from Sylvan's face and she blinked several times. '*The* Maggie Glass? As in the owner of Ghlais?'

Mrs Brown giggled behind the desk. 'That would be the one.'

'Well, it's a pleasure to meet you.'

'Likewise,' Maggie said, wishing that smile would return to Sylvan's beautiful face. 'I didn't mean to interrupt.'

'Oh, no. It's fine.' Sylvan turned back to Mrs Brown. 'I was just wondering if you knew where I'd find the files for last year.'

'Aye, I can have them brought up to your office. Did you want the entire year?'

'Let's start with October to December. If I need further back than that, I'll let you know.'

Mrs Brown picked up the phone on her desk and Sylvan turned back to Maggie. In a quiet voice, she asked, 'Tell me if you think this is inappropriate, but would you like to go for dinner sometime?'

Hell yes, she did. 'I work odd hours, Ms MacKenzie.'

'Sylvan, please.'

'Sylvan.' Maggie liked the sound of that on her lips. 'I never know when I'm going to get called out or if I'll have to work late.'

'We'll play it by ear then. I'll give you my number and, if you find yourself free, give me a ring.'

Maggie found herself whistling as she walked to her car with Sylvan's phone number logged into the contacts of her mobile. Then she had a thought. Had Sylvan asked her out for a date or for business reasons? *Well, shite.*

* * *

After picking up the cases of whisky from the loading dock, Maggie sat in her car and called MacLeod. 'Anything from forensics or the pathologist yet?'

'We should have the full pathology report by noon. In the meantime, dental records confirmed that our victim is indeed Jamie Kenmore.'

'Do you want me to do the notification?'

'No, I'll do that. I thought maybe you should go through the file on your parents' case since you're staying on this.'

'Why? Is there something in there you think I should know?' Why did she need to go through it if MacLeod already had?

There was a long pause before MacLeod answered and Maggie figured he was outside enjoying a fag.

'There are a lot of holes in the investigation, Glass. A lot we don't know. I spoke to DS Claymore this morning. You were the only witness during the investigation and you weren't able to tell him anything.'

'You're hoping reading the file will trigger my memory.' She dropped her head back against the headrest and closed her eyes, opening them again when the memory of her mother's face melting flashed before her.

'I'm sorry, Glass. The information locked in your head could be crucial the now.'

'Right.' It was worth a try if it was the only way they were going to crack this case. 'I'll head in, but I have a stop to make first.'

She hung up and called the number on the card Kaleigh Logan gave her, making arrangements to meet at a coffee shop on the Royal Mile. Apparently, Logan was keeping vigil near the crime scene.

Maggie pulled out of the Ghlais lot and began the drive back into Edinburgh's City Centre. She'd only been driving for a few minutes before she picked up the tail – a black Mercedes sedan. It wasn't close enough to read the number plate though. That's okay, she thought. I can be patient.

* * *

Maggie drove up Cockburn Street and parked at the top near the High Street. She waited while the black Mercedes parked several car lengths behind her then took out her mobile as she got out of the car. As Maggie walked down the pavement towards the Mercedes, she opened her camera app, snapping a picture of the number plate then one of the sandy-haired driver. She tucked her mobile back into her pocket and pulled out her warrant card. Then she walked right up to the driver's window holding her card up.

The driver rolled down his window and Maggie said, 'Licence, please.'

'What? I didn't do anything wrong.'

She held up her warrant card again. 'I'll say this one last

time. Driving licence, please.'

The driver huffed as he leaned forward and pulled his wallet from the back pocket of his trousers. He presented his licence to Maggie with a scowl.

Maggie took her notebook and pen out of her coat pocket, wrote down the name and address, and then passed the licence back to the driver. 'Thank you, Mr MacDonald. I like to know who's following me.' She smiled as she walked back up Cockburn Street.

Turning right, she walked up the Royal Mile until she was nearly at St. Giles Cathedral. Kaleigh Logan waited for her at an outdoor table at Caffé Nero. Maggie took the seat across from Logan and Logan slid a blue take out cup across the table.

'Chai latte,' she announced.

'Thank you.' Maggie peeled the top back and took a quick sip. 'Thanks for meeting with me.'

'I told you I'd help you with this case. I was on the scene after your parents were murdered. I was there when you were found.'

'That's not why I wanted to see you.' Maggie took a quick look around and lowered her voice. 'You didn't give me away in your broadcast about the Esplanade murder. Why?'

Logan shrugged. 'I didn't see a point.'

'You want me on this case?'

'It's not that I want you on it, specifically. Yesterday morning, I realised you don't remember everything from that horrific night. I think it may be healing for you to look into this.' She wanted Magaidh Ghlais to remember. There were a lot of unanswered questions from the Ghlais murders. Logan wanted those answers.

Maggie scoffed. 'You don't really think I believe that, do you? You have another reason. I'm just not sure what it is yet.'

The two women stared at each other over the small table. Logan was the first to break. 'I need answers. Every police detective has an unsolved case that haunts them. The same is true for journalists, Magaidh. Your parents' murder still haunts me.'

'It's Maggie. DC Maggie Glass.'

A small smile spread over Logan's face and Maggie realised she was well aware of her name change. Just how much did Kaleigh Logan know about her?

The slight smile remained as Logan took a sip of her coffee and said, 'Work with me, Maggie, and your connection to your parents' murder will remain our little secret.'

And there was the price. Maggie shook her head. 'I can't make any comments on the case to a reporter without permission from my superiors.'

'I'm not asking you to make statements. I'm asking you to share what you know and what you learn with me.'

'So you can broadcast it to the world? I don't think so.'

'What if I give you my word that I won't report anything that isn't approved through media relations?' She leaned forward, speaking in almost a whisper. 'What you tell me will remain between us until after this case is solved.'

'Why? What's in it for you?'

Logan grinned. 'A bestseller.'

If MacLeod or the Inspector discovered Maggie was sharing information with a reporter, she'd not only be off the case, she'd be up for discipline. 'I'll consider it.'

Logan rose to her feet, coffee in hand. 'You have my number.' She walked away, heading west towards the Esplanade.

Maggie remained at the café until she finished her tea, thinking about the risk she'd be taking working with Logan and how she could get around it. She could just go to MacLeod and tell him upfront what Logan wanted, but she wasn't at all sure he would keep it to himself. Actually, she was confident he would take it to the chief inspector. And what would that cost her?

Since she was close, she walked up to the crime scene. Logan gave her a nod as she walked by, but Maggie didn't acknowledge her. The forensics team continued to sift through the charcoaled remains of the fire in their white protective coveralls. Maggie stood behind one of the techs and observed, reluctant to disturb them. The tech used a small brush to clear away the black dust and debris from a small object. Maggie leaned forward for a better view. 'What have you got?'

The tech looked over her shoulder and Maggie recognised the cherubic face of Susan Walsh.

'DC Glass,' Walsh said in greeting. 'It looks like some kind of pendant. Whether it was the victim's or one of the perpetrators' remains to be seen.'

Maggie crouched down next to Susan and studied the item – a silver circle with a pentagram in the centre. 'Or the perpetrators planted it.'

'Also possible,' Walsh said as she continued to carefully brush the object.

Maggie took out her mobile and snapped a picture.

Chapter 5

Maggie hauled a case of Ghlais whisky up to the Chief Inspector's pixie admin assistant, setting it on the floor beside her desk. 'That's for DCI McTavish.'

'I'll make sure he gets it, DC Glass.' She looked up at Maggie with a cheeky little grin. 'Don't let it bother you, DC. Everyone ends up here with a wee gift for his holiness at some point.'

Maggie's brow drew in. How did she know Maggie felt guilty? 'You have me at a disadvantage. I don't know your name.'

She gave Maggie that cheeky grin again, her green eyes sparkling. 'Sapphire Dovefeather.'

Maggie barely restrained from rolling her eyes. Not only did Sapphire Dovefeather look like a pixie, but she also had a pixie name. 'Well, it's nice to meet you, Ms Dovefeather.'

'Likewise.'

Maggie walked away from the strange encounter with a strong sense she'd just made an ally in Sapphire Dovefeather. She didn't know why, but her gut told her it was important. Before she turned the corner, she glanced back at Dovefeather, who continued to watch her with that grin. Maggie smiled back and gave her a wave.

Not a pixie name, Magaidh. A faerie name.

Maggie blinked several times. Dovefeather just spoke to her telepathically about a subject Maggie had not voiced, but thought. *My apologies. I meant no offence.*

None taken. Dovefeather continued to grin and added a wink.

Maggie gave her a nod and quickly strode off. She kept her mind as blank as she could manage until she got to her desk and flopped down into her chair.

'You okay?' MacLeod asked, frowning across the desk. 'You look like you've seen a ghost.'

'I just took a case of Ghlais up to McTavish's admin.'

MacLeod laughed. 'She's quite a character, that wee sprite, is she no'?'

'Aye, quite the character.' Maggie took a deep breath in an attempt to shake off the experience and retrieved her mobile from her coat pocket. She pulled up the picture of the pentagram pendant and passed it over to MacLeod. 'What do you make of that?'

MacLeod took her mobile and studied the picture for a moment. 'Interesting, aye? A plant perhaps?'

'That was my thought.'

He passed the phone back to her. 'Send it to me. I'll talk to the husband and you can ask Kenmore's PA.'

Maggie sent the photograph to MacLeod's mobile then rang Sarah Graham at Gold Star as MacLeod went out for a cigarette.

As soon as Maggie identified herself, Graham said, 'DI MacLeod confirmed it *was* Jamie who was murdered on the Esplanade, DC Glass.' She sniffed and drew in a stuttered breath. 'We're all distraught and want to help in your investigation. You must find who did this.'

'We'll do everything we can.' Maggie couldn't promise to solve the case. It would be a promise she wasn't sure she could keep, especially as DS Claymore hadn't been able to solve her parents' case. 'I promise you that. Did Jamie wear a necklace or a pendant?'

'Aye, she wore a wee gold, heart-shaped locket.'

'Okay. That helps. Thank you.'

When MacLeod returned, he picked up a stack of file folders from his desk and placed them in the centre of Maggie's. Before she could open the top file, MacLeod slapped his hand on it and looked Maggie in the eye. 'Be sure about this, Glass. It's not going to be easy.'

Maggie pursed her lips and nodded. 'I'm sure.'

'Right.' He lifted his hand and glanced around the room, busy with the members of the Major Investigations Team. 'You'll have more privacy in the conference room.'

* * *

Having no memories of her mother and father, save the one of her mother burning, Maggie decided she could treat this objectively. They were people she didn't know, at least until her memories returned. If they returned. There were no guarantees they ever would. She took a deep breath, rolled her shoulders, and began by taking all of the photographs from the folders and spreading them out over the large table in the centre of the conference room.

'Just people,' she murmured as she spread out the gruesome photographs of her parents' charred remains.

When she came to a picture of herself at eight years of age, she sat abruptly, holding the photo up in front of her to study it. Iona said she had hypothermia when she was found. She failed to mention she'd been injured. Dark bruises circled her neck, in sharp contrast to her otherwise colourless skin. Even her lips were white. Her face was bruised and swollen, deep red blood around her nose and mouth and a deep gash over her left eye. Maggie brushed a finger over the white scar that bisected her left eyebrow, one she'd never questioned. In the photo, she lay on the ground in what Maggie assumed was

Lady Stair's Close, curled into a tight ball. Her dirty royal blue pyjamas, with a black and red-smeared Winnie the Pooh visible on the pyjama top, were soaked and no match for the cold November weather. Her long dark hair spread out in wet strands, some sticking to her pale face. Her eyes were closed. Sleeping or unconscious? she wondered. Or were her eyes swollen shut? It seemed cold that someone had taken a picture before tending to her.

The next pictures must have been taken at the hospital – close-ups of the bruises on her neck and face, bruises in the shape of fingers around both biceps, big dark bruises on her abdomen, front and back. Both knees were skint, bruising on her thighs and shins. A photograph of her entire face showed one eye open and one swollen shut. The open eye was glazed and unfocused, the white filled with the red veins of petechia, a result of being strangled. One picture focused on a large gash on her scalp and she raised a hand to trace her finger over the scar on the back of her head, another one she'd never questioned. Perhaps Iona thought she was protecting her by not telling Maggie she'd been badly beaten and strangled, but she'd asked Iona to tell her everything.

Maggie set the photos aside and leafed through the files until she found the Royal Hospital for Sick Children reports. She scanned through, noting two cracked ribs, concussion, and finally what she'd been searching for – negative for rape. Well, at least there was that. A few more pages in, she discovered a report from a psychologist describing trauma-induced memory loss or dissociative amnesia. The report described her case as generalised amnesia, meaning she couldn't remember her identity or life history. A referral was made for Maggie to see a psychotherapist, but she didn't remember ever seeing one.

Setting the papers down, Maggie sat back in her chair. Surely Iona would have ensured she got the help she needed, wouldn't she? Unless she didn't want Maggie to remember.

Fuck sake. Now Maggie didn't only distrust her uncle, but Iona too. Was there anyone she could trust?

She needed a break, needed to walk away and let everything sink in, but she feared if she did that, she'd never come back to it. Maggie picked up the file folder containing DS Claymore's reports and began reading, line by line.

* * *

DS Will MacLeod entered the conference room and waited for Glass's eyes to meet his. She looked tired, drawn. And heartbreakingly sad. When her gaze lifted to his, he said, 'Alright?'

Maggie shook her head and shrugged. 'I don't know.' She still felt numb to it all, as if her brain couldn't decide how to react. 'It's not triggering any memories if that's what you were hoping.'

He crossed the room to her and laid a business card on the table. 'In case it does. Or, even if it doesn't.'

Maggie picked up the card and snorted a quick laugh. He'd given her the card of the department psychologist. 'Think I'm crazy?'

In an unusual gesture of support, MacLeod laid a hand on Maggie's shoulder. 'No. But, we all need a bit of help now and then.'

Maggie resisted the urge to shrug MacLeod's hand away and looked up at him. 'I'm okay, but I'll give her a call if that changes.'

'Fair enough. Cause of death in Jamie Kenmore's case is carbon monoxide poisoning.'

Maggie closed her eyes for a moment. It wasn't a surprise that Kenmore had been alive while she was being burned, given that people heard her screams and Maggie wondered why no one had heard her parents. Kenmore's body had been in much better shape than her mother's and father's because

Kenmore was discovered much sooner. It was hours before her parents were discovered. 'There are too many similarities for these cases not to be related, including the pentacle pendants in the ashes.' The one found at the scene of her parents' murders was more of a melted glob, but the pentacle shape had still been recognisable.

'I agree.' MacLeod pulled out a chair and sat next to his partner. 'You've been at this for hours, Glass. Go home. Get some rest.'

Maggie picked up her mobile from the table and checked the time. She'd been studying the files for over six hours. 'Yeah.' Maggie dropped her head into her hands and scrubbed her face, hoping to revive herself. The last thing she wanted to do right now was to go home. She thought briefly about that run in the hills then had a better idea.

* * *

Maggie let Sylvan pick the restaurant and wasn't disappointed when she chose Contini, a fine Italian restaurant on George Street in the New Town. Maggie would have been happy in a pub, although she did have a fondness for Italian. Sylvan, it seemed, preferred high end. Like most businesses along George Street, Contini was in a Georgian house, similar to the ones Jamie Kenmore lived and worked in.

Sylvan waved from a table near the back when Maggie entered the restaurant and she crossed the dining room to join her, removing her coat before taking her seat. 'I hope you haven't been waiting long.'

'No, I just arrived myself.' Sylvan waited until Maggie seated herself then met her gaze. 'I'm so glad we ran into each other this morning. I've been looking for your contact information for the past few days.'

Business then. Maggie couldn't help but be disappointed. 'My uncle could have given it to you.'

The edge of Sylvan's painted mouth curled up. 'Without

involving your uncle.'

Maggie raised a brow.

'I've only been at Ghlais for a few weeks, but I like to know what I'm working with, so I've been doing some intense research. I've found some …' Sylvan's eyes turned up as if searching for something in her memory. '…discrepancies.' She focused on Maggie again.

'Shouldn't you discuss them with Alastaire?'

A young, dark-haired waiter approached the table and they each ordered a Ghlais whisky. Sylvan watched him walk away before speaking again. 'I understand you have little to do with the business, Ms Glass.'

'True.'

'There's no easy way for me to say this, so I'm just going to say it. I believe your uncle is ripping you off.'

That explained why she wasn't taking the matter to Alastaire. 'How so?'

'He's underpaying you. Considerably.'

Now she had Maggie's full attention. 'Why would he do that?'

'To fill his own pockets, perhaps. I don't know, but Alastaire's share of the profits is double compared to what he's paying you.'

Maggie supposed she only had herself to blame since she never bothered checking how much she should be receiving. She had more money than she knew what to do with. It had never occurred to her that Alastaire would short her.

'Essentially, what he's doing is embezzlement,' Sylvan said.

'You have proof of that?'

'Ms Glass–'

'Maggie, please.'

'Maggie, I'm a new employee at Ghlais. If I start making these accusations, I'll quickly find myself without a job.'

'Then why are you telling me?'

'I was hoping you could look into the matter without involving me. Your lawyers should be able to request an audit.'

'My lawyers?'

'You really have no idea?'

'I get a quarterly financial statement, but to tell you the truth, all those numbers make me cross-eyed.'

The waiter set their drinks on the table and asked if they were ready to order. Maggie told him they'd need some time and he left them again.

'Colin Eaglesham,' Sylvan stated. 'His father represented your parents' interests before Colin took over the firm.' She removed her mobile from her purse, looked up the corporate lawyer's website, and sent the link in a text to Maggie. 'Tell him what I've told you.'

'Right.' Maggie flipped her fringe out of her eyes and took a sip of her whisky. Did she want to stir this up? She had more than enough money, and Alastaire did all the work. Still, if he was embezzling funds, it needed to be investigated. If Alastaire wanted more money, all he'd had to do was ask. She would have agreed to it.

'Okay, now that's out of the way,' Sylvan lowered her chin, her twinkling blue eyes looking up at Maggie, and grinned, 'tell me all about yourself.'

Maggie laughed. Not all business then. She told Sylvan about her love of hillwalking and running, of knowing she wanted to be a police officer at an early age – as far back as she remembered. Sylvan explained she was a numbers geek at heart. She, too, loved the hills, but walking more than running. They both ordered a second whiskey and coffee at the end of the meal.

'I have to tell you,' Sylvan began. 'I'm not the type for casual relationships.'

Maggie lifted the glass of whisky to her lips and stopped, setting it back on the table. This turned serious awfully fast. 'Then I must warn you, I'm not great at commitment.' She shrugged and added, 'Abandonment issues and all that.'

'Oh?' Sylvan said with raised brows. 'Who abandoned you?'

'My parents were murdered when I was eight.' She said it matter-of-factly, still detached from the case she'd been studying just hours before.

Sympathy filled Sylvan's eyes. She reached across the table, laying her hand over Maggie's. 'I'm sorry. I knew that. How inconsiderate of me.'

'It was a long time ago.' What she felt like saying was it happened to someone else, but then she'd have to explain. Sylvan drew her hand away and Maggie instantly missed its warmth.

'Did your uncle raise you then?'

'No.' Maggie picked up the whisky again and took a slow sip. 'My Godmother.'

'So, you're not close to Alex?'

Strange reaction to her answer, Maggie thought. 'No, not particularly. Why?'

'Because I believe he's in on the embezzlement as well. Whatever your uncle is involved in, Alex is right there with him.'

Shite. If Maggie instigated an investigation into Sylvan's accusations and Alastaire and Alex were arrested for embezzlement, who the hell would run the company? This was the last thing she needed right now. 'I don't understand. If you're set on this being investigated, why not report it yourself? Surely you could protect your position at the company. Why involve me?'

'Because if the accusations are coming from you and Alastaire doesn't suspect me, I can be an asset to you inside the company.'

Okay, that made sense.

Sylvan leaned over, her hand covering Maggie's again. 'If you don't learn at least the basics of the financials and running the business, Maggie, it's too easy for people to take advantage of you.'

'Looks like it's too late for that.'

'It's never too late. You'll protect yourself from any future issues. I can help you.'

'It would be a lot easier if you'd be my eyes and ears inside Ghlais.'

'Easier, but you'd still be relying on someone else to secure your interests.'

Pouting, Maggie said, 'You know, no one asked me if I wanted a damn business.'

Sylvan broke out laughing, a beautiful musical laugh that forced a smile from Maggie. She couldn't help herself. Despite Sylvan's bluntness about not doing casual, Maggie wanted to continue seeing her. That was almost as scary as the idea of learning the whisky business.

'There's one other thing,' Sylvan said.

Good lord, now what? Maggie wondered.

'The three cases of Ghlais you picked up this morning?'

'Aye?'

'Alastaire has already deducted them from your next payment. He didn't even give you the wholesale price.'

Maggie had to laugh. She raised her hand and rubbed her forehead. 'Have I got *sucker* written up here?'

Chapter 6

Thursday nights were typically busy at the Regent, with people getting a head start on the weekend. Maggie got herself a beer from the bar and found a seat in the back. She wasn't ready to go home and sit alone with her thoughts yet. She'd parked the Range Rover at her flat in Abbeyhill and walked back to the pub after calling Nichola Dunn to meet her.

When Nichola arrived, she ordered an Irn Bru and a fish supper. 'Are you eating?' she asked Maggie.

Maggie shook her head, her fringe swaying back and forth. 'I've eaten.'

'Aren't you the big girl then? Remembering to eat at the start of a big investigation?' Nichola's brown eyes lit up with mirth. 'Did MacLeod feed you then?'

'I didn't realise I had a reputation for forgetting to eat.'

'Perhaps forgetting is the wrong word. You get so wrapped up in what you're doing, self-care takes a back seat.'

That sounded even worse than forgetting to eat. 'I take care of myself.'

'Oh, aye. Tell me, where did you have your supper?'

'I dined with the CFO of Ghlais.'

'That's unusual, isn't it?'

'It is. She believes Alastaire and Alex are embezzling funds from me.'

Nichola's mouth dropped open and her eyes widened then drew in. 'Oh, Maggie. What are you going to do?'

'I don't know yet. It's my own fault for not taking an interest.'

Nichola scoffed. 'You'd think you could trust your own uncle.'

'I'm starting to wonder if I can trust anyone.' When Nichola looked hurt by Maggie's statement, she quickly added, 'Except you. That's why I called you.' She wasn't lying. They'd been best friends since their days at the Royal High School in Clermiston. She could share anything with Nichola and know it would go no further.

'Is there anything I can do to help?'

Maggie's smile reached right up to her hazel eyes. 'You just did.'

The waiter dropped Nichola's Irn Bru off and Maggie ordered another beer. She wasn't going to get drunk, but she wanted enough to help her drift off to sleep or her active brain was going to keep her up all night with visions of the pictures she'd been looking at all afternoon.

'Something else is bothering you. Is it this case? Are they taking you off it?'

By now, Nichola would have seen the news tying this case to the Ghlais murders. She always turned on the news as soon as she woke up. 'I'm staying on it for now.'

'How'd you manage that?'

'You have to keep this one to yourself, but apparently, you can go shopping for favours from our DCI.'

'Maggie. You didn't.

'I did. But, I suspect that's not why McTavish left me on the case.'

'I don't understand. Why would they leave you on it? It's procedure. You don't investigate a case you have an emotional attachment to.'

The waiter deposited a fresh beer in front of Maggie. She downed the contents of the one in her hand and traded it out for the new one. 'I went through the files of my parents' murders this afternoon.'

Nichola gasped, slapping her hand over her heart. 'Maggie,' she yelled. 'What the hell were they thinking? What the devil were *you* thinking?'

Maggie set her beer down and took one of Nichola's hands in hers, conscious of the heads turning their way. Leaning forward, she looked straight into Nichola's eyes. 'No. Listen to me, Nic. Just like with the business, I've been taking the easy way out by not dealing with it. It's time I faced it. All of it.'

Tears formed in Nichola's eyes. 'Living through it wasn't bad enough? You have to put yourself through that again?'

'I *have* to remember,' Maggie whispered through gritted teeth. 'Do you ken? It's why they're leaving me on the case. I'm the only witness. They need to know what's locked away in my head.'

'Oh, dear God.' Nichola pulled her hand from Maggie's grasp and turned away, her tears flowing freely. She pressed the heels of her hands to her eyes and took several steadying breaths.

The strength of Nichola's reaction confused Maggie. It was as if she knew all of the details of the night Maggie's parents were killed. Then it hit her. 'You've seen the case files.'

Nichola nodded, her hands still pressed to her eyes. She'd never told Maggie, but she'd studied those files for the past five years, searching for a missed clue that may solve the case, but Maggie was right. The key to solving her parents' murders was locked in Maggie's mind.

'Then you do ken,' Maggie said quietly, calmly.

Nichola lifted her head and turned to her best friend. 'I ken why,' she said through her tears. 'But, my God, Maggie. What will it do to you when you remember?'

Maggie pulled Nichola into her embrace and held her tightly. Getting her memories back couldn't be much worse than studying the files and she survived that. 'I'll still be me,' she whispered.

Nichola wasn't so sure.

* * *

The two whiskies and four beers Maggie consumed didn't have the desired effect of turning her mind off. She lay awake all night with her parents' case, Jamie Kenmore's case, and the embezzlement accusation playing out repeatedly in her thoughts. At 05:00, Maggie gave up on getting any sleep and dressed in her running gear – leggings, long-sleeved t-shirt, fleece jacket, and her favourite trainers. She added a beanie and a head torch before going out the door and making her way into Holyrood Park. Starting at a slow jog, she made her way across the field to the hills of Arthur's Seat and the Salisbury Crags.

She turned the head torch on as she crossed Queen's Drive and began her first ascent, legs and arms pumping. The short rise gave way to a downhill slope along a path below the ruins of St. Anthony's chapel with the moon shining down from behind it like a spotlight. Then she sprinted up a steeper hill, challenging her muscles. The higher Maggie climbed, the fiercer the wind blasted her with cool, fresh air and her only thought was to wonder why she hadn't done this last night.

* * *

Iona greeted Maggie with scones and a cup of tea. They sat at the table in the kitchen with the sunlight shining through the window, Iona wringing her hands. 'I tried to call you last night.'

'I know. I'm sorry.' Maggie hadn't been ready to speak to Iona and let her calls go to voicemail.

'It's just I've been worried. Have you remembered any more?'

'No,' Maggie said with a shake of her head. 'I asked you to tell me everything the other day. Why didn't you?'

'I don't understand.'

Maggie stood, leaving her tea and scone untouched, and faced the window, staring out into the small garden with its square of green grass. 'I was injured when they found me. Strangled, beaten.' She turned back to Iona, who sat shrivelled in her chair. 'Why didn't you tell me?'

Iona's eyes flicked up to Maggie then down again. 'I was afraid I'd trigger more of your memories.'

'Why? What are you scared of?' Was Iona involved in her parents' murder? Is that why she was afraid of Maggie remembering?

'I think you need to see a therapist. I'm afraid of what will happen when you remember everything if you don't have someone to guide you, to help you.'

'The doctor recommended I see a psychotherapist after my parents were murdered. Why didn't I see someone back then?'

Iona stood and cupped Maggie's face in her trembling hands. 'Believe me, my darling, I wanted to take you to see someone. The guardianship agreement included a clause that forbade me taking you to see any form of therapist.'

Maggie clasped Iona's hands at her face. She was sure she knew the answer, but she asked, 'Who insisted on that clause?' What kind of person would refuse a traumatised child the therapy they needed?

Goddess help her as she truly believed what she was about to reveal could be her end. Iona took a stuttered breath, closed her eyes, and whispered, 'Alastaire.'

Maggie's grip on Iona's hands tightened, her jaw clenched, and her face flushed. It almost felt good, this rage building inside her after feeling numb for most of her life. 'You just recommended that I see a therapist.'

'And in doing so, broke the agreement I signed.'

'Do you have a copy of it?'

'Yes, of course.'

'Get it.' Maggie released Iona's hands. 'Now.'

Iona scurried away and returned with a manilla envelope, handing it to Maggie. 'Please be careful, Mags. Alastaire Ghlais can be quite unreasonable when he's not getting his way.'

Maggie embraced Iona, feeling she'd been too harsh with her. 'I'm sorry to put you through this. I don't want you to worry. He won't know you had anything to do with this.'

'Don't worry about me. Just look out for yourself. Please, Maggie. I couldn't stand it if anything happened to you.'

'I'll be fine, I promise.' Maggie stepped out of the embrace and headed for the front door then stopped and turned at a sudden thought. 'Oh, there's one more thing you can do for me.'

'Anything.'

'You know those old videos of my parents you have? Could I borrow them?' Perhaps the way to tease her memories out safely was with the happier memories.

* * *

It took Maggie several minutes of deep breathing to calm herself down as she sat in the Range Rover on the road outside Iona's house. Then she rang the office of Colin Eaglesham.

'Eaglesham and Associates,' a warm female voice answered.

'Hello. My name is Maggie Glass. My parents, Mairie and Malcolm Ghlais, were represented by your firm and I wondered if I could make an appointment to see Colin Eaglesham.'

'Of course, Ms Glass. I'm afraid Mr Eaglesham is tied up in court today, but he has an opening tomorrow at two o'clock. I'm assuming this is in regards to Ghlais Whisky.'

How did this woman know that? 'Tomorrow's Saturday.'

'Aye, he's working in the afternoon to get caught up. I'm sure he'd be happy to see you.'

'Alright. Two o'clock is fine.'

'He'll see you tomorrow then, Ms Glass.'

'Yes, thank you.'

* * *

Maggie left her coat at her desk and took a legal-sized notepad and the envelope Iona gave her into the conference room where she'd left the Ghlais case files. MacLeod was either out for a fag or elsewhere. She hadn't heard from him yet. She checked the time on her phone and realised it was probably because it was still early.

She took a seat at the conference table and drew a line down the centre of the notepad page. Maggie titled the left column Ghlais and the right Kenmore. Then she chronologically listed the similarities in the two cases – the foggy weather, the home invasion style abductions, the burning at the stake on the Esplanade, and the use of petrol as an accelerant. However, the use of petrol hadn't been confirmed by forensics in the Kenmore case yet. The glaring difference in the two cases was a child who survived the ordeal. Had they left her for dead on the Esplanade and she'd woken up and wandered away? Possible. In fact, she was convinced they hadn't intended for her to live. Had she seen their faces? Could she identify her parents' killers if she regained her memories? Is that why Alastaire insisted she didn't see a therapist? Did her uncle try to murder her entire family to get his hands on Ghlais? As much as she didn't want to believe it, it was the only motive she had for her parents' murders. But, and this was a big one, why would

Alastaire want Jamie Kenmore killed?

Maggie set her pen down with a long sigh and her eye caught Iona's envelope. She picked it up and drew out the papers, including several court documents and the notarised agreement signed by Alastaire and Iona. From what Maggie could gather, both Alastaire Ghlais and Iona Bryars filed for legal guardianship of her, but had settled out of court with the agreement. It wasn't just Alastaire who'd insisted on terms either. Iona had a few of her own. Most notably that Alastaire would not interfere with Maggie's upbringing and that he would abide by the terms and conditions set up by Mairie and Malcolm Ghlais regarding Ghlais Whisky. Maggie checked the envelope for more papers, but it was empty. She took out her mobile and rang Iona.

'Where would I get a copy of the terms and conditions my parents had in place for Ghlais?'

'Their lawyer would have a copy, I imagine.'

'But, you know what was in it?'

'Only that Mairie told me they'd ensured that if anything happened to them, the company would be run by her instructions and go to you, not to Alastaire.'

'So, it would be their will?'

'I don't know, Mags. Like I said, all that business and legal stuff bores me. I didn't pay much attention.'

You paid enough attention to refer to it in the guardianship agreement, Maggie thought. 'Okay, one more question.'

'Yes.'

'Why didn't they want the business to go to him and why didn't you want him involved in my upbringing?'

'That's easy. Because Alastaire Ghlais is a narcissistic bastard. I'm your Godmother, Mags. Your parents named me your guardian in their wills should anything happen to them. That bastard tried to take you from me. Alastaire had no legal right and he knew it. He would have lost in court.'

'Then why did you sign an agreement out of court?'

'He knew I couldn't afford the legal fees. He was going to draw it out until I had to sell my wee house.'

'In other words, he had you by the baws.'

'Oh, aye. A braw grip he had, too.'

Maggie leafed through DS Claymore's notes and reports again. He'd interviewed Alastaire, but he had a solid alibi. Alastaire was on holiday in Ibiza the night of the murders. Convenient. It didn't mean he wasn't involved.

Maggie's mobile rang and she picked it up from the table, checking the caller ID. She smiled, delighted to see Sylvan's name on the screen. Then delight turned to concern that she was calling about an issue at Ghlais and the smile fell away.

'Sylvan, hello. Everything alright?'

'Hello. Yes, sorry. I didn't mean to worry you. I just rang to say good morning.'

The smile returned. 'Good morning.'

'I really enjoyed your company last night. I hope we can do it again soon.'

'I'd like that.'

'Great. Let me know when you're free, even if it's just for a coffee.'

The conference room door opened and Maggie looked up to see MacLeod standing in the doorway in a baggy, wrinkled shite-brown suit. Behind him in the hallway stood a man with a round face, white hair cut close to the scalp, and kind blue eyes.

'Will do,' Maggie replied to Sylvan. 'I've got to go, but I'll call you soon.'

'Brilliant. Have a great day.'

'Yeah, you too.' MacLeod was going to know she was talking to someone she was interested in because Maggie couldn't keep the grin from her face.

MacLeod took a step into the room, waving the man

behind him to his side. 'DC Maggie Glass, this is DS Mitchel Claymore, retired.'

Maggie got up and circled the table, shaking Claymore's hand. 'Pleasure to meet you, sir.'

'And you,' he said. 'We've met before, but you were just a wee lass.'

She couldn't hide the slight wince. 'Of course.' Despite feeling oddly uncomfortable, she did have questions she wanted to ask Claymore.

MacLeod eyed Maggie from top to bottom, taking in the sage green tailored suit, pale yellow shirt, and brown leather loafers. Taking her jacket lapel between his thumb and forefinger, he said, 'Nice one. How many suits do you own?'

Maggie stared down at MacLeod's fingers until he removed them from her lapel. 'I'm not in the habit of counting my clothes. How many do you own?'

'I couldn't say, but I'd hazard a guess it's less than the number of suits hanging in your closet.'

Maggie shook her head and laughed. 'Hmmm. Perhaps. You look like you could do with some new ones.' She was sure MacLeod bought his suits from charity shops.

Claymore smiled for a moment before his expression turned sober. 'DI MacLeod shared with me what you remembered the other day. I hope you don't mind.'

Maggie spared MacLeod a quick, narrow-eyed look. 'Not at all.' What was she supposed to say?

'Have you remembered any more?' Claymore asked.

Heat spread across Maggie's face as she glared at MacLeod. 'Look, I'm not stupid. I ken you put me in here with these files,' she waved her hand at the table, 'hoping to trigger my memories, but, no, I don't remember anything else.'

MacLeod held up both hands, palms out. 'It's alright, Glass. DS Claymore came in to offer his help. We're not here to pressure you.'

'Perhaps not, but it's what you want, isn't it? It's why the Inspector allowed me to stay on the case.'

'You're the only witness,' Claymore began, 'in a case that has haunted me for the past eighteen years. I won't deny I'm hoping you remember. There's nothing I'd like more than to see those responsible for murdering your mother and father get what they deserve.'

Maggie dropped her head and stabbed her fingers into her hair, squeezing her head, wishing she could reach inside and pull out the answers. Maggie raised her head, leaving her dark hair askew, and huffed. 'Alright. I have questions.'

'Go on then, 'MacLeod said. 'I'm just away out for a fag.'

Chapter 7

Claymore took a seat next to Maggie with the contents of the Ghlais case files spread out before them.

'I want to know what's not in your notes and reports.' Maggie said. 'Your thoughts, opinions, intuition. Who topped your suspect list? What did you believe to be the motive?'

The wrinkles at the corner of Claymore's eyes deepened as he smiled. 'There's a bright lass.' He gave her a nod of respect. 'Here's what I believe happened that night after your parents were murdered. The perpetrators left you on the Esplanade, believing you dead, but you regained consciousness at some point. It didn't start raining that morning until about half five, so it was sometime after that you walked down to Lady Stair's Close as you were wet when we found you.'

Maggie had already come to that conclusion on her own. 'Who do you think did it and why?'

'Well, that's the problem, aye? The only motive I found that seemed realistic was that Alastaire Ghlais wanted the business, but he had a solid alibi.'

'He could have hired people to do his dirty work.'

'Aye, but we found no evidence of it. We went through his financials with a fine-tooth comb.'

'He could have had a hidden account.'

'If he did, we didn't find it.'

'Cash he embezzled from the company?'

Claymore raised a bushy white eyebrow. 'Now, what gave you that idea?'

Maggie wasn't about to start making accusations until she had proof. 'Is it possible?'

'I don't know. Is it?'

Maggie huffed and flopped back in her chair. Claymore leaned towards her. 'Are you suspicious of your uncle, DC Glass? Do you know something we don't?'

MacLeod picked that moment to return from his cigarette break. He took the seat across from Maggie and Claymore as Maggie glared up at him through her fringe.

'Everything alright?' MacLeod asked.

Claymore nodded. 'I was just asking DC Glass why she suspects her uncle.'

'I didn't say I suspected him,' Maggie said sternly. How did this get turned around to where she was the one being questioned?

'But, you know something,' Claymore said. 'I can see it in your eyes, lass.'

'I don't know anything.' At least until she spoke to Eaglesham. 'I'm just throwing a scenario out there.'

'What scenario?' MacLeod asked.

Claymore didn't waste a moment in catching him up. 'That her uncle paid for the murders of Mairie and Malcolm Ghlais with funds embezzled from the company.'

'*Caoch!* Is the bastard embezzling funds from you, Glass?' MacLeod's Gaelic expletive translated to *shite*.

Fuck sake! Maggie leaned forward, her forearms braced on the table. 'I don't know. It's been brought to my attention that he may be. I'm looking into it.'

MacLeod and Claymore shared a look.

'What?' Maggie asked. They were holding something back

from her. She was sure of it.

'That could be the lead we've been hoping for,' MacLeod answered. 'It fits, doesn't it? If his motive for the murder of your parents was to steal the business and you didn't die as planned, he'd find other means to get what he wanted. The motive is the money.'

Maggie disagreed. 'It doesn't explain Jamie Kenmore's murder. What would be his motive in killing her? And why risk using a method that could focus the investigation back on him.'

A sly smirk turned Claymore's lip up. 'He's playing with us. He'd want to be questioned, suspected. He thrives on attention. He'll have an unshakable alibi again, no doubt.'

Iona's comment popped into Maggie's mind – *Because he's a narcissistic bastard.* 'It still doesn't give us a motive for Kenmore. I'll go and speak to the executives at Gold Star again.'

MacLeod followed Maggie out into the hall, pulling the conference room door closed behind him. 'I don't want you to think I had anything to do with these methods of trying to jog your memory. I argued against it.'

'Well then, I suppose I owe you my gratitude. And while we're at it, thanks for giving me a heads up about the whole plan.' She spun on her heel and continued down the hall. It seemed like she was on a roller coaster the last couple of days, shifting between angry, betrayed, and elated at the prospects dating Sylvan. Except for anything involving Sylvan, she wished she could go blissfully back to numb.

She was about to grab her overcoat from the chair, but realised she hadn't checked her emails for a few days. Maggie sat down and turned on her computer, logging into her email account. It was all the usual stuff – procedural changes, memorandums, blah, blah. Then she came to a name she recognised and clicked to open the email. Her face flushed and she gritted her teeth. Apparently, she'd been scheduled for an appointment at 10:00 am on Tuesday with Dr Brenna Argyle – the department psychologist. The email had been sent not two hours after she'd told MacLeod about the memory of her parents being burned. *Fuck sake!* He'd given her Dr Argyle's card as if he was letting her decide whether or not to make an appointment. The bastard.

* * *

Maggie turned right onto St. Leonard's Street from the police station. Right about where it became the Pleasance, she noticed the tail behind her – the same black Mercedes sedan. The lad was persistent. Well, let's see how well he knows the cobbled streets of Edinburgh's Old Town. Maggie sped up, took a left at West Richmond Street, and timed a break in the traffic to make a quick right onto Nicholson. Maggie spent fifteen minutes zig-zagging between the Royal Mile, Cowgate, and Chambers Street. She was confident she lost her pursuant, but she had to be careful. She didn't want to run into him again while making her way out of the Old Town. She sped down Cowgate, turning right onto the Pleasance then right again onto Infirmary Street and another right onto South Bridge. She kept an eye on her rearview mirror as she drove across North Bridge into the New Town, then along George Street until she found a parking spot near Gold Star. She sat in the car for another five minutes, watching the traffic all around her, but she didn't spot the black Mercedes.

A light drizzle began to fall as Maggie got out of her car, pulling her mobile from her pocket. It was more of a mist than actual rain, but it was enough for Maggie to button her coat and pull her collar up. She rang MacLeod as she walked down the pavement towards Gold Star and told him about the vehicle following her since her visit to Ghlais. She gave MacLeod the number plate of the Mercedes and the driver's name and left it with him.

At Gold Star, she pushed the button on the intercom and a female voice she didn't recognise answered.

'Detective Constable Maggie Glass.' She didn't state her purpose for being there. She wanted to catch the executives off guard as much as possible. The door buzzed and Maggie entered. She drew her warrant card from her pocket, holding it up for the woman sitting at the reception desk as she passed by. 'I know my way.'

If the receptionist objected, she didn't say. Maggie took the stairs up to the top floor where she found Jamie Kenmore's PA, Sarah Graham, sitting at a desk in front of an open office door. The other two office doors were closed, guarded by two more women sitting at desks identical to Graham's.

'Sarah,' Maggie said in greeting. 'I have a few questions for Ms Dunbar and Ms Gray.' A glance over Graham's shoulder into the empty office told her forensics had picked up Kenmore's computer.

'Oh, um. Right.' Sarah picked up her phone and dialed an extension. 'Sharon. DC Glass is here to see you and Kelsey.' Graham winced and moved the phone a few inches from her ear. 'Yes, ma'am.' She set the phone back on its cradle and looked up at Maggie with sheepish eyes. 'They'll be right with you.'

'Not happy to see me?'

'It's not that. It's just been very tense around here since Jamie's passing. Our clients are questioning the future of our business without her. Sharon and Kelsey are doing their best to ensure everyone that it will be business as usual, but it's taking up all their time.'

It made Maggie wonder again who would run Ghlais if Alastaire was arrested. 'Do you know of any tension between Gold Star and Ghlais Whisky?'

'I'm sorry, DC Glass. That's a question you need to ask

Sharon.'

Sharon, Maggie noted. The one who did all the talking the last time they spoke. She'd yet to hear a word out of Kelsey Gray.

'DC Glass?'

Maggie turned to see Sharon Dunbar standing in her open doorway in a sleek grey suit and crisp white shirt just as the door to Kelsey Gray's office opened. Gray stepped out in an equally impressive suit in black paired with a black shirt. Gray closed the door behind her and brushed past Dunbar to enter her office.

'Ms Dunbar,' Maggie said with a nod as she crossed the room and stepped into the office. Gray was already seated at a round table in the corner. Maggie took the seat directly across from her. 'Ms Gray.'

Gray nodded, her expression sombre.

Dunbar sat on Gray's right and Maggie shifted her chair to her right, giving herself the optimum view of both women.

'What can we do for you, DC Glass?' Dunbar asked.

'I have a few more questions. Has there been tension between Gold Star and Ghlais Whisky in the last few months?'

Dunbar's eyes widened for a split second, but Gray didn't give anything away. Her expression remained cold and passive, but her gaze met Dunbar's.

Dunbar stared at Gray for what felt like eons and Maggie couldn't help but wonder once again if they were communicating telepathically like Sapphire Dovefeather.

Dunbar turned her gaze to Maggie. 'I suppose you could call it tension. A couple of weeks ago, Ghlais's new CFO called us requesting to cancel their contract with us. When Jamie explained the consequences, they changed their mind.'

'What were the consequences?'

'Our contract with Ghlais was arranged when the company

was owned by Mairie and Malcolm Ghlais, nearly twenty-five years ago. Mairie signed a fifty-year deal with us. The penalty for breaking it is fifty per cent of the remaining contract.'

'Fifty years? Why would she sign a contract for half a century?'

Dunbar's smile resembled the Cheshire cat's. 'Several reasons. She was impressed with the work we were doing on the Ghlais brand and she knew Gold Star was about to become very successful. Being the clever woman she was, she locked in long-term at an excellent price. Mairie was also a friend, DC Glass. For our business to go to the next level, we needed an infusion of cash. Ghlais's contract with us gave us the boost we needed. The rest is history.'

'You helped Ghlais Whisky skyrocket to success and, in turn, Ghlais did the same for Gold Star.'

'Exactly.'

'Why did Ghlais want to cancel the contract?'

'Your guess is as good as mine. The CFO stated it was a cost-cutting measure.'

'Cost-cutting?' Why the hell would they need to cost cut? Ghlais was doing extraordinarily well as far as Maggie knew.

'That's what she said.' Dunbar turned to Gray. 'What was her name, Kelsey?'

'Sylvan MacKenzie.'

'Oh, yes. Sylvan. She seemed pleasant enough, but I only talked to her on the phone.'

'What happened to their old CFO?' Maggie asked out of curiosity.

Dunbar and Gray looked into each other's eyes again before Dunbar answered. 'George Stanton? The official statement said he passed away from a heart attack right at his desk. The rumour mill says he committed suicide by overdose.' Dunbar stared at Maggie with a raised eyebrow and a smirk.

'Could I get a copy of your contract with Ghlais?'

Dunbar's smirk remained. 'Of course. As soon as you present a warrant.'

Shite. Maggie wanted to see that contract. 'What if I were the owner of Ghlais? Could you give it to me then?'

Dunbar and Gray looked at each other again, both with eyes wide open.

'Maggie Glass,' Gray whispered. 'Magaidh Ghlais.'

Dunbar rose to her feet. 'I'm sorry. I didn't put it together.' She turned to a mahogany stained filing cabinet and opened the top drawer, fishing through until she pulled out a thick file. 'Jane,' she called out. 'A moment.'

The woman sitting at the desk outside the door jumped to her feet and came to the doorway. Dunbar handed her the file. 'Can you copy that for me, please? Right away.'

'Of course.' The woman took the folder and left.

Impressive, Maggie thought. Maybe she should tell people she owned Ghlais more often.

Dunbar retook her seat. 'We knew your parents very well, DC Glass. Mairie especially. She was a great friend. Do you remember the dinner parties we shared? You were such a bright light and a great joy to your parents.'

'No, I'm sorry. I don't remember.'

'I should have known,' Gray said. 'You look just like her. I'm sorry I didn't recognise you.'

She would have had to look at Maggie to recognise her, which she hadn't until she realised who Maggie was. 'It's not a problem.'

Dunbar's arm shifted under the table. Maggie couldn't see her hand, but she figured she'd just placed it on Gray's thigh.

'Do you mind if I ask why you're not running Ghlais,' Dunbar asked.

'My mother may have had a brilliant mind for business,

but I didn't inherit it.' Maggie shrugged. 'I've always wanted to be a detective.'

'It's a shame,' Gray said. 'We'd much rather deal with you than Alastaire.'

'How so?' Maggie asked.

Dunbar and Gray shared another look.

'Let's just say that managing his public persona is a challenge,' Dunbar answered. 'He's definitely getting his money's worth from the contract your mother negotiated.'

'May I be excused, DC Glass?' Gray asked as she got to her feet. 'I've got a lot of work to get through.'

'Of course.'

Dunbar watched Gray go then turned to Maggie. 'Jamie's death has been tough on Kelsey. She's finding it very difficult just to come into the office.'

'You don't have to explain. I understand.'

'I'm sure you do. Is Jamie's death related to Mairie and Malcolm's?'

'I can't say for sure.'

'That will be the official answer, of course. The similarities are too great to ignore though.'

Maggie didn't respond.

'Perhaps once this is over, you'll join us for dinner. We'll tell you all about your mother and father. And Jamie, of course. It would do Kelsey good to remember all of the good times.'

'I'd like that.' The conversation turned too personal and Maggie still had a question. 'Will you hire a new CEO?'

Dunbar shook her head and shifted in her seat. 'No. I'll take over that role officially. She doesn't know it yet, but we're going to promote Sarah Graham to help me with that. She'll be a VP.'

That seemed just right to Maggie. Graham was probably wondering if she was out of a job. 'When will you tell her?'

'After the memorial service. We don't have a date set yet, but we're hoping for next week.'

Maggie fished in her pocket and handed Dunbar her card. 'Let me know when you have a date.'

She walked out of Gold Star with a stack of papers. All she'd asked for was the contract, but she'd been given the entire Ghlais file. It might be interesting reading to see what predicaments they'd had to get Alastaire out of anyway.

Chapter 8

Maggie turned onto St. Leonard's Lane next to the police station and spotted the black Mercedes at the curb. She slowed down, grinned, and waved at MacDonald as she rolled past. He scowled at her and she laughed.

MacLeod and Claymore were huddled over the table in the conference room. Maggie entered the room and asked, 'You find anything on Robert MacDonald?'

Macleod and Claymore looked at each other and laughed. 'You really should learn a wee bit about the company you own,' MacLeod said. 'You sign the man's paycheques.'

She didn't actually sign anyone's paycheque, but she knew what he meant. Technically, MacDonald worked for her and that gave Maggie an idea. 'I'll be right back.'

MacLeod called out after her, 'Oh, and you own the car he's driving.'

Maggie shook her head. How crazy was that? She went out the side door to the street, not surprised to see MacDonald still sitting in the Mercedes. She approached the driver's window as MacDonald stared straight ahead, ignoring her. That's fine. He could hear her through the window.

'I assume you know I own Ghlais Whisky.'

No response.

'If I catch you following me again, I'll terminate your

77

employment with my company.'

That got his attention. He flung his head around and glared out the window. 'You can't do that.'

'Did you miss the part where I said I own the company? Which also means I own this fine car you're driving. Maybe you should get out of my car and give me my keys.'

His mouth dropped open. 'You can't do that. I need it for work.'

'For following your boss?'

'I work for Alastaire Ghlais.'

'Alastaire doesn't own the company.'

The window rolled down. 'Look, miss–'

'Detective Constable.'

'Right. Anyway, I'm just following orders. I was told to keep an eye on you and Alastaire's not pleased that I got caught the other day. He's really not going to be happy I lost you this morning. I may get sacked anyway.'

'He'd fire you for losing me?'

'Oh, aye. Alastaire doesn't tolerate mistakes.'

'What's your job title?'

'Security Manager.'

Maggie snorted a quick laugh. 'Tell Alastaire I went to a crime scene on the Esplanade.'

'But, you didn't. I checked there.'

'You want to stay out of trouble or not?' She turned and walked back into the station.

MacLeod and Claymore looked up at her with broad smiles as she entered the conference room. 'What did you do?' MacLeod asked.

'I threatened to fire him if I caught him following me again.' Maggie pulled off her coat and sat opposite the two men.

'Can you do that?'

'What, fire him? I own the company, don't I?'

'Aye, but do you actually have powers in the running of it?'

Maggie stared at MacLeod with a blank expression. *Well, shite.* 'I have no idea.'

MacLeod shook his head and sighed. 'Alastarie Ghlais could have been robbing you blind this whole time and you'd have no idea.'

Maggie lifted her elbows to the table and rested her chin in her hands. She really was going to have to get more involved in Ghlais. Unless... 'I may have someone on the inside to monitor things for me.'

'Is this the same person who warned you about embezzlement?' MacLeod's brow lifted as he waited for Maggie's answer.

'Aye.'

Claymore cleared his throat. 'If you don't mind me putting my nose where it doesn't belong, be very careful who you trust there. Your uncle could be up to something.'

'Point taken.' Maggie raised her head before she dozed off. The lack of sleep was catching up to her. 'Anyone want a coffee?'

When Maggie returned with three coffees, she presented an overview of her interview with Dunbar and Gray.

'Do you think they would murder Kenmore to get her shares of the company?' MacLeod asked.

'It's possible.'

MacLeod shook his head. 'What does your gut tell you, Glass?'

He always seemed interested in what her gut told her. To date, she'd humoured him, but one of these days, she was going to ask him why he put so much stock in her intuition. 'My sense is that they were a close-knit group, loyal and supportive of each other. So, no, I don't think they would murder their friend and associate.' She couldn't get a good read on Dunbar's grief, but Gray's was genuine. Either that or she was drowning in guilt. Still, Maggie didn't get the sense that they were capable of burning their friend alive.

'It's time you had a talk with Alastaire Ghlais,' Claymore said to MacLeod. 'He'll have his alibi at the ready, but you'll be able to get a sense of him through his reactions to your questions.'

'We'll question this new CFO while we're at it,' MacLeod said.

Shite. This was going to be awkward as hell, Maggie thought. 'Any chance we can leave the embezzlement accusations out? I don't want to tip Alastaire off about that as yet.'

MacLeod studied Maggie for a moment. 'Aye, okay. But, you need to look into it, Glass.'

'No bother. I'm doing just that.' Odd that MacLeod seemed to have her back. They hadn't been working together all that long, but he felt like her protector. Almost like a father figure, she thought, even though he wasn't old enough to be her father. It gave her a weird sense of comfort given that she couldn't trust those closest to her. 'But, thanks for your concern.'

'Nae bother,' MacLeod said with a nod and added a tight-lipped smile.

* * *

'This is proper luxury.' MacLeod's eyes roamed the interior of the Range Rover before focusing on the dash. 'Did you need to take a course to figure out all they buttons and knobs?' He leaned forward, reaching for the radio controls when Maggie slapped his hand away.

'Look, but don't touch. I have everything set just right.' It took her ages and she probably could have used a course, but the manual had gotten her to where she wanted in the end.

MacLeod shifted in his seat, twisting to get a look at the

plush leather seats in the back. '*Póg mo thóin!* Is that a footrest?'

Maggie didn't speak Gaelic, but she was becoming well-versed in the sweary phrases of the language. She recognised this one as *kiss my arse*. 'Aye. The seats back there also have hot stone massage.'

'Well then,' he said as he undid his seatbelt. 'I'm sitting in the back.' He got out and into the back seat as Maggie laughed.

Maggie pulled out of the car park and raised her hand, wiggling her fingers at Robert MacDonald as she drove by the black Mercedes. She wasn't bothered about him following her to Ghlais.

MacLeod fiddled with the ten-inch screen on the seatback, then reclined his seat and turned on the hot stone massage. 'Why the devil would you buy a car with all this in it when you can't enjoy it yourself?'

Maggie glanced at him through the rearview mirror, reclined and relaxed. He looked very content. 'You're using it.'

'In that case, I appreciate you buying this car. We'll take your vehicle whenever we go out in the field together.' He lifted the lid on a compartment in the centre console and gasped. 'Glass! You've got a bloody fridge in your backseat.'

Maggie threw her head back and barked out a loud laugh.

'Go on then,' MacLeod said with a pout. 'Have a go at your financially challenged DS. My wee car is on its last legs. Poor Buttercup.'

Maggie laughed harder. 'You named your car Buttercup?'

He mumbled something under his breath that Maggie couldn't hear.

MacLeod picked up the stack of papers on the seat next to him. 'What's all this then?'

Maggie glanced in the rearview mirror as MacLeod held

up the reams of paper. 'It's Gold Star's file on Ghlais.'

'They gave it to you?'

'They did when I mentioned I owned the company.'

'Right.' MacLeod fanned through the pages. He wasn't quite sure what a media relations company did. It would be interesting, he thought, to see what they did for Alastaire Ghlais. 'Mind if I take a wee look?'

'No, go ahead. I haven't had a chance to look through it yet.' As much as she enjoyed the laugh, Maggie was relieved when silence descended in the vehicle. She let her thoughts drift as she drove through the traffic, leaving Edinburgh and out onto quieter roads. Her mind kept bringing her back to Sylvan and her attraction to the beautiful, sophisticated woman. There was no other way to broach the subject of Sylvan asking to break the contract with Gold Star than to bluntly ask. Maggie only hoped Sylvan wasn't playing her and that this investigation wouldn't ruin their chances of getting to know each other.

They were nearly at Ghlais when MacLeod interrupted the peaceful quiet. 'Glass? There's a problem here.'

Maggie glanced at him in the mirror, his face drawn, his mouth pursed in a fine line. 'What problem?'

'There are dozens of accusations against your uncle for sexual harassment or sexual assault from female employees at Ghlais – everything ranging from grabbing an arse to rape. The complaints were all handled with monetary settlements and the victims signing non-disclosure agreements.'

Maggie's stomach roiled. For a moment, she thought she may have to pull over to be sick. Was this the motive they'd been searching for? Did Alastaire order Jamie Kenmore's murder to keep his dirty secrets?

'It adds up to a shite ton of money, Glass.'

Maggie did pull over to the side of the road then. She stopped the car and turned in her seat, her face ashen. 'How much are we talking about?'

'I haven't gone through them all, but I'm up to about three million quid.'

Maggie stabbed her fingers in her hair and curled them into a fist. 'Fuck sake.'

'Do you suppose Jamie Kenmore threatened to expose him?'

Maggie could see her threatening to do just that if Alastaire didn't clean up his act. Gold Star must have been sick covering up these allegations. 'I want to speak to Dunbar and Gray again before we speak to Alastaire.'

'Right. Back to the city centre then.'

Maggie made a U-turn and headed back towards Edinburgh. The black Mercedes passed her, but it wouldn't be long before he turned around and caught up. It would be easier to lose him on the busy streets in the city centre, but she sped up, hoping he wouldn't catch up before she could find an alternate route and some side roads to evade him.

'What's the hurry,' MacLeod asked.

'I need to lose MacDonald.'

MacLeod had been enjoying the luxuries of Maggie's Range Rover so much, he hadn't even realised they were being tailed. 'Right,' he said, as if he'd known all along.

Why hadn't Dunbar just told her about Alastaire's issues instead of handing her the file and leaving her to find out on her own? Or not find out. There were no guarantees that she would read the files. The more she pondered the whole thing, the higher her blood pressure rose. For a company that thrived on keeping drama under wraps, Gold Star certainly seemed to enjoy creating it.

It was nearly 2:00 pm when Maggie pulled into a parking spot on George Street, having successfully lost the Mercedes. She identified herself on the intercom at Gold Star and didn't bother to show her warrant card. She charged up the stairs with MacLeod huffing and puffing behind her. Dunbar and Gray stood in front of Dunbar's office door as Maggie marched into the room.

Dunbar pulled a £20 note from her pocket and passed it to Gray. 'Seems I lost the bet, DC Glass. Kelsey said you'd be back today. I figured Monday.'

'Do you think this is a game?' Maggie growled through gritted teeth. 'Jamie Kenmore is dead.'

Dunbar's smug expression dropped away and her face paled.

'I asked you point-blank if there was anyone who may be a threat to Gold Star or to Jamie Kenmore. Why the hell didn't you mention Alastaire Ghlais?'

Dunbar and Gray shared one of their annoying looks before Dunbar answered. 'Alastaire Ghlais may be a sexual predator, but we don't think he's capable of murder.'

'*You* don't think he's capable? It's not up to you to decide that.' Maggie stabbed her finger towards the two women. 'Your job is to answer our questions so we can conduct our investigation. Lying by omission is still lying. I could charge you both with obstruction of justice.'

Sarah Graham and the other two personal assistants looked on with eyes ping-ponging between the two parties. MacLeod stepped forward, placing a hand on Maggie's forearm. 'Perhaps we'd be better discussing this in your office, Ms Dunbar.'

Dunbar stood with a hand over her heart and said nothing. She walked into her office with Gray on her heels. Maggie and MacLeod followed, MacLeod closing the door behind him. Everyone remained standing. Gray swayed from foot to foot with her eyes cast on the plush, charcoal grey carpet. Dunbar stood with one arm hugging her abdomen and one hand still firmly on her chest.

Maggie waited for MacLeod. Her ire would only have her

yelling at the two women again.

'Did Ms Kenmore threaten to expose the sexual harassment complaints against Alastaire?' MacLeod asked in a calm, even tone.

'No,' Dunbar shook her head firmly. 'She didn't threaten to reveal anything, but she did tell him we wouldn't cover for him again. It was a decision we made together. In the beginning, it was one or two instances within a year. Even those first cases took a toll on each of us. It's been getting progressively worse and more frequent ever since. We couldn't in good conscience continue to make deals to cover up for his … indiscretions.'

'Why the hell didn't you just tell me?' Maggie asked again.

'Oh, believe me, DC Glass, we wanted to. We're bound by a non-disclosure agreement with severe consequences for breaking it. We couldn't tell you and we couldn't give you Ghlais's file without a warrant. That is until we realised you are Magaidh Ghlais and own the company.'

'So when I asked you for the contract, you gave me everything hoping I'd read it?'

'We knew you'd read it. We just didn't know when.'

'How did you know?' Maggie didn't know herself, although she had been intrigued by the idea of reading about the shenanigans Gold Star fixed for Alastaire.

Dunbar and Gray shared that look again. It was Gray who answered this time. 'Like your mother, I have the gift of sight.'

Like my mother? 'My mother was psychic?'

'As are you,' Gray answered. 'You may not use it to the best of your ability, but your intuition is powerful and true, is it not?'

Maggie shrugged. Was it? It was something Maggie took for granted and assumed everyone's intuition was relatively the same. 'Did you foresee Jamie Kenmore's death?'

'Not specifically. We knew something dark was coming. It's one of the reasons we decided to take a firm stance against Alastaire Ghlais. Perhaps in doing so, we caused Jamie's death.'

Was that why Gray looked guilty? 'You can't blame yourself. The only ones to blame are the people who killed her.' Or conspired to do so, Maggie thought.

'Perhaps.'

Gray didn't look like she believed it, but Maggie let it go. It would take time for her to heal and maybe then she would feel less guilty. 'Is there anyone else who may have had a reason to murder Jamie that you can't tell me about?'

'No. Not that we can think of,' Dunbar answered. 'Except for Alastaire Ghlais, our clients are law-abiding citizens. We're not in the habit of covering up crimes.'

'When exactly did Ms Kenmore tell Alastaire Ghlais that Gold Star wouldn't be covering for him again?' Maggie asked.

'Two weeks ago this past Monday,' Dunbar answered.

'We'll let you get back to your business then,' MacLeod said.

Maggie waited until they were outside on their way to the car before speaking. 'You knew my mother was psychic.' She didn't know how he knew, but it was why he was always asking about her gut reactions. Maggie was sure of it.

MacLeod stopped walking and lit a cigarette, blowing out a long stream of smoke. 'I was in my first year in uniform when you're parents were murdered. I was one of the first on scene. I wasn't assigned to the case, but Claymore used my partner and me to do a lot of the witness interviews and leg work.'

'And one of those witnesses told you my mother was psychic?'

The edges of MacLeod's mouth curled up. 'A lot of the

people we talked to said she was psychic. We heard many stories of how she told people things she couldn't possibly know or predicted things that often came true. Many said Mairie Ghlais could have made a good living as a psychic, but of course, she wasn't interested in that. The whisky business was her forté.'

From the sounds of it, MacLeod knew her mother better than Maggie did just based on the people he'd talked to. 'Why didn't you tell me this before now?'

'It's an awkward thing to bring up, isn't it?'

'You knew the Kenmore case was related to my parents' case from the get-go.'

MacLeod took a last haul on his cigarette and snuffed it out on the sole of his shoe. 'That was also awkward. I didn't know how much you knew about their murders or how it would affect you. I contacted DS Claymore and we discussed both cases.'

'So, you had their file before I told you about the memory?'

'Only just.'

'Were you and the Inspector discussing pulling me from the case from the start?'

'I didn't speak to him until after you rang me about your memory. I was the one who argued you should be taken off the case, Glass. The Inspector insisted we attempt to jog the rest of your memories.'

'And who notified the psychologist?'

MacLeod's eyes widened. 'I didn't contact the psychologist. I just gave you her card.'

Maggie couldn't be angry with him. He was looking out for her by trying to get her off the case. 'If we're going to work together, I need you to be upfront with me. No more hiding stuff from me.' They were a good match, with Maggie preferring the field and MacLeod preferring to ride his desk and computer, but Maggie couldn't tolerate him working behind her back.

MacLeod met Maggie's gaze. 'You've my word.'

'I should make you pay for the case of whisky I paid McTavish.'

'How much is a case worth?'

'About twenty-three hundred pounds.'

MacLeod's eyes bugged out. '*Pòg mo thòin!* That's three months rent.'

'Three months? Where the hell do you live? In a cardboard box?'

Chapter 9

On the drive back out to Ghlais, MacLeod sat upfront. Maggie contemplated the other question burning in her brain until she couldn't hold it in any longer.

'The witness interviews you did during the investigation of my parents' murders weren't in the files. What else is missing?'

MacLeod let out a loud sigh. Not much got by his partner. He had to give her that. 'I'll see that you get the rest.'

Maggie nodded, tapping her fingers on the steering wheel. 'All of a sudden, I'm not sure who I can trust. I need to know that I can trust you, MacLeod.'

'I've got your back, Glass. I promise you that.'

If she was going to put as much stock in her gut as everyone else seemed to, she could rely on MacLeod. Despite questioning him about it, Maggie knew he'd been watching her back all along. 'I've got yours, too.'

Maggie parked in a visitor's spot at Ghlais. On the way across the car park to the entrance, MacLeod reminded her to let him do the talking with Alastaire.

'Right. I'll just be arm candy.' She got a laugh out of MacLeod.

Maggie led MacLeod up the stairs to Mrs Brown at the reception desk. 'Is he in?' Maggie asked

Mrs Brown smiled up at Maggie and MacLeod, her brown eyes twinkling through her red frames. 'Aye, away you go then.' She waved them towards the hallway on her left.

Maggie preceded MacLeod down the hall, tapped on the double doors, then stood aside to let MacLeod pass through before her as she opened the door.

'Mr Ghlais,' MacLeod began as he drew out his warrant card and held it up. 'DI Will MacLeod. We have a few questions.'

Maggie closed the door behind her, noting the fire roaring in the fireplace and Alex sitting in front of her uncle's desk again. Did the two of them spend all day in here chatting?

Alastaire rose from his chair wearing black trousers, a pressed white shirt, and a tartan tie. 'Questions?'

'Aye. Can you tell me your whereabouts on Wednesday night from nine o'clock to six on Thursday morning?'

Alastaire smiled, but his eyes looked colder than a Canadian winter. 'I was home with my wife.'

'All night?'

'Yes. My wife can confirm that for you, DI MacLeod. She was up in the night with me as I was feeling poorly. Food poisoning, perhaps. At any rate, she got up with me at around half one and we were up until my stomach settled around half three or four.'

Convenient, Maggie thought.

'Now, if that's all, we've a lot of work here.' Alastaire retook his seat and pulled a file folder from the corner of his desk, opening it in front of him.

'Sorry,' MacLeod said. 'Just a few more questions.'

Alastaire looked up at him with a smirk. 'About?'

'Was there any tension between you and Gold Star Media Relations, Mr Ghlais?'

'Gold Star has been representing Ghlais since before I took the helm.'

MacLeod raised an eyebrow, waiting for Alastaire to answer the question. The two men stared at each other for a long moment. If Maggie had to place a bet on who would break first, her money would be on her uncle. MacLeod had the patience of a saint when he wanted to.

'No, there was no tension. Gold Star does a fine job managing our brand.'

'The brand or your indiscretions?' MacLeod asked, watching closely for Alastaire's reaction. He wasn't disappointed.

Alastaire shot to his feet, his face turning beetroot. 'I beg your pardon?'

'You know what I'm talking about, Mr Ghlais. Gold Star has been putting out fires for you for years, covering up the numerous accusations of sexual harassment and assault you've accumulated.'

'How dare you? Those accusations were false. It starts with one employee getting away with a false accusation and word spreads. It's easy money. They make a false complaint with pound signs in their eyes.' He slammed his fist on his desk, making Alex jump in his seat. 'Where did you get this defamatory information? I'll have their heads.'

'Their heads?" MacLeod waited a moment for effect. "Or burn them at the stake?'

Alastaire's face turned so red it was closer to purple. He spat through clenched teeth, 'I'll have your job, MacLeod. My own brother was murdered in that manner.'

MacLeod offered him a pleasant smile. 'You could try, Mr Ghlais. And you needn't worry about Gold Star. I didn't get the information from them.'

'Then where the hell did you get it?' Alastaire yelled. 'I demand an answer.'

MacLeod wasn't going to answer that particular question, so he ignored it and the demand. 'Is Ghlais having financial difficulties with the money you've paid out in settlements?'

Maggie was standing a fair distance from her uncle, but she could still see the line of sweat over his lip and across his brow. She'd also been watching Alex's reactions. He hadn't gone red, but white, and his eyes were bulging as they bounced back and forth between Alastaire and MacLeod.

'I run a very successful company and I'm getting bored of your accusations. If you're not here to arrest me, you know where the door is.' Alastaire dropped back into his seat, huffing.

MacLeod turned to Maggie and nodded his head at the door. She let MacLeod walk out first then turned back. 'Oh, I'll be in on Monday to start learning the business. Have a good weekend.' Before she closed the door, Maggie was sure she saw steam coming out of Alastaire's ears.

In the hallway, MacLeod whispered, 'What was that about?'

'Sorry, I'm playing with him a bit.' She was only half-serious. It was time she learned the business. At least, enough to ensure he wasn't ripping her off.

Maggie approached Mrs Brown at the reception desk again. 'Is Ms MacKenzie available?'

'Yes, do you know where the CFO's office is? It's the first door on the right.' She waved towards the hallway they'd just come from.

'Brilliant, thanks.' Maggie leaned over the desk and whispered. 'Listen, if Alastaire is prone to temper tantrums when he's upset, it may be a good idea if you took the rest of the day off.'

'I've been working here for nearly twenty-five years, dear. I can handle Alastaire Ghlais.' She winked through her bright frames.

Maggie had no doubts she could do just that. They strode back down the hall and Maggie tapped on the first door on her right before opening it. Sylvan sat behind a solid antique desk in dark wood with a forest view behind her through floor to ceiling windows. She looked up and her bright blue eyes glimmered as a wide smile spread across her face.

'Ms MacKenzie, this is my partner, DI MacLeod. We have a few questions for you.'

The smile dropped from Sylvan's face at the formal introduction.

Maggie felt terrible not giving Sylvan pre-warning, but it wasn't something she could have avoided. 'A couple of weeks ago, you called Gold Star Media Relations to cancel Ghlais's contract with them. Can you tell me why?'

'Of course. It was at Alastaire's request. He wants to go with another company. I tried to talk him out of it as the contract with Gold Star is an excellent one. He won't get another deal like that.'

'What company did he want to switch to?'

Sylvan picked up a notepad from her desk and leafed through it. 'Here it is. Thomas Campbell PR.'

There's that name again, Maggie thought. Dunbar stated Campbell was harassing Jamie Kenmore to sell Gold Star to him.

'Is Ghlais having financial issues?'

Sylvan's bright eyes turned cool. 'You own the company, Maggie. You should know the answer to that.'

'I don't know that I can trust the statements I receive. I'm asking you. Is Ghlais in trouble?'

The icy eyes softened. 'No. I'm still working my way through all of the financials, but as far as I can tell, Ghlais is doing just fine. Better than fine.'

Maggie nodded, debating whether to say what was on her mind. In the end, she had to put it out there. 'I'm going to tell you something that's confidential for now.'

Sylvan nodded, a serious expression on her face.

'There are substantial allegations against Alastaire Ghlais for sexual harassment and sexual assault. Be careful around him.' Maggie expected a little fear to show on Sylvan's face, but what she saw there was anger with Sylvan's pursed lips and narrowed eyes.

'Thank's for the warning.'

'Maybe you could do me a favour as the owner of Ghlais,' Maggie said.

'Of course.'

'Start looking for large sums of money paid out to previous female employees.' If the company was paying to bail Alastaire out of his criminal behaviour, Maggie would damn well make him pay it back.

Sylvan's eyes narrowed even more. 'Settlements for keeping quiet?'

'Yes. They could go back as far as when Alastaire took over for my mother.'

Sylvan dropped her elbow on the desk and slapped her palm to her forehead. 'Jesus Christ.'

Maggie stopped to see Mrs Brown on the way out. 'Do you recall when I asked you if anyone was inquiring about purchasing Ghlais around the time my parents were murdered?'

'Yes, of course.'

'Does the name Thomas Campbell sound familiar?'

'Thomas Campbell? I don't know if he's inquired about purchasing Ghlais, but he's a good friend of Alastaire's. Tam often drops by to see Alastaire.'

'When was the last time he was here? Do you remember?'

'Of course. Tam was in with Alastaire when I arrived yesterday morning.'

The morning after the murder of Jamie Kenmore. Interesting. 'Does he usually drop in that early?'

'No, actually. That's the first time he's beat me in. I'm here

94

by half seven. Mr Campbell likes to come in the late afternoon so they can have a wee dram together. As a matter of fact, he was in the afternoon before that. Wednesday afternoon.'

'Thanks, Mrs Brown.'

As soon as they stepped outside, Maggie said, 'You've been awfully quiet since we left my uncle's office.'

Macleod smiled and patted his pocket before pulling out his cigarettes and lighting one. 'There was nothing for me to say. You handled it all just fine. Do you think this Thomas Campbell is involved?'

'I don't know, but it's worth questioning him. He was pressing to purchase Gold Star, but Jamie Kenmore told him she wouldn't sell to him. Now he's hanging out with my uncle right before and after her murder.' Maggie pulled out her mobile and rang Gold Star, asking for Sharon Dunbar. 'Hello, it's DC Glass. Have you heard from Thomas Campbell since Ms Kenmore's murder?'

'No, but if we do, I'll let you know.'

'Great. Thanks.' Maggie ended the call, shaking her head to let MacLeod know Dunbar's answer.

'Drop me off at the station and see if you can catch up to Mr Campbell, then call it a day. I don't know about you, but I'm scunnered.'

They got in the car and started back towards Edinburgh. Maggie kept her eyes open for a café since MacLeod mentioned he was tired. The long night of no sleep was catching up to her as well.

'The cute blonde CFO?' MacLeod said out of the blue. 'She's your source for the embezzlement allegations?'

'How'd you come to that conclusion?'

'She's new to the company and her eyes lit up like Guy Fawkes day when she saw you.'

'How does that figure into her being my source?'

'She's new, but she's met you and you've spent more time together than a quick conversation. She likes you.'

'So?'

'It was good of you to warn her about Alastaire.'

Maggie glanced over at him, but MacLeod was staring straight ahead, no readable expression on his face. 'I couldn't not warn her.'

'No, I suppose not.' MacLeod tapped his fingers on his knee and glanced over at Maggie. 'She's not the only one who may be in danger, aye?'

'What do you mean?'

'If Alastaire is responsible for killing your parents and Jamie Kenmore, he won't think twice about getting rid of you if you're in his way.'

Shite. She hadn't gone there yet. 'I'm careful and I have a state of the art alarm system. No one is getting into my flat in the middle of the night.'

'Aye, well. Have a care.'

A chill ran up Maggie's spine and made her wonder about Kelsey Gray's statement that she was psychic. Was that chill a warning? The only way to ensure her safety was to put the bastards responsible for Jamie Kenmore's murder, and possibly her parents' murders as well, behind bars. 'It's all well and good to suspect Alastaire and Thomas Campbell, but we've got no evidence. Nought. Have you heard anything from forensics yet?'

'I'll give them a ring when we get back to the office.'

Maggie wasn't confident they'd have anything as all the evidence was burnt to a crisp. Her only hope was the pentagram pendant. 'If they have nothing, what's our next step?'

'I still haven't looked at the CCTV footage from the First Minister's residence. That may give us something. I'll do that before I go home.'

'And if we get nothing from that?'

'Start again from the beginning. Re-question the witnesses. See if there's anyone we missed. We keep digging until we do find something.' MacLeod leaned his head back against the headrest and sighed.

MacLeod was quiet the rest of the drive back to St. Leonard's. Snippets of conversations over the past couple of days prickled Maggie's thoughts. Kelsey Gray – *Like your mother, I have the gift of sight.* Iona – *Mairie told me they'd ensured that if anything happened to them, the company would be run by her instructions and would go to you, not to Alastaire.* The two comments triggered something in Maggie and she used the car system to ring Iona.

MacLeod stirred next to her at the sound of the phone ringing over the car speakers. When Iona answered, Maggie said, 'My mother knew they were going to die, didn't she? She arranged for me get the company instead of it going to uncle Alastaire because she knew she and my father were going to be murdered.'

There was a long silence then a sigh. 'Aye, she knew.'

'Did she know who was going to kill them?'

'No. Mairie tried, but that and the date eluded her.'

'But she suspected uncle Alastaire.' It was a statement, not a question.

'She wasn't sure, Mags. She didn't trust him or like him particularly, but she could see nothing to indicate he was behind it.'

Maggie pulled into the car park at St. Leonard's Police Station. She had more questions for Iona, but not in front of MacLeod. 'Alright, I have to go. I'll ring you later.' She ended the call and turned to MacLeod. 'Did you know?'

MacLeod answered in a quiet, calm voice. 'Iona was one of the people I interviewed back then, so aye, I knew.'

Maggie had a strong urge to slap him up the side of the

head. Why did it feel like both MacLeod and Iona were withholding information from her? *Duh.* Because they were. She pulled free of her seatbelt with a little too much force. 'I'll see you tomorrow.' She got out of the car and slammed the door behind her. When she heard MacLeod close the passenger door, she hit the door lock button on her remote and kept walking until she was inside the building. She didn't want to see or talk to MacLeod again until she calmed down. It wouldn't do to punch her superior.

* * *

Maggie set the VHS player she'd signed out for the night in the back of the Range Rover next to the box of VHS videos and the two cases of Ghlais whisky. Why did she ask for a few cases? Maggie certainly didn't need twenty-four bottles of whisky. She put the thought out of her head and sat in the driver's seat, going over the Kenmore case from the beginning in her head. Her first reaction had been that the murder had been perpetrated by misogynists. If her uncle and Thomas Campbell were both involved, was it possible that some kind of secret misogynistic society was punishing women who dared to thrive in a male-dominated world, threatening the patriarchy? Certainly burning a woman at the stake was putting her in her place. Many, if not most, of the women put to death between the sixteenth and eighteenth centuries in Scotland accused of being witches weren't witches at all. An estimated four thousand women were killed during those times, accused of anything from strange behaviour to healing with herbs. All it took was someone with a grudge accusing you of witchcraft. And burning at the stake wasn't the only method of punishment.

Maggie got out of the car and marched back into the police station, her ire towards MacLeod forgotten. She found him out back, puffing on a fag, and she paced back and forth in front of him. 'We need to search for cases where successful business or career women were drowned or hung. Think about it. Both Jamie Kenmore and my mother were women succeeding in a man's world. Their businesses were at the top of their specific fields, outdoing similar businesses run by men. They could be viewed as a threat to the patriarchy. If we've got some sort of secret misogynist society murdering women using the same methods used during the witch hunts, then we can't just look at burning at the stake. There were many other methods like tying their thumbs to their big toes, throwing them in the Nor Loch, or hanging them at the gallows.' She stopped pacing and faced MacLeod, threw up her arms then let them fall to her sides. 'We need to widen the methodology on similar cases.'

MacLeod took another long haul on his cigarette then whispered, '*Mhac na galla.*' As much as he didn't like it, Glass had a point. 'How many more murders are we going to find related to this case and your parents'?'

'And how long has it been going on?' Maggie added.

'*Mhac na galla.*'

* * *

Maggie removed her coat and sat at her desk across from MacLeod, who updated the search parameters for like cases in the ViCLAS database, the Violent Crime Linkage Analysis System, the system utilised by the Serious Crime Analysis Section of the National Crime Agency to identify similar violent offences. Maggie placed a call to Mrs Brown at Ghlais, asking if any more of Alastaire's friends visited him in his office regularly.

'Oh, yes. Several.' Mrs Brown lowered her voice, 'Sometimes they come all together.'

'All together?' Maggie repeated.

'Aye, a group of eight of Alastair's friends. They meet once a month. Not always here, mind. They only meet here about every six months or so.'

'What kind of group is this, Mrs Brown?'

'Just a group of friends, dear. What's odd about it is the regularity in which they meet. First Thursday of every month at six o'clock. I only know as Alastaire has me book the time in his schedule and make arrangements when the meetings are held here.'

'I'm going to give you my email address. Could you send me the list of men who attend these meetings?'

'Aye, of course.'

'You might not want to mention it to Alastaire.'

'Understood.'

'Do you know where their next meeting is being held?' The first Thursday of the month would be next week, the first Thursday in December.

'Oh, aye. It's the last meeting of the year which always takes place here, in the conference room downstairs. A right celebration, if the cleanup is any indication. An event planner manages the decorations and catering and such.'

'He uses an event planner for a party for eight of his friends? Who pays for that?' Maggie knew the answer, but wanted confirmation.

'The company, dear. And it's not just eight of Alastaire's friends for the December meetings. I believe the number attending this year is around two hundred.'

'Two hundred!' How could Alastaire justify Ghlais picking up the tab for that? 'Are any Ghlais staff invited?'

'Just Alex. He attends all of the meetings with his father.'

Maggie ended the call and scrubbed her hands over her face. What an idiot she'd been to let Alastaire run the business without any checks in place. That Alastaire was charging his private party to the company stoked her fires. However, if the company was paying for it, nothing could stop her from attending.

'You get something?' MacLeod asked as he continued to

type, his eyes flicking between his computer screen and Maggie.

'Perhaps. A group of Alastaire's friends who meet once a month like clockwork.'

'Could be a group of misogynists then?'

'Yeah. Could be.' Then again, it may just be a group of mates meeting up for drinks. 'I'll email you the list.'

MacLeod leaned back in his chair, rubbing the scruff on his chin. 'You'd be a feminist, I suppose?'

'Why do you ask?' MacLeod's question prickled the hairs at the back of Maggie's neck.

'It's just you seem proper repulsed by the notion of misogyny and patriarchal societies.'

The hair on the back of Maggie's neck prickled again and her muscles tensed. Misogyny was still rampant in police services, but she hadn't thought of MacLeod as one. 'Does that make me a feminist, MacLeod? Perhaps it does, but if you want to label my beliefs, it would be egalitarian. I believe in equal rights for all people – men, women, nonbinary, gays, trans, heteros, whites, people of colour, abled, disabled, rich, poor, no matter their religious beliefs. I believe in an egalitarian society where *everyone* has equal rights. I can only hope that I'll witness something close to that in my lifetime. We have a long way to go.'

MacLeod leaned forward, placing his forearms on the desk and staring into Maggie's stormy eyes. They tended to turn more green than brown when she was angry and they looked bottle green now. He hadn't meant to upset her. 'I agree with you, Glass. I'd like to see that as well.'

She felt a bit of a fool for allowing MacLeod's question to rile her, thinking him a misogynist. 'The rise and popularity of the feminist movement threatens misogynists and patriarchal cultures who objectify women and believe it's a woman's place to serve men.'

'And you believe Alastaire Ghlais is a misogynist?'

'It fits with all of the sexual harassment and sexual assault claims against him. Misogyny normalises the rape culture. A misogynist believes it's his right to take any woman. When I say they believe women are here to serve them, I mean in every way.'

'He just hired a female CFO.'

'Right. Perhaps, Alastaire believes Sylvan will be easy to control.' Maggie offered MacLeod a tight-lipped smile. 'I think he'll find he's very wrong there.'

'Aye, I hope so.'

'Do you consider yourself a feminist then?'

A small smile formed on MacLeod's lips. 'I think I prefer the term you used. Egalitarian, was it? But, yes, I believe in equal rights for women. For everyone.'

'Well, aren't you the rare policeman?'

With a laugh, MacLeod said, 'It's not as bad as it used to be, believe me. Progress is slow, but there's been some progress, aye?'

'Some.' Not nearly enough in Maggie's view. Especially in male-dominated institutions like policing.

'Still, I fear as long as there's a feminist and equality movement, there will be opposition to it.'

Maggie supposed he was right.

Chapter 10

Maggie left the box of VHS tapes and the VHS player on the kitchen island when she entered her flat and changed out of her suit into a comfortable pair of worn jeans and a faded Police Scotland jumper. She'd also brought home the legal pad where she'd started to write out the similarities between the Kenmore case and her parents'. It helped her formulate ideas and theories when she wrote things down while working on a case.

In her office, she gathered the documents she wanted to take to her meeting with Colin Eaglesham, the corporate lawyer, the next afternoon – the file from Gold Star and the past year of financial statements she'd received from Ghlais. She put the documents in a leather messenger bag and left it at the front door. Then she grabbed her laptop and made herself comfortable on the sofa in the lounge.

Opening her email, she was pleased to find the email from Mrs Brown listing the names of Alastaire's friends who attended these meetings. Aside from Alastaire and Alex Ghlais and Thomas Campbell, she recognised several names – politicians and prominent business owners. All men with some power. Did it burn Alastaire's baws that he didn't own the company he ran? Maggie bet it did. All the rest on the list seemed to either own their businesses or hold lofty positions within the government. Self-made men, it seemed, except for Alastaire and Alex.

She made a note of that on her legal pad. Then added a note to interview the family of George Stanton, Ghlais's last CFO, who either died of a heart attack or an overdose. She was undecided about interviewing the men on Mrs Brown's list. It would inform Alastaire that she was on to his group if they were what she thought. On the other hand, it would put some pressure on Alastaire. She'd discuss the matter with MacLeod.

At the sound of the lobby door intercom chiming, Maggie set aside her laptop and legal pad and got up to let Nichola in. She'd invited her over for two reasons. One was that discussing the case with her may trigger a lead. The other was that she didn't want to watch the old home videos alone and the only person she was comfortable watching them with, aside from Iona, was Nichola.

After checking it was Nichola at the door, Maggie pressed the button to release the door lock. She had a minute or two while Nichola made her way up the stairs, so she popped into the kitchen, opened two bottles of beer, and set them on the table in front of the sofa before going down the hall and opening the front door. Nichola reached the top stairs and rounded the railing carrying two parcels in her arms.

'I brought fish suppers,' she said, passing them off to Maggie. 'I assume you haven't eaten.'

Nichola rolled her blue eyes and Maggie laughed. 'No, I haven't. You alright? You look tired.' There were dark smudges beneath those rolling eyes.

'I'm always tired after a stretch of nightshifts. I think I may have found someone to switch them off to, though. Gerrard Duncan doesn't like days. Bless him.'

Nichola began her police career at the same time as Maggie. They'd gone through high school together, as well as uni and the Scotland Police College in Kincardine. Nichola could have written the exam to become a detective by now, but preferred the variety and excitement of working the streets. Maggie had her sights set on detective from the beginning and the Major Investigations Team was precisely where she wanted to be.

Maggie plated the fish and chips and brought them through to the sofa along with a bottle of brown sauce. Nichola was already cosied on the couch with her legs tucked under her, sipping from a beer bottle.

'How's your investigation going?' Nichola asked as she accepted a plate from Maggie. 'Any closer to finding who burned that poor woman?'

While they ate their fish suppers, Maggie updated Nichola on the investigation.

'You know they're going to pull you from the case,' Nichola said. 'Even with the bribe of a case of Ghlais, McTavish can't keep you on it. The more it looks like Alastaire Ghlais is involved, the more they're risking having the case thrown out because of your involvement. I'm surprised they've kept you on it this long.'

'They've kept me on it because they're hoping to jog my memory of my parents' murders. Which brings me to those old home videos.' Maggie motioned to the box and VHS player on the kitchen island. 'If I'm going to trigger my childhood memories, I'd rather it be with the good memories.'

'You've never watched them before?'

Maggie shook her head. 'No. Iona always told me they were there when I was ready. I wasn't ready.'

'Are you now?'

'Doesn't matter. It's time.' Maggie loaded their plates into the dishwasher and grabbed two fresh beers. Then together, they hooked the VHS player up to Maggie's 85 inch Sony

Bravia TV.

They'd just gotten it set up when Maggie's mobile rang and Sylvan's name displayed on the screen. Maggie swiped to answer the call and held the phone to her ear. 'Hello?'

'Maggie, it's Sylvan. Can we meet?'

'Ah, um.' Maggie glanced at Nichola, curling back up on the sofa with her beer. 'I'm home for the night. You're welcome to stop by if you want.' This was turning into a regular party. She gave Sylvan the address and ended the call.

Nichola looked at Maggie with a smirk. 'Girlfriend?'

'No. Sylvan's the CFO at Ghlais. I asked her to work on something for me.'

Nichola hadn't missed the glow in Maggie's eyes when she read the caller's name on the screen of her mobile. 'I know that look, Glass. You're hoping to get her into your bed if you haven't already.'

'I haven't.' And probably wouldn't after today, she thought.

'Does she know you don't do relationships?' It was her polite way of asking if Sylvan knew that sex was just a physical release for Maggie. There were no emotions involved. Nichola would know. They'd been together in uni, but it became apparent that Maggie had no feelings other than friendship towards her and Nichola needed more than that. So, they remained best friends. As far as Nichola could tell, Maggie's heart was frozen. She was incapable of loving. A fact that tore at Nichola's heart. Not for her own sake, she'd moved on years ago. But, for Maggie and what she was missing – that hurt Nichola.

Maggie screwed up her nose. 'She knows I don't do commitment. It's a moot point, anyway. With this investigation, I ruined my chances.' She still had the expression on Sylvan's face when she questioned her about

Gold Star etched in her mind. Sylvan wasn't impressed, to say the least. It was probably for the best, as Sylvan had made it clear she didn't do casual. Still, Maggie felt a tug of disappointment. Unusual for her, but it was there.

* * *

Maggie welcomed Sylvan into her flat. She still wore her crisp suit under a royal blue wool overcoat and clutched a brown leather briefcase in her right hand. Maggie took her coat and waved her towards the lounge. 'Can I get you a drink?'

'Whisky, if you have it.'

While Maggie went to pour a whisky, Sylvan entered the lounge, spotting Nichola curled up on the couch like a cat. 'Oh, hello.'

Nichola uncurled herself and stood to shake Sylvan's hand. 'Hi. Nichola Dunn.'

Sylvan returned the firm handshake. 'Sylvan MacKenzie.'

'Please,' Nichola said as she waved a hand at the sofa. 'Make yourself comfortable.' Nichola sat in a chair, giving Sylvan MacKenzie a good once over as she set her briefcase down and perched herself on the edge of the sofa.

'Here you go,' Maggie said, handing Sylvan a crystal glass containing two fingers of Ghlais whisky. 'Have you met Nichola?'

'We've introduced ourselves, yes.' Sylvan accepted the glass and took a generous sip. 'I had hoped to speak to you alone.'

Maggie took her seat next to Sylvan and picked up her beer. 'Nichola's my best friend and a police officer. I trust her completely, but if you want to speak to me alone, we can use my office.'

'No, it's fine.' Sylvan gave Nichola a thin-lipped smile. 'I'm sorry if I offended you. It's just been a difficult day.' She sighed and set her glass on the table before pulling her briefcase to her lap and opening it. 'You asked me to have a look for large payments to women who worked at Ghlais.' She took out a file folder and handed it over to Maggie. 'I found several just in the past year. Going further back than that is going to take me more time.' Then she pulled a single sheet of paper from her briefcase. 'I also found this. I don't know if it means anything, but it's peculiar to find large payments like this in even numbers – in this case, precisely one hundred thousand pounds paid to a numbered account this past Wednesday morning.'

'A numbered account?' Maggie asked as she took the paper and studied it. The payment had been sent from the Ghlais business account to a numbered account at approximately 7:40 on Wednesday morning. Right about the time Thomas Campbell visited Alastaire in his office. There was no description of what the payment was for. 'How do I find out who this account belongs to?'

'Did you contact that lawyer I mentioned?' Sylvan asked.

'Yes, I'm seeing him tomorrow afternoon.'

'Good. Ask him if he can have it traced. I feel like I'm a spy working deep cover. Paranoid. Like I'm being watched.'

Maggie noted the tremor in Sylvan's hands. 'If you feel unsafe, you can get out of there. Quit. Don't go back.'

'No. I'm not prepared to do that as yet. When I discovered Alastaire Ghlais may be embezzling funds, I was determined to get to the bottom of it. But, when you told me he may be paying off women who worked at Ghlais ... well, let's just say I'm like a dog with a bone. I'm not letting it go.'

Maggie nodded. She had to respect Sylvan's determination and grit. 'Fair enough. But, if you feel you're in danger at any time, ring me or 999. And be careful, aye?'

Maggie showed Sylvan to the door a while later. Sylvan stopped in the doorway and whispered, 'Is she your girlfriend?'

'No,' Maggie said with a shake of her head. 'I told you, she's my best mate.'

'But, you've been together.'

Where the heck did she come up with that? Maggie wondered. And how did she answer? 'For a short time whilst at uni. We both realised we were better off as friends.'

'Because of your commitment issues. What was it? Abandonment issues?'

Maybe Sylvan was a bit too bright for her own good. 'Aye, I suppose. I don't seem to feel emotions like most people.'

A slow, sad smile drew the corner of Sylvan's lips up. 'I find your honesty refreshing. Tell me, Maggie, am I a fool for still wanting to explore a relationship with you?'

Now she had no choice but to be honest. 'I don't have an answer to that. All I can tell you is I feel something for you that I've never felt for anyone before.' And it was the truth. There was a visceral attraction, which may be more hormonal than emotional, but it was there.

'Are you free tomorrow evening? There's a pub close to here that I hear is quite good. The Regent?'

'It's my local.'

'Ah, perhaps somewhere else then?'

'I'm okay with it if you are.'

'Right. The Regent then. Seven o'clock?'

'I'll be there.'

There was no kiss, no touch. Maggie simply watched Sylvan walk to the staircase and disappear with a wide grin on her face.

When Maggie returned to the lounge, Nichola had retaken her curled up spot on the sofa and eyed her with a raised eyebrow and a smirk.

'She's hot.'

Maggie flopped onto the sofa and chucked a pillow at Nichola. 'Shut up.'

'If we're going to watch your videos, we should get started, or we'll be here all night.'

Maggie got up again and began sorting the videos from the box by date. They went back thirty years, the first being her parents' wedding. In the first video Maggie picked, she was a newborn in her mother's arms in the hospital. Mairie grinned down at the tiny bundle in her arms with a head full of short dark hair, longer on top and sticking up in all directions.

Nichola guffawed as she pointed at the telly. 'You've still got the same haircut.'

Maggie burst into laughter with Nichola.

In the next video, Maggie was two years old. She wouldn't remember anything before that, even if her memories returned, so there was no point in watching the earlier years.

They watched videos of family holidays, special occasions, and clips of ordinary days at home and at Ghlais. To Maggie, it was like watching a stranger's life. She had no memories of any of it and none were triggered. Several men from the list Mrs Brown sent were in some of the videos of events at Ghlais or parties at Alastaire's. She also recognised Jamie Kenmore, Sharon Dunn, and Kelsey Gray at many of the events.

'One more?' Nichola asked as a video ended.

'Last one then,' Maggie answered. She changed the videos and pressed play before settling back on the sofa next to Nichola. It seemed such a waste of time.

The scene that came to life on the large screened TV showed Maggie on her eighth birthday, running into her father's arms. He picked her up and swung her around before snuggling her in his arms. He was a handsome man with curly, dark brown hair and loving hazel eyes, several shades darker than Maggie's. 'There's the love of my life then.'

Maggie's mother entered the frame and leaned in behind Malcolm, pressing a kiss to Maggie's cheek. 'And here I thought I was the love of your life.'

'Oh, aye, you are. See, I'm the luckiest man alive as I have two loves of my life.' Malcolm turned his head and shared a rather hot kiss with Mairie.

'Och, it's your two loves who're the lucky ones. You're a rare man, Malcolm Ghlais.'

'A rare daddy,' Maggie said and patted Malcolm's cheeks with a giggle.

As the tape played on, Maggie couldn't help but think of the loving relationship her parents shared and that it was just a few months after this moment that their lives were so cruelly taken. No one had the right to steal their lives like that, no matter the reason. Her heart rate sped up and her face flushed. She jumped to her feet and crossed to the VHS player, stabbing the stop button before ejecting the tape and throwing it back in the box.

Nichola watched Maggie with her mouth gaping. 'What did you do that for?'

'There's no point in watching any more. It's not triggering anything.' Maggie paced back to the sofa and threw herself down on it.

'Except your temper,' Nichola said. 'What part upset you?'

'All of it. I don't know those people, that beautiful, loving family that was snuffed out and for what? What did they do to anyone?'

Nichola stared down at the beer in her hands and Maggie huffed. She was acting like a spoiled child and making Nichola feel awkward. 'It's not fair, is all.'

'No, it's not. They stole that from you. That lovely childhood.' She couldn't imagine. She still had both her parents and she knew how deeply affected Maggie was over the loss of hers, whether she admitted it or not. It had damaged Maggie in ways she may never heal from, like her inability to love. And that was a sad, sad thing.

'I'm not angry about that. What my parents shared seems extraordinary, doesn't it? They didn't deserve to have that ended in such a horrific manner.' It made her wonder if that was part of why they were murdered. Was someone jealous or envious of what they shared? Alastaire? Did he resent that Malcolm loved Mairie unconditionally and was quite happy for her to run Ghlais while he slaved away in the distillery? 'I've had enough of watching home videos for the night.' *For the month, maybe even the year.*

Nichola wondered if Maggie realised that underneath that anger was a deep sadness bleeding through her eyes. She may be shocked to discover she was capable of feeling something other than anger. Nichola would have brought it up, talked to her about it, but it seemed Maggie had had enough for one night.

'How about we have a wee dram of whisky to end the night then?' Nichola asked. 'And you can tell me all about the elegant Sylvan MacKenzie.'

Maggie picked up a throw pillow and slapped Nichola's shoulder with it. 'There's nothing to tell.' *Yet.* She dragged herself up off the sofa and poured two whiskies.

Chapter 11

Maggie's sleep was restless with dreams of her parents from the videos. Her mother's long jet black hair, bright Celtic blue eyes, and a smile that lit up the room. She was beautiful, a tall woman with delicate features and a great sense of humour. Her father shared that sense of humour and the two of them seemed to constantly be laughing. And, like Iona always said, they loved their daughter so very much.

Mairie sat on the edge of Maggie's bed, curling Maggie's long hair between her fingers. Maggie's hair was a shade of dark brown somewhere between her father's and her mother's. Nearly black, but not quite.

'It's time to sleep, Magaidh darling.'

'Can I have one more story, mummy?'

That dazzling smile shone down on Maggie and she smiled up at her mother's lovely face. Then flames leapt up and the broad smile turned into a horrible scream, the face melting away before Maggie's eyes.

Maggie shot up in bed, her breath coming in ragged pants as sweat coated her skin. She dropped her face into her hands and cursed. The last bit of the dream with her mother sitting on her bed hadn't been from the videos. Was it a memory or just a dream? She didn't know how she knew, but Maggie was sure it was the last night Mairie put her to bed, just hours before they were taken from their home and murdered.

She shoved the duvet aside and went into the en suite, squinting against the glare when she flicked on the lights. The room was earthy with granite counters and shower tiles in rusty browns and slate greys. Lush plants hung down from shelves in the corners and a copper, claw-footed tub sat in front of a large window facing Arthur's Seat. The shower itself was a wonder with a waterfall shower head at ceiling level and five pulsing heads shooting out from different levels from two walls. She turned the water on and stripped off her t-shirt and boxers, stepping into the glassed enclosure with a sigh. Usually, she could care less about the money Ghlais provided her with, but luxuries like this and her car were things she was supremely grateful for. For several minutes, she just stood in the sprays from the multiple heads, letting the heat of the water relax her muscles and wash the tension down the drain.

She took some deep breaths, trying to expel the image of her mother's burning face from her mind, but the more she tried, the clearer it became. She heard the screams and the roaring flames as if they were real, happening at that moment. The stench of burning flesh and wood filled her nostrils and Maggie gagged. She darted out of the shower, dropping to her knees in front of the toilet. She heaved, purging everything from her system.

Leaning her forehead on her arm, Maggie rested for a moment. At least when she'd been throwing up, her mind had been blank. She berated herself for thinking that because the image returned as soon as she did. And then another – *dark figures in the thick fog, moving around a stack of wood set around a vertical pole. Someone was holding her arms, preventing her from moving as she struggled to free herself and screamed for her mother and father.*

'Don't worry, bairn,' a rough voice said. *'You'll see them in a*

minute.'

Wicked laughter surrounded her.

Despite being wet, naked, and cold, sweat broke out over Maggie's skin again. She drew herself up and back into the warmth of the shower. This was what she wanted, wasn't it? For the memories to return? So why did it feel so awful? And why the hell couldn't she at least remember something useful?

She lowered herself to the floor under the spray, drew her knees up to her chest, resting her cheek on her knee. 'Mum? Da? If you can hear me, help me to remember something that will get you the justice you deserve.'

Maggie would have sworn she heard her mother's voice answer, *'Patience, Magaidh darling. Everything in its proper time.'*

* * *

She'd gone back to bed and slept fitfully, tossing and turning with dozens of images playing in her mind. Running in the hills in the Highlands with her father chasing her; sitting on the floor in her mother's home office with a colouring book and crayons; holding her father's hand as he walked her through the distillery, explaining the process with pride. But, memories from that macabre last night were as murky as the thick Scottish haar. Dark figures faded in and out of the fog. Someone's steely grip on her arms. Her parents, dark hoods covering their heads, shoved out of a van towards that horrible spike reaching out of the woodpile.

Maggie sat up in bed again, calm and determined. The van. Focus on the van. It was the kind of van you might see refurbished into a camper van. White with an extended roof and a gold logo on a black background that she couldn't quite bring into focus. She closed her eyes and tried to zoom in on it. Why was it she could see her mother's face in that fire so clearly, but she couldn't make out a logo?

Maggie threw the white duvet cover with ivy designs in varying shades of green off her legs and got up, dressing in grey jogging bottoms and a warm wool jumper. She went into the lounge, where she'd left her laptop and a legal pad, and turned to a fresh page. She drew an oval, labelling it black, then wrote *Gold Letters* in the centre. There was a gold design within the lettering, but the lettering itself evaded her. It could be anything from a plumbing company to a delivery service. She could only hope that the words would come to her eventually, but she felt like she should know it.

She turned to her laptop, opened the browser then searched for work vans. It didn't take long to identify the van she'd seen as a Mercedes-Benz Sprinter, although the one she'd seen was much boxier with sharper edges than the modern versions. And none of it mattered without that logo, Maggie thought.

* * *

Maggie set a coffee on the desk in front of MacLeod, peeled back the lid on her own, and took a quick sip before settling at her desk. 'Anything on similar cases involving drownings or hangings?'

MacLeod stopped typing and looked over the desk at her. 'I'm still waiting on a response from the ViCLAS team.'

'Forensics?'

'Ah.' He picked up a clear plastic evidence bag and tossed it onto her desk. 'Two possible shops it came from – the Cadres and Witchery shop on Lower West Bow Street or the Wyrd Shop on Canongate. Maybe you could pop into those shops and figure out which one sold that item and to whom.'

Maggie picked up the bag and examined the pentagram pendant inside. 'No fingerprints on it?'

' No. Nary a one.'

Maggie scoffed. 'Figures.' She set the pendant down and took another sip of her coffee, eyeing MacLeod as he went back to his typing. Usually, when she arrived in the mornings, he'd give her an update and ask her for hers. Having to pry anything out of him was new. 'How long have I got?'

MacLeod stopped typing again. 'Pardon me?'

'How long before the Inspector pulls me off the case?'

'Och.' MacLeod screwed up one side of his face and scratched the back of his neck. 'I've no answer to that, Glass. But, if I had to guess, a matter of hours.'

Maggie sat back, tapping the side of her cup with her fingers. They weren't going to solve this case in a matter of hours. She debated whether or not to divulge what she had or keep it to herself and let the bastards try to solve it on their own. In the end, she didn't have a choice. She couldn't hold back. 'Here's what I have – a white Mercedes-Benz Sprinter van drove my parents to the Esplanade that night. I don't remember if I was driven there in the same vehicle or not.'

'You remember?'

'Not enough, unfortunately. There was a logo on the side of the van, but I can't see it clearly. A black oval and gold lettering with a horse in the middle. I can't see what the letters are.'

MacLeod stared at Maggie with his mouth slightly open. 'Really? You don't know what that is? You really don't remember your childhood, do you?'

That feeling that she should recognise the logo returned with a vengeance, but she still couldn't place it. 'Did you think I was lying?'

'No. It's just bizarre.'

Maggie just stared at him. How did you explain what it felt like not to remember your own family?

MacLeod waved her over to his side of the desk and began tapping his keyboard. He pulled up Google on his browser and typed in *Ghlais Whisky logo circa 2002*. When the page loaded, he clicked *images* at the top and dozens of black ovals appeared with the word *Ghlais* in scriptive letters with a gold unicorn set inside the G. Beneath it, in smaller letters, it read *Scotch Whisky* and below that *Est. 1996.*

'Fuck sake! They used a Ghlais van!' Maggie leaned in for a closer look.

'Ghlais changed the logo after your parents' deaths.' MacLeod leaned back in his chair with his eyes on the computer screen. 'Chances of us finding out who had access to that van eighteen years ago are slim to none.'

'Not necessarily. Mrs Brown may just remember.' Maggie turned her head and MacLeod met her gaze, a small smile on his face. It was the first real break they had. The first glimmer of hope. 'Trouble is,' Maggie continued. 'She's off for the weekend.'

'Well then.' MacLeod interlocked his fingers and stretched his hands out, cracking his knuckles and making Maggie cringe. 'Let's see where Mrs Brown lives. First name?'

Maggie thought about it for a moment. 'I have no idea.'

MacLeod opened the Ghlais website in the browser with a shake of his head and looked for an employee listing. Under Administrative Assistant, he found a photograph of Mrs Brown with the name Charlotte Brown printed beneath it. He looked up at Maggie. 'How long have you known her?'

'Shut up. She's always just been Mrs Brown.' She returned to her seat, booted up her own computer, and searched the system for Charlotte Brown. 'I need more,' she said. 'Do you know how many Charlotte Brown's are in the system?'

MacLeod shook his head at her. 'Try Facebook. If you find her on there, it should give you a birthdate.' MacLeod's chair made a loud scraping noise as he pushed back and got to his feet, then picked up the cup of coffee Maggie had set on his desk. 'I'm away for a fag.' He stopped beside her chair and gave her a soft cuff up the back of the head.

Maggie's hand flew to her nape. 'Hey, what was that for?' It hadn't hurt, but it startled her.

'For someone who's pure brilliant, you're a right idjit.' He started for the exit then turned back, tapping a finger to his temple. 'When you catch up to Mrs Brown, ask her if the vans Ghlais is using these days are a dark colour – black or navy blue. The CCTV footage from the First Minister's residence showed a dark sedan and a dark van pulling up in front of Kenmore's house. Three individuals got out and stormed the front door wearing dark clothes and balaclavas. They were in and out in less than five minutes.'

'Did you get the number plates?'

MacLeod shook his head. 'The video was grainy due to the haar, making the plates unreadable. Even if they hadn't been wearing balaclavas, we wouldn't have gotten a good look at the perpetrators.'

Maggie stared after him, not sure whether to be flattered or insulted by the brilliant/idjit comment. Then, with a shrug, she opened up Facebook and began searching through Charlotte Browns for a profile picture resembling her Mrs Brown.

* * *

The Wyrd Shop on Canongate near the bottom of the Royal Mile had the distinction of being the oldest pagan shop in the city. It was a small shop with bright red trim around the window and door, its shelves jam-packed with pagan products like tarot cards, crystals, cute little faeries, and pagan jewellery. Maggie showed the pendant to the teenaged clerk, who took her to the jewellery section and pointed to exact replicas of the pendant in the evidence bag – a silver circle with the pentagram in the middle.

'Have you sold any of these recently?' she asked as she scanned the shop for surveillance cameras, spotting one in the front corner aimed at the till from behind.

The young woman with one side of her long hair jet black and the other bleach blonde rolled her eyes and strode back behind the counter. She tapped away on the computer then asked, 'How recently?'

Maggie thought for a moment. Dunbar stated Kenmore told Alastaire they wouldn't be covering for his indiscretions anymore two weeks ago from last Monday, so she answered, 'In the past three weeks.'

'Hmmm.' The clerk leaned closer to the monitor, squinting her eyes. 'We sold one on the twenty-eighth of November.' She looked up at Maggie, the silver loop in her left eyebrow twinkling in the glow of an overhead light.

'Was it a credit card sale? Do you have a name?'

The girl's eyes narrowed, but she pushed her nose to the monitor and squinted her eyes again. 'Visa purchase. Donna Braemore.' She popped her head up and asked, 'Anything else?'

'Yes.' Maggie pointed at the video camera in the corner. 'Any chance you have CCTV for twenty-eight November?'

She straightened and blew a raspberry. 'I'll have to ring my mum for that.'

It took some time that Maggie didn't have to waste, but she eventually left the Wyrd with a CD of the video footage of Donna Braemore purchasing the pendant and a printout of the transaction. On her way out the door, she said to the young clerk, 'You may want to get your eyes checked.'

'Oh, she has glasses,' the mother responded. 'She's too cool to wear them.'

Her next stop was the Cadres and Witchery Tours shop at the bottom of Victoria Street near the Grassmarket. This shop was as small as the Wyrd, if not smaller. The trim around the window and door was black and a man and woman sat behind the counter. They greeted Maggie with smiles and a kind hello. She showed them her warrant card and the pendant.

'Ah, yes,' said the male, an older gentleman with kind brown eyes and wire-framed glasses. 'Just there.'

He pointed to a display on the wall behind Maggie and she turned to see several of the pendants hanging from a peg.

'Have you sold any in the past three weeks?' Again she eyed the shop for a video camera and wasn't disappointed. They had also set theirs up facing the till from behind.

The woman, partially hidden behind the counter and computer, tapped the keyboard. 'Two in that period, one paid by debit card and one by cash.'

Which meant they wouldn't have names on file. MacLeod could work his magic with the banks from the debit card purchase, but they were out of luck with the cash purchase. Maggie asked for printouts of the transactions and if they had the CCTV footage for the times of the transactions. The male clerk led her to a back room, where they reviewed the footage together. The first purchase was made the previous weekend by a young woman with long dark hair who paid by debit card. The second purchase was made last Monday by a man who appeared to be in his thirties wearing a well-tailored business suit and what Maggie would call a nerdy haircut. He didn't look like the type to be buying a pentacle pendant. And, he paid cash.

She had another thought before she left the shop and was given the distributor of the pendant's information.

She dropped everything off to MacLeod to identify the purchasers. If she was still on the case once he'd done that, she'd visit all three and ask to see the pendants. If they didn't pan out, she'd go to the distributor.

Next, she drove over to Stockbridge to the address she'd found for Mrs Brown. Her flat was on the top floor in a row of grey stoned Georgian style tenement buildings with massive windows overlooking the Water of Leith. The front door was unlocked, so Maggie walked up the three flights of stairs and knocked on the flat door. She waited a few minutes and knocked again, a bit louder. No answer.

The door across the hall opened six inches and a tiny grey-haired woman with a face mapped with wrinkles peeked out. 'Are ye looking for Mrs Broon then?'

'Aye.' Maggie pulled her warrant card out of her coat pocket and held it up.

The woman studied it for a long moment and said, 'She's away oot to the garden with her washing.'

'Right. Thank you.'

Maggie went back down the stairs and out the door leading to the small square of a garden. Mrs Brown wasn't the only one catching up on her washing this Saturday morning. Sheets and clothes hung from lines crisscrossing most of the garden. Maggie found Mrs Brown behind a pale blue duvet cover, slipping a clothes peg onto one side. 'Mrs Brown?'

Mrs Brown looked over as she pulled another peg from the pocket of her pale peach cardigan. She continued to place pegs as she answered, 'Oh, hello Maggie. Did you get the email alright then?'

'Yes, thank you.' Maggie stepped around the sheets. 'I have another question for you. One that may test your memory.'

'Away you go then. I love a challenge.' Mrs Brown picked up a pole leaning against the line and used it to raise the line, bracing the pole in the green grass.

'Who would have had access to a white Ghlais company van just before my parents were murdered?'

Mrs Brown faced Maggie, tapping her forefinger against her lips as she thought back eighteen years. 'Well, there would have been two vans back then. Your da had access to them, of course. And Alastaire, but he was away on vacation.

They were used for deliveries, aye? Let me see,' she said as she continued to tap. 'Who were the drivers back then? Oh, Bobby MacIntyre. Young lad who was working his way through uni. The other would have been old Jock Hunter. He passed a few years ago.'

'Just those four?'

'Your da allowed employees to borrow them from time to time on evenings and weekends, for moving house and such. They'd have to sign them out, but those records would be long gone by now. Anyway, it was rare anyone borrowed them.'

'Your memory is exceptional, Mrs Brown.' But it didn't help Maggie any. Anyone working at Ghlais could have used the vans that night.

Mrs Brown tapped her temple. 'Still sharp as a tack.'

'What sort of vans are used now?'

'Oh, we still use Mercedes Sprinters, but there are five now.'

'White?' Maggie couldn't remember seeing any when she'd been at the loading dock.

'Alastaire prefers black, I suppose. He's been ordering black since he took over running Ghlais.'

'Do you know if anyone signed one out on Tuesday evening?'

Mrs Brown shook her head with a small smile. 'Your da allowed employees to borrow the vans. Alastaire is strictly against the practice. Only the drivers and Alastaire would have access to them.'

Chapter 12

Maggie returned to the office to update MacLeod. There was a hitch in her step as she spotted DCI McTavish sitting in her chair. She walked past him to MacLeod's side of the desk, crossed her arms over her chest, and waited. The scowl on McTavish's face accentuated his sagging jowls. The purpling of his bulging nose gave away years of alcohol consumption.

'You can take the rest of the weekend off, Glass,' he said. 'I have to take you off the case due to the connection of your parents' murders and your business.'

Even knowing it was coming didn't soften the sting. Maggie couldn't help but feel she'd failed. 'Right,' she said, her face betraying none of this. 'I'll need my case of whisky back from you.'

McTavish's wide eyes blinked several times and he sputtered. 'You ... You can't ask for it back.'

'I can and I am. You had no intention of leaving me on this investigation when you accepted that case of whisky from me. You were just buying time to try to trigger my memories of the night my parents were murdered.' If Maggie hadn't been so determined to remain on the Kenmore case, she would have realised he didn't have a choice in leaving her on it. Her personal connection and potential bias put the investigation at risk of being thrown out of court when it came time to prosecute. She couldn't blame McTavish, but she wasn't going to let him keep the whisky either.

McTavish gaped like a fish for a moment. 'I can't give it back now.' He'd opened one bottle already and given several away. 'Consider it credited to your account for the next time.'

'The next time?' Maggie stuffed her hands into her trouser pockets to stop herself from reaching over the desk, grabbing McTavish by the shirt front, and giving him a good shake. She'd be damned if she put herself in this position with him again. 'I can assure you, DCI McTavish, I won't be offering you another bribe.'

McTavish narrowed his dark eyes at Maggie, his face reddening and his scowl deepening.

'If you can't return the case, you can reimburse me for the amount my uncle charged me for it,' Maggie said, undeterred by McTavish's dangerous expression.

'And how much is that?' he asked with a growl in his voice.

Maggie gave him a small smile. Who knew she'd enjoy the fact that her uncle had charged her full price? 'Two thousand, two hundred, and eighty pounds.'

McTavish coughed and sputtered, giving Maggie the urge to go over and whack his back, which she resisted. His face turned an even darker shade of red and Maggie glanced at MacLeod as if to say, *do something*.

'Alright, sir?' MacLeod asked.

McTavish held up a hand and got himself under control. Glaring up at Maggie, he yelled, 'You own the company. You couldn't possibly have paid that much.'

'Sorry, but my uncle insists on charging full price. I can provide you with a receipt if you like.' She'd have to ask Sylvan for that as she wouldn't see it until she got her next financial statement.

Hefting himself out of Maggie's chair, McTavish bellowed,

'You'll have your case of whisky back on Monday morning.' He'd look like a fool, but he'd ask for the bottles he'd given away back and buy a new bottle to replace the one he'd opened. 'It's a good thing you don't plan on offering another, Glass, as I'd be damned if I accepted anything from you again.' With that, he marched his heavy body out of the room.

MacLeod waited until he was out of sight. 'You've bigger baws than I, Glass.'

She didn't need or particularly want the case of whisky back. It was the principle of the whole thing. McTavish never should have made her offer a bribe when he had no intention of honouring it. She wasn't about to let McTavish walk all over her just because he was her superior, no matter the cost.

Maggie looked down at MacLeod and shrugged. 'When he calms down, you can let him know if I remember anything else, I won't be sharing.'

MacLeod flinched back ever so slightly before his brow furrowed. 'You're not going to co-operate with the investigation into your own parents' murders?'

It wasn't that she didn't want to co-operate. She wanted the murders solved, but she felt betrayed by the underhanded manner they'd played her and tried to force her memories back. MacLeod had backed her up, but McTavish had basically thrown her to the wolves in the hopes of solving an eighteen-year-old cold case. He didn't deserve to know whatever information remained locked in her mind. 'You'll just have to solve both cases without the benefit of my memories, won't you?' She started across the room to the exit, calling out, 'Have a nice weekend. I know I'm going to.' It probably wasn't fair to rub MacLeod's nose in it, but Maggie couldn't help herself.

* * *

Maggie stepped outside into a stiff wind and took a deep

breath of cool, damp air. It wasn't raining, but the grey, rolling clouds didn't look like they'd hold off much longer. She buttoned her coat, pulled up the collar, and shoved her hands in the pockets as she started towards the car park, wondering what the heck to do with herself now. It was a strange feeling, having time on her hands and nothing to do with it. As she approached the Range Rover, she spotted a tall, slim figure in a long, cream-coloured coat leaning against the back. *Shite.* 'If you've scratched my car, I'm sending you the bill.'

Kaleigh Logan pushed off the car with a grin. 'Maybe I should send you a bill for polishing it.' Logan stood back as Maggie inspected the rear door for scratches. 'You haven't been returning my calls. I thought we had a deal.'

Satisfied there were no scratches, Maggie straightened and turned to Logan. 'I never said we had a deal. I said I'd think about it.'

'And have you?'

'It's a moot point. I've been removed from the case due to the possible connection to my parents' case and Ghlais Whisky.'

Logan appeared to deflate as if the air was slowly being released from her. 'That's a shame.'

Maggie shrugged and returned her hands to her coat pockets. 'Nothing I can do about it.'

Logan glanced around the car park. 'Are you going to continue to investigate on your own?'

'That would get me into trouble,' Maggie answered with narrowed eyes. Besides, she'd probably have her hands full trying to get to the bottom of Alastaire's embezzling, if that was what he was up to.

The icy wind picked up and Logan put her hands in her own pockets, mirroring Maggie's stance. 'You were near death when PC MacLeod found you.'

'MacLeod found me?' Another wee tidbit he'd neglected to tell her.

'He checked for a pulse then removed his coat, wrapping you in it before he called for an ambulance.'

The old softie, Maggie thought. What she couldn't fathom was Logan's reasons for telling her this.

'I followed the ambulance to the hospital, but no one was holding out much hope. They didn't expect you to make it through to day's end. Then to the next morning.' Logan's gaze remained locked on Maggie's, a fierce glimmer in her eyes. 'You're a fighter, Magaidh Ghlais. I thought you'd fight to obtain justice for your parents.'

Maggie's head flinched back as if she'd just been struck in the face. She felt like she had been. She clenched her teeth and narrowed her eyes. 'That's a low blow.'

'Don't you want justice for them?'

'Of course, I do. I trust the Major Investigations Team to get justice for Jamie Kenmore and my parents.'

'Do you?' Logan raised an eyebrow. 'That's interesting.'

'What's that supposed to mean?'

Logan glanced around the car park again. 'Maybe we could go somewhere else and talk. Somewhere warmer?'

Maggie looked around the lot and over to the St. Leonard's Police Station. If she got caught speaking to a journalist, she'd be up a burn. 'You suspect a coverup from inside Police Scotland? On my parents' case?'

'I'd rather not speak here.'

Hadn't she just been wondering what to do with her unexpected free time? Logan's inferences were too intriguing to ignore. 'Right. Name a place.'

'Edinburgh Press Club on Cockburn Street.'

Maggie scoffed. It sounded like a nest of reporters. 'Fine. I'll see you there.' Maggie turned and started for the driver's door.

'Oh, but …' Logan said with a bashful grin. She waited for Maggie to turn again. 'I'll need a ride.'

'How did you get here?'

'My driver dropped me off. I could call him back, but why waste time when we're both going to the same place?'

Maggie rolled her eyes, but popped the door locks. 'Get in.' The last thing she needed was for McTavish to see Kaleigh Logan getting in her car.

* * *

Nichola Dunn spent the morning catching up on the cleaning and laundry that she neglected during night shifts. She'd just sat down with a cup of tea when her mobile rang. She didn't recognise the caller's number, so answered hesitantly. 'Hello?'

'Nichola Dunn?'

'Yes.'

'It's Will MacLeod. Glass's partner.'

Nichola sat up straight, wondering if MacLeod was calling to pass on bad news. 'Oh. Everything alright?'

'Aye. I'm calling in an official capacity. We're a bit shorthanded with all of the investigations in MIT. Are you interested in coming on board for the Kenmore investigation?'

'Me?' This was odd. It wasn't a secret that Maggie and Nichola were best mates, making Nichola an unlikely choice. Still, the experience would look good on her service record and she'd enjoy working with Mags as long as she wasn't off the streets for too long. 'What is it you'd need from me?'

'I need someone willing to do the fieldwork, tracking down leads and conducting interviews.'

Even stranger, Nichola thought. 'Isn't that what Maggie does?'

There was a short silence, then MacLeod whispered, 'Can we meet somewhere?'

* * *

Maggie expected the Edinburgh Press Club to be a stuffy, dark room with reporters huddled in dark walled booths, whispering about the day's rumours and headlines. Instead, she walked into a modern space, two rooms connected by an opening in a brick wall, with furniture, walls, and lighting giving the impression you'd just walked into a cup of café au lait. They each ordered coffee and a sandwich at the counter and took them to an adjoining room, sitting at a small round table for two in the back corner. Instead of reporters, it seemed to be tourists occupying most of the tables.

'Why do you suspect a coverup?' Maggie asked, then took a bite of her hummus and roasted red pepper sandwich. She had to admit this café was a good choice. The sandwich was fresh and flavourful.

'Perhaps the better question is why don't you?'

A familiar prickle raised the hairs on the back of Maggie's neck and heat spread over her cheeks. 'Stop being so evasive and answer the question.'

Logan added half a teaspoon of sugar to her coffee and stirred slowly. 'Tell me, Magaidh, what's your overall impression of these cases?'

The first thought that popped into Maggie's mind was that she was being kept in the dark regarding some facts. But her overall impression was that the murders were carried out by a misogynistic group. 'Your still not answering my question.'

'I don't answer yours; you don't answer mine?'

'Exactly.'

They ate their sandwiches surrounded by the clatter and chatter of the café and didn't speak again until they were finished. Logan dabbed the corners of her mouth with her napkin. 'Why do you suppose Police Scotland hasn't been able to solve your parents' murders these last eighteen years?'

Maggie shrugged. 'Not enough evidence.' She took a sip of her coffee then added, 'And my memory loss.'

Logan stared Maggie in the eye. 'I believe that's what kept you alive.'

'Stop playing games and lay it out for me.' Tired of the evasion and cryptic comments, Maggie was about ready to walk out of the café.

Logan lifted her handbag from the floor and sat it on her lap, removing her mobile. 'I'm texting you a link to a page that contains the videos of my reports from the Ghlais murders.' Once she'd sent it, she looked back up at Maggie. 'Watch them. Then give me a call.'

Maggie rolled her eyes. 'Talking to you is maddening.'

'Watch the videos, then I promise it won't be.'

* * *

As Maggie stepped out of the café, an alert sounded on her mobile. She pulled it from her pocket to see that an alarm had been triggered at her flat. Opening her security system app to a video of her front door, Maggie observed three men wearing black balaclavas trying to jimmy the lock. Brazen, she thought as she confirmed the alarm, triggering the alarm company to dispatch the police. Then she jogged to the Range Rover and sped off towards her flat in Abbeyhill.

Maggie rounded the corner onto her street as a black sedan began to pull out from the kerb. Recognising the car as the Mercedes Robbie MacDonald drove, she angled the Range Rover to block its exit. Three men in balaclavas jumped from the car and took off in different directions. Maggie stayed on the driver, sprinting after him. He dashed down a walkway leading into Holyrood Park and Maggie grinned. She loved a good run in the hills.

Unfortunately, she didn't get it. The suspect made it halfway across the field then doubled over, bracing his hands on his knees as he huffed and puffed. Maggie slowed, shaking her head. She hadn't even worked up a sweat. She pulled the balaclava from the suspect's head and said, 'Hello, Robbie.'

'Fuck,' he said through panting breaths.

Maggie took hold of his arm and walked him back to their vehicles. 'Why are you trying to break into my flat? What is it that Alastaire wants?'

'No comment.'

'Who were the two people with you?'

'No comment.'

'Security staff from Ghlais?' It wouldn't surprise her.

'No comment.'

A police patrol car had arrived when they got back, the two constables circling the vehicles left in the middle of the street. Maggie walked MacDonald over to them. 'Mr MacDonald and two others tried to break into my flat. You can take him in for attempted home breaking.' He'd be out in a few hours, but he'd have a problem renewing his security licence with that kind of charge on his record.

The constables placed MacDonald in the back of the patrol car and Maggie played the video from her front door. 'I'll send you the video for evidence.' She wanted to check her door for damage as well. They didn't manage to get through her locks. Amateurs. It wasn't easy, but possible if someone knew what they were doing.

'What are we going to do with his car, ma'am?' one of the constables asked.

'It's owned by Ghlais Whisky, which I own, so I'll take possession of the car.' She called in to dispatch requesting a fingerprint tech. She wanted the other two lads.

Maggie went to the back of the patrol car to get the keys from MacDonald and found him sweating profusely. She opened the door and leaned down to his eye level. 'What's wrong with you then?'

'No comment.'

Maggie rolled her eyes. 'Right. I'll need the car keys.'

MacDonald sneered at her. 'No.'

Straightening, Maggie nodded for the constables to come over. 'Let's get him out and give him a good search.'

While the constables searched MacDonald, MacLeod's bright yellow car rumbled around the corner and came to a stop behind the patrol car. Maggie narrowed her eyes as she spotted Nichola in the passenger seat. She was supposed to be off this weekend, so what was she doing with MacLeod? When Nichola stepped out, her eyes seemed to be pleading with Maggie.

'PC Dunn,' Maggie said coldly.

'DC Glass.' Nichola gave her a short nod then lowered her eyes.

MacLeod hefted himself out of the small car and yanked up his creased brown trousers before lighting a cigarette. 'Glass,' he said with a nod. 'We heard a call about a home breaking.'

Maggie glanced at Nichola because MacLeod wouldn't have recognised her address. Nichola would. 'Is that so?'

'Aye.' He looked up, studying Maggie's posh building for a moment. 'What do you suppose they were after?'

That was the question, wasn't it? What did she have that Alastaire wanted? The only thing that made sense was the financial reports Ghlais sent her every quarter. They were the only items she had related to Ghlais or Alastaire. 'Good question. The suspect isn't talking.'

MacLeod drew on his cigarette with his brow furrowed. 'I don't like it, Glass. You need to be careful, aye?'

'No bother. I can take care of myself.'

MacLeod stubbed out his cigarette on the ground and took a few steps toward Maggie. 'Don't be upset with Nichola,' he began in a quiet voice. 'I asked for her. It's the only way I can keep you in the loop without it looking like I'm keeping you in the loop.'

'Nice,' Maggie said as that prickle crept up the back of her neck. 'Protect yourself and leave Nic in the line of fire.'

'They'll be watching me, Glass. They won't be watching Dunn.' He'd already said more than he should. He kept his eyes on Maggie's, hoping she'd understand what he was trying to convey.

Fuck sake, Maggie thought. Logan was right. Something was going on inside the MIT. 'Any chance you can wait here for the fingerprint tech to get here and print that car.' She hiked a thumb over her shoulder at the Mercedes. 'I've got an appointment, but I want all the doors printed so we can try to identify the two who got away.'

'Aye, nae bother.'

Chapter 13

Eaglesham Commercial was located in a Georgian New Town house much like Gold Star. To Maggie's surprise, Colin Eaglesham, a golden-haired man with a light scruff, answered the door. He couldn't have been much older than Maggie.

'Ms Glass. It's a pleasure to meet you at last,' he said with an extended hand.

Maggie placed her hand in his, noting the firm, confident grip. 'Likewise.'

He waved her into a bright lobby, closing the door behind her. 'My office is in the back.' He led the way to double doors guarding a very masculine office with large Georgian windows overlooking a tidy garden. The room was bright and airy despite the dark wood trim and bookcases covering the walls.

A silver-haired man in charcoal trousers and a navy blue jumper over a white button-up shirt sat in a seat facing the antique mahogany desk.

'My father,' Colin began, 'Derek Eaglesham.'

The senior Eaglesham stood and bowed slightly. 'Magaidh. You've grown a bit since last we met,' he said with a twinkle in his eyes.

Maggie had no memory of meeting this man, but smiled.

When he would've known her, she was just a small child. Now she had a good few inches on him. She slipped the messenger bag from her shoulder and set it on her lap as she took the seat next to the senior Eaglesham and Colin took his seat behind the big, solid desk.

'My father is retired now, Ms Glass, but he's asked to be here as he represented your mother and father and knows the details much better than I.'

'Right,' Maggie said and gave them a small smile. 'The reason I'm here today is it has been brought to my attention that my uncle, Alastaire Ghlais, may be embezzling from Ghlais Whisky and/or myself. I should also mention that someone tried to break into my flat about an hour ago, a representative of Alastaire's.' She opened the messenger bag in her lap and drew out a thin stack of papers, handing them over the desk to Colin. 'The only thing I can imagine he'd be after is my financial statements from Ghlais.'

Colin's brow furrowed as he accepted the papers. 'That wouldn't make much sense, as we receive copies of the same statements.'

That was news to Maggie. These statements focused on her earnings based on the company's profits. 'Why would you receive copies?'

Colin looked up from the paperwork. 'We represent your interests in the company, Ms Glass. We have done since the passing of your mother and father.'

Maggie felt the fool for not knowing that. Before embarrassing herself further, she explained, 'I'm afraid I've never taken any interest in the business, Mr Eaglesham. An error that I'm coming to regret.'

'What makes you think Alastair is embezzling?'

'I've been told that he may be underpaying me and taking the balance for himself. I have no proof of that. Just the word of a Ghlais employee who I'd rather not name.'

'Uh-huh.' Colin studied Maggie's financial reports, then set them down and opened a file folder on the desk in front of them. He picked up the first sheet of paper from the folder and the lines across his brow deepened. 'Well, well.' He looked over at his father. 'It looks like Ghlais may be keeping two sets of books. Our reports differ from Ms Glass's by a substantial amount.'

Derek reached out a hand and Colin passed him the two sets of reports. He slipped on a pair of reader glasses and studied them with a grim expression. 'Dear Lord.'

Maggie glanced back and forth between the two men. 'So he is stealing from me?'

'Now it makes sense why Alastaire sent someone to your home to get your statements back. Did he know you were coming to see me, Ms Glass?' Colin asked.

Maggie shook her head. 'Not that I'm aware of.' How would Alastaire have found out she'd made an appointment with Eaglesham? The only person other than herself who knew about it was Sylvan. The back of Maggie's neck prickled. Had Sylvan warned Alastaire? She rubbed her nape and asked, 'What do we do about it?'

Colin looked to his father. 'How should we proceed?'

'That depends on Magaidh,' Derek answered and turned to Maggie. 'Would you like to initiate legal proceedings at this time?'

'Is that what you'd suggest? Are there other options?' As versed as she was in criminal law, Maggie knew nothing about business law.

'We could confront Alastaire and request a full audit,' Derek said.

That was what Sylvan had asked her to do – request an audit. Still, she wasn't sure of the correct answer. 'If we do that and he refuses, is it too late to proceed legally?'

'Not at all, but we risk giving him time to cover his tracks,'

Colin said.

Maggie pointed to the documents still in Derek's hands. 'Won't those serve as proof?'

'They prove we received significantly different statements, but what's happened with the funds you appear to have been shorted? If we file the case with the courts, Ghlais's financial records will be seized for examination. They'll be able to trace the movement of funds and determine if there are indeed two sets of books.'

Derek Eaglesham noted the indecision in Maggie's pinched expression. 'You don't have to decide right away, dear. Think about it and let us know.'

Maggie turned to this gentle man who'd known her parents and called her by her birth name. 'What would my mother have done?'

A wide smile spread over Derek's lined face and his eyes flashed bright. 'She'd have gone after him with the full force of the law. No one fucked with Mairie Ghlais. Pardon the language.'

Maggie snorted a quick laugh. 'Then that's what we'll do. No one fucks with her daughter either.'

Derek reached over and patted Maggie's hand. 'She'd be proper proud of you, Magaidh.'

Maggie was confident she'd made the right decision, but she wasn't done yet. 'There's another issue.' She pulled the Gold Star file from her messenger bag along with the list of large payments to female employees over the past year and passed them over to Colin. 'Gold Star Media Relations has represented Ghlais since not long after it was established. Apparently, they've been helping to cover up sexual harassment and sexual assault complaints brought against Alastaire Ghlais by female employees for years. It appears he's been using company funds to pay for the silence of his victims. I don't know if there's anything I can do about it, but

I don't believe Ghlais should be paying Alastaire's hush funds.'

Derek got up and circled the desk, leaning over his son's shoulder as he flipped through the pages in the file. Glancing up at Maggie, he asked, 'How did you come into possession of these files?'

Odd question, Maggie thought. 'I own the company. When I told the executives at Gold Star this, they were only too happy to turn them over to me.'

Derek straightened with a wide grin. 'You obtained them legally then. This is tremendous.'

Colin looked over his shoulder at his father with a scowl. 'Tremendous? The man is assaulting young women.'

The smile dropped from Derek's face. 'That part's not tremendous, no. But,' he raised his pointer finger in the air, 'Alastaire Ghlais has broken the terms of the agreement.'

'The agreement?' Maggie asked. This had to be the document Iona spoke of.

'Aye.' He walked over to a filing cabinet in the corner of the room and began leafing through the folders in the second drawer. He pulled a file folder out and returned to the seat next to Maggie, opening it in his lap. He flipped through the first few pages then pulled out several pages stapled together. 'The agreement,' he said and passed it to Maggie with a look of pride. 'Mairie Ghlais was a woman not only of great intellect, but great intuition and sight. She was well-prepared to protect Ghlais should she and Malcolm leave this world before you were ready to take the reins, Magaidh.'

Maggie flinched inwardly at the last bit of Derek's statement, having no desire to take the reins at Ghlais.

Derek leaned over and tapped a finger on the top page. 'Here. Number five.'

As Maggie read it to herself in legalese, Derek recited it from memory in laymen's terms. 'If anyone holding a leadership position behaves in a manner that may damage the good reputation and standing of Ghlais Whisky, they will immediately resign without compensation, or their employment will be terminated immediately with cause. I'd say sexual harassment and assault of employees qualify, wouldn't you?'

'Who will run the business?' Maggie asked, although she didn't expect an answer. 'I can't do it. I don't know anything about it.'

'You simply hire a new CEO, my dear,' Derek said with a warm smile. 'You'll have your mother's gift of intuition and sight to help you choose a suitable replacement for Alastaire.'

Maggie spent the next couple of hours with the Eagleshams, brainstorming and organising a plan to address Alastaire Ghlais. She could see why her mother put her trust in Derek Eaglesham. He was a gem and his son hadn't fallen far from the tree.

Maggie took all of the original documents home with her and spent an hour scanning all of her Ghlais financial statements and saving them onto a USB drive which she then placed in the fireproof safe hidden in the floor of her bedroom closet. Now who was paranoid? she wondered. With that done, Maggie emailed a request to use a week's holiday time. She didn't think she would have a problem getting it as DCI McTavish would want her out of the way of the Kenmore investigation. She took the documents Colin Eaglesham copied for her and settled on the sofa with a cup of tea.

The agreement crafted by Maggie's mother began by defining that the terms were legal should she, Mairie Ghlais, die or not be able to function as CEO of Ghlais. In the event of Mairie's death or disability, Malcolm Ghlais would run the business. If both Mairie and Malcolm died or could not function as CEOs, Alastaire Ghlais would run the company until Magaidh Ghlais came of age and was ready to take over.

Well shite, Maggie thought. Her mother had inadvertently given Alastaire Ghlais the motive to murder Malcolm right along with her. Could it be that simple? Had Alastaire orchestrated her parents' deaths simply to gain control of Ghlais? Would he murder his own brother over a business? *Wicked. Evil.*

The agreement stated that should Magaidh Ghlais, upon her twenty-seventh birthday, decide she did not want the business, Alastaire Ghlais had the option to buy her out at full market value in cash.

Maggie was months away from her twenty-seventh birthday. Was that why Alastaire was embezzling funds from her? To buy her out? Why hadn't anyone informed her of this stuff? Why hadn't her mother left her something about it? Or had she?

Maggie rang Iona. 'Did my parents leave a letter or anything for me to open when I became an adult?'

'Not that I know of, hen. There may be something in with all the stuff we packed from the house after Mairie and Malcolm passed.'

'Their stuff is still around? Where?'

'In storage at Ghlais.'

Which meant Alastaire had access to it all these years. *Shite.* 'Who helped you pack up the house?'

'Alastaire and Eilean,' Iona answered. 'Oh, and Jack.'

'Jack?'

'Aye, he's a good friend of Alastaire's. Jack Taggart. You'll know him, of course. He's with Police Scotland.'

She didn't know him personally, but she knew of him. He was the Assistant Chief Constable for Major Crime. Was Jack Taggart the mysterious Jack Lord, the one name Maggie hadn't been able to identify on the list of Alastaire's group of friends that Mrs Brown had emailed to her?

After she ended the call, Maggie set the agreement aside and picked up the other document Colin and Derek had copied for her – the contract Alastaire Ghlais signed to accept the position as CEO of Ghlais Whisky. Maggie couldn't help but smile as she skimmed through the document. Alastaire Ghlais had to follow Mairie's instructions for running and growing Ghlais Whisky to a tee until Maggie took over the running of the business. Failing that, the contract would continue to be enforced unless Alastaire purchased the company outright from Maggie.

* * *

Maggie sat at a small table at the back of the Regent, sipping her whisky as she watched Sylvan cross the room to her. Despite Maggie's lack of trust, her reaction to Sylvan was deep and visceral every time she saw her. Arousal flared between her thighs and her belly quivered. Sylvan's short hair, shiny Doc Martin boots, faded and well-worn jeans, and button-up shirt under a wool blazer were masculine, but it didn't distract from her exquisitely feminine air as she sailed across the room.

'You've started without me,' Sylvan said with a nod to Maggie's whisky as she took the seat next to her and leaned over to peck her cheek.

'Sorry,' Maggie said. 'I wasn't sure what you wanted.'

'I never turn down a good whisky.'

The pub was busy, as usual on a Saturday evening, but Maggie didn't have any trouble getting the attention of a server and ordering a Ghlais for Sylvan. Sylvan had her drink within a couple of minutes and took an appreciative sip.

'How was your meeting with Eaglesham?'

'About that,' Maggie said as she turned her glass in slow circles on the table. 'You didn't happen to mention my meeting with them to anyone, did you?'

Sylvan's mouth dropped open, then abruptly closed. 'Of

course not. Why do you ask?'

Maggie watched Sylvan closely as she explained the attempted break-in at her flat earlier and what she suspected they were after.

'Why would Alastaire go to that length to get the statements back?' Sylvan asked.

Maggie narrowed her eyes. 'I think you know why.' After three weeks of examining Ghlais's financial records, Sylvan had to know they had two sets of books. 'My financial statements don't match the ones sent to Eaglesham.'

Sylvan closed her eyes for a moment and sighed. When she opened them, she focused directly on Maggie's eyes. 'So, I was right? He's embezzling funds by sending you less than you should be getting and syphoning the rest into his own pockets?'

'I don't know, is he?' Maggie kept her face expressionless and her eyes cold. 'What was it that tipped you off to Alastaire embezzling funds?'

'At the same time that your dividends cheque goes out every three months, an equal payment goes to an undisclosed numbered account.' Sylvan took a generous swig of her whisky. 'Stupid mistake, really. It would be less glaringly obvious if he staggered the amounts. I can get you the account number on Monday, if you like.'

'Aye, do that.' Maggie wouldn't need Sylvan to get the account number for her, but she wasn't about to tip Sylvan off in case it got back to Alastaire. She still didn't know how Alastaire knew about her meeting with Eaglesham, if he even did. Maybe he was just becoming paranoid himself and wanted the statements destroyed. Or, there may have been something else he was after, although she had no idea what it could be.

'Are you alright?' Sylvan asked, drawing Maggie from her thoughts. 'You seem ... distracted.'

'It's been a crap week,' Maggie answered and tried to smile. She wasn't feeling very jovial. 'I've got a lot on my mind. Sorry, I'm not very good company.'

'It's been a crap week for me as well. I'm still trying to get my feet at Ghlais and the more I see, the more I'm regretting taking the job.' Her smile was as unconvincing as Maggie's.

'Still feel like you're being watched?'

Sylvan gave a short laugh. 'This morning, I checked my office for hidden cameras. How paranoid is that?'

'Trust your gut,' Maggie said and had Sylvan raising a brow. Maggie reached out and took her hand, giving it a squeeze. 'Don't give up, just yet. Trust me.'

'I do,' Sylvan answered. 'I just wish you trusted me back.' She squeezed Maggie's hand in return. 'You can, you know? My loyalty is to you, not Alastaire.'

'People I thought I could trust have been holding things back from me this week and doing things behind my back to the point I'm not sure who I can trust anymore. I've even been questioning the loyalty of the woman who raised me.' She shook her head and stared down into her drink. 'That's pathetic and shameful.' Iona had given up her life to raise Maggie. She was a free spirit with a wanderlust that she'd had to suppress to make a stable home for a traumatised child.

'Tell me about her,' Sylvan said. Maggie hadn't pulled her hand away, so Sylvan kept it cradled in her own.

Maggie looked up from her drink and smiled genuinely. 'She's a character. Picture a hippie or a gypsy and you've pretty much got it. She had the patience of a saint those first few years while I adjusted. I couldn't have been easy or fun. They say I didn't even remember my own name after my parents passed.'

'You had amnesia?'

'Still do,' Maggie answered then added, 'Mostly.'

'Is that why you say you don't feel emotions like other people do?'

'No, I say that because I don't feel emotions like most people. Anger,' she said with a nod and a laugh. 'I feel that one just fine. All the others seem to be numbed or dormant.' Sylvan's expression seemed to sag and Maggie gave her hand another squeeze. 'That bothers you.'

Sylvan shook her head. 'It's just that I've only ever been in love once and that person had no real feelings for me.'

'She hurt you.'

Sylvan shrugged and tipped the last of her drink down her throat. Maggie waved for the server to bring them another round. Leaning forward, she took Sylvan's hand in both of hers and looked into those fathomless blue eyes. 'I know dating me scares you and you're questioning if you should. I can only tell you that I *do* feel something. If you decide I'm not worth the risk, I'll understand. I won't like it, but I'll understand.'

Sylvan threw her head back and laughed. 'Oh, something tells me you're well worth the risk.' Maggie was right. She was constantly asking herself if she was making a big mistake going out with Maggie Glass, if she was setting herself up for another horrible heartbreak. But, the truth was, she couldn't stay away from Maggie if her life depended on it.

'We could go back to my flat and test that theory,' Maggie said with a grin, enjoying Sylvan's melodic laugh and beautiful smile.

Sylvan laughed again, staring into Maggie's hazel eyes, which had turned more green than brown and sparkled. 'We could, but we're not going to. Not until I'm good and ready.' It wasn't that she didn't want to go there with Maggie. She just wanted to make sure she'd captured her heart first.

'Just how long do you plan on making me wait?' Maggie asked, still grinning.

'As long as it takes.'

Now Maggie laughed. 'Who knew flirting about *not* having sex could be so hot?'

Chapter 14

Their parting kiss lingered on Maggie's lips long after she returned home. A sweet, soft kiss that sent tingles down her spine. Their first kiss. She didn't usually get sentimental about such things, but this was different. Sylvan was different. Perhaps, after all these years, Maggie's heart was beginning to thaw. And she wasn't sure she wanted it to. That layer of ice encapsulating her heart offered protection and Goddess only knew what would happen to her without it.

Maggie put the kettle on, made herself a cup of tea, and settled on the sofa with her mobile. She opened the link that Kaleigh Logan sent her and scrolled through the webpage with links to videos of the news coverage from the Ghlais murders.

In the first video, Logan stood at the top of the Royal Mile, whisps of smoke visible behind her through the haar hanging heavily over the Esplanade. She described the grisly scene and announced the discovery of two bodies, suspected to be Mairie and Malcolm Ghlais, in the coal and ash remnants of a significant fire.

The scene changed to the Lawnmarket area of the Royal Mile, the camera following a Police Scotland Constable in his dark uniform and black and white checker rimmed cap. As he approached Lady Stair's Close, he peered around its corner then shouted as he burst forward, disappearing from view for a moment.

The camera rounded the corner, zooming in on the constable bent over a small body curled up on the ground in the narrow close, the building housing the Writers' Museum peeking through the fog beyond them. A young Will MacLeod gently pressed two fingers to the neck of the pathetic small body curled into the foetal position in blood and soot-stained blue and yellow pyjamas. MacLeod keyed the mic at his shoulder and called out, 'I've got her. Lady Stair's Close. I need medics.' He began to remove his coat and noticed the camera pointed at him as clomping footsteps grew louder. 'Get that camera out of here,' MacLeod yelled and two uniforms came into view, pushing the cameraman back.

The view inside the close remained, but the child's body was blocked from view by the bodies of the additional police constables. MacLeod gently wrapped the small figure in his coat.

Nothing new there, Maggie thought. She moved on to the next video with Logan back at her original spot with the Esplanade behind her, the majestic, medieval Edinburgh Castle barely visible through the haar. A thin man in a Police Scotland uniform came into view. Logan called out, 'DCI Taggart? Can you confirm that the victims are Mairie and Malcolm Ghlais?'

A memory flashed into Maggie's brain. *Her parents' dead bodies, consumed by the wicked flames of the roaring fire. Maggie stood frozen in terror, a vice-like grip on her arms and tears streaming down her smoke-stained face. One of the dark figures turned to her, the light from the flames dancing over him. He reached up and drew off his balaclava, scowling at Maggie. 'Kill the bairn,' he said, then turned and walked off, disappearing into the fog. Maggie recognised the man. He'd been in her own home for suppers, attended events at Ghlais, and parties at uncle Alastaire's. She knew the horrible man who brutally murdered mummy and daddy and forced her to watch.*

Maggie flinched as if she actually felt that first blow to the back of her head. Oh, aye, she recognised the monster who ordered her death. Assistant Chief Constable Jack Taggart.

Maggie told MacLeod that she wouldn't be sharing if more memories returned, but she had to do it. She came out of the web page and rang MacLeod. He answered in a raspy voice as if wakened from a deep slumber. She was probably about to ruin his night's sleep.

'I've got something.'

* * *

The sun shone through Maggie's bedroom windows and although she felt a slight twinge of guilt for not getting up and enjoying a rare, sunny day off, she decided to lounge in bed for just a wee while longer. She could indulge herself in a lazy morning and still have time for a good run over the hills and valleys of Arthur's Seat.

Maggie just about nodded off again when her mobile alerted her to someone at the front door. She pulled it from the charger on her bedside table and opened her security app to see Nichola holding a banker's box at her door. Maggie got up and padded down the hall to answer the door in bare feet, boxer briefs, and a sleeveless t-shirt. She swung the door open to find MacLeod and Claymore standing behind Nichola, MacLeod with a laptop bag slung over his shoulder and Claymore carrying a bakery box and a tray of coffees.

Both MacLeod's and Claymore's eyes bulged while Nichola burst into laughter.

'Wearing your Sunday best?' Nichola asked.

It was too late to be modest now, so Maggie ignored Nic's comment. 'What are you doing here?'

'We need a place to run our investigation away from prying eyes and ears,' MacLeod announced.

'So you decided to help yourself to my flat?' Rather presumptuous of them, Maggie thought.

'And you,' MacLeod said. 'Unless you don't want to be involved.' When Maggie didn't answer right away, MacLeod smiled widely and added, 'We have cakes and coffee.'

Claymore held up the box and matched MacLeod's grin.

So much for her day off and lazy morning. Maggie opened the door wider and waved everyone in. 'Dining room,' she said to Nichola.

'Great legs,' MacLeod said with a wink as he strode past.

'Shut up.' Maggie closed the door then slipped back into her bedroom to make herself presentable. She took a quick shower and dressed in jeans and a long-sleeved t-shirt. When she entered the dining room, she asked, 'What are we doing here?'

With icing sugar in the corner of his mouth, Claymore said, 'If Taggart is involved in these murders, we need to conduct our investigation in secret.'

'Our investigation? Aren't you retired?' Maggie raised an eyebrow as she waited for his response.

'Aye, and haven't you been pulled from the case?'

Touché, Maggie thought.

'We don't know who we can trust,' MacLeod said as he slid a coffee across the table to Maggie. 'I trust Claymore and the two of you.' He nodded toward Nichola, then Maggie.

Maggie had to trust his judgement on Claymore as MacLeod had worked closely with him in the past. Maggie didn't know him. 'If I'm going to do this, you can't hold anything back from me anymore.'

'It's not just that I've been holding back,' MacLeod began. 'Things are being held back from me as well. We're not getting answers from forensics except for that pendant and I still haven't received an answer back from ViCLAS concerning like cases.'

Maggie pulled out a chair and sat next to Nichola with MacLeod and Claymore across the table from them, the videos of Logan's coverage of the Ghlais case that she watched after speaking to MacLeod the night before forefront in her mind. 'Taggart is preventing information from being released to you?'

'Someone is,' Macleod answered. 'I've no proof it's Taggart.'

Maggie pulled up the website with the videos of Logan's coverage of the Ghlais murders on her mobile and scrolled down to the one she wanted. Then she passed the phone across the table to MacLeod. 'Take a look at that.'

The video showed Logan outside the St. Leonard's Police Station, stating that four weeks after their deaths, the investigation into the murders of Mairie and Malcolm Ghlais seemed at a standstill. She stated that answers from the investigators were limited and when questioned, DCI Taggart would only say that the investigation was ongoing. Logan took it a step further, hinting that Taggart was stalling the investigation. She looked straight into the camera and said, 'Who benefits from the murders of the Ghlaises? I'll tell you who. Alastaire Ghlais. Why hasn't he been brought in for questioning? Yes, he has an alibi, but that doesn't mean he wasn't involved in the organisation of these gruesome murders. A source inside Police Scotland informs me that reports from forensics, pathology, and other sources are being sent to DCI Taggart and aren't getting to the investigating detectives. What is it you're trying to hide, DCI Taggart?'

MacLeod stopped the video and looked at Claymore.

'It's true,' Claymore said. 'We weren't getting the reports. After that bit from Logan aired, we started receiving them, but they were incomplete. Some were missing pages or had sections redacted. I expressed my concerns to Taggart and was told the orders came from higher up and what we didn't receive wasn't relevant to our investigation.' He raised both his hands up. 'What was I to do?'

'Someone higher up than Taggart at the time must have been protecting him if he didn't get any kickback from Logan's accusation,' Maggie said. 'I mean, that was aired nationally and no one investigated him? Anti-Corruption should have been all over that unless they had someone high up in Anti-Corruption as well.'

'Actually, we've called someone from Anti-Corruption to meet us here,' Claymore said. 'Someone we trust implicitly.'

'Do we know anyone in forensics or ViCLAS who would talk to us?' Maggie asked.

'I'm working on that,' MacLeod answered. 'I should know more tomorrow. In the meantime, I thought we'd run through everything we have to date, beginning with the footage from the First Minister's home security system.' He pulled his laptop out of his bag, set it on the table, and inserted a USB key.

'Wait.' Maggie extended her hand across the table, wiggling her fingers. 'Give me the USB.'

MacLeod frowned at Maggie, but ejected the USB and handed it over. Maggie took it through to the lounge, inserted it in her laptop, and connected wirelessly to her huge-screened TV.

The others followed her into the lounge and MacLeod headed for the vast windows looking out over Holyrood Park and Arthur's Seat.

'Och. Would you look at this view?' MacLeod turned to face Maggie and the others. 'Do you know what I see when I look out my window? A stone wall.'

Maggie rubbed the back of her neck as she tried to stifle a

laugh. 'Would that be from your cardboard box?'

'It may as well be compared to this place.' He pointed at her TV. 'That monstrosity wouldn't even fit in my lounge.'

Maggie started the video before MacLeod could say any more. It was true she had a ton of money that she did nothing to earn, but she wasn't about to let anyone make her feel like shite for it. She stood near the TV to get a good view of the vehicles pulling up outside Jamie Kenmore's home. The darkness and fog made it difficult to see any detail. Maggie hoped to see the shape of the Ghlais Whisky logo on the side of the van, but the van was black and the logo that replaced the one she remembered from her parents' murder scene was a dark hunter green background with golden yellow type. Alastaire had also removed the whimsical unicorn from the newer logo. 'It's definitely a Mercedes-Benz Sprinter, but I can't make out the logo or the number plate.' She turned her attention to the black sedan. 'The car looks like a Mercedes, doesn't it?'

Nichola stepped closer to the screen. 'Look at the shape of the taillights. Mercedes C-class.'

'That fits with what Robbie MacDonald is driving – Black Mercedes CLA. But, we can't prove it's the same vehicle without the number plate.'

'I'll send the video to my tech guy to see if he can enhance it,' MacLeod said. 'Let's take a look at the videos from the sales of those pentacle pendants.'

They watched all three sales, although Maggie thought it was unnecessary. 'If it's any of these three, it's going to be the guy,' she said. 'Cash purchase and he's male.'

'They could have sent a woman to buy it for them,' Claymore said.

Maggie shook her head. 'Not for this. They're not going to trust a woman to carry out their nefarious deeds.'

'He's the only one we haven't been able to identify,'

MacLeod said. 'We traced the other purchase from the Witchery Tours shop through the debit card purchase.' He nodded towards Nichola. 'Maybe you can pay her and the woman from the Wyrd Shop a visit and ensure they still have their pendants.'

Nichola made a little note in the small pad on her lap.

'What about our mystery man?' Maggie asked MacLeod. 'Does your tech guy have a facial recognition program?'

'I'll ask and I'll look at CCTV footage in the area around the time of the purchase to see if we can spot him in a car.'

Maggie thought about the fact that the pendant was the only piece of evidence forensics had released to them to date. It could be because it was known she'd seen it at the crime scene, or it could be that the perpetrators weren't worried about them tracking it down. 'If it's not one of these three, we need to trace the source of the pendant. Who makes it? How long have they been producing them? Does it match the one found at my parents' murder scene? Have there been bulk sales to any of the men on our list from Mrs Brown? We have the name and contact information from the Witchery's distributor.'

Nichola scribbled notes on her pad. 'I'll look into it.'

'There's something else,' Maggie said. She went through to her office and withdrew the sheet of paper Sylvan had given her from her messenger bag, then brought it out and presented it to MacLeod. 'Ghlais sent a payment of exactly one hundred thousand pounds the morning after Kenmore's murder to a numbered account.'

'That's odd,' Claymore said and circled MacLeod to look over his shoulder at the document. 'We didn't find any payments after the murders of Mairie and Malcolm Ghlais.'

'I wonder if that payment came from Thomas Campbell's business,' Maggie said. 'Like a shell game. They cover the payments by one of the other's making it.'

'You're saying it was Campbell who wanted Kenmore killed?' MacLeod asked.

'It's just a theory,' Maggie said. 'But if I'm right, Alastaire made a grave mistake in thinking he wouldn't be a suspect.'

'Mhac na galla.' MacLeod blew out a long breath. 'We need the ViCLAS report.'

'And forensics,' Maggie said. 'The amount of wood they used for the fire was significant. What type of wood was it? Where did it come from? Were there fingerprints on the broken vase in Kenmore's lounge? Was the blood hers or a suspect's? What other evidence was found at the crime scenes?'

'Too many unanswered questions,' Claymore said and lowered himself to the sofa. 'I may be an old man, but I've still got connections. I'll start reaching out to one or two of them in forensics and the National Crime Agency.'

An alert sounded on Maggie's mobile and she opened her security app to a video of a young woman with short sandy hair standing at the building's front door. 'This would be your anti-corruption officer,' Maggie announced.

'Oh, aye,' Claymore said with a wide smile and puffed out chest. 'DI Liz Claymore. My daughter.'

* * *

DI Liz Claymore was none too pleased with her father's involvement in an investigation, never mind one with a high ranking police officer as a suspect. She was a compact little spitfire. Athletic and full of energy. Maggie could almost see the sparks flying off her. She was cute, Maggie decided. Not beautiful, but definitely appealing to the eye. Maggie couldn't pin it, but thought that energy added to her allure.

Maggie wrote an official statement documenting her memory of ACC Taggart's involvement in her parents' murders and ordering Maggie's death.

Once Maggie signed her name to it, she slid it across the

dining room table to Liz Claymore. 'Can you charge him based on my statement?' What she was really asking was if her memories could be trusted.

'We'll need more, of course,' Liz said, much calmer after having a private discussion with her father. 'But, it's enough for us to begin an investigation and bring him in for questioning.'

'If you bring him in for questioning and release him, we could have a major problem,' Maggie said.

Liz tucked the statement into her brown leather satchel and eyed Maggie with a closed mouth smile. 'Then I suggest you solve these murders quickly, DC Glass.'

Maggie barely restrained herself from rolling her eyes. She didn't mention she was technically off the cases. 'If Taggart's involved, he may have other police officers under his thumb.' Maggie had DCI McTavish in mind for one. If you were as comfortable accepting bribes as McTavish was, who knew how far over the line you'd go.

'I'm aware of that, DC. This isn't my first investigation.' Liz kept that smile in place as she stood and picked up her coat from the back of her chair. She bent over, pressed a quick kiss to her father's cheek, and whispered in his ear, 'Stay away from this. Taggart is dangerous.'

Maggie heard her words despite the low whisper and wondered just how much DI Claymore and the Anti-Corruption Unit knew about ACC Jack Taggart. 'Have you ever heard of Jack Lord?' she asked Liz on impulse and watched closely for her reaction. To her credit, Liz kept her face expressionless, but Maggie saw the flash of recognition in those big brown eyes and fluttering long lashes.

'Jack Lord? No. Should I have?'

Maggie shrugged. 'It's just a name I'm trying to identify.'

'Well, good luck then.' Liz shoved her arms into her coat, then slung the strap of her satchel over her shoulder.

The senior Claymore waited until he heard the door close behind his daughter and asked, 'Who's Jack Lord?'

'I think it's an alias Taggart uses,' Maggie answered.

Claymore nodded, his mouth pressed into a tight line. 'Liz recognised the name, which means Anti-Corruption already know about Taggart.'

'Which begs the question,' Maggie began, 'who's still protecting him?' The only people above him in rank were three Deputy Chief Constables and the Chief Constable himself.

MacLeod got up from his seat and put his own coat on. 'Let's leave that mess to Anti-Corruption. We've enough on our plate.' He patted his pocket and pulled out a crumpled pack of cigarettes. 'I'm away for a fag.'

Maggie put the kettle on and made a pot of tea. When they were all seated around the table again, they talked through the case while MacLeod penned a to-do list. Maggie's tasks included finding out anything she could at Ghlais and tracking down where the Ghlais vans were on the night of the murders.

Nichola was checking into the pendants and, along with MacLeod, interviewing Thomas Campbell.

Both MacLeod and Claymore were to feel out contacts at the National Crime Agency and Forensic Services to see if they could get the reports they desperately needed. MacLeod was also going to review the footage from the First Minister's home security system to see if anyone was casing Jamie Kenmore's residence in the days leading up to her kidnapping and murder.

By the end of their session, they had more questions than answers, but a plan to move forward under the nose of ACC Taggart and anyone who may be loyal to him.

Chapter 15

Maggie opened the door to Sylvan dressed in running pants and a warm fleece. She wore a black knit beanie over her short blonde hair and matching gloves on her hands. 'Ready?' Sylvan asked with a glowing smile.

It had taken Maggie ages to get MacLeod and the others out of her flat, but now she had the rest of the afternoon free to take a run in the hills with Sylvan. She grinned back at Sylvan in those tight trousers. 'Ready.' She had to remind herself it was a run she was ready for and not another form of very satisfying exercise. She tucked her keys in her pocket and led the way through the building and out to Holyrood Park.

They stretched in the field before starting out a slow jog, crossing Queen's Drive and into the hills. The sun continued to shine as dark clouds rolled in from the west behind Edinburgh Castle, sitting regally atop its extinct volcano. To the east, the Firth of Forth glimmered with the rolling green hills of the Kingdom of Fife as a backdrop.

Maggie admired Sylvan's stamina as it was a good forty minutes of intense running before she began to show signs of struggling up the inclines. Maggie slowed to a walk at the top of a long climb near the summit of Arthur's Seat.

'Thank God,' Sylvan wheezed as she reached the top of the

climb.

Maggie couldn't help a laugh. 'I'm sorry. Did I push you too hard?' Perhaps she should have kept a slower pace.

Sylvan waved her off. 'No, but much more and I won't be walking tomorrow.'

'Hot bath in Epsom salts,' Maggie suggested. 'It works wonders.'

Sylvan didn't have the heart to explain that the flat where she rented a room didn't have a bath, just a tiny box of a shower stall. She threaded her arm through Maggie's as they made their way down a slope and to the right with a view of the Pentland Hills and the dark, brooding clouds hovering just above their numerous peaks.

No one had ever held Maggie in that manner before. It made her feel as though Sylvan was relying on her for support and, for some reason, made her feel ten feet tall. As they strolled, Maggie wondered about Sylvan's life. She'd asked Maggie all about hers, but had offered very little in return. 'Did you grow up in Edinburgh?' she asked, deciding that was a relatively easy place to start prodding into Sylvan's background.

'No, I moved here at sixteen when I started at the University of Edinburgh.'

Maggie glanced at Sylvan, expecting her to continue the story, but she didn't elaborate. 'Do you go back home to see your family?'

A small smile appeared on Sylvan's face and her eyes sparkled as if she knew she was keeping Maggie in suspense. 'No. All I ever wanted was to move here to the city and never look back. Edinburgh held so much potential in my mind back then.' Her smile faded and her eyes lost some of their lustre. 'It held my dreams, my future.'

The sadness emanating from Sylvan was so palpable Maggie wanted nothing more than to hug and comfort her, but she held off, not knowing if she would make Sylvan feel worse. 'And it let you down?'

'No.' Sylvan shook her head. 'Edinburgh didn't let me down. Just one person in it.'

'One day,' Maggie began, thinking of words Sylvan had spoken to her, 'perhaps you'll trust me enough to tell me the story.' She knew Sylvan spoke of the woman she loved who didn't love her back, but that seemed to be as much as she was willing to say on the matter.

'Sorry,' Sylvan said and tightened her hold on Maggie's arm. 'I suppose it's still a sore spot.'

'Understood, but when you're ready to talk about it, I'm here.'

Maggie continued to lead Sylvan to the right with the strong wind whipping at them, invigorating them. She took the path through the valley between Arthur's Seat and the Salisbury Crags, the view of the Firth of Forth and the Kingdom of Fife spread out before them. Maggie was a bit disappointed that Sylvan hadn't opened up about her family or childhood, but had to let it go and hope Sylvan would open up in time. Sylvan was wounded. Deeply hurt. Maggie imagined Sylvan had wrapped herself in a cocoon of safety and would emerge, healed and strengthened in time.

They walked in silence for several minutes while Maggie tried to think of a topic that may draw Sylvan out instead of shutting her down. She finally settled for education. 'So you studied finances at uni?'

'Business, economics, and finances, yes.'

Maggie screwed up her nose, red from the cold. 'How did you stand it? I never would have made it through the first year.' She would have died of boredom or her head would have exploded from looking at all the numbers.

Sylvan laughed. Finally, that beautiful, musical laugh was back.

'I told you, I'm a numbers nerd. Numbers never lie.'

Maggie wondered who had lied to Sylvan. Her family or her lover? 'Where did you work before Ghlais?'

The flush in Sylvan's cheeks from the run and the cold wind drained from her face. After a long silence, she said, 'It's difficult to talk about. I owned a letting company with a partner. We were doing quite well, but a fair amount of the money in our account was rent we were holding for the landlords. My partner emptied our account and disappeared.'

Maggie's mouth dropped open. 'And left you owing the landlords?'

'Among other business expenses, yes. I lost everything. My house, the business, my savings. My pride.' The only reason she kept her car was that it was leased. She would be paying for her error in judgement in trusting her partner for years to come. But, that was her cross to bear and not something she would burden Maggie with. 'Anyway, when Alastaire hired me, it was a relief. I'd been turned down for several positions. Losing a business doesn't look good on one's CV, especially when you're in finance.'

'Well, I'm glad he did.' Maggie wondered if that was why Alastaire had hired Sylvan. Did he think she'd be pliable because she was so grateful for the job? It must have been scary when Sylvan realised that Alastaire was embezzling funds. 'I appreciate you giving me a heads up about the discrepancies you found.'

'Numbers never lie.' Sylvan offered Maggie another weak smile.

'The partner who stiffed you, she was the woman you loved?'

Sylvan looked down at her feet as they continued to walk down the path, the wind calmer lower in the valley. 'Loved. Trusted.'

'I'm sorry you had to go through all of that.'

'I don't need sympathy, Maggie. I was a fool. I won't make the same mistakes again.'

'Which is why you want to take things slow and be sure before we sleep together.' Maggie wanted to promise Sylvan that she would never leave her, never hurt her. But, how could she make that promise when she didn't know if she was capable of loving her?

'I suppose.' Sylvan never jumped into a relationship, but she was more cautious than ever. They walked a few minutes in silence again with their arms still hooked together then Sylvan started laughing. 'I've been calling you out on your commitment and abandonment issues and here it seems I may have the same issues.'

'You haven't really called me out on them. You stated, quite clearly, what you wanted. I think that's important if we're going to try to have a relationship.' As crazy as it sounded, that was precisely what Maggie wanted with Sylvan.

Sylvan was a bit surprised that Maggie, a self-admitted commitment-phobe, was willing to give a relationship a go. But, she was right. If they were going to do this, communication was vital and there was so much she hadn't said. 'I haven't exactly been forthcoming today. I'm sorry.'

Maggie smiled at Sylvan and patted the arm linked with hers. 'We've got time. You don't have to spill everything in one day.' Besides, she wasn't being entirely forthcoming herself. She hadn't told Sylvan anything about her plans with the Eagleshams.

As they neared Maggie's flat, Maggie invited Sylvan in, but she declined, stating she needed to prepare for work in the morning. Maggie walked her to her car.

'Don't forget the bath in Epsom salts.'

Sylvan laughed. 'I'm afraid I'll have to settle for a hot shower. I don't actually have a bathtub.'

Maggie grinned and wiggled her eyebrows. 'You're welcome to use mine.'

Sylvan came close to accepting the offer. What she wouldn't give to soak in a hot bath. Instead, she leaned in and pressed a kiss to Maggie's waiting lips, slow and sensuous.

Maggie returned the kiss, lazy and lingering. Then she wrapped her arms around Sylvan, rested her cheek against Sylvan's, and just held her. Sylvan's arms wrapped around her waist and Maggie didn't think she'd ever felt so content. She could have stood there on the pavement like that for hours, breathing in the scent of Sylvan's hair – green apples and fresh air. All too soon, Sylvan stepped back, gave Maggie a quick peck, and got in her car. Maggie leaned over as she started the car, and Sylvan rolled the window down.

Maggie didn't really have anything specific to say. She just didn't want Sylvan to leave yet. 'Thanks for coming for a run with me.' She knew it wasn't Sylvan's forte, but she'd come along anyway.

'Thanks for inviting me. I thought I was fit, but I've got a ways to go to catch up to you.' Sylvan enjoyed the run in the hills more than she thought she would. 'I hope I didn't slow you down too much and that you'll invite me again.'

'Next weekend then?' Maggie would have said tomorrow if it didn't get dark so early.

'It's a date.'

Maggie leaned through the window and kissed the smile from Sylvan's face, then reluctantly took a step back and watched Sylvan drive away until her car disappeared around the corner.

* * *

Maggie arrived at Colin Eaglesham's office promptly at eight in the morning wearing a crisp suit of charcoal pants, charcoal shirt, and purple and black checked blazer wrapped under her black wool coat and tartan cashmere scarf. A pair of shiny, dark purple oxfords completed the outfit. Maggie was greeted by the woman she spoke to on the phone on Friday to book the appointment with Colin. She introduced herself as Kathrine Doyle and reminded Maggie of Mrs Brown, although slightly younger and slimmer.

Doyle led Maggie through to a conference room and released her into the jam-packed room. Colin took charge and introduced Maggie around the room to a team of auditors, private security officers, and a Detective Inspector from the Economic Crimes Unit. Derek Eaglesham sat at the head of the table.

The Eagleshams had been busy assembling this team over the weekend. Maggie didn't usually get nervous, but she felt a little shaky and queasy at the moment, thinking about what they were about to do. The senior Eaglesham laid out the plan, with Maggie going into Ghlais with Colin and the private security team. The auditors and the Detective Inspector would follow half an hour later.

'We'll provide security services at Ghlais until you're able to hire your own security staff,' Iain Blackwell, head of the security team, stated. He was a broad-shouldered man with military short dark hair and bright blue eyes.

The white line above Blackwell's left temple reminded Maggie of the scar bisecting her left eyebrow. Like hers, it wasn't recent and she wondered if it was a relic of his childhood or serving his country. 'Appreciated, Mr Blackwell. Once your staff arrives at Ghlais, their priority will be to secure the CCTV systems. I need all of the surveillance systems intact. We also need to ensure nothing is taken from the property.'

Blackwell gestured to a female member of his team, a woman with long dark hair tied back in a ponytail. 'Reid, you're responsible for the security systems.' He assigned two others to cover the front door and two to cover the loading dock area in the back.

Derek Eaglesham brought an image onto the screen behind him through his laptop. The map Maggie had sent to him of the layout at Ghlais displayed on the screen and she stood, moving to the screen. 'The security office is here.' Maggie highlighted the location on the main floor not far from the front entrance. Then she pointed out the main entrance and loading dock area. Finally, she instructed the auditors and Detective Inspector to assemble at the reception desk on the second floor upon their arrival.

DI Lindsay Ross, a mid-forties woman with short red hair, cleared her throat. 'I'll have three constables from the Penicuik Police Station meeting me upon our arrival. We'll be taking Alastaire Ghlais, Alex Ghlais, and Sylvan MacKenzie in for questioning.'

'Ms MacKenzie is not involved,' Maggie said. 'She's a new employee who warned me of the embezzlement of funds.'

'Understood, DC Glass, but we still need to question her.'

Maggie breathed a sigh of relief that she hoped no one noticed. She had a strong urge to warn Sylvan of what was coming and pushed it away. 'You may also want to question the wife of George Stanton. He was the previous CFO and apparently died of a heart attack or drug overdose at his desk. If he was under a lot of stress, his wife might be able to shine some light on it.'

Ross took a notebook out of her pocket and made a note.

'Right then,' Derek said, rubbing his hands together. 'Let's get this show on the road.'

Maggie, Blackwell, and Colin Eaglesham headed out of the room, followed by the security team. Maggie passed the keys for the black Mercedes she'd driven to Eaglesham's to Blackwell. 'You'll have use of this vehicle while you're heading up security at Ghlais.'

Blackwell stared at the keys, then at Maggie. 'That's not

necessary, DC Glass.'

'Perk of the job,' she said and dropped the keys into his hand.

Maggie got in the passenger side while Colin got in the back and waited for Blackwell to get in and adjust his seat and mirrors. Blackwell lifted his hand to show Maggie the black dust on his fingers.

'Is that fingerprint dust?' he asked with a frown.

'Sorry,' Maggie said with a snort. 'I thought I got it all.'

'That's a story I think I need to hear.'

Maggie explained the attempted break-in at her flat and how she'd come into possession of the Mercedes. Blackwell's frown lines deepened, but he said nothing.

Maggie kept an eye on her surroundings on the drive to Ghlais, but she hadn't noticed a tail since Robbie MacDonald's arrest. They pulled into the Ghlais car park and Maggie directed Blackwell to the visitor parking. She waved her hand at the two cars parked in the spots designated for the CEO and VP Marketing – a sleek silver Jaguar XE and a flashy royal blue Jaguar F-Type. 'Those vehicles belong to Ghlais. I'll need the keys from Alastaire and Alex.'

Blackwell answered with a short, crisp nod.

Maggie led the way through the entrance doors and started to her left, but stopped when Blackwell kept walking forward. He peered around the corner to where the security offices were, noting the closed door, then turned back to follow Maggie.

Mrs Brown must have sensed the seriousness of the situation as she stood when Maggie and her companions crossed the lobby towards her desk.

'Is he in his office?' Maggie asked.

'Yes, along with Alex.'

'Thank you, Mrs Brown.' Maggie gave her a quick nod then started down the hallway, taking a couple of deep breaths as she approached the double doors at the end of the hall.

Colin laid a hand on Maggie's shoulder. 'We're right here with you.'

Maggie tapped her knuckles on the door with one last deep breath and opened it.

* * *

As soon as she heard the door close at the end of the hall, Mrs Brown shuffled down to Sylvan's office and let herself in. 'Something's going on,' she whispered with wide eyes behind her thick red frames.

Sylvan looked up at her with raised brows. 'What's that?'

Mrs Brown waved over her shoulder at the closed door behind her. 'Maggie just came in with two men. They looked … professional. And very serious. They went into Alastaire's office.'

Sylvan was aware Maggie and Eaglesham were looking into the embezzlement of funds at Ghlais, but she certainly didn't expect a response this quickly and Maggie hadn't mentioned anything. 'Alright.' There was nothing she could do until after the meeting in Alastaire's office. 'Business as usual, Mrs Brown. Unless we hear different.'

'Right.' Mrs Brown pursed her lips, but did as she was told. She began to close the door behind her when Sylvan asked her to leave it open.

* * *

Maggie stepped into Alastaire's office with Colin and Blackwell behind her, one at each shoulder. She noted the roaring fire in the fireplace and Alastaire and Alex in their usual spots with their coffee cups in front of them.

'Maggie, pet,' Alastaire said. 'If you're here for training, I'm afraid you're a bit overdressed. You'll be learning the business from the ground up, starting in the distillery.'

Maggie ignored his derogatory tone and crossed to his

desk as she drew several documents from her messenger bag. 'I have a few questions first, uncle Alastaire.' She laid the first document on his desk containing several sexual assault complaints against him.

Alastaire scanned the document and scoffed. 'I explained to you that these are false allegations by greedy little witches.'

Interesting choice of word, Maggie thought. The prickle at the back of her neck had her taking a deep breath before she set the next document on the desk. 'If they're false allegations, why are you using Ghlais funds to pay them off?' She started laying papers on his desk, one by one, from the stack in her hand. 'To the tune of millions of pounds over this past year alone?' She pulled another stack from her bag, fanning them out before laying them over the documents piling up on the desk, one by one by one. 'And why are all these women signing non-disclosure agreements?'

With each document that landed in front of him, Alastaire's face turned a darker shade of red. 'Because we can't have these stupid whores damaging the good reputation of Ghlais.' He raised his fist and smashed it down on top of the stacks of papers as he rose to his feet.

Blackwell stepped in front of Maggie, towering over Alastaire. Alastaire glared up at him, his body shaking with anger and his fists clenched tightly at his sides.

From behind Blackwell, Maggie recited paragraph five from the agreement Alastaire signed when he accepted the role of CEO of Ghlais. 'Any behaviour that damages the reputation of Ghlais Whisky or that is reasonably assumed to cause damage to the reputation of same will result in the immediate resignation of said CEO without compensation.'

'I will not resign,' Alastaire shouted. 'This is absurd. You have no right to come in here and make these defamatory allegations. I'll not have it.'

'Failing resignation,' Maggie continued, 'said CEO will be

terminated immediately with cause.'

Alex began to rise from his seat and Maggie stabbed her finger towards him, her eyes still locked on Alastaire. Alex sat back down like an obedient dog.

Colin laid a document on top of the others on Alastaire's desk and Alastaire swiped his arm across the desk, sending documents flying through the air. Spittle flew from his mouth as he screamed obscenities, denials, and refusals.

'I suggest you calm down, sir,' Blackwell said in a relaxed tone. 'You're liable to give yourself a heart attack.'

'Da, please,' Alex said, his face sheet white.

Alastaire was nearly hyperventilating, panting in and out. He grabbed the handset on his desk and dialled an extension. 'Get my solicitor on the line,' he barked and hung up. He dropped back into his chair, still vibrating and red. 'We'll just see about all of this when my solicitor arrives. In the meantime, get the hell out of my office.'

'I'm afraid we can't do that, sir,' Barkwell said. 'You're no longer an employee of Ghlais Whisky.'

The door burst open and Maggie turned to see Sylvan and Mrs Brown in the doorway with bulging eyes.

'What's going on here?' Sylvan asked. 'We heard all the yelling.'

'Get out,' Alastaire screamed, sending Mrs Brown shuffling quickly down the hall.

Sylvan remained rooted in the doorway, her wide eyes on Maggie. Maggie gave her a quick nod and Sylvan turned, closing the door gently behind her. When Maggie turned back around to face Alastaire, he glared at her with nothing short of loathing in his eyes.

Chapter 16

Maggie checked her watch. Surely thirty minutes had passed ages ago. Leaving Alastaire and Alex in Blackwell's capable hands with Colin to back him up, she excused herself and went out to the lobby. There was no sign of DI Ross and the auditors yet, so she approached Mrs Brown. 'I'm expecting some police officers and a few others. Can you show the police officers into Alastaire's office when they arrive?'

'Yes, but what's happening, Maggie?'

'I'll explain later,' she said and headed for Sylvan's office. Maggie found her pacing back and forth behind her desk, silhouetted by the forest scene behind her. 'I've only got a moment, so please listen.'

Sylvan stopped walking, faced Maggie, and nodded, but she continued to knead her hands in front of her.

'They're going to take you in for questioning, but as a witness. You're not a suspect, do you ken?'

'Aye, of course.'

'It's better that you're taken in with Alastaire and Alex. It will take any suspicion away from you.' The last thing she wanted was Alastaire setting his minions on Sylvan.

'Am I in danger, Maggie?'

'No.' She was sure Alastaire would focus his ire on her, not Sylvan, so long as he didn't suspect that she gave him up.

'Just co-operate with the police when they arrive and everything will be fine.'

'Of course.'

Maggie returned to Alastaire's office, where no one seemed to have moved.

'This is ridiculous,' Alastaire said. 'You're going to stand there staring at us until my solicitor arrives?'

'Aye,' Maggie answered.

Alastaire scoffed. 'He hasn't called back yet, so you'll be waiting a while.'

'I've got all day,' Maggie said with a sweet smile.

Alastaire picked up his phone again and stabbed several numbers. 'My office,' he said and hung up.

Maggie hoped that was Alastaire's security team he'd just called. She wasn't disappointed. Moments later, Robbie MacDonald came through the door, followed by two young men – one with short red hair and one dark-haired with a long gash and a black and purple bruise on his forehead.

'Sir?' Robbie said as he looked around at the people in the office.

'Get these idiots out of my office,' Alastaire demanded.

'Robbie MacDonald?' Colin asked.

'Who's asking?' Robbie said with a scowl at Colin.

Colin passed him a document which Robbie accepted and began to read.

'Your employment with Ghlais Whisky is hereby terminated,' Colin said.

Robbie's head whipped around to Alastaire. 'Sir?'

'You do not have the authority to terminate my employees, Mr ...?' Alastair glared at Colin.

'Eaglesham. Colin Eaglesham.'

Recognition flared in Alastaire's eyes and he turned them on Maggie. 'You wee whore. You're no better than the rest of those witches. You will not get away with this.'

At that moment, DI Ross strolled into the room with her three constables, followed by several of Blackwell's security team.

Finally, Maggie thought. She addressed two of the security officers. 'I'll need the ID's checked on these two,' she said, motioning to the two security guards who accompanied Robbie MacDonald. 'Then these three gentlemen can be escorted from the premises.' Turning to the two men, she added, 'In case you hadn't sorted it out yet, your employment with Ghlais is also terminated.' She pointed to the dark-haired man's forehead. 'By the way, how'd you injure your head?'

His hand went to his forehead as if to cover the wound. 'Bumped it.'

Maggie just bet he did. Bumped it on a crystal vase, no doubt.

DI Ross crossed straight over to Alastaire and before he could ask her what the devil she was doing, she said, 'Alastaire Ghlais, you're being detained on suspicion of embezzlement.'

'No,' Alastaire screamed as he shot up from his seat, his eyes wild like a spooked horse. 'This is outrageous.' As Blackwell took hold of his upper arms, Alastaire flung his head around to his son. 'Alex.'

Alex shot out of his chair and sprinted for the door, but one of the police constables quickly took control of him. 'Alex Ghlais, you're being detained on suspicion of embezzlement. You do not have to say anything.'

'Sylvan,' Alastaire yelled, his voice cracking. 'Sylvan!'

'She's being detained as well,' Maggie said, her eyes cold as her uncle glared at her. He was desperate now, panic burning in his wild eyes. Maggie had no doubt Alastaire was looking for someone to start deleting files. She was only surprised that he didn't start screaming for Mrs Brown.

As DI Ross slapped handcuffs around Alastaire's wrists, Maggie said, 'I'll need any keys he has on him and his mobile.' Then she turned to the officer cuffing Alex. 'Him too.'

'My personal keys are on there,' Alex complained. 'My house and my car.'

'You'll get your house key,' Maggie said. 'But the car belongs to Ghlais.'

'You can't take our phones,' Alastaire yelled.

'I can,' Maggie stated calmly. 'They belong to Ghlais as well.' Stupid of them, Maggie thought. If they'd paid for their own mobile phones, she wouldn't be able to take possession of them without a warrant.

DI Ross began to lead Alastaire out and he skidded to a stop next to Maggie, his head shaking and red as he spat, 'You have no idea what you've done, who you've messed with. You will pay for this.'

'What are you going to do, uncle?' Maggie whispered. 'Burn me at the stake?'

He lunged forward with a primal growl, but Ross caught him and pulled him back, then shoved him towards the door. She passed him off to one of her constables then returned to Maggie. 'Is he a suspect in the murder of Jamie Kenmore?'

Maggie shouldn't have said what she did, but she couldn't help herself. She nodded at Ross. 'Jamie Kenmore and the murder of my mother and father eighteen years ago.'

'Fuck me,' Ross said.

* * *

DI Ross went to Sylvan's office next. A constable stood just inside the doorway as Sylvan paced in front of the windows. 'Sylvan MacKenzie, you're being detained on suspicion of embezzlement.'

So, not a witness then, Sylvan thought as she turned to face Ross. 'I'd like to come in for questioning voluntarily, but I'd appreciate it if you'd put me in handcuffs.' She'd seen Alastaire and Alex being led out in handcuffs and had to ensure they knew she was being arrested as well. She undid a couple of buttons on her shirt and reached into her bra, pulling out a USB drive which she held out to DI Ross. 'You'll find all the evidence you need on here.'

Ross accepted the USB with a raised eyebrow. 'DC Glass insisted you were a witness in all of this. I hope you understand that, as CFO of Ghlais, we have to treat you as a suspect until we can rule you out.'

'Understood.'

Ross nodded to the constable, asking him to handcuff Sylvan and escort her to the police station.

* * *

With just Colin, Blackwell, and Maggie left in Alastaire's office, Maggie strode over to the desk and deposited Alastaire and Alex's keys and mobiles on the desktop, then eased herself down into Alastaire's chair. She didn't like the feel of it. It was more a chair for lounging in than working. She sat back and the chair reclined, taking her off guard and she lurched back to an upright position. Oh, aye, didn't like the chair at all.

Mrs Brown popped her head in the doorway and gasped, her hand slapping against her chest. 'Oh, dear. It's like seeing your mother sitting there again.' She fanned her hand in front of her face for a moment. 'Are you taking over then?'

'No,' Maggie said with a shake of her head. 'I'll have to hire a new CEO. I don't know the first thing about running a distillery.'

'That's a shame. You're mother and father would be so proud to see you sitting there, Magaidh.'

Maggie ran her hand over a clear space on the desk, smooth and polished. 'Do you remember what it looked like in here back then?'

'Oh, aye. I've pictures if you'd like me to bring them in.'

'I'd like that.' She had a vague idea from the few memories that returned and the videos she watched, but a photograph would be much better.

Mrs Brown smiled, although a sadness lingered in her eyes. 'Is there anything you need?'

Maggie motioned towards the leaping flames in the fireplace. 'Could you get someone to extinguish that fire for me?' She couldn't take much more of its crackling or the scent of burnt wood. She stared at the offensive flames for a moment, questions forming in her head that would have to wait until whoever Mrs Brown sent up arrived.

Colin began to gather and sort all of the paperwork strewn over the desk and floor as Blackwell left to check on his employees.

Maggie turned her attention to Alastaire's desk drawers, opening each one and fishing around. She had no idea what she was looking for, only that she'd know if she found it. When she got to the bottom right door, she discovered it locked and thought *bingo*.

Maggie checked all of the keys on Alastaire's keyring to no avail, then began searching through all of the other drawers again for an old fashioned skeleton type key. She scanned the desktop and eyed the wooden box that always sat in the far right corner of the desk. Opening it, Maggie studied the fat cigars. She'd never known Alastaire to smoke a cigar, yet she remembered this box always being on his desk. Maggie picked up the box and tipped it over on the desk as Colin cleared away the last of the papers. A shiny brass skeleton key fell out on top of the heap of cigars. Maggie grinned as she held it up for Colin. 'Not the smartest hiding spot, is it?'

'Apparently not.' He tapped the stack of papers on the desk to straighten them then left them sitting neatly near the corner. 'I'll go and check on the auditors then.'

'Right,' Maggie said, her concentration now on the bottom drawer again. She slid the key in and it turned like a hot knife through butter – smooth and easy. Maggie pulled the drawer open slowly, revealing a stack of thin white file folders. She lifted the top folder out and spread it on the desk in front of her. It contained a single sheet of paper with a logo at the top – a scroll with the words *Lords of Edinburgh* in an Old English font. Under the logo was a photograph of Alex with his name beneath it, followed by a list of items beginning with the date initiated and level achieved. It was like some deranged playing card, Maggie thought. She stood, picked up the two sets of keys and the mobiles from the desk, and backed away, picking up her coat from the back of the chair.

'Ma'am,' a fair-haired young man said from the doorway. 'I was asked to put the fire out.'

'Yes, please,' Maggie waved to the fire as if he'd need directions. 'What's your name?'

'Davey, ma'am.'

'Pleased to meet you, Davey. I'm Maggie.'

'Yes, ma'am.' He nodded and bent to deal with the fire.

Maggie walked over to the side of the fireplace, staying a good few feet back. 'I assume there's wood stored somewhere for this,' she said.

Davey separated the burning logs, moving them off the coals with the poker. 'Yes, ma'am. There's a woodpile out back.'

'Right. Thanks, Davey. And you don't need to call me ma'am.' It made her feel ancient. 'Maggie's fine.'

'Yes, ma'am.'

Maggie waited until Davey had the fire out then followed him out of the office, closing the door behind her. Then she pulled her mobile from her pocket and rang MacLeod.

'Any chance you can come to Ghlais with forensic techs you can trust?'

'What have you found, Glass?'

'I've only just started, but I've got a drawer full of file folders that appear to be fact sheets for each member of the Lords of Edinburgh.'

'Interesting.'

'Yeah. And I may have a lead on the wood used in Kenmore's murder.'

'Right. I'm on my way.'

Maggie used Alastaire's keys to lock the office door and started down the hallway. At Sylvan's door, she stopped and leaned against the doorjamb, watching the man typing on Sylvan's computer as Colin and a police constable looked over his shoulder. 'I assume you'll want access to Alastaire's computer,' she said to Colin.

Colin looked up and smiled. They were copying the files on Sylvan's, Alex's, and Alastaire's computers before being seized as evidence by DI Ross. The police constable ensured they only copied files and didn't delete any. 'Aye. We were just waiting for you to finish in there.'

'It's going to be a while longer. I've got a detective coming in with a forensics tech.'

'For the embezzlement case?' Colin asked, a frown marring his forehead.

'No. They're investigating the murders of Jamie Kenmore and my parents.'

Colin's mouth dropped open and he stood there, unmoving. The auditor stopped typing and looked up, staring at Maggie with a similar expression.

'I've locked Alastaire's office. I'm going to lock Alex's as well.'

'Right,' Colin said, shaking his head. 'This just keeps getting more and more surreal.'

* * *

Maggie made her way downstairs. Had she thought to

bring some nitrile gloves with her, she could have continued to search Alastaire's office. Without them, she'd have to wait for MacLeod to arrive. In the security office, Blackwell and Reid sat in front of a wall of CCTV monitors.

'Is there a camera on the Sprinter vans?' Maggie asked as she entered the room.

'Aye,' Reid answered, pointing to the monitor second from the left on the top row. It was split into four views, two of them displaying two vans parked in the back of the loading dock area.

'Perfect,' Maggie said. 'Can you bring up the coverage on these cameras from last Wednesday afternoon through Thursday morning?'

Reid typed on the keyboard then pointed at the monitor directly in front of her. 'I'll bring it up on here,' she said. The camera angle facing the vans popped onto the screen then Reid used the mouse to scroll to the date and time she wanted. 'I'll start at fifteen hundred hours. Is that okay?'

'Perfect,' Maggie said. 'I'm looking for anyone taking one of the vans out after operating hours.'

'That's fifteen hundred hours,' Reid said as the monitor displayed what appeared to be the same two vans parked in the same spots. 'The cameras are motion sensored, so we can move ahead to when there's activity in the lot.'

It was dark at 1635 hours when an identical black van pulled in and backed into one of the empty spots. The driver got out, a man in his mid to late thirties with a knit beanie on his head, wearing the Ghlais driver uniform of black pants and a black jacket with the Ghlais logo over the left breast and Ghlais in gold letters printed across the back. He removed his trash from the cab then did a quick circle check before locking the van and wandering into the loading dock through a side door.

A few minutes later, a fourth van pulled in and the driver

went through a similar series of actions before heading into the distillery loading dock.

The fifth van pulled in just before 1700 hours. Between 1700 and 1730 hours, several employees exited the loading dock door and drove off in their personal vehicles. It was quiet until 2043, when a fox trotted through the lot. Then three men exited through the loading dock door and walked to the row of vans. Maggie recognised Robbie MacDonald and the two security staff who'd accompanied him to Alastaire's office. Lights flashed on the van parked in the centre and the three men got in and drove the van off camera, but not towards the street. They drove deeper on the property, towards the warehouse building.

'See if you can pick them up on another camera,' Maggie said.

Reid surveyed all the monitors, selected a view, then scrolled back to 2100 hours on Wednesday.

The van pulled over beside a woodpile and all three men got out and began loading wood into the back of the van, mostly split logs, but they also loaded two logs that were about seven feet long. The three men got back inside the cab and turned the van around, driving out towards the front of the distillery. Switching to the front car park view, the van pulled up by the main entrance. Robbie got out of the van and into the Mercedes. The two vehicles then pulled out onto the road.

Reid returned the original camera view to the monitor in front of her and scrolled back to the time they'd left off. The van returned at 0615 on Thursday, driven by the ginger-haired security guard. The dark-haired guard with the gash and bruises on his forehead wasn't with him. Maggie made a mental note to check where he got his stitches.

'Could you make a couple of copies of that on USB for me?' Maggie asked.

'Yes, ma'am. I'll have that ready for you in about half an hour.'

'Thanks.' Yeesh. Why was everyone calling her ma'am all of a sudden?

'A moment, DC Glass?' Blackwell said as Maggie started walking away. He followed her out into the hallway. 'I've got two guards coming in for the three to eleven shift and two for the eleven to seven shift, then Reid and I will be back in at seven. One should suffice, but given the circumstances, I thought it best to double up for the next few days.'

'Sounds like a good idea,' Maggie said. 'Thanks, Blackwell.'

He gave her that short nod of his, then said, 'Alastaire Ghlais's security staff may turn up for duty as well.'

'Right. I'll make sure I'm here for the shift changes.'

Maggie headed through a set of double doors leading to the main floor of the distillery, which housed six massive copper stills, three on each side. There were three more floors above them. Production began on the top floor with the malting and germination of the barley. The barley then went to the third floor for kilning over peat fires. Then to the mashing stage where the malt grit was mixed with water from a Highland spring. The fermentation process followed and this was where yeast was used. Often, you could smell yeast in the air all over Edinburgh from the various distilleries in the area. Maggie wasn't sure if the yeast smells from Ghlais contributed to that or if they were too far away, but every time she smelled it, she thought of Ghlais. After the fermentation process, the whisky entered the stills and then into wooden barrels for the maturing process. Ghlais currently offered three different whisky ages – three, twelve, and eighteen years. Next year, in time for Ghlais's twenty-fifth anniversary, their first batch of twenty-five-year-old whisky would be ready. There were barrels in the warehouse, a massive building behind the main building, marked to be aged for fifty years to mark their fiftieth anniversary. Maggie's knowledge of the whole process was vague at best as, just like reading the financial reports, it tended to fry her brain.

Once through the distillery area, she entered the bottling room where employees were busy bottling, inspecting, and labelling the bottles before boxing them. From there, they went to the loading dock where they were picked up by lorries or the Ghlais vans took them out for local deliveries.

As Maggie walked through, conversations came to a halt and heads turned to stare. No doubt word of the three members of upper management being taken into custody had made it down here. She continued through to the loading dock and out the side door to the wooden shelter housing firewood and peat. All of the wood was split into fireplace sized logs. She circled the structure and found a stack of about ten seven-foot-long logs behind it. She returned to the shelter's front and stood staring at the massive stone building that housed Ghlais with the wind whipping through her hair. She'd have to deal with the production end of the business, but how did she know who she could trust and who was loyal to Alastaire?

Chapter 17

Next on Maggie's agenda was speaking to the production manager, but first, she needed to talk to Mrs Brown. She went back up to the second floor and approached the reception desk. 'I have a few questions,' she said.

Mrs Brown looked up through her red-framed glasses. 'Can you tell me what's happening first?'

Maggie explained the embezzlement accusations.

'Alastaire and Alex make good wages. I don't understand why they'd risk embezzling funds.'

Maggie didn't have time to stand there and explain. 'You've worked here since Ghlais opened. You must know the employees well.'

'Oh, aye. I suppose I do.'

Maggie leaned over the counter, lowering her voice. 'Would you be able to make me a list of the employees you believe are loyal to Alastaire?'

Mrs Brown's eyes widened. 'I don't understand.'

Maggie wanted to roll her eyes, but held back. She whispered, 'I need to know who I can trust.'

Mrs Brown's brow furrowed, then a slow smile spread as she looked into Maggie's eyes. 'That's a list I can make for you.'

Sometimes, getting what you needed was a matter of

rephrasing the question, Maggie thought. 'Mrs Brown, who's in charge of production and the distillery?'

'Will. William Fergus.'

'Where would I find Mr Fergus?'

'He could be anywhere in the distillery or in his office.' Mrs Brown rose to her feet. 'Shall I take you down to his office?'

Maggie didn't want to waste time if he wouldn't be there. 'Is there a way to get hold of him if he's in the distillery?'

'Oh, aye. I can use the public address system to page him to meet you here.'

Maggie nodded. 'Do that.'

When Mrs Brown had called for Fergus, Maggie leaned over the counter. 'Ghlais's last CFO? Do you know what happened to him?'

'George?'

Maggie nodded and Mrs Brown looked around to ensure they were alone.

'Well, the official statement is that he passed away at his desk from cardiac arrest, but I was the one who found him. There were empty tablet containers covering his desk and a half-empty glass of water.'

'So he committed suicide?'

'I spoke to Brennagh, his wife, at the funeral. Apparently, he left her a voicemail after he took the tablets. He couldn't cope with the stress of working for Alastair anymore.'

Maggie just nodded again as she wondered if that stress was caused by covering up Alastaire's embezzling. She glanced around the reception area then asked, 'Where can I make a cup of tea?'

* * *

Maggie managed several sips from her steaming mug of tea before Will Fergus lumbered up the stairs in green coveralls. He removed his Ghlais cap as he reached the top, releasing a wiry mop of russet hair, and grinned at Maggie, his hand slapping over his heart.

'Och, you're the spit of your mother.'

Will was embroidered in a script font over the Ghlais logo on the left breast of his coveralls, revealed when he dropped his hand and offered it to Maggie. Fergus gripped her hand and pumped it up and down, his grin firmly in place. For a moment, Maggie wondered if he was insane.

'The old bastard's been arrested then, has he?' Fergus asked. 'Brilliant.' He released Maggie's hand and turned to Mrs Brown. 'A bonnie day, aye?'

That wasn't the reaction Maggie expected, but it made her trust Fergus, if only a little. 'Mr Fergus, I was hoping we could discuss the running of the distillery.'

'Oh, aye.' He motioned to the stairs with his cap. 'I'll take you through the whole process.'

'That won't be necessary,' Maggie said. 'I need to know that production will continue without any disruptions until I can hire a new CEO.'

Fergus nodded vigorously. 'Oh, aye, dinnae fash, lass. Ghlais will run nae bother without Alastaire.' He winked at Mrs Brown. 'Smooth as glass.'

Satisfied with that, Maggie said, 'Then perhaps you can show me where my parents' belongings are stored.'

Fergus tilted his head. 'Your parents' belongings?'

Maggie found herself hoping Alastaire hadn't disposed of her parents' things. 'Apparently, the contents from their house are stored here somewhere.'

'Right,' he said and pulled his cap over his unruly hair. 'That'll be over in the warehouse then. You'll need your coat, lass.'

Maggie left her mobile number with Mrs Brown to ring her when DI MacLeod arrived then followed Fergus out to the loading docks and across the yard to the warehouse. He removed a set of keys from his pocket and unlocked a door in the far corner, behind rows and rows of ageing barrels.

Tilting his cap to her, he said, 'I'll leave you to it.'

'Thank you, Mr Fergus.' Maggie stood in the doorway, watching Fergus walk away before turning into the room and flicking the light switch on the wall. The overhead florescent lights flickered and sizzled to life, illuminating the thirty by sixty-foot storeroom. A good portion of the room was empty, save the corner crammed with furniture covered in white sheets and dozens of boxes stacked in rows. Where to start? She wasn't even sure what she was looking for.

Maggie wandered over to the boxes and lifted one off the top of a stack, lowering it to the floor before studying it for markings. Kitchen was written in black block letters on the top of the box. She set it off to the side, starting a new row, and took down the next box until she came to one labelled 'Office – Mairie'. She cut through the tape with her flat key and opened the box, sifting through the items and papers inside. The silver frame holding a picture of Mairie, Malcolm, and Maggie must have sat on Mairie's home office desk. They looked so happy, eyes bright and smiles wide. Maggie could only wonder what life would have been like had their lives not been snuffed out.

Pulling a sheet aside to reveal the corner of a white sofa, Maggie sat and stared at the picture. She studied the sloping hills in the background, deciding it must have been taken in the Highlands, but she had no memory of it. Setting the frame aside, Maggie began looking through the paperwork, most of which were household bills and files. Near the bottom of the box, she discovered a locked metal box and gave it a light shake. Whatever was inside was relatively lightweight and clattered against the sides of the box. She'd need a key or something to break the lock.

She was about to start on the next box when her mobile

rang and Mrs Brown informed her that DI MacLeod had arrived. With the metal box and the framed photograph tucked under her arm, Maggie turned out the lights and closed the storeroom door, making a mental note to get Fergus's key for the room.

* * *

Maggie picked up two USB drives containing the video footage she'd requested from the security office before heading to the second floor. MacLeod stood in the reception area with DS Claymore, Nichola, and a handful of forensic techs.

'We'll start in Alastaire's office,' Maggie said and led the way down the hall. Once she unlocked the door, she took a pair of nitrile gloves from MacLeod and put them on before entering the office and heading straight for Alastaire's desk. Alex's file still sat on top of the desk and she opened it for MacLeod.

MacLeod leaned over to study the single sheet of paper. 'Lords of Edinburgh? Jack Lord?'

'Aye. Fits, doesn't it?' Maggie set the metal box and frame on the desk and pulled the rest of the files from the bottom drawer, carefully sifting through them until she came to the one she hoped to find. She'd assumed the Lords of Edinburgh was a society started by Alastaire, but this sheet made it clear he wasn't the founder or the man in charge. 'You may want to call in your daughter, DS Claymore.' Maggie spread the open folder on the desk for everyone to see. A photograph of Jack Taggert sat above the text, 'Jack Lord – founding member and President of the Lords of Edinburgh, established 1992.'

While Claymore placed a call to DI Liz Claymore, Maggie sat at Alastaire's desk and moved the mouse to wake the computer. A screen with the Ghlais logo appeared, asking for a password. *Shite.* 'You'll need to take the computer into evidence,' she said to MacLeod. 'I don't know his password.' Somewhere, Alastaire would have records of the Lords of Edinburgh's activities and she figured it would be on his computer. 'You'll need to coordinate that with DI Lindsay Ross from the Economic Crimes Unit. She's the officer in charge of the embezzlement case against Alastaire.'

One of the forensic techs called out for DI MacLeod from the far side of the room. Maggie looked up just as the tech pulled a painting of Edinburgh's skyline as if it was a door on hinges, revealing a dark grey safe embedded in the wall. Maggie picked up the phone and hit the button marked 'reception'. When Mrs Brown answered, she asked, 'You don't happen to know the combination of Alastaire's safe, do you?'

'Sorry, dear. That was something Alastaire kept to himself.'

It was the answer Maggie expected, yet it left her feeling deflated. She crossed the room to join MacLeod and the tech, studying the numbered keypad and LCD display screen on the one foot wide by two foot high safe. 'Any suggestions?'

The tech leaned in closer to the keypad, noting the keys more worn than the others. 'It may take me a while, but I think I can crack it.'

* * *

DI Liz Claymore read the one-page document detailing Jack Lord's statistics with the Lords of Edinburgh. 'This isn't even enough to bring him in for questioning unless you have evidence tying the Lords of Edinburgh to the murders of Jamie Kenmore and the Ghlaises.'

MacLeod rubbed the scruff on his chin. 'Aye, that's what I suspected. I'll get Alastaire Ghlais's computer off to my mate in IT.'

Despite DI Claymore's declaration that the document wasn't enough, Maggie watched her take out her mobile and capture a quick picture of it before handing the file folder back.

'Got it,' the tech working on the safe called out from across the room.

Maggie looked up to see him swing the safe door open then stand aside, gesturing to the open safe with a wide grin. From where she was sitting, it looked empty. She slowly pushed to her feet, her eyes locked on the safe, but still, there appeared to be nothing inside. *Shite*. Perhaps she'd put too much faith in what they might find in that damn safe.

MacLeod made his way over to the safe and removed a single envelope bearing the old, elegant and fanciful Ghlais logo and *Magaidh* written in an elegant script on the front of the envelope. He turned to Maggie, standing behind her uncle's desk and held up the envelope. 'It's addressed to you.' He crossed the room and placed the envelope in Maggie's hand.

Maggie stared at the elegant script and knew it must be her mother's handwriting. Her eyes watered and she reached up to touch the corner of her eye, wondering what was happening. Maggie didn't cry. That would require emotions. She looked up into MacLeod's compassionate eyes.

'Why don't you find somewhere quiet to read it?' he said in a soft voice and nudged his head towards the door.

The envelope shook in Maggie's hand as the first fat tear slid lazily down her cheek. Maggie marched out of the office on stiff legs wishing she'd brought her own vehicle so she could sit in its comfort and privacy to read whatever was contained in the envelope.

As Maggie rounded the corner into the reception area, Mrs Brown stood, extending a sheet of A4 paper, proudly announcing, 'The list.' Then, catching Maggie's watery eyes, Mrs Brown lowered her hand. 'What's wrong, dear? Is there anything I can do?'

'I need somewhere private,' Maggie said, glancing around

the reception area.

'The conference room is empty. End of the hall across from Alex's office.' Mrs Brown motioned to the hallway in the opposite direction of Alastaire's office with the sheet of paper in her hand.

Maggie turned and quick-stepped down the hall until she found the conference room. Closing the door behind her, she leaned against it and took a deep breath. What the devil was wrong with her that the sight of an envelope could reduce her to tears? She grounded herself by studying the room, the huge mahogany table the focal point in an otherwise unremarkable room. There was a service area along the wall to her right, windows straight ahead looking out over the car park and the road, and a massive portrait painting of Alastaire taking up most of the wall to her left. One of Iona's comments came to mind. *Narcissistic bastard.*

Twelve high-backed leather chairs surrounded the majestic table – five on each side and one on each end. The chair on the end near Alastaire's portrait was even plusher than the others. Maggie pulled out the chair closest to her, placing the envelope on the table in front of her.

All she had to do was read its contents with the same disconnection as when she watched the videos and looked over the case files from her parents' murders. So why did a simple envelope with her name written on it strike her heart with a ferocity she'd never experienced? At least, not that she remembered. Was it her intuition telling her what was contained in this envelope was an emotional letter from her mother? Is that what had brought tears to her eyes?

Maggie stood, leaving the envelope where it was, and walked around the table to stare out the window at the green grass and denuded trees across the road. What was she so afraid of? And why did she feel so … vulnerable? She drew her mobile out of her pocket and rang the only person she could think of who she wouldn't feel embarrassed to speak to.

'Hello, darling,' Iona answered.

Tears welled in Maggie's eyes again and it was a moment before she could speak. 'I need you.' Maggie's breath hitched before she could get out the rest. 'Can you come to Ghlais?'

Iona heard the hitch and a sniffle and her heart sank. In all the years she'd known Maggie, she'd never known her to cry. 'I'm on my way.'

* * *

Maggie sat at the table with her back to the door and her head hung low as Iona entered the conference room. She closed the door behind her and pulled out the seat next to Maggie, eyeing the envelope sitting on the table. Iona put her arm around Maggie's shoulders. 'What's happening? The place is crawling with polis.'

Maggie closed her eyes and gave her head a bit of a shake. She'd been so focused on that envelope and what it evoked in her that Maggie nearly forgot everything else going on. 'It's a long story, but it seems dear Uncle Alastaire has been embezzling funds, among other things.'

Iona's mouth dropped open. 'That...that...' Iona couldn't think of a word vile enough to describe how she felt about Alastaire Ghlais.

'That's not why I asked you here,' Maggie said, her head dropping low between her hunched shoulders. 'I've been a selfish coward, refusing to remember what happened that night.'

'No.' Iona scooted forward in her chair and turned to face Maggie, gathering Maggie's hands into her own. 'Don't you dare blame yourself for that.'

Maggie raised her head enough to meet Iona's gaze. 'All these years, I've taken the easy way out, letting the memories remain buried in my brain. I've been an eejit, letting Uncle

Alastaire run the company with no checks in place.' She knocked a fist against the side of her head. 'I'm still a stupid coward because, goddess help me, I don't want to remember.'

'Then why are you trying so hard to stir your memories?'

'I've failed them. My mother and father deserve justice for what was done to them and I've failed them. However painful it is to remember, it's nothing compared to what they were subjected to.'

Or what you were subjected to, Iona thought. 'You've remembered more?' She asked with a pinched brow.

'Some. Not nearly enough.' Maggie wouldn't burden Iona with the few memories that had surfaced, even if she didn't need to keep them confidential for the investigation.

'Do you know why I've never encouraged you to remember, hen?' When Maggie shook her head, Iona continued. 'It's what kept you safe. Have a care, aye? If the people responsible for murdering Mairie and Malcolm and nearly killing you learn that your memories are surfacing, you could be in grave danger. They won't hesitate to finish what they started to protect themselves.'

Now it made sense why Iona accepted Alastaire's terms that Maggie didn't see a therapist. And why she always insisted that Maggie carry a protection spell, something Maggie continued to this day. She slipped her hand from Iona's and into her trouser pocket, fingering the small pouch containing herbs and a protection spell. 'I'm careful.' She met Iona's gaze again. 'And I ken who to watch out for.'

Iona gasped, her grip on Maggie's remaining hand tightening. 'You know who murdered Mairie and Malcolm?' She narrowed her eyes, emphasising the fine lines at their corners. 'I wouldn't be surprised if Alastaire Ghlais had his filthy hand in it.'

'It's an ongoing investigation. I can't comment. Besides, that's not why I asked you here.'

Iona placed her hand on the envelope and whispered, 'Mairie's handwriting. This is what's upset you.'

'I haven't even opened it yet. I don't understand why it's making me … feel.' Maggie looked up at Iona and pointed to the watery eyes that she thought she'd managed to get under control before Iona walked in. 'What's happening to me?'

'Darling, you're feeling the power of your mother's and father's love.'

'Why now? Why haven't I felt it before? And why does it hurt so damn much?'

'I don't have answers to the first two questions, but the third may be because the love your parents had for you is not entirely forgotten somewhere in your lost memories.'

Not forgotten, or Iona never letting her go a day without reminding her? Maggie wondered. She drew a deep breath and blew it out as she picked up the envelope, tapping it on the table. At least if she fell apart whilst reading it, Iona was there to pick up the pieces.

'Would you like me to read it to you?' Iona asked.

Maggie shook her head. 'No, but maybe you could read it with me.' Iona released Maggie's hand and Maggie opened the unsealed envelope, drawing out a single sheet of cream paper folded in thirds. Maggie unfolded the page with great care, then stared at the elegant script in confusion. 'It's written in Gaelic.' Three words spanned the middle of the page – *An Dhuibh Brighde*. Oddly, Maggie found she could translate the words – The Black Bride. But, what was the Black Bride? It sounded like the name of a pub.

'Can you not read it?' Iona asked. 'You were fluent in Gaelic when you were a wee bairn. Mairie made sure to pass the language on to you. I suppose I should have done more to ensure you didn't lose it.'

Perhaps that explained why she didn't have a problem translating those three words into English, but she didn't recall doing that before. 'Would Alastaire have been able to read it?'

'Not unless he had someone translate it for him.'

Maggie sank back in her chair, knowing that's precisely what Alastaire would have done.

'Why? What does it say?' Iona asked.

Maggie spoke the words in Gaelic and Iona nodded with a smile.

'The Black Bride. I haven't heard her name in years.'

'Her name?' Maggie asked as she flipped the paper over to ensure nothing was on the other side. It seemed strange that her mother would write those three words with no explanation. 'Who is she and how do I find her?'

'Well, you'll have to go up to the house in Ballachulish. Your caretaker there will be able to direct you to The Black Bride.'

Maggie continued to inspect the sheet of paper. 'Mrs Leòideach?' She stood and moved to the window, holding the paper to the natural light. The indentations from someone writing on a page on top of this sheet were evident in this light, but she couldn't quite make them out. The lab would be able to recover them. Or, she could try rubbing a pencil over it. Maggie turned to find Iona staring at her, head tilted. 'Who's The Black Bride? A witch?'

'Aye, a witch.'

'How'd she get the name?'

The corner of Iona's mouth quirked up. 'Her husband suffered a heart attack and died moments after their marriage was consummated.'

Maggie held up the sheet of paper. 'So, why would my mother leave her name on a piece of paper for me?'

'I couldn't say, but I do know that Mairie was close to Isla.'

'Isla?'

'Aye. The Black Bride's real name is Isla Caileanach.'

'So why didn't she just write that?'

'Because your uncle would have been able to find Isla by her given name. Only a witch would know her as The Black Bride and I can't see Alastaire contacting a witch to decipher the words on that page.'

Maggie folded the paper and carefully returned it to its envelope. She didn't quite agree with Iona. The words Mairie Ghlais wrote on that page held enough significance for Alastaire to keep it locked in a safe all these years. She was sure he'd take any measures necessary to decode it. And, she had no doubt he destroyed whatever had been written on the page above it.

Chapter 18

'I was beginning to think you weren't coming back,' MacLeod said from behind Alastaire's desk as Maggie returned, the envelope and Mrs Brown's list of employees loyal to Alastaire tucked safely into her inside blazer pocket.

Maggie took a moment to survey the room. Nichola stood next to an extensive bookcase, leafing through a book with gloved hands, while Claymore and MacLeod lounged in Alastaire's and Alex's usual spots, the forensics techs they'd brought with them nowhere to be seen. Colin Eaglesham and the auditors were missing as well. 'Did you find anything useful?'

'Couple of things.' MacLeod leaned back in the chair, making himself comfortable as if he owned it. 'I spoke with DI Ross. As she has actual warrants, she gets first dibs on the computers, but she said, as the owner of Ghlais, you could consent to Eaglesham's auditors providing us with a copy of the hard drives.'

'Of course,' Maggie said.

'That's what I figured, but Eaglesham won't pass them over until he has your consent.'

'I'll give him a ring. What else?'

MacLeod nodded towards Nichola who grasped onto the side of the bookcase, sliding it across the wall and revealing another safe. This one black, standing four feet high and two feet wide.

'We're waiting on a safecracker for this one. It requires a digital code and a fingerprint.' MacLeod pointed to the bureau next to the bookcase containing a fancy coffee machine and all the fixings. 'While we're waiting, could we get a cuppa?'

Maggie muttered, 'Help yourself,' as she approached the safe and studied it for a moment. 'Do me a favour, Nic. Put the bookcase back.' While Nichola did as bid, Maggie strode to Alastaire's desk and used the phone to summon Mrs Brown. When she arrived, Maggie asked, 'Where's Alastaire's safe?'

'Oh, I thought you'd found it.' She marched over to the far wall and pulled the painting open on its hinges, pointing to the first safe they'd discovered. 'Your mother had it put in.'

'Does he have any other safes on the property?' Maggie asked.

'No.' Mrs Brown shook her head. 'Not that I'm aware of.'

'Okay. Thank you,' Maggie said, dismissing Mrs Brown.

MacLeod shuffled back to the desk with his full attention focused on the four coffee mugs in his meaty hands and set them on the desktop. 'So, what does that tell us?'

'My uncle trusted Mrs Brown enough to handle his schedule and his meetings with his Lords of Edinburgh friends, but he didn't want her to know about the second safe in his office.' Maggie eased her hip onto the desk as MacLeod retook Alastaire's seat, sliding one of the mugs in front of him. 'Because there's something other than Ghlais business in there? How long before the safecracker arrives?'

'They said within the hour. That was about twenty minutes ago.'

'This is interesting,' Nichola said, walking towards the others as she continued to leaf through a book. She held it up for the others to read the cover – *Scottish Witch Hunts*. 'The bookmarked pages detail the various methods used to put convicted witches to death.' She placed the book on the desk, opened to the pages describing burning witches at the stake. The sections highlighted in yellow outweighed the areas with no highlighting.

* * *

There were only five names on Mrs Brown's list, four of whom Maggie had already terminated their employment – Alex and the three security guards. The fifth name was someone she didn't know, so instead of waiting around for the safe guy to show up, she went out to the reception area and asked Mrs Brown who the fifth name was.

'Richie Perstock?' Her big brown eyes did an impressive roll behind her specs. 'His official title is distillery aide, but we call him the town crier. He's Alastaire's eyes and ears in the distillery and warehouse. Writes everything he sees and hears in a wee notebook and reports to Alastaire every Friday at eleven o'clock.'

'And no one has killed him yet?'

The edge of Mrs Brown's mouth quirked up. 'They're too afraid of Alastaire.'

Now that was an interesting tidbit. 'Why?'

'They're afraid of losing their jobs and it doesn't take much for Alastaire to put them out of one.'

'Where would I find this Richie Perstock?'

'He could be lurking anywhere.' Mrs Brown glanced over her shoulder as if checking he wasn't hiding behind her. 'I'll page him for you.'

* * *

Richie Perstock looked just as Maggie pictured him – like a weasel. Tall and thin with a long, pointy nose and mousy brown hair. He couldn't have been more than eighteen. Maggie showed him into the conference room and shut the door. 'Take a seat.'

Richie slumped into the first chair he came to.

Maggie circled the table so she could face him, but remained standing. 'I assume you know who I am.'

'No, ma'am.'

She didn't believe that for a second. Word had spread throughout the distillery and this boy would have heard everything. Maggie reached her hand out across the table. 'Your notebook, please.'

Richie's mouth dropped open and he met Maggie's gaze for the first time. 'No. It's mine.'

'Let me explain something to you, Richie. You use that notebook to write down things occurring or said here at Ghlais, making the notebook Ghlais property.'

'Aye, I'm to give the notebooks to Mr Ghlais and Mr Ghlais only.'

'Except that Mr Ghlais no longer works here and I own the company, so you'll turn it over to me.' When he didn't respond, Maggie held out her hand again and said, 'Now.'

'I'm sorry, ma'am. I'm only to give it to Mr Ghlais.' Richie squirmed in his seat, a line of sweat beginning to spread over his upper lip.

Maggie pulled out a chair and sat across from the boy, resting her forearms casually on the table. 'Do you know where Mr Ghlais is right now, Richie?'

'No, ma'am.'

'He's in police custody. You don't want to end up there with him, do you?' It was an empty threat, but the kid didn't know that. To exaggerate it, Maggie laid her warrant card on the table.

Richie looked from the warrant card up to Maggie with wide, pleading eyes. 'He's really not coming back?'

'No, Alastaire Ghlais is done here.'

Richie leaned forward and withdrew a small, fat notebook

from his back pocket, then hesitantly handed it over the table to Maggie. Before he released it into her grasp, he asked, 'You're sure?'

'Aye, pal. I'm quite sure.' As soon as Maggie took possession of the notebook, Richie seemed to deflate into the chair.

'I don't have to do that anymore, do I? Write down what people are doing and saying?'

Until that moment, Maggie planned to terminate his employment. And, given how the other employees must feel about him, she couldn't imagine why he'd want to stay. 'No, I don't want you doing that again.'

'Thank you, ma'am.' Richie held his hands up in front of him as if he was praying. 'Thank you.'

'No bother.'

Maggie pushed her chair back, getting ready to leave when Richie asked, 'I suppose, since your the polis, you'll be wanting the books I didn't give to Mr Ghlais, ma'am?'

That stopped Maggie in her tracks. 'What books would those be?'

'The one's where I wrote the things Mr Ghlais did and said.'

* * *

Sylvan MacKenzie paced back and forth with her arms wrapped around her middle. This wasn't the first time she'd been locked in a cell. The last time, she'd been released once the police could find no proof of her involvement with the theft of funds from her business. This time, she wasn't sure she'd be so lucky. Surely, they couldn't believe she had anything to do with the embezzlement of funds at Ghlais, yet she had the stigma from what happened with her own business hanging over her head. It made her look guilty. Hours had passed since she'd been put in the cell and they'd yet to question her. All they had to do was look at the USB she provided them and they'd see she'd been collecting evidence since she first noticed a discrepancy in the Ghlais accounts. What could possibly be taking so long?

* * *

While Sylvan paced her cell, DCC Jack Taggert, dressed in his crisp uniform with silver buttons and the decorative rope on the peak of his cap and lapels shining brightly, arrived at the Penicuik Police Station demanding to speak to DI Ross. He removed his cap, tucked it under his arm, and glared down at the sergeant staffing the desk.

Ross was preparing to bring Sylvan MacKenzie into the interview room when DCC Taggert arrived at the desk she'd been loaned. She stood, straightened her back with her arms hanging stiffly at her side. 'Sir?'

'DI Ross.' Taggert gave a slight nod of his head. His path had never crossed Ross's before today, but her service record was exemplary. Shame he may have to mar it. 'You can drop the case you're working on and release Alastaire and Alex Ghlais immediately.'

Ross pressed her lips together to keep herself from releasing the string of expletives itching to escape. She allowed herself one deep breath before speaking. 'I'm sorry, sir. I can't do that.'

'Of course, you can. You can't have a shred of evidence to support these ridiculous accusations.'

'Oh, but we do, sir. All of the i's are dotted and the t's crossed.'

She had a good set of baws on her, this wee woman, Taggert thought. 'Fine. Send all the evidence to my office and release Alastaire and Alex Ghlais. I'll handle it from here.' With that, he turned on his heel and marched out of the room.

Ross allowed herself one more deep breath, then released all of the expletives sitting on her tongue. Taggert made a mistake though. He hadn't ordered her to release Sylvan MacKenzie.

* * *

The technician from Burg Wachter had the safe open and the digital code and fingerprint reprogrammed to Maggie's in a matter of minutes. Maggie scribbled her signature on the tech's job sheet and off he went, leaving them staring at the safe door.

It was a moment before Maggie realised they were waiting for her to do the honours. She pulled the safe door open, exposing three shelves. On the top shelf, two USB keys sat next to a wooden box similar in shape to the cigar box on Alastaire's desk. The middle shelf contained two stacks of notebooks matching the ones Richie gave Maggie. The rest of the middle and bottom shelves held a vast rainbow of coloured file folders.

Maggie donned a pair of purple nitrile gloves, picked up the USB keys and passed them to MacLeod as Nichola photographed the safe's interior and everything being removed from it.

'If you find anything on those relating to Ghlais's accounts, you'll pass it on to DI Ross?' Maggie asked.

'Aye,' MacLeod said as he sealed the USB keys in an evidence bag.

Next, Maggie removed the small wooden box and teased open the lid. It contained several plastic sealable bags containing various items of jewellery. Maggie scanned the pieces on top – a woman's wedding ring and engagement ring, a tennis bracelet she was pretty sure consisted of genuine diamonds, a pair of pearl earrings. Then she came to an item that sparked a memory – Jamie Kenmore's PA stating she always wore a wee gold locket. 'We'll need to get these to the lab for DNA testing.' Maggie turned to MacLeod, holding the box open in front of her. 'I'm pretty sure that locket belonged to Jamie Kenmore.' Was this a box of souvenirs from the women Alastaire and his band of misogynist friends murdered? There had to be a couple dozen trinkets in the box.

'Mhac na galla,' MacLeod said on a loud exhale. 'How many women have they murdered?'

'Is there someone you can trust to do the testing?' Maggie asked, ignoring his disturbing question. 'Or do we need to take them to a private lab?'

'We'll need the results run against our DNA database,' MacLeod replied and glanced over at Claymore. 'We've someone we trust who'll do it quietly.'

Maggie glanced between the two men, her eyes narrowed. 'What are you two up to then?'

Claymore raised his hands, palms out. 'Nothing sinister, lass. We've just been assembling a team loyal to the case. To the truth.'

Satisfied with Claymore's answer, Maggie turned back to the safe. 'The notebooks will be Richie Perstock's. He was Alastaire's eyes and ears in the distillery.' Maggie would go through them, but she wasn't much interested in the gossip and piddly wrongdoings of the staff. Ghlais was about to begin afresh, with a clean slate. 'The file folders we'll need to go through.'

'We'll each take a stack then,' MacLeod said.

'Aye. Why don't we make ourselves comfortable in the conference room?' Maggie pulled a stack of folders from the safe and passed them off to Claymore while Nichola continued to take photographs. Once all the folders were removed, she closed and secured the safe, then led everyone to the conference room.

* * *

DCC Taggert waited in his car outside the Penicuik Station. When Alastaire and Alex finally emerged, he gave his horn a short blast. Alastaire got in the passenger seat as Alex slid into the back. As soon as they were seated, Taggert pulled out onto the road. 'What the devil are you playing at, pal?'

Alastaire's temper was at the boiling point, but he couldn't lose it with Jack. 'Simply trumped-up accusations from my dim-witted niece.'

'Trumped-up?' Taggert yelled. 'The inspector investigating the case is confident she's got enough evidence.'

Alastaire's face turned purple, the veins in his neck straining and pulsing. How the hell would Maggie obtain evidence of his embezzling?

'They'll have seized your office computers for evidence,' Taggert continued. 'Is there anything incriminating on them? Anything concerning the Lords?'

'I'm not that stupid, Jack. Anything to do with the Lords is locked away in a safe.' Even if Maggie managed to find the safe, she couldn't access it without his thumbprint. The files in his bottom drawer on each of the Lords of Edinburgh didn't contain anything incriminating and he doubted dunderhead Maggie would find the key to the drawer anyway.

'A safe in your office?'

'Aye.'

'You better go there now and retrieve whatever's in that safe. Get everything to a safe place where the police can't access them.'

'Ah…' Alex said from the back seat. 'We can't go to Ghlais. Maggie's fired us.'

Taggert slammed his clenched fist down on the dash. 'Fuck sake, Alastaire.'

Alastaire could have murdered his son at that moment. Anything to do with Ghlais was none of Jack's business. 'We'll go in tonight and remove any sensitive materials.' And then some, he thought. Then he'd burn bloody Ghlais Whisky to the ground.

Chapter 19

As Maggie settled at the conference room table with a stack of file folders, her mobile rang.

'Glass.'

'It's DI Ross. I'm afraid I've some bad news.'

Ah, shite. Maggie's heart sank. 'What is it?'

'This is strange, but I've just had a visit from DCC Jack Taggert.'

Double shite. 'Let me guess. He's interfering with the investigation?'

'Oh, aye. And then some. Taggert shut me down and ordered all evidence sent to his office.'

Triple shite. 'Fuck sake.'

'My feelings exactly. I've had to release Alastaire and Alex, so I thought I better give you a heads up in case they turn up at Ghlais.'

'I appreciate it. Ms MacKenzie has been released as well then?'

There was a moment of silence before Ross responded. 'Well, see, that's where Taggert made a mistake. He didn't order her release, so I'm about to question her now.'

Maggie glanced at her watch. Sylvan had been in their custody for several hours already. 'Right. Could you do me a favour? Could you let me know when she's released? I need to speak with her regarding Ghlais.'

'Aye. Will do.'

Maggie ended the call and blew out a raspberry before updating MacLeod, Claymore, and Nichola. Then she rang Iain Blackwell and asked him to look out for Alastaire or Alex returning. Then Maggie started on the file folders and was distracted by Nichola pushing to her feet, arms waving frantically as she spread the file folders out on the table in front of her. Nichola picked out a file, opened it, then let out a low growl as she slammed the cover closed again and fished another folder out of the pile.

'The blue folders,' Nichola screeched as she opened another one, her eyes darkening. 'Fuck sake, the dark blue folders.'

Maggie pulled a dark blue folder from her pile and opened it. Printed on Lords of Edinburgh letterhead was a headshot of a woman. The name Mary Arbroath Graham was centred below the photo, followed by a short list:

Crime – Witchery

Verdict – Guilty

Sentence – Death by Drowning

Bingo, Maggie thought. She opened another dark blue folder. They were all women accused and found guilty of witchery. The sentences were all death by drowning or hanging. The only ones where the punishment was death by burning were Mairie Ghlais and Jamie Kenmore. There was no mention of Malcolm Ghlais. Had her father's murder been spur of the moment? An accident during the abduction?

As Maggie read further down the page, she thought again, *bingo*. Not only had Alastaire listed the crime and punishment, but a detailed account of how the sentences were carried out, by whom, and how they were paid. She looked up and met MacLeod's gaze across the table.

A slow smile spread across MacLeod's face. 'Lock the

feckin' door and throw away the key.' There was still a lot of work to do, but, by God, Alastair Ghlais and the Lords of Edinburgh couldn't escape justice now. 'We'll make copies and store them somewhere safe before I turn these files in as evidence.'

Maggie nodded. No sense in risking Taggert destroying the evidence. And she knew just the place to keep them safe. 'Alastaire will be anxious to get his hands on these,' she said.

'Aye. You think Alastaire will try to break in?' It's what MacLeod would do – come back in the middle of the night to secret them out while nobody's looking.

'If he does, he's going to get a wee surprise.' Maggie looked forward to the look on Alastaire's face when he realised he couldn't open the safe.

* * *

Dusk began its daily ritual, smothering the Pentland Hills in a shroud of grey clouds and darkness as Maggie stared out the conference room window. And still, Sylvan failed to return to Ghlais. The messages left for DI Ross went unanswered and Maggie grew agitated. She needed to speak to Sylvan before going home and try to get a few hours rest before returning to Ghlais. Not that rest was going to be easy. MacLeod, Claymore, and Dunn had commandeered her flat as their base while they sifted through the evidence and decided on next steps. They had enough to detain every member of the Lords of Edinburgh, but executing their detention was tricky. They couldn't allow DCC Taggert to quash their investigation.

Maggie turned on her heel and left the conference room. Staring out at the car park wasn't going to bring Sylvan back any sooner.

Mrs Brown had called the remaining security staff, telling them not to come in for their shifts today and making appointments for each of them to meet with Maggie individually. Maggie would make a decision about whether they would keep their jobs once she'd spoken to them one on one. In the meantime, Iain Blackwell's staff would protect Ghlais through the next 24 hours.

Maggie and Mrs Brown prepared four ads to post on job listing websites, but they couldn't post them until Maggie spoke to Sylvan. Now there was nothing left to do but wait. She made her way down to the security office, surprised to find Reid sitting at the CCTV monitors. 'What are you still doing here?'

'Ah, glad you're here,' Reid said as she pointed to the CCTV screens. 'Since you were interested in the delivery vans, I thought I'd take a closer look at them.'

Maggie cocked her head, not sure where Reid was going with this. 'And?'

'Well, there's a pattern, aye?' She pointed to the large monitor directly in front of her as she brought up an image of all five vans parked in the lot at the back of the loading dock. 'See these two?' She pointed to the two vans parked closest to the camera. 'They don't get used for deliveries. They don't seem to be used much at all.'

Maggie leaned in closer to the screen. 'Isn't that one of the vans used the night I asked you to look at?'

'Aye. There are other nights one or the other were used. Always by the same lads. Always late at night, returning by early morning.'

MacLeod hadn't taken the one van into evidence as yet. They had to be sure the evidence wouldn't be destroyed before they did so. Maggie made a decision based on Alastaire and Alex being released from custody. 'Could you get me a list of the dates and times those two vans were used?'

Reid smiled up at Maggie and handed her a USB key. 'Already done.'

Maggie grinned. 'You wouldn't be interested in the Chief of Security position here at Ghlais, would you?'

'Ah.' Reid winced, squirming in her seat. 'I'm sorry, no.'

'I get it. You've got bigger and better goals than babysitting a distillery.' It only made sense. Reid's skills would be wasted at Ghlais.

'Aye, something like that.'

'Well, if you ever need a recommendation, I'm happy to give you one.'

'Appreciated. Thank you.'

Maggie placed her hand on Reid's shoulder. 'No, thank you.' She waved the USB key and made her exit, walking to the back of the distillery where she picked up the keys for the two vans then drove them to the warehouse, locking them inside for safekeeping.

* * *

After receiving the call from DI Ross that Sylvan had been released, Maggie waited at the reception desk for her return. She turned as she heard footsteps on the stairs to find a woman who looked as though she was climbing the last few steps of a Monroe with a heavy rucksack on her back. Sylvan's slumped shoulders and lowered head had Maggie taking a step towards her before remembering where she was. Sylvan dragged herself up the last couple of steps and raised her head. She looked pale and drawn. 'Alright?' Maggie asked.

Sylvan smiled ever so slightly and nodded. 'Aye, just tired. But, I'll stay until I've made up the time I've missed today.'

'I don't think so.' How could she even think she needed to make up for the time she'd spent in police custody? Maggie wondered. 'I have something I need to discuss with you and then you'll go home.'

Sylvan didn't have the energy to argue. The heightened state of anxiety and stress over the long day completely drained her. 'Alright, fine.'

Maggie led her into Alastaire's office and motioned for Sylvan to sit in front of Alastaire's desk. Instead of taking Alastaire's chair, Maggie sat next to Sylvan, turning her chair to face her. 'I'd like to offer you the position of CEO.'

Sylvan just stared at Maggie for a moment before her words registered in her tired brain. Her mouth dropped open. 'What? I don't know the first thing about running a whisky business.'

'You said you have a business degree though, aye?'

'Well, yes, but–'

'And my mother left detailed instructions on how to run the business.' Maggie leaned over the desk and pushed the two contracts Colin Eaglesham had drawn up for her across the desk to face Sylvan. 'One is a contract for the position of CEO. The other is for the position of CFO. The choice is yours, but I'd be most grateful if you accepted the CEO position.'

Sylvan scanned both contracts, noting the salaries. Even if she accepted the CFO position, it was a significant increase. She was well aware that Alastaire Ghlais was paying her less than half of what he paid his previous CFO, but it was a foot in the door. He'd given her a job in her field when no one else would. The contract before her raised her current salary to one exceeding what Alastaire paid the previous CFO. The contract for CEO would give her a salary she'd never dreamed of. Numbers floated around in her brain as she calculated expenses. She could pay off her debts in less than a year. And then she'd be free from the shackles her ex-partner had locked her in. 'This is very generous.'

Maggie's hand covered Sylvan's on the desk before Sylvan had time to add a *but*. 'What you did for me, for Ghlais, is very much appreciated, Sylvan. The offer is not generous. It's well-earned and well-deserved.' Maggie scooted to the edge of her chair and waited until Sylvan met her gaze. 'Please. I need someone I trust running Ghlais.'

Sylvan's blue eyes widened. 'You trust me, knowing what happened with my business?'

'I trust you, knowing what your partner did to your business and knowing what you've done for mine. I'll meet with you once a month and you can update me on what's going on with the business, so long as you don't throw a bunch of figures at me.'

What Maggie was offering her was more than a job, a career. It was an opportunity to prove herself in the business and financial world after being doubted for so long. Sylvan picked up the CEO contract, read through every line, then placed it back on the desk. 'Got a pen?'

As soon as Sylvan signed the contract, Maggie withdrew her mobile from her pocket and opened the photos app, displaying the original Ghlais logo. 'As CEO, there are two things I'd like you to do for me.' She handed her phone to Sylvan. 'I know it will be a bother, but I'd like the Ghlais logo changed back to the one my mother had designed.' Labels would need to be redesigned, as would signage and advertisements and who knew what else.

Sylvan studied the image on the phone. The gold unicorn and lettering on the black background was whimsical yet elegant. 'It's beautiful. I don't understand why anyone would change the logo from this to the current design.' In stark contrast, the newer Ghlais logo was dull and drab. For the first time in days, weeks perhaps, Sylvan's nerves settled. This was something she could do and just looking at this logo gave her a sense of hope for the future – not just for herself, but for Ghlais Whisky. 'I'll take care of it. What's the second thing?'

'I don't remember what this office looked like when my mother occupied it, but I'm sure it didn't look like this.'

Maggie waved her hand out to her side. 'I'd like you to hire an interior decorator and have the office redone to your taste.'

Sylvan blinked, adding numbers up in her head. 'You want me to have the office completely redecorated?'

'Aye. It's your space now, Sylvan. Make it your own.'

Chapter 20

Sylvan pulled to the kerb in front of Maggie's building and Maggie reached over to take her hand. 'Thanks for driving me home. I know it's out of your way and you're exhausted.'

'It's no bother.' It was the least Sylvan could do. 'I'll see you in the morning?'

'I've got an appointment at ten, but I'll be in as soon as I can manage.' Maggie wanted nothing more than to blow off the appointment with the psychologist, but she had to see if Dr Brenna Argyle could trigger any more of her memories. As much as she didn't want to remember that awful night, she wouldn't forgive herself if she couldn't testify in court. Maggie needed to be part of bringing her parents' murderers to justice. She owed it to her mum and da not to hide from the truth any longer. 'I know there's a lot to be done at Ghlais, but I have to go up to Ballachulish on Friday for a few days. Would you come with me? It would do us both good to get away.'

'Ballachulish?'

'Aye. Glencoe. We have a house there.' Maggie would never get used to calling it her own. It had been her mother's and her mother's mother's before her for how many generations Maggie didn't know.

'But, there's so much to do.' Sylvan already had several

lists going in her head. She needed to start writing them down, organise them into doable steps.

'It's just for a couple of days. Ghlais can wait.' Sylvan looked like she was in a different world, staring out the windscreen, so Maggie squeezed the hand she continued to hold. 'You'll have your own room, if that's worrying you.'

Sylvan tilted her head back on the headrest with a long sigh. God, she was tired. She hadn't been away in years, hadn't been able to afford it. This was a golden opportunity to get away without it affecting her budget. 'Okay, let's do it.'

Maggie couldn't suppress her grin. She leaned over and touched the tip of her nose to Sylvan's. 'Thank you.'

Sylvan raised her hand to Maggie's face, her thumb caressing Maggie's cheek. 'It's me who should be thanking you. You turned a horrible day into a pure brilliant one. Thank you.'

* * *

Maggie opened the door to her flat expecting to be greeted by what sounded like a party, but it was quiet. She rounded the corner into the dining room to find MacLeod and Nichola slouched over the table scattered with papers. 'Alright?' she asked.

MacLeod scrubbed his hands over his face before looking up at Maggie with dark circles shadowing his eyes. 'Seems we've hit a wall.'

'How so?'

'The forensics reports and pathologist's report were ordered sent to DCC Taggert only. Same goes with the ViCLAS results. Even with contacts in each department, we're unable to get our hands on them.'

Maggie motioned towards the file folders stacked on one of the chairs. 'You have enough evidence to detain all of the Lords of Edinburgh for questioning.'

MacLeod and Nichola shared a look and he gave her a

nod. 'What happens if Taggert, or someone protecting him, kibosh it?'

'You think the Chief Constable is protecting Taggert?'

'That's the question,' MacLeod said. 'If we bring in all of those high-level professionals, we need to know it's going to stick, but who do we trust? If we go over Taggert's head and take what we have to the Chief Constable, what happens if he is crooked?'

'What about Anti-Corruption?'

'Same issue. We don't know who we can trust. Does Taggert have people in Anti-Corruption? In the Fiscal's Office?'

Maggie pulled out a dining room chair and sank into it. 'So, where do we go from here?'

MacLeod raised his hands in a shrug then let them fall to his lap. 'We keep investigating, keep putting the case together and hope we figure out a way to get around Taggert.'

'Have you talked to Liz Claymore?' Maggie just couldn't believe there wasn't some way to ensure Taggert paid for his crimes.

'All she will say is that Anti-Corruption is reluctant to get involved,' Nichola answered.

Maggie screwed up her face. 'What does that even mean?'

'Who knows,' MacLeod answered. 'Taggert could have something on one of the higher-ups in AC. He's had decades to build alliances and collect dirt.'

The more Maggie thought about it, the hotter her blood boiled. 'I'm not going to accept that Taggert and his band of murderers are untouchable. There has to be a way. They deserve justice. Not just my parents and Jamie Kenmore.' Maggie stabbed a finger at the navy blue file folders piled up on one of her dining room chairs. 'But every single person those bastards have murdered.'

'We're not giving up, Mags,' Nichola said. 'We just have to find the right avenue to take this down.'

'Well, find it, damn it.' Maggie surged to her feet, her chest so tight it felt as if someone was sitting on it. 'Find it.' She dashed down the hall to her room, slamming the door behind her, then opened the window, leaning out to suck in deep breaths. She hadn't meant to go off on Nichola. She was just so damn frustrated. Maggie leaned her forearms on the window sill and let the cool air soothe her. There had to be an answer, but she couldn't see it. MacLeod was right. They'd hit a damn wall. A bloody blast-proof one.

At the soft knock on her door, Maggie glanced over her shoulder, expecting to see Nichola, but it was MacLeod who stood in her doorway.

'Alright?'

'Aye. Sorry.'

'You've nothing to apologise for. We're all frustrated.' MacLeod had never felt more impotent in his life. The one victim he most wanted justice for stood across the room from him, leaning out the window. 'We'll figure something out, Glass.'

Maggie glanced over her shoulder again and gave MacLeod a short nod, although she wasn't sure she agreed.

'I'm away home, but if you need anything, give me a ring.'

Maggie straightened and turned to face MacLeod. 'I know I haven't shown it, but I appreciate everything you're doing.'

'Ah, well, it's no bother.'

Maggie knew better. Both MacLeod and Claymore were going above and beyond and Claymore was retired. He didn't have to do anything.

* * *

Maggie was back at Ghlais before 21:00. She'd known she wouldn't get any sleep after fifteen minutes in bed with her brain refusing to turn off. All the evidence against the Lords of Edinburgh whirled in her head while she tried to figure out a way over that damn wall. She'd given up on getting some rest, showered, changed into jeans and a jumper, and had some supper before heading back to Ghlais.

She met with Iain Blackwell, who brought her up to speed on the security details spread throughout the property. Blackwell would monitor the CCTV system with Reid and give Maggie a heads up should Alastaire and Alex turn up.

Maggie would wait in Alastaire's office, which Blackwell didn't like as it left her vulnerable, but Maggie was confident she could handle Alastaire and Alex. Besides, Blackwell and his team wouldn't be far and he'd set up night-vision cameras around the office, so he would see everything from the CCTV room.

Maggie went upstairs and sat at Mrs Brown's desk. It could be hours before Blackwell gave her the heads up that Alastaire was on the property, if he showed up at all. She took the envelope with her name written on it out of her coat pocket and removed the sheet of paper, then took a pencil from the holder on Mrs Brown's desk. Maggie placed the pencil on an angle against the page, rubbing it back and forth until the indents became visible words – *My darling daughter*. Maggie's heart rate increased and she rubbed the pencil faster and faster until she covered the entire page.

My darling daughter,

Happy eighteenth birthday. Your father and I are not there to celebrate with you, but be strong, my wee love. Although we're not there in person, we're here in spirit and will watch over you all your life. We love you with all of our hearts. When you're ready, contact our solicitor, Derek Eaglesham. He will be able to bring you up to speed on Ghlais Whisky, which you own in full. This business was our passion, our legacy. It is up to you whether you choose to follow in our footsteps and take the reins at Ghlais or not. I don't want you to feel pressured into something that is not in your heart.

In all of my visions, you're wearing a police uniform, but a mother can still hope. Just please remember that Ghlais Whisky is very special to us.

I trust your intuition as you have the gift, but please be wary of your Uncle Alastaire. I'm not at all convinced he has the business's interests at heart. He cares more about himself and his own personal gains than the business as a whole. Your father would scold me for saying so, but my gift hasn't steered me wrong yet. You will find the same, my dear Magaidh. Trust your intuition. Trust your heart. They will serve you well.

I've left a wee gift for you, hidden in your favourite toy.

Blessed be, my wee darling,

All my love,

Mummy

Maggie read the letter a second time, then a third. Then she pulled out her mobile and rang Iona. 'What was my favourite toy? Do you remember?'

'Of course. Rufus.'

Maggie's eyes lit up. She had a floppy-eared, stuffed dog named Rufus well into her teens. He sat on her bed and she cuddled him at night. Strange for a teenager, but she hadn't been able to let him go. Rufus was her security blanket until she went off to college. 'Do you still have him?'

'Oh, aye. I've kept everything.'

'I'll drop by in the morning.'

'Alright. I'll dig through the boxes tonight then.'

Maggie checked her watch. 'I can do that in the morning.'

'It's no bother, hen. There's nothing on the telly anyway.'

When Maggie ended the call, she tucked the letter back into the envelope and put it in her coat pocket. Had Alastaire kept the letter from her because her mother said not to trust him? It was the only explanation Maggie could come up with. Cruel. He could have blacked that part out and given it to her.

She went down the hall and let herself into Alastaire's office. No, not Alastaire's, she told herself. It was Sylvan's office now. She looked around the dark room, searching for a suitable spot to wait. He would go to the desk to retrieve the Lords of Edinburgh files and to the big safe. She crossed the room to the far corner and made herself comfortable on a black leather sofa.

Maggie took out her mobile and checked her emails to pass the time. Then she opened her Kindle app and started a new crime fiction novel by one of her favourite authors. It wasn't long before her eyelids fluttered closed and she drifted off to sleep.

Her mobile ringing on her chest had her jumping to her feet, her heart in her throat. 'Shite.' How long had she been out? 'DC Glass.'

'It's Blackwell. Alastaire and Alex walked into the car park, carrying petrol cans. We'll have eyes on them at all times, but have a care, aye?'

'Petrol cans? Are they planning on burning the place down?'

'Let me worry about the petrol cans. You worry about Alastaire and Alex.'

Maggie rubbed her sleepy eyes. 'Right. I'm going to leave the line open so you can hear.'

'I'll put my earphones in. If you need assistance, yell, 'Red'. I'll be right outside the door.'

'Aye. Hey, Blackwell?'

'Aye?'

'Thank you.'

'No bother, ma'am.'

Maggie sat on the floor between the side of the sofa and the wall and set her mobile on the floor, face down so it didn't light up. Then she checked her watch. Three forty-five. She'd slept for a good five hours. Sitting in the dark, she became hyper-focused on her hearing, listening for the door opening or footsteps on the carpet. The first noise she heard was a key sliding into the door lock. Maggie figured Alastaire had a second set of keys, but left the door open just in case. There was barely a creak as the door opened.

'I'll start at my desk. You get the envelope from the small safe,' Alastaire said.

There was a rustling from the direction of the desk, then the key sliding into the lock, turning, and the drawer sliding open. Maggie heard Alex tapping on the safe keys to her left.

'Fuck,' Alastaire yelled. 'The little witch got the Lords files.' The drawer slammed closed and a loud bang sounded on the desk.

The safe door creaked open. 'Ah, da? There's nothing in here.'

A loud bang rang out from the direction of the desk again. Maggie pulled her legs in tight as a torch beam crossed the floor in front of her.

'At least she couldn't have gotten in here,' Alastaire said.

The book case slid on its rollers and Maggie heard beeping as Alastaire pressed his thumb to the small digital screen. It beeped again. Then again.

'That fucking bitch. I'll have her head. I'll have her fucking head.'

Maggie slowly rose to her feet. Alex and Alastaire stood silhouetted with their torches aimed at the digital display on the second safe.

'Get the crowbar,' Alastaire ordered and Alex jogged back to the door. He bent over with his light shining on a black bag, pulling out a crowbar before dashing back to his father and passing it to him. Alastaire took the crowbar and tried to wedge it into the safe's door.

Maggie took several steps forward, her focus on Alastaire. Alex wasn't as much of a threat. 'Alastaire and Alex Ghlais.'

The pair swung around, their torches hitting Maggie in the face.

Blinded, Maggie kept her focus above the torch on the right. 'I'm arresting you on suspicion of breaking into a building and presence with intent to commit an offence.' She couldn't see the damn crowbar with the lights in her face.

'Like fucking hell you are, you wee witch. I'll send you to your whore of a mother.'

The light on the right advanced towards her and Maggie called out, 'Red.' Her only hope was to get in close. Maggie shot forward, smashed her right arm down on Alastaire's left, dislodging the torch, and grabbed for his right arm with her left. Alex's torch was now on Alastaire's back, lighting up the crowbar for Maggie. She spun and gripped onto it with her right hand as it swung towards her head, then yanked it to her as she stepped back, pulling Alastaire forwards. He stumbled and sprawled on the floor. Maggie grabbed his right wrist and pulled it behind his back while she pulled her handcuffs from the waist of her trousers. 'You are not obliged to say anything, but anything you do say will be noted and may be used in evidence. Do you understand?'

'You just signed your fucking death warrant. Do *you* understand?'

'I'll take that as a yes.' Maggie glanced over her shoulder at Alex to find Blackwell handcuffing him. He'd also managed to turn on the lights. 'You have the right to have a solicitor informed of your arrest and to have access to a solicitor.' Maggie helped Alastaire to his feet.

Alastaire snarled at Maggie. 'I won't need my solicitor. We'll be out before you finish your paperwork.'

He was probably right, but she bet he shat himself not getting into the big safe. 'Does Taggert know what you kept in that safe? What do you think he'll do when he realises what we have?' Maggie almost felt bad for him when

Alastaire's face drained of colour. 'Aye, it's sinking in, is it?'

'You're a dead woman.'

'Will that be by drowning, hanging, or burning at the stake?'

Maggie flinched when Alastaire spat in her face. She leaned into him and wiped it off on his fleece at his shoulder. 'We'll add inhuman or degrading treatment to the charges.'

Reid came in with two uniformed police officers in tow.

Maggie nodded at them. 'I'm DC Maggie Glass and the owner of Ghlais Whisky. These two men have broken into the building with intent to commit theft and this one tried to hit me with a crowbar and spat in my face. They also carried two petrol cans in with them. Their employment at Ghlais was terminated yesterday.'

Alastair sneered at Maggie. 'We'll be out by dawn and we're coming for you, witch.'

Maggie motioned to the two officers. 'Get them out of here, will you?'

Chapter 21

Alastaire was right. Maggie received a call from the Penicuik Police Station before the sun rose to inform her that Alastaire and Alex were released on the orders of DCC Jack Taggert. Still, there would be a record of the arrests and Taggert's orders. She had copies of the CCTV footage and the footage from the cameras Blackwell had set up in the office. Reid had even managed to record the audio from Maggie's mobile. Blackwell had left his mobile in the CCTV office with her and when Maggie called out, 'Red', Reid radioed Blackwell the signal.

Maggie arrived at Iona's to the aroma of sizzling sausage. She made her way to the kitchen, where Iona plated square sausage, scrambled eggs, fried tomatoes, and potato scones. A steaming pot of tea sat in the centre of the dining table on the far side of the kitchen. Iona laid the plates at the settings on the table, then embraced Maggie and kissed her cheek.

'Good morning, hen. I hope you're hungry.'

'Aye, famished. It smells brilliant.' Maggie removed her overcoat and took her usual seat at the table across from Iona. 'Did you find Rufus?'

'Aye. He's in the lounge. Why do you want Rufus after all this time?'

Maggie told Iona about the letter from her mother and its

contents.

Iona closed her eyes and took a deep breath. When she reopened them, her face was flushed, her lips pursed. 'He's a right bastard, isn't he? Keeping that from you all these years.'

Iona didn't know the half of it. 'Aye. Seems Mum was right about him.'

That brought a smile back to Iona's face. 'Mairie was rarely wrong.'

After breakfast, Maggie went into the lounge and picked up Rufus with his curly, sandy fur, long floppy ears, big brown eyes, and shiny black nose. She hugged him to her, her nose buried in his fur. It was like coming home.

Iona leaned her shoulder against the door jamb and crossed her ankles, tea towel dangling from her hand. 'Missed him, did you?'

Maggie turned, her nose still pressed to the wee dog, nodded, then held the dog up. 'I'm sorry, Rufus, but we're going to have to perform surgery.'

'There's no need for concern, Rufus. Dr Iona will stitch you up afterwards, good as new.'

Maggie flicked her eyes to Iona. 'You will?'

'Oh, aye. Let me get my medical bag.' Iona pushed off the door jamb and returned a few minutes later with her sewing kit. She sat on the sofa next to Maggie and placed Rufus in her lap. She squeezed the dog's middle, feeling for something inside. 'You're sure there's something in here?'

'The letter said she left me a gift in my favourite toy.'

'Has to be Rufus then.' Iona selected a seam ripper from her kit and carefully cut the stitches on the dog's side until she had a two-inch opening. She picked up the dog and placed it in Maggie's lap. 'I'll let you to the honours, Dr Mags.'

Maggie stuck two fingers inside the toy and rooted around in the stuffing. 'Sorry, Rufus.' Her fingers touched what felt like a foam cylinder. 'There's definitely something there. I'm going to have to turn it.'

'Pull out some of the stuffing if you need to. We can put it back in.'

Maggie was hesitant to pull poor Rufus's innards out, so she pulled the bottom of the cylinder and pushed at the top, frustrated when she wasn't making any progress. She apologised to the wee dog again and pulled out the stuffing in the way. When Maggie pulled on the bottom of the cylinder again, it swung towards the opening in the seam. She pulled out a five-inch long piece of foam wrapped around an object of some weight secured with tape.

Iona retrieved a pair of small scissors from her sewing kit and snipped the tape. Maggie unrolled the foam to reveal a five-inch long brass skeleton key. 'It's a key.'

'An old one,' Iona said.

'Aye, but what does it open?'

Iona smiled at Maggie. 'A door, I suspect. To determine what door, I think you will have to take the key to the Black Bride.'

* * *

Dr Brenna Argyle wasn't what Maggie expected. She wore a tight-fitting skirt that ended just above the knee and a billowy silk blouse with one too many buttons undone. Her long dark hair flowed like a dreamy waterfall to the underside of her breasts, which Maggie was definitely not ogling. Deep, green eyes peered at Maggie through black-framed glasses.

'DC Glass, please come in.' Dr Argyle waved toward two chairs set at right angles with a small circular table between them.

Maggie made her way to the chairs with Argyle's heels clicking on the floor behind her. She perched herself on the edge of the chair on the right and watched Argyle lower herself to the other chair, lean back, and cross her long, elegant legs. She smiled at Maggie. Maggie smiled back, tapping her hands against her thighs.

After a long moment of awkward silence, Dr Argyle said, 'So, why don't you tell me why you wanted to see me?'

Maggie shrugged. 'I didn't make the appointment.' She'd asked the receptionist who had, but the receptionist was under the impression that Maggie had called herself to schedule the appointment.

Argyle cocked her head. 'It's not a mandated appointment. Is someone concerned about your mental health?'

Obviously, Maggie thought. But who? It wasn't MacLeod. At least, he said he didn't make the appointment. 'Aye, perhaps.' Time to jump in and see what flew. 'My parents were murdered when I was wee. I have no memories of that night or the first eight years of my life up until that point.'

'You witnessed the murders?'

The vision of Maggie's mother burning, her face melting, surfaced. 'Apparently. What I'd like to know is can you restore my memories.'

Argyle leaned forward, her hands clasping her knees. 'Are you sure you want to remember?'

Maggie pursed her lips, turned her head to the left and closed her eyes. The image of her mother's face melting sharpened. Her eyes flew open and she turned them on Dr Argyle. 'I have to remember or my parents won't get the justice they deserve. Their murders will remain unsolved.'

'And you think remembering will reveal the killers?'

'I *know* who killed them. I need to be able to testify in court.'

Argyle leaned back in her chair and blew out a long breath. 'I can help you, DC Glass, but it will take time. I can't restore your memories with a snap of my fingers.'

'How long?'

Argyle raised her hands, palms up. 'It could be weeks, months, years. There are no guarantees when or if your memories will return.'

Not good enough, Maggie thought. She needed those guarantees. 'Right. Can I get back to you?'

Argyle uncrossed her legs and rose from the chair like a sexy phoenix. 'Aye, of course.'

Maggie followed Argyle to the door. 'Do I pay the receptionist?'

'There's no charge to you, DC Glass. It's all part of the service.'

'Aye, but I'd rather Police Scotland isn't billed.'

'My fees are £100 an hour, DC.'

Maggie snorted. 'You don't know who I am.' At Argyle's slight shrug, she said, 'Maggie Glass?'

Argyle shook her head.

'Magaidh Ghlais?'

Argyle's eyes bulged. 'As in Ghlais Whisky Magaidh Ghlais?'

'Aye, that one.'

'Well, like I said, my fees are £200 an hour.'

Maggie laughed. 'Of course, they are.'

'I'm joking,' Argyle said with a mischievous grin.

Who knew therapists had a sense of humour? Maggie couldn't help but like Dr Brenna Argyle. 'Listen, if I need someone to talk to when my memories come back, can I see you without it being reported to my employer?'

'Anything we talk about in this room is confidential, whether your visits are mandated by Police Scotland or not. Your visits would go no further than this office if you want to see me of your own accord. There would be no reason for me to report to anyone.'

'Good to know. Thanks.'

Maggie left Argyle's office and, since she was so close,

popped into the police station to check in with MacLeod. She found him at his desk, a massive sticky bun and a cup of coffee in front of him. 'Breakfast of champions.'

MacLeod looked up with a twinkle in his eyes. 'Jealous?'

'I had square sausage, eggs, fried tomatoes, and potato scones.'

MacLeod scowled. 'That wasnae very nice.'

'You asked for it.' Maggie gave him a cheeky grin.

'How was Dr Argyle?'

'Sizzling hot.'

'Oh?' MacLeod's scowl was replaced with a cheeky grin.

'Aye. Are you suddenly coming down with a case of excess stress and anxiety then?'

'It wouldn't be a stretch the now.'

Maggie pulled out the chair at her desk and sat. 'Any ideas on how to get around you know who?' She glanced around to be sure there weren't any ears close by.

MacLeod shook his head, scowling again. 'We've been ordered to back off the case.'

'By whom?' Maggie knew the answer, but had to ask.

'The DCI, who, by the way,' MacLeod hitched his thumb over his shoulder at the case of Ghlais Whisky sitting on top of a filing cabinet, 'had that dropped off for you yesterday.'

Maggie eyed the case and rose from her chair. 'Did the DCI say why?'

'Oh, aye. On the orders of DCC Taggert.'

That was the answer Maggie expected. She made her way to the filing cabinet and flipped open the box's flaps. There were twelve bottles inside, but three had a different coloured cap. 'Cheap bastard. He returned nine of the eighteen and three of the three-year-old.' She huffed out a laugh. Served her right for giving in to DCI McTavish's bribe. She lifted the case and set it on MacLeod's desk. 'Here. A wee bit of something to help with the stress and anxiety.'

MacLeod gaped at Maggie. 'I thought you said that was worth a couple thousand quid?'

'Well, not quite that much now that there are three bottles of the three-year-old in there.' Maggie shrugged. 'What am I going to do with it? I've got enough whisky.' She turned and headed for the door.

'Where are you off to?' MacLeod called after her.

'Ghlais. I've got a business to attend to.'

With a broad smile, MacLeod picked up the case of whisky and slid it underneath his desk. 'There now. That's the Christmas shopping done.' He chuckled and added, 'Hallelujah.'

* * *

Maggie stopped by the reception desk when she arrived at Ghlais. 'Good morning, Mrs Brown.'

'And a fine one it is.' Mrs Brown grinned, her red-framed glasses glinting in the overhead lights.

Maggie frowned and glanced over her shoulder out the window. 'It's baltic and blowin' a houlie out there.'

'Oh, aye, but it's grand in here.' Mrs Brown wiggled her eyebrows. 'I'd say there's been a ninety per cent increase in the morale around here overnight.'

Maggie laughed. 'Well then, let's see if we can keep that going. You know the party Uncle Alastaire had planned for Thursday night? I imagine it's too late to cancel the caterers and all that.'

'Aye, I suppose. I'll have to check with the event planner.'

'Do that. Make sure they can still put on the party, but let's make it a staff Christmas party and send an invitation for all the staff and a plus one.'

The twinkle in Mrs Brown's eyes brightened. 'That's still quite short of the number Alastaire had attending.'

'If there are leftovers, we'll offer them to the guests to take home. I'll probably invite two of my friends and their dates and we should probably invite the Eagleshams and the staff from Gold Star. And any other business contacts you think are appropriate.'

Mrs Brown scribbled on her notepad. 'We've not had a staff Christmas party since your parents passed.'

No wonder morale was so low. 'Well, it's about time then. Ms MacKenzie in her office?'

'Aye, away you go then.'

Maggie strolled towards the hallway with a spring in her step, then stopped and turned back to Mrs Brown. 'Oh, perhaps we should ask the staff to RSVP so we can have a guest list at the door. In case any of Alastaire's friends turn up.'

'Consider it done.' Mrs Brown rubbed her palms together with glee. 'Right then. Party planner first.'

Maggie cocked her head as she strode down the hallway. As far back as she could remember, she'd never walked down this hallway to open doors at the end. They'd always been closed. Sylvan sat at her desk, tapping away on a laptop with the phone tucked between her ear and shoulder.

'Aye, you and me both,' Sylvan said with a laugh. 'I'll see you at three then. Bye.' She hung up the phone and grinned up at Maggie. 'That was Sharon Dunbar from Gold Star. She and Ms Gray are coming in for a meeting about rebranding Ghlais. They're very excited.'

Maggie took a seat facing Sylvan's desk. 'You notice anything different around here?'

'Aye.' Sylvan raised her arms in the air and spun in a circle in the chair she'd retrieved from her old office. 'It's grand, isn't it? The atmosphere has completely changed. We've ordered Christmas decorations for the lobby and I've found an interior decorator. I'm meeting with her early next week.'

Maggie wished her chair swivelled because she felt like doing exactly what Sylvan had just done. Instead, she laughed. 'Grand indeed. Listen, I should have talked to you about this before I did it, but you know that party Alastaire had planned for Thursday evening?'

'Aye?'

'I'm changing it to a staff Christmas party.'

Sylvan grinned. 'The only negative I can see is that I didn't think of it first. We'll make it an annual tradition.'

'The other thing I was wondering about is staff Christmas bonuses. Ghlais is doing so well. Our employees should share in our success.'

Sylvan leaned back in her chair, studying the gorgeous woman before her. 'I have a feeling we're going to work very well together. I'll take care of it.'

'Brilliant. Any response to the ads for CFO and Marketing VP yet?'

'A few. Mrs Brown is collecting the CVs in a file for me. I'll review them once we've had the ads up for a week and then begin scheduling interviews.'

'Anything else I need to know?'

'That just about brings you up to speed.' Sylvan raised her eyebrows. 'Is there anything you need to tell me?'

Maggie winced. 'Are you talking about last night?'

'Aye, I'm talking about last night. Blackwell briefed me when I came in this morning.'

'Well, it's not good news, I'm afraid. They've been released and the charges quashed.'

'Why?' Sylvan asked. 'It's the same thing that happened with the fraud charges, isn't it?'

'They've got a deputy chief constable in their pocket. We're trying to figure a way around that.'

Sylvan sat forward. 'Do I need to be concerned for my safety?'

Maggie still couldn't think of any reason they would target Sylvan. 'I don't think so, but it's better to take precautions. I can have Blackwell put one of his officers on you.'

Sylvan's face paled. 'Maggie? Are *you* in danger?'

'It would seem so, if what Alastaire said last night carries any weight.'

'Perhaps we should go up to Glencoe earlier.'

'That would be nice, but we've got a Christmas party to attend on Thursday. I thought we'd close Ghlais down for the day on Friday and give the staff a paid day off after the party. We can head up to the Highlands first thing Friday morning.'

The desk phone rang and Sylvan picked it up. 'Yes, Mrs Brown?' She frowned, her eyes flicking up to Maggie's for a moment. 'Get her on the line for me, will you? Thanks.' Sylvan replaced the receiver in its cradle. 'Apparently, Alastaire has given the party planner a venue change.' She smiled wickedly. 'The problem with that is Ghlais is footing the bill for this party, so I'll set her straight.'

Maggie laughed. 'Something tells me you're going to enjoy that.'

* * *

Maggie spent a few hours meeting with the security staff and kept them all on, confident they had no loyalty to Alastaire Ghlais. She was so impressed with two of them in particular that she invited them to apply for the Security Manager position. It was posted on the job website, but she'd prioritise the two employees depending on their CVs and interviews.

Just before three o'clock, she joined Sylvan at the reception desk as the group from Gold Star arrived. Sharon Dunbar led the way and introduced herself to Sylvan.

'It's a pleasure to meet you.'

'Likewise,' Sylvan said.

'I'll be taking over as CEO of Gold Star along with my assistant.' Dunbar waved her hand at Sarah, Jamie Kenmore's PA.' Vice President Sarah Graham.' Dunbar placed her hand on Gray's lower back. 'And this is our Chief Operations Officer, Kelsey Gray.'

'It's a pleasure to meet all of you,' Sylvan said with a warm smile. 'We've a lot to discuss, so I'll take you through to the conference room.'

As Sylvan led the way, Maggie hung back, stepping beside Sarah. 'Congratulations on your promotion.'

Sarah lowered her head. 'Thank you. I wasn't expecting it. Honestly, I had no idea.'

Maggie laughed. 'No bother, Sarah. I don't suspect you of killing your boss to get a promotion. If they've given you the position, it's because you've earned it. I imagine you know Jamie's job as well as she did.'

'Thank you for that. I'd rather have Jamie back, believe me. She was a brilliant woman. We all loved and respected her.'

The Gold Star women sat on one side of the table with Maggie and Sylvan at the other. Sylvan used a remote to close the blinds on the floor to ceiling windows and turned on the projector. 'As you know, Alastaire and Alex Ghlais are no longer with us. Maggie and I would like to rebrand Ghlais Whisky, beginning with this.' Sylvan hit a button on the projector remote and the old Ghlais Whisky logo with the gold lettering and whimsical unicorn appeared on the screen.

Dunbar and Gray shared a look, both of them grinning. Then Dunbar clapped her hands. 'We've missed that logo. Mairie Ghlais designed it herself.' Dunbar's eyes welled up. 'If only Jamie were here to witness this.'

Maggie smiled at Dunbar across the table. 'Who says she's not?'

After the meeting, Maggie made her way down the stairs with her overcoat slung over her arm, intending to go home. When she got to the bottom of the steps, the aroma of yeast hit her nose and brought with it a sense of home, of belonging, of comfort. She had a memory flash of walking with her da, her hand in his, her hair in pigtails. They walked the length of the distillery, both Maggie and her da chatting to employees as they passed.

Maggie turned to her right and headed for the distillery. She'd just walk the length of the ground floor and back to see if it triggered any more memories. She swung the door open and walked down the centre past the stills. On either side of her, employees worked bottling, labelling, and packing stations. Maggie could almost feel the warmth of her da's hand in hers.

Someone shouted, 'Long reign the Queen. The Queen of Ghlais.'

Maggie stopped in her tracks as someone began applauding and it spread like wildfire. Maggie's blood heated. Not at the staff's reaction, but Alastaire's treatment of them bringing them to this the day after his dismissal. She didn't deserve the appreciation these people were showing her. She should have ensured they were well taken care of long before now. She waved her hands back in forth in front of her, trying to get them to stop. When the applause finally died down, she raised her voice so that most of the room could hear her. 'Please, I don't deserve that. I've owned this company since I was eight years old. The way you just reacted shows me I've been negligent in my duty to ensure a safe and enjoyable work environment.'

A bald man with a round face stepped forward. 'You cannae blame yourself. You were just a wee lassie who horrifically lost her ma and da.'

That may have excused her initially, but not since she became an adult. 'I used to come in here with my da.'

'Your memories are back then?'

Maggie shook her head. 'Just a few.'

'When did you remember coming here with your da?'

Maggie hiked a finger over her shoulder. 'Just now, when I

came down the stairs and smelled the yeast.'

'You were here with him at the end of every day, saying thank you for a good day's work, enquiring about our families, or just saying have a good night. Danny McLean used to sneak you sweeties when your da wasnae looking.'

Maggie laughed, remembering the man with the big red nose and white whiskers. 'Dolly mixtures. He looked like Santa.'

'Aye, that he did.'

'And you had wavy blond hair and a goatee.'

The man rubbed his hand over his bald head. 'Now there's a memory.'

'Mr Glendale. Laughlin Glendale.'

Glendale's blue eyes twinkled. 'Aye, that's me.'

'And your wife. You called her your bonnie Donna.'

'She's still my bonnie Donna.'

Maggie drew in a stuttering breath, desperate not to burst into tears in front of all of these people. 'Thank you, not just for the work you've done today, but the work you've done here over the past eighteen years. Please, bring your families to the Christmas party on Thursday, so I can meet them. I hope you can forgive me for taking so long to find my way back here. And I wish you all a good night.'

Maggie turned, walking to the door on stiff legs, her blurry eyes trained on the woman standing in the doorway, smiling.

When Maggie stepped through the doorway, Sylvan put an arm around her. 'I'll drive you home.'

'My car's here.'

'You can pick it up tomorrow. I'll give you a ride back in the morning.'

Maggie stopped at the front door, sniffing and hiccuping, and struggled into her coat. 'I just made a fool of myself.'

'No. You showed them that the owner of Ghlais cares about them as individuals. That boosts morale more than a

Christmas party or bonus ever could.' Sylvan wrapped Maggie in her arms and let her sob on her shoulder. 'No feelings, eh?' This was not a woman who didn't feel emotions. This was a woman who felt deeply.

'I don't know what's happening to me.' Every time she thought of walking down that aisle with her wee hand enveloped in her da's big hand, her heart clenched and the tears flowed faster.

'Are you getting your memory back?'

'Some.'

'Perhaps your emotions are returning as well.'

'I don't think I want them. It's so embarrassing.'

Sylvan ran her hand over Maggie's short locks. 'You've nothing to be embarrassed about. Let's get you home.' She opened the front door and led Maggie out.

'I just need to grab something from my car,' Maggie said as she veered to the visitor parking. She unlocked the Range Rover and picked Rufus up from the passenger seat, burying her nose in his fur. Maggie closed and locked the door and walked to Sylvan's car with Rufus clutched to her chest. When she was in the seat with her seatbelt on, she glanced over at Sylvan eyeing her with one brow raised. 'Don't say a word. He's comforting.'

'Are you sure you haven't reverted to your eight-year-old self?'

'Shut up.'

Sylvan laughed. 'See what I mean?'

Maggie pressed the dog to her face and mumbled, 'You have to be nice to Rufus. He had surgery this morning.'

Chapter 22

Sylvan escorted Maggie into her flat and helped her out of her coat. 'I'll run you a hot bath.' She glanced down the long hallway. 'If you show me where the bathroom is.'

'I can run the bath. I'll be fine.'

'Aye, you will be.' But at the moment, Maggie looked like she was asleep on her feet and miserable on top of it. Since Maggie didn't show her, Sylvan marched down the hall, glancing into the rooms. When she came to a bedroom with a king-sized bed and white duvet with green ivy designs, she entered. It was a bright room with huge windows, a settee centred between them. A television hung on the wall opposite the bed with a long dresser of dark wood beneath it. Sylvan walked to the open door next to the bed and found the en suite. It nearly took her breath away when she flicked on the lights with its earthy tones, lush greenery, and a gorgeous view from a large window above the copper clawfoot tub. The walk-in shower was a dream. The only place Sylvan had ever seen a bathroom like this was in magazines. What she wouldn't give for a soak in that tub?

Sylvan started the bath and found a bottle of lavender bath oil in a cupboard. The tub was nearly full when Maggie appeared in the doorway.

'You don't have to do this.'

Sylvan turned the taps off. 'You, my dear, are in desperate need of some TLC.' She smiled at Maggie and nodded her head to the tub. 'Enjoy your bath. I'm going to make you supper.'

Maggie snorted. 'I probably don't have anything worth cooking.'

Sylvan had grown accustomed to cooking with next to nothing over the past few years. 'Well, let's see what we can come up with.'

As much as Maggie liked Sylvan and enjoyed her company, she wanted nothing more than solitude tonight. But, she took the bath, dressed in flannel pyjama bottoms and a warm jumper, and ate the meal of lentil soup, cheese omelette, and frozen peas that Sylvan cooked for her. When Sylvan finally left her, Maggie climbed into bed, cuddling Rufus. At the expense of her dignity, she learned a valuable lesson today. Ghlais wasn't just a company. It was the people who worked there. Her parents left her Ghlais, entrusting their employees into Maggie's care. And she'd let them down. She pressed her nose into Rufus and hoped for the oblivion of sleep.

* * *

After a night of tossing and turning, Maggie rang Sylvan to tell her she was taking the day off to indulge in that TLC she was apparently in desperate need of. She started the day with a run on Arthur's Seat, bracing herself against the cold North Sea wind. Then she showered, dressed in jeans, a warm jumper, black puffer jacket and a wool beanie and went out to walk the streets of Edinburgh, which usually helped to clear her head.

She took Regent Road to Princes Street, admiring the giant Ferris wheel next to the Sir Walter Scott Monument and had a wander through the Christmas Market in the East Princes Street Gardens. Maggie hated Christmas shopping. She never knew what to buy people. Thankfully, her list wasn't long – Iona and Nichola. She should probably pick something up for MacLeod and she found herself wanting to purchase something for Sylvan.

Maggie left the Christmas Market and walked up to George Street, window shopping as she walked along. When she got to the ice rink at the west end of the street, she bought a hot chocolate and spent a good half hour laughing at the spastic movements and dramatic falls.

Maggie was surprised to hear voices as she entered her flat after her walk. She rounded the corner to the dining room to find Nichola and MacLeod. 'I thought you were ordered to back off the investigation.'

'Aye.' MacLeod stared up at her with tired eyes. 'We're not giving up, Glass. We were just debating whether to request an audience with the Chief Constable to feel him out.'

'What about the Fiscal?' Maggie asked.

'He's not bothered about the investigation being quashed, so we don't think we can trust him.' MacLeod flopped back in his chair. 'It's either the Chief Constable or we're buggered.'

There had to be another way. They just hadn't found it yet. 'I think the Chief Constable is a bad idea. Someone like Taggert doesn't get to where he is without someone having his back.'

'A lot of someones.' MacLeod sneered, then shook his head. 'How are things at Ghlais?'

'Very good, actually. And since we're on the subject, we're having a staff Christmas party tomorrow night at Ghlais if the two of you and your plus ones would like to attend.'

'Open bar?' MacLeod asked with a grin.

'Of course. And food.'

'Count me in.' MacLeod looked over at Nichola.

'I'm working tomorrow. Evening shift.'

'You can find someone to switch with you,' Maggie said.

'Are you joking? At this time of year, on short notice?' She stood and bent over to kiss Maggie on the cheek. 'I'm away to get ready for work the now. I'll ask around and see if I can find a numpty with no plans.'

'Alright. I'll put your name on the guest list just in case.'

'Ooh, hear that?' Nichola winked at MacLeod. 'We're on the guest list.'

MacLeod scowled at Nichola's back as she walked out, then turned narrowed eyes on Maggie. 'Do I have to dress up then? Fancy like?'

Maggie laughed. 'You can come in your pyjamas if you like. Just come and have a good time.'

'That's alright then. I suppose I better get back.' MacLeod began to gather the papers spread out over the table and Maggie covered his hand with hers.

'We'll figure out a way, aye?'

MacLeod turned his hand and gave Maggie's a squeeze. 'Aye, like I said, we'll not give up.'

Because her eyes began to burn, Maggie stood and crossed the living room to the window, staring blindly out at the view of Arthur's Seat.

MacLeod took a step into the living room and shifted from foot to foot. 'Alright?'

'Aye.' Maggie scrubbed a tear from her cheek with a clenched fist. 'They deserve justice. Not just my parents, but all of the women they murdered.'

'Aye, they do. Dinnae fash, lass. We'll find a way.' It was a promise he didn't know if he could keep, but he hated seeing Glass like this. The way she stood looking out that window with her arms wrapped tightly around her middle made him think of the wee lass he found in Lady Stair's Close, a whisper away from death. It made him even more determined to figure out how to get to Taggert and the rest.

* * *

Maggie waited on the pavement as Sylvan pulled up in front of her flat the following day. She got into the passenger seat and looked over at Sylvan as she clicked into her seatbelt. 'Morning.'

'Morning. Alright?'

'Aye, better. Everything alright at Ghlais?' Maggie didn't want to dwell on her state of mind at the moment.

Sylvan pulled away from the kerb. 'Aye, I spent most of yesterday going over your mother's notes. She was very meticulous and organised with a great vision of where she wanted the company to go, much of which hasn't been done.' She glanced over at Maggie with a smile. 'We've a lot of work to do to catch up with her plans, but she's left step by step instructions, not only for running Ghlais but achieving her dreams for it.' Sylvan's concerns about running a company she knew little about vanished on reading Mairie Ghlais's notes.

'I should probably read it.' Another thing Maggie should have long since done.

'I'll have Mrs Brown print you off a copy.' They drove along in silence before Sylvan said, 'You didn't bring your little dog today.'

Maggie rolled her eyes with a laugh and told Sylvan the story of how she came to have Rufus again.

'So, he really did have surgery the other day. What was inside him?'

'A key.'

'A key to what?'

Maggie' shrugged. 'I'm hoping to find out in Ballachulish.'

The event planner was waiting for them when they arrived at Ghlais. She introduced herself as Lynn Bell and asked to see them in the event space. Maggie and Sylvan followed her to a set of double doors next to the CCTV office. They stepped inside a massive room with a gorgeous floor of polished planked wood where dozens of people were busy setting up tables and decorating. Across the room, a wall of windows displayed a forest view. The rest of the walls were bare, painted off white. Maggie looked up, admiring the open ceiling with exposed beams and a massive iron chandelier hanging in the centre.

'Alastaire had precise instructions on how to set up the room. I just wanted to ask if you wanted any changes.' Bell held her clipboard out to Maggie and Sylvan with a map of the room showing the placement of tables, food, bar, and stage.

Maggie shrugged. She didn't care how it was set up. 'Looks fine to me.'

Sylvan studied the map. 'What's this?' she asked, pointing to a rectangle drawn in front of the stage.

'That's the head table. Twelve place settings.'

'I think we can do away with that. Otherwise, it looks fine.'

Bell was called away by one of the decorators and Maggie called Fergus over. He stopped helping set up a table and walked to Maggie and Sylvan.

'What's this room used for?' Maggie asked.

Fergus removed his cap before he spoke. 'Other than Alastaire's annual party in December, it sits empty, ma'am.'

'Seems a waste, aye?'

'Aye, ma'am.' Fergus smiled and returned to help with the tables.

Maggie studied the room once again, forming a picture in her mind. 'Ghlais is one of the few distilleries in Scotland that doesn't offer tours. There's enough space here for a tasting area, bar and restaurant or a wee café, and a gift shop where we could sell exclusive blends and Ghlais merchandise.'

Sylvan smiled, her blue eyes glittering. 'Maggie, that's exactly what your mother had planned for this space. It's on my list of things to discuss with Gold Star.'

'Huh.' A slow smile spread as Maggie wondered if her mother would be proud that they shared the same vision. How could she have gone so long with no interest in Ghlais? Just being here seemed to improve her mood. 'Do you need me for anything?'

'Not unless you want to stay available for the event planner's questions.'

'I'll give her my mobile number, then I'm going to head out to the warehouse and go through the boxes of stuff from my parents' house.' She would donate some things to charities, but she needed to go through everything to see what she wanted to keep. It was time to clear out that space and see how it could be better utilised.

Maggie walked over to Fergus this time and asked him to unlock the storage room door for her. He pulled out his keyring and removed a shiny brass key from it.

'I forgot to give you this. I had your own key cut, so you can go in there without having to chase me down.' He handed Maggie the key.

That gave Maggie an idea. She'd given Alastaire's keys to Sylvan and had kept the spare set they'd taken from him when he broke in the other night for herself. 'You don't happen to know what keys Alastaire had, do you? I've given his keys to Sylvan, but we don't know what key is for what.'

'Alastaire had master keys, so there will be one for all of the offices, one for the exterior doors, one for the distillery and warehouse doors. I'm not sure about the rest.'

'Brilliant. Thank you.'

'No bother, ma'am.'

* * *

Maggie had the car service pick up Iona first. She slipped into the back seat of the silver Jag limo dressed in a black tux with tails. Leaning over, she gave Iona's cheek a quick kiss.

'You look amazing.'

Iona flung her sage cashmere shawl over her shoulder. 'This old thing?' She wore a long, flowy dress bleeding shades of hunter green, which set her long red locks aflame. On her feet, she wore dark green Doc Martens.

Maggie laughed. 'You just bought it, didn't you?'

'Aye, it's Chrismassy.'

Maggie gave the driver Sylvan's address and they headed south. She frowned out the window when the driver pulled up in front of a derelict building and Sylvan emerged in a form-fitting dress of shimmering ice blue and matching high heels. The dress ended mid-thigh.

'She's gorgeous,' Iona said, breaking Maggie out of her spell.

'Aye. Beautiful." Maggie made sure her tongue wasn't hanging out, then got out of the car to let Sylvan in. When she got back in, she introduced Sylvan to Iona. Maggie was dying to ask Sylvan why she was living here, but didn't want to embarrass her in front of Iona.

When they got out of the car in front of Ghlais, Iona stared up at the building with watery eyes. 'It's strange being here without Mairie and Malcolm.'

Maggie slung her arm around Iona's shoulders and Sylvan said, 'I feel like I've gotten to know Mairie a wee bit over the past couple of days. She was an extraordinary woman.'

Maggie screwed her nose up at that. Sylvan was another one who probably knew Maggie's mother better than she did at the moment. 'Well, tonight, let's celebrate Mum and Da and all they've taught us and given us.'

'And what they created with Ghlais,' Sylvan added. 'And the future they wanted for their business.'

Maggie wrapped her other arm around Sylvan's shoulders and guided the two women into her parents' legacy, confident Ghlais was finally in the right hands.

* * *

After dinner, Sylvan stepped onto the stage and accepted a cordless microphone from the DJ before taking centre stage. She waited until the din of conversation died down. 'Good evening. I'm Sylvan MacKenzie, the new CEO of Ghlais Whisky.'

The crowd burst into applause and people began rising to their feet until the entire room stood, clapping their hands and cheering. With her face flushing, Sylvan waited for the room to calm. 'Thank you, but I haven't earned your applause yet. I will. We have big plans for Ghlais going forward. Plans originally set out by Mairie Ghlais herself.' Once again, she had to pause for the applause to die down. 'Ghlais wouldn't be what it is without all of you and tonight is about expressing our appreciation. I'm sure you've all noticed the change in atmosphere here in the past few days. We don't want that to change. I can't tell you how wonderful it is to come to work and be bathed in your excitement for the changes happening and for those to come. Mairie and Malcolm would be so proud of you all.'

'And you,' someone shouted.

Sylvan smiled. 'Thank you. I hope so. Anyway, I'm sure you've heard enough from me, so I'm passing the mic to the owner of Ghlais, Ms Maggie Glass.'

The room filled with applause again and Maggie shook her head at Sylvan. She hadn't expected this.

Iona placed her hand on Maggie's forearm. 'Go on, hen. You can't let them down the now.'

Shite. Maggie didn't know what to say to the staff and their families. She stepped onto the stage and took the mic from Sylvan, grateful when Sylvan stayed at her side. It seemed to take forever for the applause to die down, giving Maggie time to think of something to say. 'Let me start by addressing those of you who weren't on the ground floor of the distillery on Tuesday afternoon because I owe you an apology. I should have taken an interest in Ghlais long before now and for that, I am genuinely sorry. I have another job, but I'll be here when I can and I'm leaving you in the best hands with Sylvan MacKenzie. She sees my Mum's vision for Ghlais and plans to honour it.' She turned to Sylvan. 'For that, I am truly grateful.' Maggie lowered the mic and said, 'Thank you.' She laid her hand over her heart. 'I truly mean that. I'm so grateful you're here.'

'It's me who should be thanking you.' Maggie had no idea how much of a difference she was making in Sylvan's life.

Maggie gave a slight shake of her head and turned back to the crowd. 'Enjoy tonight and the paid day off tomorrow.' Hoots and hollers emerged from every corner of the room. 'And thank you for making Ghlais Whisky the best damn whisky Scotland has to offer. I can't wait to see what we can achieve together.' The room erupted in applause and shouts as everyone got to their feet again. Maggie shook her head, face flushed. 'Let's get this party started then.'

Maggie handed the mic back to the DJ as Adele's latest song burst from the speakers and Maggie took Sylvan's hand. 'Care for a dance?'

Chapter 23

Maggie woke with a start, her head pounding and her mouth fuzzy. She eased one eye open to check if the warm body she was spooning and cuddling was Sylvan. By the view of the back of her head, Maggie was pretty sure it was. She hoped they hadn't made love last night because Maggie wanted to remember their first time. She wanted it to be memorable.

'You awake,' Sylvan whispered.

'If you can call it that. Did we …?'

Sylvan's musical laugh embraced Maggie in its warmth. 'I poured you into bed and you were asleep before your head hit the pillow.' She hadn't meant to sleep in the same bed as Maggie. She'd just laid down for a moment to watch her sleep and had nodded off herself. 'Sometime in the middle of the night, you wrapped yourself around me.'

Maggie scooted even closer to Sylvan and stuck her nose in Sylvan's hair. 'I'm sorry. Did you want me to move?'

Sylvan laughed again. 'You're fine where you are.' Sylvan was content to stay right where she was all day. 'There's someone else in the bed with us.'

Maggie popped her head up and groaned. 'Who?'

Sylvan lifted Rufus over her shoulder. 'You want your wee pal?'

'No.'

'Hear that, Rufus? You've been dumped.'

'I'm not dumping him. I just don't want to let go of you.'

'How are you feeling?'

'Like I've been hit on the head with a hammer.' Maggie ran her tongue over her teeth. 'And my mouth tastes like an ashtray. Did I have a fag last night?'

'Several, I think. MacLeod is a bad influence on you.'

Maggie didn't remember that. She remembered meeting as many employees and their families as she could, dancing with Sylvan, and … 'Was Nic there?'

'Aye, she came after her shift.' Sylvan didn't tell Maggie about her conversation with Nichola Dunn. Nichola told Sylvan that she liked her and approved of her as a partner for Maggie, but Sylvan would have Nichola to deal with if she ever hurt Maggie. Maggie had been through enough pain in her life. Sylvan responded with a quip about them all having gone through difficult times. So Nichola told her about Maggie witnessing her parents' murders and all of the gory details until Sylvan fled to the ladies' where she lost the contents of her stomach. Sylvan stopped drinking at that point.

Sylvan turned to her other side, so she was facing Maggie. 'She's a good friend.'

'Aye, we've been friends since we were wee.' Sylvan had the face of an angel with her long, thin nose, sharp cheekbones and very kissable lips. Her eyes were the most striking blue Maggie had ever seen.

'You look like shite.'

Maggie laughed, then slapped a hand to her head, wincing. 'Why aren't you hungover?'

'Because I stopped drinking around midnight.' And everything she'd drank before then ended up in the toilet.

'Why didn't I do that?'

Sylvan snickered. 'Why don't I find you some ibuprofen?'

She rolled to the side of the bed and got up.

Maggie watched her emerge from under the duvet in a black lace bra and matching boy shorts. Sexy as hell. 'There should be some in the bathroom cabinet.'

Sylvan retrieved the bottle of ibuprofen from the bathroom and got a glass of water from the kitchen. She placed them on the nightstand next to Maggie while Maggie pulled herself into a sitting position, one hand plastered to her forehead. She took the pills and laid down again on her back with her arms and legs sprawled out.

'If I manage to keep those down, it will be a miracle.'

'Poor wee bairn. Do you mind if I borrow some clothes and take a shower?'

With her eyes still closed, Maggie pointed to the opposite side of the room. 'Socks and underwear are in the top left drawer. There should be a few pairs of brand new pants still in the package.' She moved her arm to the left. 'Closet is there. Help yourself.'

Sylvan went to the closet and opened the door, expecting an ordinary closet. What she got could have passed for another bedroom. It was massive. She walked in, turned the light on, and stood gaping at the clothes hanging all around her. Maggie had to have dozens of suits hanging on the left and the right-hand shelves were filled with designer trousers, shirts, and jumpers. The back wall was row upon row of shoes, including dozens of different styles and colours of oxfords, ankle boots, and lord knew how many trainers. One whole section was devoted to high tops. 'Holy shite.' What she wouldn't give for a couple of those suits. She went to the section holding jeans and pulled a pair of faded Levi's from a hanger. She nearly chose a comfy hoody, but couldn't resist a soft, grey cashmere sweater. She closed the closet door behind her after one last longing look, grabbed socks and underwear, then made her way into the bathroom. She was going to enjoy this. It was a long way from the cramped stall and trickle of water Sylvan was used to.

* * *

Maggie pulled into the car park at Sylvan's building, gawking at the line of cars with their windows and mirrors smashed, tires slashed, and rude graffiti. Sylvan directed her to the visitor's parking then said, 'You may want to wait in your car. Who knows what condition it will be in when we come back down.'

Maggie wasn't sure if she was concerned about the car or Maggie seeing her flat. 'Aye, no bother.'

'I'll be quick. My bag is packed. I just need to change my coat and shoes.'

When Sylvan got back down to the car park, she couldn't see Maggie in the car. She peered in the window to find Maggie reclined back in the seat, eyes closed and mouth agape. Sylvan went around to the driver's side and knocked on the window. Maggie's body jerked, then she thrust up to a sitting position and fumbled for the door locks. Sylvan opened the door. 'Out you get. You're going in the passenger seat.'

'I'm okay,' Maggie said as she rubbed her eyes.

'Oh, aye, you're brilliant. Out you get.' Sylvan had never been to Glencoe, but she knew they had a nearly three-hour drive ahead of them. She wanted to arrive alive.

Maggie did as she was told and, to make it easier on Sylvan, entered the North Ballachulish address on the SatNav. 'Why are you living here? Surely you can afford a flat in a better neighbourhood than this.'

'I don't have a flat here. I let a room.' Sylvan pulled out onto the road, chewing on her lower lip. 'I have some hefty debts.'

'You? The financial whiz?'

'I told you about my letting business.'

Maggie scowled at Sylvan. 'You're paying back the money your partner stole? Wouldn't your insurance cover that?'

'It didn't cover theft by one of the owners, no.'

'Geez. Is Ghlais going to lose all the money Alastair stole?'

'No, Ghlais's insurance policy covers a lot more than ours did. Besides, Alastaire didn't own any part of the business.'

Maggie didn't know how much Sylvan was stuck paying back, but surely there was a better plan. 'Could you not have claimed sequestration?'

'Aye, I could have, but I chose to pay back what we owed.' It was a matter of pride, what little of it Sylvan had left.

'I have a spare room you can let for free.' Maggie tilted her head towards Sylvan. 'Until you're back on your feet.' She would have offered to pay off Sylvan's debts, but didn't want to offend her.

It was the most tempting offer Sylvan had ever received and, for that very reason, she declined. 'I'll be fine. Less than a year now and I'll be free and clear of it.'

'How long have you been paying it off?'

'Three years or so.'

'You've lived in that building for the past three years?'

Sylvan chewed her lip again, deciding whether to answer or not. The woman sitting next to her had never known poverty. Would she understand? 'The past two years.'

'Where were you before that?' Maggie couldn't imagine anywhere worse than that neighbourhood.

Sylvan glanced over at Maggie with her face screwed up. 'In my car.'

Maggie's mouth dropped open. How the hell had Sylvan coped with going from a business owner to living in a car? She must have been absolutely devastated. 'I won't take no for an answer. When we get back from the Highlands, we'll stop by to pick up your stuff and move you into my spare room. It has its own en suite and sitting area, so you'll have all the privacy you want.'

'Maggie?' Sylvan huffed. She was having a difficult time coming up with an argument. She wondered if the en suite was anything like Maggie's. That would be too difficult to resist. Her shower that morning was divine. 'I can't impose on you.'

Maggie snorted. 'Impose on me? I'm rarely home with my job.'

Sylvan didn't answer yes or no. She'd see how the weekend went. After nearly three hours of driving, Sylvan gawked out the windscreen at the tremendous views of snowcapped mountain peaks on either side of the road. Maggie directed her to pull into a car park on the left. They got out of the car and met at a low stone wall in front of the vehicle. Before them, the land dipped down to a deep valley before rising up to a multitude of peaks.

'It's beautiful.'

'One of my favourite views on the planet.' Maggie stepped in behind Sylvan and circled her arms around Sylvan's waist. 'The Three Sisters of Glencoe.' She pointed to her left and drew her hand up a slope between two peaks. 'If you take that trail there along the ridge, you'll come to Coire Gabhail, the Lost Valley. It's where the MacDonalds hid their cattle. How they got them up there, I've no idea.'

'The same MacDonalds who were massacred by government forces?'

'Aye, on the thirteenth of February 1692, about thirty members of Clan Macdonald were killed, their houses burned. The survivors fled into the mountains during a winter storm.'

Sylvan leaned back into Maggie. 'You may not be very good with numbers, but you know your history.'

'History is a hell of a lot more interesting than numbers.' Scottish history, in particular, fascinated Maggie. It was full of captivating characters and enchanting stories, although some were gory and despairing, like the Glencoe Massacre. Maggie brushed her lips over Sylvan's slim neck and gloried in Sylvan's shudder.

'It's bloody baltic out here,' Sylvan said. She wasn't really feeling the cold, only the heat of Maggie's body and the touch of her lips. 'Let's get back in the car.'

Maggie went to the driver's side. 'I can take it from here while you enjoy the scenery.'

'Feeling better?'

'Marginally. We're only a few minutes away now.'

Maggie drove west through Ballachulish, then north across the Ballachulish Bridge. She turned right, driving down the single lane road for a few minutes before turning into a driveway on the right.

Sylvan gaped at the three-story stone house cradled in a glen in the embrace of a small forest of trees with a backdrop of snow-capped mountains. 'Wow.'

'It's been in my mum's family for generations, passed down from mother to daughter. I don't know how many times.'

'Mother to daughter?' That was odd, wasn't it? Didn't the men in the family inherit?

If she wanted a relationship with Sylvan, Maggie would have to come clean at some point. She just wasn't sure how Sylvan would take it. Better to get it out there now, before things got serious. 'I come from a long line of witches.'

Sylvan laughed until she realised Maggie wasn't laughing with her. 'You're serious? You're a witch?'

'Not a practising one at the moment.'

'I don't even know what that means.' Witches were a thing of fairy tales – mythical, like vampires and werewolves. Maggie couldn't be serious.

'It's a pagan religion. We worship the Goddess and Mother

Earth. It's a very nature-based practice. There are rituals and celebrations like Esbats, Sabbats, and the solstices.'

'My God. You are serious.'

Sylvan's disbelief was a wee bit endearing. 'You have witches in Aberdeen, so it can't be that much of a surprise.'

Of course, Sylvan had heard all sorts of witch stories, but she thought they were just that – stories. And those who claimed to be witches, she thought eccentric weirdos. 'So, do you put spells on people?'

Maggie laughed. 'I'm not going to put a love spell on you, if that's what's bothering you. Like I said, I'm not practising at the moment. I've no time for it with my job. But, I do have to meet with a witch while we're here or, at least, try to track her down. It's why I needed to come up. You remember that letter I told you about from my mother?'

'Aye.'

'There was one page that simply said *An Dhuibh Brighde*. It translates to *the Black Bride*. Iona told me she's a witch and that I'd find her here in Glencoe.'

Sylvan wondered what the hell she'd gotten herself into. 'Alright.'

Maggie reached over and took Sylvan's hand in hers. 'Are you sure? You look a bit like a deer in the headlights.'

'I suppose I am. I'm not sure what any of this means.'

'It's just me coming clean about who I am, what I am. If we're going to be together, you need to know.'

That, Sylvan respected. The honesty of it. 'Right, well, since we're putting our cards on the table, I'm not a witch or anything else. I'm just a numbers geek.'

Maggie laughed. 'I'll try not to hold that against you.' She tugged on Sylvan's hand. 'Come on. Let me show you the house.'

* * *

As soon as Maggie opened the front door for Sylvan, Mrs

Leòideach appeared at the bottom of the stairs. 'Welcome back, Maggie.' She walked to Sylvan and took one of her hands in both of hers, holding them for a moment. 'You must be Sylvan. Welcome to Gleann Sìthichean.'

'Thank you.' Sylvan glanced over at Maggie, hoping for a translation.

'It's the name of the house, Fairies Glen.' Maggie gave Mrs Leòideach a quick hug. 'Sylvan, this is Mrs Leòideach, keeper of Gleann Sìthichean.'

'Och, so dramatic.' Mrs Leòideach gave Maggie's arm a light slap. 'I'm the housekeeper, lass.'

'Isn't that what I said?' Maggie laughed.

'Aye, I suppose it is. I'll take your bag up to your room, Sylvan.' Mrs Leòideach took Sylvan's bag from her then turned to Maggie. 'Your guest is waiting for you in the lounge.'

'My guest?'

'Aye, Isla Cailennach,' Mrs Leòideach said as she started up the steps.

'Who's Isla Cailennach?' Sylvan asked.

Maggie watched Mrs Leòideach's retreating form, wondering how Isla Cailennach had known she was here to see her. 'The Black Bride.' She took Sylvan's hand and led her up to the first-floor lounge with floor-to-ceiling windows overlooking Loch Leven and the mountains beyond. The woman standing by the windows had long, curly, jet black hair. When she turned to face Maggie, her eyes flashed with the colour of an azure sea. Maggie estimated her to be in her late forties and one of the most beautiful women Maggie had laid eyes on.

'About time, lass,' Isla said with a smirk. 'I was expecting you over eight years ago.'

'I only just found the letter from my mother.'

Isla's smirk turned to a sneer. 'Let me guess. That bastard

Alastaire Ghlais?'

Maggie nodded as Isla crossed the room to them. She took Sylvan's hand in both of hers. 'I'm Isla.'

'Sylvan.'

'Aye, I know,' Isla said, still holding Sylvan's hand. 'You've been through a lot these past few years, but don't let it prevent you from accepting the gift you're being given. She's the right one for you.' She released Sylvan's hand and took Maggie's, smiling into Maggie's eyes. 'You're so like Mairie. So beautiful. You haven't lost them, Magaidh. They're with you every day. Did you not feel the warmth of your da's hand just a few days ago?'

Maggie flashed back to that sensation of warmth as she walked through the distillery. Was it possible her da was right there with her?

'You've never been abandoned, do you ken? There's no reason to worry that she'll leave you. She's the one.' She nodded her head towards Sylvan. 'And she's the reason that lump of ice in your chest is beginning to thaw.'

Maggie's eyes burned, her lip quivered. 'Why are you doing this?'

Isla flashed a wicked grin. 'I'm only telling you what you need to hear, aye? Now, let's get down to business. Did you bring the key?' She released Maggie's hand and held hers out, palm up.

Maggie drew the skeleton key out of her pocket and placed it in Isla's palm. 'What does it open?'

'Your legacy.' Isla walked to the stairs, started down, and then stopped and looked over her shoulder. 'Come on then. I've no' got all day.'

'Where are we going?' Maggie asked as she followed Isla.

Isla stopped on the stairs again and turned to Maggie. 'We're going to give you your memories back. It's long overdue, aye?'

'How can you give me my memories back?'

'By undoing Mairie's spell. It's why she sent you to me.'

Maggie's head reeled. 'My mum took my memories?'

'Aye. It was the only way she could save your life, Magaidh. If you had remembered what you saw that night, those murdering bastards would have come back to finish the job they botched.'

Since Isla seemed to know so much, Maggie couldn't resist asking, 'Will I ever get justice for them? Will their killers be sent to prison?'

Isla smiled. 'The answer to that, my dear Magaidh, is in here.' She tapped a finger on Maggie's forehead. 'So, let's get on with it, shall we?' Isla started down the stairs again, with Maggie and Sylvan following behind. She led them down the hall to the wine cellar and swung one of the shelves aside to reveal an old wooden door with black iron hinges.

'Where does it lead?' Maggie asked as Isla turned the key in the door.

'To your legacy, as I've already said.' Isla swung the door open and waved Maggie and Sylvan through. 'There may be a few cobwebs. No one's been in here since Mairie's last visit.'

Maggie took one step down the stone steps and stopped. 'I'm going to need a torch.'

'Oh, right.' Isla crossed to an electrical panel on the wall and threw up the switch.

There was an electrical buzz, then dull bulbs spaced at six-foot intervals along the curving stone wall flickered to life. Maggie still felt like she needed a torch, so she used the torch app on her mobile to light her way down the circular stairway, swiping cobwebs out of her way when necessary. When she reached the bottom, Maggie couldn't help but grin. This was Mairie's domain. The sanctuary where she practised her craft. Wooden shelves lined the walls on either side, holding books, supplies, and glass jars containing her herbs and oils. Dried flowers hung down from the ceiling on twine. A large wooden table sat on the stone floor in the centre of the room. Mairie's alter. On it lay a witch's most sacred items – mortar and pestle, wooden board with the pentagram carved into it, athame, silver chalice, black marble scrying bowl, and, Mairie's most treasured item, her wand, carved from the branches of a rowan tree.

A large, leather-bound book sat at one end of the table and white candles with dripping wax frozen in time dotted the surface.

A large stone hearth sat empty on the far wall with wood stacked at its side.

Isla passed Maggie and laid her hand on the leather-bound book. 'Your family grimoire.'

It would contain all of the spells passed down from generation to generation but, more importantly, it was a first-hand account of Maggie's family history. She didn't know much about her da's side of the family, but she learned bits and pieces of her mum's from Iona. The grimoire would give her so much more.

Isla placed some logs in the hearth then, with a flick of her hand, had a fire glowing brightly.

Maggie flinched inwardly at the leaping flames. She'd always hated fires, but now she knew why. She might have complained, but the room needed the heat.

'Right then.' Isla glided to the table and opened the grimoire, leafing through the last few pages. 'Let me just find the spell, then we can undo it.' She glanced up at Maggie. 'Don't fash, lass. The memories of your first eight years will return immediately, but the memories of that last night will come more slowly. Of course, you can choose not to remember that night at all.'

Maggie moved next to Isla. 'I need that night back. Sooner rather than later.' She peered down at the page of the grimoire written in her mother's hand. At the top, Mairie had written *Magaidh's Memories*. Below that was a detailed description of the spell. Halfway down the page was the title *Reversing the Spell* and another detailed description.

'I won't give them back to you all at once, Magaidh. It's too much. What you witnessed that night was very traumatic. But, we can choose the time frame.'

'By tomorrow morning?' Maggie asked.

'That's still awfully fast, lass. Are you sure?'

Something inside Maggie emphasised the urgency of getting those memories back. She couldn't explain it. She just knew it had to be now. 'Aye. I'm sure.'

'Right.' Isla slapped her hand down on the book. 'Let's get started.' She pointed to the verse written below the *Reversing the Spell* title. 'We need to change the wording a bit here, so you get the memories of that last night back by morning. Then you'll recite the spell four times, once to each direction, and bibbity bobbity boo, your memories will be returned to you.' Isla grinned at Sylvan, who stood staring at them with a pale face. 'There's a stool over there if you need it, lass.'

Sylvan was still trying to process how Isla lit the fire, never mind all of the bibbity bobbity boo stuff.

Maggie took one look at Sylvan and went to retrieve the stool herself. She placed it next to the table and took Sylvan's arm. 'Here, have a seat.' Once Sylvan was seated, Maggie whispered, 'You alright?'

'I have no idea.' This was not what she expected when she agreed to a weekend in the Highlands.

Chapter 24

Isla split the list of herbs to be collected from the shelf, giving Maggie the first half while she took the second. Then she told Maggie not to bother as she pulled a glass jar from the shelf and handed it to Maggie.

Maggie read the label written in Mairie's elegant script – *Magaidh's Memories, Reversal Spell.*

'That's even better as they were collected by Mairie's own hand. Now, we're going to need boiling water. Sylvan, would you go up and boil the kettle and bring it down?'

Maggie waited until Sylvan's footsteps faded and asked, 'Why did you have to say those things to us when we were standing right next to each other?'

Isla smiled. 'The secret to a great relationship is to have no secrets.'

'Fine, but Sylvan's a bit skittish about getting involved with me. I don't want to scare her off.'

Isla splayed her hand at the side of Maggie's neck and brushed her thumb over Maggie's cheek. 'She knows in her heart she can trust you not to betray her. The best way to assure her is to be yourself and not keep anything from her. Your honesty is what she needs most.' That said, Isla went back to the shelves and began opening the drawers of a small chest, selecting different coloured four-inch long thin candles.

She placed the candles, one at a time, in holders on the table circling the wooden board engraved with a pentagram. 'White for protection, understanding, clarity, truth, and peace. Yellow for mental clarity. Orange for clearing the mind. Red for courage.' Placing the last one in its holder, she said, 'And violet for awareness.'

Next, she went to a larger cabinet and opened drawers filled with all manner of gemstones. 'While I'm doing this, why don't you rinse out the chalice. I'm sure it must be dusty.'

Maggie took the silver chalice to a small sink, gave it a good rinsing, then a shake as she didn't have anything to dry it with. She placed the chalice back on the table and wiped her hands dry on her jeans. When Sylvan returned with the boiling kettle, Maggie emptied the contents of the glass jar into the chalice and filled it with boiling water to let it steep.

Isla began placing gemstones onto the wooden board. 'Fluorite to strengthen the conscious mind. Rose quartz for healing and balance. Ruby for mental clarity. Opal for improved memory. Diamond for bravery, strength, and clarity. Aquamarine for awareness. Calcite for inner healing.' She went to Sylvan and placed the last gemstone in her hand, closing Sylvan's fist and wrapping it with her hands. 'Tiger's eye for self-confidence. Carry it with you as it allows you the freedom to follow your own path.' She winked at Sylvan and returned to the shelves where she retrieved a yellowed pad of paper and a pen which she set down in front of Maggie. 'We're going to rewrite the spell with some minor changes. It's better if it's written by your hand.'

When everything was ready, Maggie waved her hand from the small white candle to the violet one, setting their wicks alight with dancing flames. Then Maggie stepped to the centre of the room and drew a pentagram in the air with Mairie's wand to open a door to the sacred circle. Entering the circle, Maggie closed the door in the same manner and faced west. She didn't need a compass to tell her the correct directions as they were etched into the stone floor. Nor did she need the paper she'd written the spell on as Isla had made it as simple as can be.

'Guardians of the west, hear my plea. Return my memories to me. By the rising of the morrow's sun, let this task be done.' She repeated the verse, addressing the guardians of the north, east, then south and finished with, 'As I will, so mote it be.'

Her childhood memories flooded her mind in a torrent of images, sounds, smells, and emotions. Tears spilled to her cheeks at the enormity of the love and happiness she was immersed in as a child. Her parents had surrounded her in love and laughter. Maggie had a good idea of the memories that would return after viewing the home videos. What she hadn't been prepared for was the overwhelming depth of emotions. With determined force, Maggie held herself together until she respectfully exited and closed the circle.

Isla wrapped Maggie in her embrace. 'It's alright to cry, Magaidh. What was stolen from you was immense.' She took Maggie's hand and placed the white calcite gemstone in her palm. 'Carry it with you until you're feeling stronger. When you're particularly down, place it on your third eye and sit with it for a while.' She wiped the tears from Maggie's face. 'Now, I think I've earned a wee dram of your Ghlais whisky.'

* * *

Maggie saw Isla out and made her way back up to the first floor, where she found Sylvan staring out the window in the lounge. Big, fat snowflakes drifted down and Maggie could barely see the loch, never mind the mountains behind it. She walked over and stood behind Sylvan, wrapping her arms around Sylvan's waist. Maggie loved holding her like this. Loved when Sylvan leaned back into her, trusting her.

'It's so beautiful,' Sylvan said. 'I don't know how you ever leave here.'

'It's a great place to visit, but it gets lonely after a while.' Although, she supposed, if she had Sylvan here with her, it wouldn't be lonely at all.

Sylvan peered over her shoulder at Maggie. 'Is it weird? Getting all of your childhood memories back?'

There were so many memories whisking in and out of Maggie's head, it was challenging to keep up. It wasn't just memories of her parents, but of school, pals, and her grandparents on her mum's side. Her da's parents passed before Maggie was born, so there were no memories of them. She remembered the day she got Rufus. She'd just had her tonsils out and her Gran and Granddad came to see her, with Rufus as a gift. It wasn't long after her Granddad passed then her Gran shortly after that. She wondered if that was why she always treasured the wee dog. 'A bit, aye.' She still didn't have any memories of the night her parents were murdered though.

'You know what would be nice? Cuddling by the fire to watch a movie.'

It sounded romantic, but the fire part made Maggie cringe. 'We've got a cinema downstairs.' And there was no fireplace in there. Bonus. 'I'll make the popcorn.'

'A cinema? In your house?' That was another thing Sylvan had only seen in magazines.

'With big comfy chairs. You'll love it.' Maggie pressed a kiss to Sylvan's neck then headed for the kitchen pantry.

The first floor was an open floor plan with the lounge, kitchen, and dining room. Across the hall was a music room where Maggie's father used to play the violin, piano, or guitar. A water closet and utility room with the washing machine and tumble dryer were at the end of the hall. Upstairs there were four bedrooms. Two with their own en suites and two with a shared bathroom. On the ground floor, the cinema shared space with the library, which had served as Mairie's office. Across the hall were a home gym and a shower room, next to the wine cellar.

Maggie remembered her mother's room in the basement now. She'd spent hours and hours in there, learning the craft with her mum. Maggie even had her own book of shadows down there, where she recorded her own spells before they were added to the family grimoire. She was looking forward to having a good look through the grimoire, but now wasn't the time. Sylvan still seemed a bit tentative about her being a witch. Besides, reading through the grimoire was something Maggie wanted to do privately.

When the popcorn was popping, Maggie called out to Sylvan. 'What would you like to drink?'

'What have you got?'

'Wine, beer, cider, tea, coffee, water, juice. And whisky, of course.'

'White wine would be lovely.'

Maggie retrieved a bottle of wine from the fridge and poured a glass for Sylvan. Maggie made a cup of tea for herself as she was still hungover. With the bowl of popcorn and the drinks on a tray, she said, 'Alright. Let's head down.'

Sylvan took the glass of wine from the tray so it didn't topple over and followed Maggie down the stairs. She opened the door to the right of the entrance and they stepped into a massive room with a gigantic white screen at one end with two rows of fat leather chairs facing it. To the right, bookshelves encircled a beautifully carved wooden desk.

'Make yourself comfortable.' Maggie set the tray down and picked up a remote to turn on the projector. 'What do you feel like watching?'

Sylvan shrugged. 'Something light.' She was worried about Maggie's memories of her parents' murders coming back, so she didn't want anything too heavy.

They settled in to watch a romantic comedy featuring two women with the usual trope of one of them not being out. At some point, someone would start making movies about gay people that weren't coming out stories. It was getting boring. Sitting side by side in the reclining chairs, they ate popcorn, sipped their drinks, and laughed at the comical antics of the two main characters. Near the end of the movie, the memory of Maggie's mum putting her to bed on that last night surfaced. Maggie tuned the film out and closed her eyes. She could see her mum's lovely face as if she was sitting right there, telling her one last story. Mairie's favoured fragrance of jasmine was a soothing balm. When Maggie realised what her mum's story was about, she bolted straight up in her chair. Mairie was warning her about the Lords of Edinburgh. She let the story play out in her head then whispered, 'The key to justice is through a woman named Allan.'

Sylvan laid her hand on Maggie's thigh. 'What is it?'

'A woman named Allan. I don't know any women named Allan.'

Sylvan shrugged. 'The only one I know of is Kaleigh Logan.'

Maggie turned to Sylvan with a frown. 'How is Kaleigh Logan named Allan?'

'She's married to James Allan.'

'James Allan?'

'Aye, the owner of ACN.' When Maggie stared at her with a look of confusion, Sylvan elaborated. 'Allan Communications Network? He owns the telly station that Kaleigh Logan reports for.'

Maggie could have cared less what he owned. The answer to getting past DCC Jack Taggert had been right in front of her this whole time. She patted her pockets for her mobile then remembered placing it on the kitchen counter when she was looking for the popcorn. 'I need to get my mobile.' She jumped up and ran up the stairs, grabbed her mobile, and rang MacLeod. When he answered, Maggie said, 'I know how to get around Taggert. I know how to expose him.'

'How?'

'We take the case to the media. Tell them everything.'

'Maggie, we cannae do that. We'll lose our jobs.'

'Let me rephrase that then. I'll take it to the media. I'll do an interview with Kaleigh Logan and give her everything. The whole damn story and the evidence we have so far. I don't want to lose my job, MacLeod, but at least I've got Ghlais to fall back on.'

'Be sure about this, Glass, because you will lose your job.'

Maggie wanted to be a detective since she was a wee lass. It was all she wanted to do, and still did, but she had to do this for her parents, regardless of the consequences. 'I'm sure. I have to do this, MacLeod.'

'Alright. What do you need from me?'

'I'll need copies of the files on the women they've killed. The ones we got from the safe. That will be enough evidence. I won't give them anything that's been collected in an official capacity to keep you and anyone else who's worked on the case safe. I'll make sure it's only my arse on the line.'

'You may need more than that.'

'I have more than that. I have my story. I have what I witnessed the night my mum and da were murdered.' At least she should have by morning.

Maggie's next call was to Kaleigh Logan. Logan answered with, 'I've been trying to track you down all week.'

'I was busy at Ghlais.' Why she felt she needed to give Logan an excuse, Maggie had no idea. 'I've got something for you.'

'Oh, what's that?'

'The interview of your life. I'm going to give you

everything I know. Proof of who killed my parents and more than forty other women over the past twenty years.'

'Jesus Christ. Where are you? I'm on my way.'

'I'm in Glencoe for the weekend. I'll have to drive back down in the morning.' Maggie winced when she caught the look on Sylvan's face. She hated disappointing her.

'No, wait. Where are you staying?'

'I have a house in North Ballachulish.'

'Perfect. I can be up there with a small film crew around noon tomorrow.'

Even better. Maggie could salvage some of her weekend with Sylvan. 'I'll need you to pick up a package from DI Will MacLeod before you come up.' Maggie gave Logan her address then rang MacLeod back to ask him to get the files to Logan in a sealed envelope. When she ended the call, she turned to Sylvan. 'I'm so sorry.'

'No bother.'

'Aye, it is. I promised you a weekend away. Logan is going to come up here with a camera crew. We'll have tomorrow morning and evening and all of Sunday.' She reached her hand out and waited for Sylvan to come to her. 'And the rest of today. The snow is piling up out there.' She tugged on Sylvan's hand and headed for the stairs. 'We're going out to play in it.'

'What? It's baltic out there.'

'No bother. I've extra gear in the drying room.' She glanced over her shoulder and eyed Sylvan up and down. 'And it seems my clothes fit you well enough.' Maggie pulled Sylvan all the way to the drying room then kitted them both out with ski trousers, jackets, boots, wool beanies, and mitts.

'This is mad,' Sylvan said as she pulled the trousers up. 'I haven't played in the snow since I was a wee lass in a school uniform.'

'That's what makes it fun.' Maggie finished dressing and

pulled a beanie over her ears. She took Sylvan out to an open space at the side of the house and scooped up some snow, forming it into a ball.

'Don't you dare.' Sylvan took several steps back from Maggie.

Maggie grinned at her. It was tempting, but throwing a snowball at Sylvan was not what she had in mind. She scooped up more snow, packing it onto her ball. 'We're building a snowman, you numpty.' Maggie continued adding snow to her ball until she deemed it ready to roll on the ground, building up snow as she went. When she glanced over at Sylvan, she stood in the same spot staring at Maggie. 'Come on, you. I'm not building it myself.'

Although she didn't know why, Sylvan bent over and scooped up some snow. What was the point of freezing yourself to build an inanimate person? She would have preferred a stroll through the forest. Once she got rolling the ball over the ground, she realised she was much warmer for the activity, but still couldn't understand the point. When her ball was nearly a foot and a half wide, she rolled it over to Maggie's.

When they had the entire snowman assembled, they gave it a pine cone nose and stone eyes, then Maggie rolled two smaller balls of snow.

'What are they for?' Sylvan asked.

Maggie picked up a ball in each hand and plastered them to the snowman's chest. Sylvan doubled over laughing and Maggie giggled like a schoolgirl as she packed more snow around the breasts to keep them in place. 'If you're going to build a snow person, why not a snow woman?'

'If that's the size of boobs you like, Maggie, I'm not the woman for you.'

Maggie laughed. 'You know what they say? More than a handful's a waste.'

'Or, in my case, more than a mouthful.'

Maggie grabbed a handful of snow and chucked it at Sylvan, hitting her in the chest.

'Oh, you devil.' Sylvan scooped up snow and placed the snow woman between herself and Maggie for protection. She packed her snow into a ball and took a few steps to the side before heaving it at Maggie. She'd been on the cricket team at school and had damn good aim. The snowball hit Maggie on the side of the head.

Maggie grabbed her head and fell to the ground, landing face up.

'Oh, God.' Sylvan ran to Maggie's side and dropped to her knees. 'Maggie. Oh, God. I'm so sorry.'

Maggie played unconscious for a moment, then grabbed Sylvan and pulled her down for a kiss, laughing as their lips met. Sylvan punched her shoulder, but Maggie kept kissing her and rolled in the snow until Sylvan was beneath her. The kiss deepened, intensified. Maggie raised her head slowly, her hazel eyes on Sylvan's blues.

Sylvan raised a snowy mitten and brushed Maggie's fringe from her eyes. 'I told you this wasn't going to happen until I'm good and ready.'

'Mmm. You're waiting until I've fallen in love with you.'

'Maggie, I–'

'You won't have to wait much longer. I fall for you more every day.' Maggie searched Sylvan's eyes as if she would find all the answers to the universe there. 'You're a rare woman, Sylvan MacKenzie.'

Sylvan raised her snow encased mittens to cup Maggie's face and thought, to hell with it. She pulled Maggie's lips to her own, her taste becoming familiar now. Intoxicating.

'Here, you two. Your supper's ready,' Mrs Leòideach called down from the balcony.

Maggie broke the kiss, grinned down at Sylvan, and they

burst out laughing.

* * *

Maggie was halfway through her bowl of stew and dumplings when another memory returned.

She awoke to her father shouting, 'Run Magaidh, run.' Magaidh knew he didn't really mean for her to run. She was to go straight to her hiding place and be quiet as a mouse until mummy or da came for her. If it wasn't mummy or da, they had to give her the secret password or she wasn't to make a sound. Magaidh got out of bed in her Winnie the Pooh pyjamas with Rufus clutched to her chest. Mummy and da were shouting and loud noises were coming from their room. Magaidh was only a few feet from the hidden door in the wall when she heard a horrible scream from mummy. She froze, unable to move, her eyes locked on the secret door. Run Magaidh, run, she told herself, but she couldn't move. What was happening to mummy? Who was shouting at da?

Someone grabbed Magaidh's arm and yanked. She dropped Rufus and tried to get him back, but the person pulled her out to the hall and down to mummy and da's room. A man dressed in black with a black hat over his face held da to the floor. Da's hands were tied with ropes and there was tape over his mouth.

'Da,' Magaidh screamed and tried to run to him, but the man holding her wouldn't let her go. Magaidh burst into tears, trying to pull her arm free and kick the man gripping her arms. It hurt. She wanted mummy. Where's mummy?

'You've gone quiet,' Sylvan said, eyeing Maggie across the table.

'Eh?' Maggie blinked several times and focused on Sylvan. 'Sorry, just thinking.'

Sylvan cocked her head. Maggie's rosy cheeks from being out in the cold had gone white. She was doing more than thinking. 'I know this is going to be a difficult night for you. I'm here, Maggie. You don't have to go through it alone.' She didn't know whether to come clean about knowing the details of that night or not.

Maggie attempted a smile. 'Thanks. It's appreciated.' She'd already seen the worst of it with her mother's face melting. It couldn't get worse than that. 'I'm not a very good host, am I? I'll make it up to you another weekend.'

'It's fine. You've nothing to make up.'

Maggie thought about all of the money Sylvan was paying back and asked, 'When was the last time you had a weekend away?'

Sylvan shrugged and took a sip of her wine. 'It's been a while.'

Her first weekend away in who knew how long and Maggie was ruining it. Whether Sylvan thought she had to make up for this weekend or not, once the Lords of Edinburgh were locked up, she'd treat her to a weekend at a nice hotel somewhere. She'd even get separate rooms, if that's what Sylvan wanted. 'I'm a real shite. I'm sorry.'

'Would you stop that. It's no' bother.'

Chapter 25

Sylvan went looking for Maggie early the next morning. She knocked on the bedroom door and got no answer, so she opened it. The bed looked slept in, but Maggie wasn't in it. Sylvan stepped into the room and heard the shower running, the en suite door on the other side of the room ajar. She went to the door and called Maggie's name. When she got no answer, she raised her voice. 'Maggie?'

Still no answer. Sylvan eased the door open to the sight of Maggie sitting on the floor of the glass-enclosed shower, her knees tucked into her chest and her arms around her lower legs. Her head was bowed and her shoulders heaved. 'Jesus. Maggie?' Sylvan reached into the shower and turned the water off, soaking the sleeve of her jumper. She pulled a warm, fluffy towel from the radiator and wrapped it around Maggie.

'I'm alright,' Maggie said as she tugged the towel tighter. 'I just … can't stop …crying.'

Sylvan helped Maggie to her feet and drew another towel from a shelf, then fluffed Maggie's hair dry.

'Really … I'm fine.' Maggie took the towel from Sylvan and finished the job, her shoulders still heaving.

Sylvan put her arm around Maggie's waist and guided her back to the bedroom, sitting her on the side of the bed.

'Where's the stone Isla gave you?'

Maggie pointed to the nightstand and Sylvan retrieved the small gemstone, placing it in Maggie's hand. 'You're supposed to hold it to your third eye, aren't you?'

Maggie did as she was told, placing the calcite on the centre of her forehead just above her eyebrows. She began to feel a tingling sensation, then a mild sense of euphoria, like being at home with her mum and da. Her shoulders relaxed, her breathing returned to normal, and the tears dried up. She lowered the stone and Sylvan dabbed her cheeks dry with a tissue.

Sitting on the bed next to Maggie, Sylvan wrapped an arm around her and Maggie rested her head on Sylvan's shoulder.

'You know what the saddest part of what happened that night is? Not only did my mum and da love each other so much, but they really enjoyed each other's company. They were always laughing, joking, teasing. And they always made me feel a part of it. We were a unit. A happy family. The Lords of Edinburgh ripped that away from us. My da worked as hard as my mum to build Ghlais into what it is, but he stayed in the background, my mum taking the glory and accolades while he cheered her on from the sidelines. He was the opposite of Alastaire.'

Sylvan rested her cheek against Maggie's wet hair and hugged her a little tighter. 'My parents barely tolerated each other. They didn't tolerate me.'

'How so?'

'They sent me to one of those conversion camps when I came out.'

Maggie raised her head and met Sylvan's gaze. 'I'm so sorry you had to go through that. It must have been awful.'

'I can't say as I enjoyed it. I left home as soon as I got out. I haven't seen my parents since.'

Maggie returned her head to Sylvan's shoulder. 'Do you

know what I want for us, Sylvan? I want what my parents had. I want to spend our days laughing and loving each other. I want to support you in achieving all your dreams. I want to be able to talk to you about everything, never holding back. I want to be the one you turn to whenever you need anything and give you everything you need without you ever having to ask.'

Sylvan closed her eyes and a tear escaped the corner of her eye. 'That sounds perfect.' The only problem with it was that perfection didn't exist.

Maggie sensed Sylvan's hesitancy. 'I'm sure we'll have the odd argument or disagreement and that's okay. That's what make-up sex is for.'

Sylvan laughed. 'That sounds even better.' They sat in silence for a bit before Sylvan realised Maggie had fallen asleep on her shoulder. She removed Maggie's towel, eased her head down to the pillow, and raised her legs onto the bed before covering her with the duvet. Then she pressed a kiss to Maggie's forehead and whispered, 'I'm falling for you more every day as well.'

Sylvan closed the door gently and the edges of Maggie's mouth curled up as she drifted back to sleep.

* * *

Maggie spent the entire afternoon with Kaleigh Logan. As Logan's two-man crew set up three cameras, lighting, and sound equipment, Maggie filled Logan in on firing Alastaire and Alex, their arrests on suspicion of embezzling, and DCC Jack Taggert ordering their release and quashing the investigation. Maggie opened the envelope MacLeod sent up and showed Logan the files on the members of the Lords of Edinburgh and the files of each of their victims.

'I knew the bastard was corrupt, but even I didn't expect it to be this bad.' Logan leafed through the victims, her brow furrowing more with each. 'I knew a lot of these women. Not all personally, but they were top of their fields. Dr Phillipa Sands was a top scientist in cancer research. Some of the drugs she developed are responsible for saving thousands of lives. I went to her funeral. None of us could believe she committed suicide, but no foul play was suspected. Jenny McCrae was a close friend expected to become the next First Minister. She's been missing over ten years.' Logan dropped the papers to her lap, her eyes watery. This whole thing had just become personal. She wanted to see Jack Taggert pay for his crimes more than ever, and that was saying a lot as she'd wanted him bad since she realised he was withholding evidence in the Ghlais murders.

'I'm so sorry.' Maggie didn't know what else to say.

'At least now there will be some closure for the families and verification that their loved ones didn't take their own lives or wander away, leaving them behind.' Logan sighed, then stacked all the papers and returned them to the manilla envelope. 'Let's get on with the interview then. I'll have a lot of research to do afterwards.' Logan planned on researching every single case before she aired Maggie's interview. Maggie was right when she said she was giving her the interview of her life.

Maggie often dressed to suit her moods. She chose charcoal trousers, a grey button-up shirt, and a charcoal cashmere jumper. Despite the newly fallen snow sparkling in the sunshine, it felt like dark clouds hovered over her.

Logan's crew had set two living room chairs in front of the fireplace. Logan and Maggie took their seats, waited for the sound and lighting tech to give them the thumbs-up, and Logan began the interview with a brief introduction. Then she left Maggie to tell her story, beginning with the embezzlement suspicions at Ghlais, the discovery of the Lords of Edinburgh files, and then the documentation of their victims. She spoke of crucial reports being held back from the investigators of Jamie Kenmore's case, likening it to the issues with the investigation of her parents' murders.

The last part of Maggie's story was a surprise. Logan didn't know Maggie's memories of that night had returned.

'A white van pulled up. A Ghlais van with the Ghlais logo on the side. Gold lettering on a black background with a unicorn inside the letter G. The side door opened and the other two men dressed in black with black balaclavas over their heads pulled out my mother, then my father. They both had what looked like black pillowcases over their heads and their hands were tied behind their backs. One of the men, short and stalky, pulled my mother towards the stack of wood on the Esplanade and the other, a tall thin man, walked behind them with my father.

'My father bent at the waist and charged headfirst into the man pulling my mother, hitting him in the middle of the back. He dropped to the floor. The tall man hit my da over the head with something and my da dropped. I screamed for him, fighting the man who was holding me, but I couldn't get free. The tall man chased my mother and tackled her to the floor. He tied her to the post sticking up from the middle of the pile. Then he grabbed my da under the arms and pulled him behind the woodpile where he tied him up behind my mum. The short man was still on the ground, yelling that he couldn't move his legs.'

That rang bells in Logan's head. Graham Lange, one of the men listed as a member of the Lords of Edinburgh and the owner of a chain of clothing shops, was a paraplegic.

'The tall man went back to the van and came out with a petrol can, pouring its contents over the woodpile. My mother yelled, "Jack Taggert, Tam Campbell, Graham Lange, you are cowards, so afraid of women you resort to murdering them. You may get away with this for many years to come, but, mark my words, justice will be served. And you *should* fear women, you bastards, as it will be two women who are responsible for your arrests. Two women who will see you locked in cells for the rest of your miserable lives." Then she laughed wickedly and said, "And, it will be a woman you must stand before in judgement for your crimes."'

Logan was sure the first two women in Mairie's prediction were herself and Maggie Glass.

'The tall man struck a match and tossed it onto the woodpile as if it were nothing. My mother said, "Magaidh, darling, close your eyes and sing your favourite song in your head. Can you do that for me, my wee darling?" I squeezed my eyes shut and sang, louder and louder trying to block out the roar of the flames. My mum never screamed or cried. I heard her say, "I love you, Mal. I'll see you on the other side." And then, "Magaidh, darling, we will be with you always. We love you so much."

Maggie gasped and slapped her hand over her mouth, her shoulders heaving and eyes streaming. Logan waited a few moments, then signalled to the cameraman to cut before handing Maggie a box of tissues. Even Logan couldn't hold back her tears at Maggie's words. Once Maggie had taken a couple of tissues, Logan took one for herself before returning the box to the coffee table. 'We'll take a break.'

Sylvan darted across the room and crouched in front of Maggie, her hands on Maggie's knees. 'It's alright. Let it out.'

Maggie leaned forward, wrapping her arms around Sylvan and struggled to get control of herself. 'Eighteen years, I didn't shed a tear. In the last few days, I've cried enough to fill Loch Ness.'

'Tears are healing, Maggie. You've eighteen years of healing to make up for.' And the wounds were more profound than Sylvan could have imagined.

Maggie thought she should be dehydrated by now.

Mrs Leòideach came in carrying a tray with a pot of tea

and several mugs as one of the techs went out for a cigarette. Maggie felt like joining him, despite not smoking since she was a teenager, except for the other night with MacLeod. She couldn't stomach the tea, but sipped from the glass of water Logan had set on the table before they began recording.

When the lights and cameras came back on, Maggie hoped it was almost over. She was completely drained.

'I was screaming the song in my head at that point and the man holding me shook me really hard and said, "Look at her, you wee witch. Look at her." He grabbed my jaw and squeezed hard, shaking my head until I opened my eyes and I saw … I saw …' Maggie shook her head, unable to continue as silent tears soaked her face. She swiped at them with the tissue in her hand.

Logan leaned forward. It was torture putting Maggie through this, but this part of the interview would cement the public's sympathy. 'What did you see, Maggie?'

'M-m-my mother's face. M-m-melting in the flames.' She broke down again, shoulders heaving, head bent low with her hands covering her face. Her mother hadn't screamed. It was Maggie's own screams that she'd heard when she first remembered seeing her mother burn.

This time, Logan let the cameras roll while Maggie struggled to regain her composure. She wanted viewers to see the pain the Lords of Edinburgh caused.

Maggie was still crying when she continued. 'The tall man pulled off his balaclava and I recognised him. Jack Taggert. He was a friend of my uncle's. He sneered at me and said, "Kill the bairn." The man holding me lifted me into the air then threw me to the floor. My head cracked against the ground.' Maggie raised her hand and slid her fingers into her hair, tracing the long scar on her scalp. 'That's the last thing I remember. I must have regained consciousness at some point and walked down to where they found me in Lady Stair's

Close, but I don't remember it. The next thing I remember after that, I was living with Iona, my godmother.'

Logan got her questions in then. She didn't have many as Maggie had laid out her story so well. She ended the interview with, 'Why are you coming forward with your story now?' Logan wasn't naive enough to believe this wouldn't negatively affect Maggie's career with Police Scotland. She was hoping this question would help.

'Jack Taggert interfered with the investigation into my parents' murders, Alastaire Ghlais's embezzlement, Jamie Kenmore's murder, and who knows how many others. If I don't make what I know public, he and the rest of the Lords of Edinburgh continue their killing spree with impunity. Forty-five people's lives were ended by these men to date and why? Because they're threatened by successful women? Intelligent women? Those forty-five victims and their families deserve justice. The Lords of Edinburgh deserve to be locked away for the rest of their pathetic lives. The only way to ensure that was for me to go public.'

'Thank you, DC Maggie Glass, for your integrity, your strength, your courage.'

Maggie didn't feel strong or courageous. She felt defeated. She felt like she'd just kissed her career goodbye. But, she would do it all over again because she knew in her heart, in her gut, she'd done the right thing.

Chapter 26

The rest of the evening was hazy. Maggie went through the motions at supper, pushing her food around the plate, then sat cuddled with Sylvan watching the telly in the lounge. She couldn't even remember what they watched. Nor could she be bothered to complain when Sylvan lit a fire in the hearth.

Maggie got into bed and lay in the dark staring up at the ceiling. She wasn't there long when the door opened and Sylvan came in wearing boxers and a t-shirt. She slipped under the duvet and cuddled in close to Maggie. Maggie turned onto her side, facing Sylvan in the moonlight. 'Hi.'

'I thought you could use a cuddle tonight.'

'You realise this is the second time we've slept in the same bed without making love.' When had she started referring to sex as making love? Maggie wondered.

'Perhaps next time, but tonight you need a cuddle.' Sylvan was ready to go there, but not tonight. What Maggie needed now was comfort.

Maggie couldn't complain. Her sex drive at the moment was hovering around zero. 'Thank you, for knowing what I need.'

Sylvan raised her head from the pillow and placed a chaste kiss on the tip of Maggie's nose. When she laid her head back down, she closed her eyes.

'Sylvan?' Maggie whispered.

'Aye?'

Maggie had never said these words to a woman in her life, other than her mother and Iona, but she couldn't deny she felt them down to her soul. 'I love you.'

With her eyes still closed, Sylvan smiled. 'Aye, I know.' Her smile grew wider. 'I love you, too.'

* * *

Determined to salvage some of Sylvan's weekend away, Maggie loaded Sylvan's bag into the Range Rover after breakfast. Dressed in their winter gear again, they got into the car and Maggie drove Sylvan to the Glencoe Mountain Resort. They took the chairlift up the northern slope of Meall a Bhuridh, then walked hand in hand up to Craeg Dhuibh to take in the spectacular views of Rannoch Moor and the surrounding hills covered in a blanket of snow.

'It's beautiful,' Sylvan whispered. 'Bloody baltic, but beautiful. I wish I had a camera.'

'Use your mobile.'

'It takes crap pictures.' She didn't want to admit how old her mobile was.

Maggie made a mental note to ensure Sylvan received a brand new iPhone on the Ghlais account. Then she took out her mobile and turned, facing away from the views, holding her mobile up in the air. 'Come on. Selfie time.'

Sylvan laughed and smiled up at Maggie's mobile, then leaned in close to admire the photo with the stunning views behind them. They looked ridiculous in their wool caps, but she loved it. 'Will you send me a copy?'

'Aye.' Maggie took a few photographs of the views, including a couple of Sylvan gazing out at the snowy vistas. Then she took Sylvan's hand. 'Come on. We're going sledging.'

'Sledging?' Another thing Sylvan hadn't done since

childhood. 'Are you joking?'

Maggie laughed and led Sylvan back down the trail, then to the right, where they each picked up a small round sledge with a pole sticking up in the middle. They took them to the top of the hill and sat side by side. 'Race you,' Maggie said with a laugh.

'Oh, a race, is it?' Sylvan used her hands to propel herself forward, laughing as Maggie called out behind her.

'Hey, you're cheating.' But Maggie bubbled with laughter as she pushed herself forward.

They flew down the hill, Sylvan in the lead, laughing their heads off. Maggie crashed at the bottom, lying in the snow on her back. She couldn't remember the last time she went sledging and lost count of the number of times they went up and down the sledging hill before they finally made their way back to the chair lift.

'That was brilliant,' Sylvan said. She hadn't felt so alive in a very long time. 'Thank you.'

'My pleasure. It was the least I could do after the rest of the weekend.' Maggie pointed off to their right. 'Look. Deer.'

'Oh.' Sylvan sat up straighter in her seat. 'Can you get pictures with your mobile?'

Maggie did as requested, taking a few of Sylvan while she was at it. Then she raised her mobile to take another selfie of them in the lift.

When they arrived back in Edinburgh, Maggie pulled up in front of Sylvan's building, turned the car off, and put on her hazard lights. 'We'll pack up your things and take them to mine.'

'Maggie,' Sylvan huffed.

'You don't have to share my bed. You'll have your own room.' Maggie couldn't stand for Sylvan to spend another night in this place. 'Please.'

Sylvan struggled to find an excuse and could only come up

with one. 'You don't think we're moving too fast?'

'We don't have to move fast. I told you I'd wait as long as you need. I meant it. Just because we'll be living in the same place doesn't mean we have to speed things up.'

The thought of spending one more night in her rented room when she could be at Maggie's was too much to resist. Sylvan gave in. 'Okay.'

They took the stairs to the fifth floor as the lift bore an out of order sign. Maggie covered her mouth and nose and they climbed the steps, the smell of stale urine assaulting her. Sylvan let them into the flat with her keys and introduced Maggie to her landlady, Mrs Roberts. The flat was icy cold and Maggie felt for the older woman. While Sylvan went to her room to pack, Maggie took out her wallet and withdrew all of the cash inside it. She handed it to Mrs Roberts and said, 'That should cover Sylvan's notice.'

Mrs Roberts spread out the notes and gaped. 'That's far too much, dear.' She handed most of it back to Maggie.

Maggie raised her hand, palm out. 'Keep it, please.' She hoped it would help pay for a bit more heat.

Sylvan came out of her room pulling one suitcase.

'That's it?' Maggie asked.

'Aye, that's it.' Sylvan crossed to Mrs Roberts and gave her a hug. 'Thank you, for everything. I'll get the rent I owe to you tomorrow.'

'You're friend took care of it, dear.' She patted Sylvan's shoulder. 'Take care, aye?'

Maggie carried Sylvan's case down the stairs and insisted on driving her round to her car in the car park. It was dark and who knew who was lurking in the shadows. She waited until Sylvan was safely in her vehicle and led the way home.

While Sylvan was unpacking, Maggie fetched her spare set of keys, wrote out the security codes on a piece of paper, and took them to Sylvan's room. 'Here. You'll need these.' She set the keys and codes on the dresser.

Maggie's guest room was kitted out nearly as wonderfully as Maggie's room and en suite. The only thing Sylvan lacked was the copper tub, but she had a jacuzzi tub, so she wasn't going to complain. 'This is gorgeous, Maggie.'

Maggie studied the few outfits hanging in the walk-in closet. 'We'll take you to my tailor this week and get you fitted for a few suits. The CEO of Ghlais should be well-dressed. In the meantime, you can borrow anything in my closet.'

Sylvan shook her head. 'No, you've done enough.' Although, she'd be happy to borrow some of the suits in Maggie's closet until she could afford her own.

Maggie shrugged. 'It's nothing, really. I've got more money than I'll ever need and it will make me happy spending some of it on you.'

Sylvan stared at Maggie. She couldn't even comprehend more money than she'd ever need. 'No. I don't mind borrowing some of your clothes, but you've done enough, Maggie. I mean it.'

'So, you're going to deny me a wee bit of happiness when I need it most.' Maggie faux pouted. She'd just get a gift certificate and give it to Sylvan for Christmas.

At eight o'clock, they got comfortable on the sofa with a cup of tea to watch Maggie's interview with Kaleigh Logan. It began with an image of Logan standing outside with the Three Sisters of Glencoe as a backdrop.

'I'm in Glencoe for an exclusive interview with one of Scotland's finest, Detective Constable Maggie Glass.'

They must have used a drone to shoot the footage as the view retreated from Logan and raised up in the air, giving them a spectacular view of the valley with the mountains behind it. Then the words, 'An ACN Special Report with Kaleigh Logan' appeared on the screen with Logan's trademark intro music, shifting to her regular intro reel before zooming in on Kaleigh Logan sitting at her desk in the newsroom. She gave a brief introduction then rolled the footage of Maggie's interview. After the interview, Logan appeared in the newsroom again. She displayed an image of each of the victims, giving a brief description of who they were and whether they were listed as suicides or missing persons. Then she showed the corresponding page from Alastaire's files on Lords of Edinburgh letterhead, showing the victim's photograph and the charge and verdict, which were always *Witchery* and *Guilty*. The sentence of hanging or drowning followed, except for Jamie Kenmore's burning at the stake. Then the description of who carried out the sentence and how.

Logan saved Mairie and Malcolm Ghlais for last. Mairie's photograph appeared on the screen behind Logan and she described her as the CEO and owner of Ghlais whisky, a woman of vision. Maggie wasn't sure if Logan referred to her mother's dreams for Ghlais or her psychic abilities. Then Mairie Ghlais's Lords of Edinburgh sheet came on screen. When Logan got to Malcolm Ghlais, she posted his photograph and said, 'Malcolm Ghlais, the only male murdered by the Lords of Edinburgh. Was he a mistake? There's no file on him or on the Ghlais's eight-year-old daughter, Magaidh Ghlais, who they brutally beat and left for dead. Magaidh Ghlais, for those of you who don't know, is Detective Constable Maggie Glass.' She let that hang in the air for a moment.

'Forty-five murders. Zero convictions. Clearly, it's time for change within the higher ranks of Police Scotland.'

Maggie blew out a long breath and turned off the telly. It was ten o'clock. The program ran for two hours. She could just imagine the shite hitting the fan at Police Scotland Headquarters. She'd had to turn off her phone not long after the start of the program as it wouldn't stop ringing. The first few calls had been people she knew, then unknown numbers began displaying on her screen. Maggie assumed they must be reporters. That's when she'd shut it down.

Sylvan squeezed Maggie's thigh. 'Alright?'

'I don't know.' She didn't know how she felt at that moment. She was just glad she wasn't crying. 'Tomorrow will tell.'

'How do you mean?'

'I'll probably lose my job tomorrow. I broke the rules, crossed the line.'

'But–' How on earth could she lose her job for doing the right thing? 'That's not right.' Sylvan leaned forward and wrapped an arm around Maggie's slumped shoulders.

Right or wrong, Maggie couldn't, and wouldn't, change it now.

* * *

Maggie came out of the en suite after her shower just as Sylvan emerged from her closet, dressed in a charcoal suit with royal blue pinstripes and a royal blue shirt. She leaned her shoulder against the door jamb. 'You know, I really like seeing you in my clothes.'

Sylvan glanced up and smiled. 'Good, because I really like wearing them.' She turned in a circle, modelling the suit. 'You haven't worn this one to Ghlais lately, have you?'

'No, I haven't worn that one at all.'

'Oh, I'm sorry. I'll find something else.'

'No, it's fine. I haven't worn it because blue's not my colour. You can have that one if you like.'

'How is blue not your colour?' With Maggie's dark hair, Sylvan imagined she would look great in blue.

Maggie pointed to her eyes. 'Hazel looks shite with blue.'

Sylvan crossed the room and kissed Maggie. She could tell by the way Maggie kissed her back she still wasn't herself. 'I bet you look hot no matter the colour.'

'Hmm. We'll see what you think when I'm actually wearing something blue. I can get away with navy, but not royal blue.'

Sylvan kissed her again and brushed her thumb over Maggie's cheek. Dark circles shadowed her eyes and she looked exhausted. 'What are you wearing today?'

'Black.'

'Just … black?'

'Aye, what else would I wear to my career's funeral?'

'Oh, Mags.' Sylvan hugged Maggie, rocking back and forth. 'Will you call me when you hear anything? Or come to Ghlais if you need me?'

'Aye.' Maggie pressed her nose in the crook of Sylvan's neck, breathing in warm lavender. She wanted to remember that scent, carry it with her throughout the day. Sylvan's embrace was always comforting and she may need to draw on that warmth, that wonderful scent, to get her through the morning.

She walked into the St. Leonard's Police Station an hour later, keeping her head high as she endured the stares of her fellow officers. She made her way to the Major Investigations Unit and removed her black overcoat, revealing her black suit, black shirt, black tie.

'Who died?' MacLeod asked from his desk.

'My career?'

'Shite, Glass.' He hoped to hell it didn't come to that. 'For whatever it's worth, I'm behind you.'

'Thanks, MacLeod.'

He pointed to the ceiling with his pen. 'They're waiting for you in McTavish's office.'

'Right.' Straight to it then. Maggie laid her overcoat over her chair and made her way up the stairs, dragging her feet. Sapphire Dovefeather looked up from her desk with a sad smile. 'You can go straight in, DC Glass.'

Maggie nodded and started for DCI McTavish's door. Dovefeather's voice sounded in her head. *Bravo, Maggie. Bravo.* Maggie closed her burning eyes for a moment to fight back her tears, then took a deep breath and opened the door. McTavish stood behind his desk, glaring at her, and the Chief Constable himself, Stephen Stewart, stood by the window with a woman at his side, both in their polished uniforms. Maggie walked to the centre of the room and stood at attention.

Stewart eyed her up and down before speaking. 'I'm here to inform you that DCC Jack Taggert has been taken into custody and we're in the process of rounding up the rest of the Lords of Edinburgh. All reports pertaining to the Kenmore investigation are being released to the investigating officers and Chief Superintendent Kathryn Drysdale,' he motioned to the woman at his side, 'is assembling a team to investigate the deaths and disappearances of the other women you've accused the Lords of Edinburgh of murdering.'

The fact he said she'd accused the Lords of Edinburgh said a lot. She didn't make the accusations. Alastaire Ghlais's own files did. CC Stewart and CS Drysdale walked out, closing Maggie in with McTavish. She faced him and waited as he glared at her, red-faced. He looked like he was about to spit on her.

'Effective immediately, you're on suspension pending a disciplinary hearing. You'll be notified where and when to attend the hearing. No one likes a rat, Glass. Now get your arse out of my office.' McTavish thrust his pointer finger at the door and shouted, 'Get out.'

Maggie turned and walked out the door, closing it none too gently behind her, and faced CS Drysdale standing at Dovefeather's desk. She came to attention again. 'Ma'am.'

Drysdale walked to Maggie. 'DC Glass, before I say what I want to say, it's important you know that later this afternoon, there will be an announcement that I'm being promoted to Deputy Chief Constable Major Crimes. I'm telling you that because I want you to know it's not the reason I'm saying this. I will do whatever I can to ensure you keep your job. I admire and respect what you did. You deserve to be celebrated, not punished.' With that, Inspector Drysdale turned and walked out.

Maggie stood where she was for a moment, not sure what to do, when she heard Dovefeather's voice in her head again. *Most of Police Scotland are applauding you, Maggie. Remember that over the next several days.*

Maggie wasn't sure how to take that. It implied the next few days were going to be shite. She nodded at Dovefeather and made her way back downstairs to retrieve her coat.

* * *

Across town, Kaleigh Logan picked up the newspaper on her desk with a scowl, disgusted at the headline. 'Seriously? This is Police Scotland's response? Label DC Glass as a whistleblower, a rat? They're making a serious fecking mistake.' She launched the newspaper into the bin. 'Serious fecking mistake.' Logan dropped to her chair, picking up the desk phone. Last night's report wasn't the end. It was just the beginning.

Chapter 27

Maggie walked to her desk with the control on her emotions dangling from a thin thread. She'd hoped MacLeod would be out for a fag, but he was at his desk and rose to his feet when he saw her coming.

'Well?'

'Suspended pending a disciplinary investigation.' She grabbed her coat and stuffed her arms into the sleeves. At least at the hearing, she'd have a chance, slim, but a chance, to fight for her job.

MacLeod's instincts were to bring Glass up to speed on the investigation, but he'd been ordered not to say a word to her. She'd broken this case wide open, put her career on the line, and he couldn't respect her more. 'If there's anything I can do … anything you need.'

Maggie just nodded and walked away. She just wanted to get to her car and go home. Maggie didn't want to see anyone, never mind talk to them. She endured the stares and marched out the station's front door only to be engulfed by video cameras and fuzz-covered microphones.

'DC Glass? How do you feel about being labelled a whistleblower?'

Whistleblower? She supposed she should have expected that one. 'I did what I had to do to get justice for forty-five victims. I'd do it again.'

'Have you been dismissed from your job?'

The thin thread unravelled. With a quivering lip, Maggie said, 'I've been suspended pending a disciplinary investigation.' With that, she charged forward, expecting to have to fight her way through the mob, but they parted, providing her with a clear path. She got in her car and headed home, the road blurry through her watery eyes. When she walked in her door, Iona came down the hall towards her, closely followed by Nichola.

'You weren't answering your mobile,' Iona said as she wrapped Maggie in her arms.

'Sorry, I had to turn it off.'

Iona held her tight and whispered, 'You're a hero, Mags. A bloody hero. I don't care what anyone says.'

Maggie closed her eyes and blew out a stuttered breath. 'That bad, is it?'

Nichola wrapped her arms around both Maggie and Iona. 'It's not what the majority are saying, Mags. It's just the misogynists getting their two pence in.'

It was time for Maggie to see for herself. She pushed out of the group hug, headed for the lounge, and picked up the telly remote, turning it on. The telly sprung to life, revealing Kaleigh Logan mid-report. 'Whistleblower? DC Glass is a hero. She's got more integrity and courage than any police officer I've ever met. How would you feel if the police were covering up the murders of your loved one? What would you do to ensure your loved one received the justice they deserved? I'll tell you what you'd do. Anything you damn well had to.' Logan glared into the camera. 'And as for Chief Constable Stephen Stewart, let me ask you this? How does a corrupt police officer who reports directly to you go undetected for so many years unless you're complicit? Or blind? Which one is it, Chief?' Instead of her usual smile,

Logan ended her report with a scowl. 'This is Kaleigh Logan reporting.'

Knowing Sylvan was probably keeping an eye on the news reports, Maggie borrowed Nichola's mobile to call her and let her know she was okay.

For the rest of the morning, the news seemed to play an endless loop between Maggie leaving the police station and Kaleigh Logan's rant. But, when the mid-day news came on at one o'clock, there were a few developments. Logan announced CC Stewart had resigned from his position. They ran a clip of him leaving police headquarters, but he refused to comment. She also reported every single one of the Lords of Edinburgh had been arrested and detained on suspicion of multiple murders and conspiracy.

Near the end of the news hour, Logan announced they'd just received a statement from Stephen Stewart stating he was not complicit with DCC Taggert, but as his direct superior, took responsibility for not detecting his corruption. Logan scoffed and tossed the sheet of paper she'd read from over her shoulder. 'Perhaps a disciplinary hearing is in order, former Chief Constable.' Logan sighed with a shake of her head.

'I'm really starting to love her,' Nichola said, making Maggie chuckle.

'I leave you with this live shot from outside the Scottish Parliament. This is Kaleigh Logan reporting.'

The screen switched to a view of the Scottish Parliament building at the foot of the Royal Mile, where crowds of people gathered. It took Maggie a minute to decipher their chant – *Reinstate DC Glass.*

By mid-afternoon, tensions rose all across Scotland to the point the First Minister made a live broadcast promising a full investigation into the conduct of DCC Jack Taggert. When asked if Maggie would be reinstated, the First Minister responded that she'd reinstate DC Glass immediately if it were up to her. But, she had no influence over the internal policies and disciplinary procedures of Police Scotland. Tensions continued to rise.

Maggie changed into her running clothes and pulled a beanie over her ears. She needed to get out in the open and breathe fresh air and she couldn't stand to see one more news report. Maggie headed for Arthur's Seat and ran, her legs burning, up and down the slopes, until she was ready to drop. Then Maggie climbed to the summit and sat on a rocky ledge overlooking her city as the sunset. The protests had spread to include every police station in Edinburgh and many more across Scotland. Somewhere down there, people were holding up signs and chanting. Some would be there just for the sake of protesting. A lot were outraged that so many murders were allowed to go unquestioned for far too long.

Maggie made her way back down to Holyrood Park and wandered to the Parliament building, pulling her hood up over her hat. She stood across the road, watching. A woman holding a sign near the back of the crowd turned her head, her eyes locking on Maggie. She started walking towards her and Maggie was about to turn and leave when she recognised the photograph on the woman's sign. It was one of the victims listed as a missing person. The Lords of Edinburgh had tied cement blocks to her before throwing her into a loch. Maggie stood her ground.

When the woman got to Maggie, she pointed to her sign. 'My mother.'

'I'm so sorry for your loss.'

'And I yours.' The woman glanced around them. 'Don't worry, I'm not going to give you away. I just wanted to say thank you.' Tears streamed down the woman's face. 'Thank you for sacrificing everything to get justice for my mum.'

Maggie's own tears started once again. She nodded at the woman and turned, walking into the night. When she arrived back at her flat, Sylvan was home, Nichola had gone off to work, and Iona was in the kitchen making supper.

Sylvan noted Maggie's slumped shoulders, her red-rimmed eyes, and said, 'What do you need?'

Maggie shook her head and shrugged. 'I don't know what to think, what to do. It's like the world's gone crazy.' She stepped into Sylvan's embrace and leaned her cheek on Sylvan's shoulder. 'I don't know if all these protests will help my case or hinder it. Whoever's investigating my conduct,' and she hoped to hell it wasn't McTavish, 'may take offence to the protests.'

Given that the police force was still a male-dominated institution, Sylvan wouldn't be surprised if it was a misogynist who was responsible for Maggie's discipline, but she couldn't see them terminating Maggie's employment without a public outcry. 'Well, maybe give it a few days for things to calm down.'

* * *

Maggie spent most of her days over the next couple of weeks wandering the city. She hadn't heard one word from MacLeod, which wasn't like him. Nichola claimed not to know anything about the Lords of Edinburgh cases. It was like she couldn't pry information from anyone. Even Kaleigh Logan's reports didn't contain much new information. All she did know was that the Lords of Edinburgh had all been charged and remanded in custody.

The longer she went without word about her disciplinary hearing, the more convinced she was that her job was lost.

Maggie looked up, realising she was on Alastaire's street in an affluent neighbourhood in Morningside. She walked to his house and stood looking up at it from the pavement. On a whim, Maggie decided to knock on the door and check on her

Aunt Eilean. The woman had lost her husband and her son, and she was very likely about to lose her lovely house since all of Alastaire's assets would have been seized or, at the very least, frozen. DI Ross had reopened the fraud investigation against Alastaire and Alex after Maggie's interview with Logan aired. Maggie thought the least she could do was pay the mortgage on Eilean's house.

Eilean answered the door wearing a pale pink dress with a half apron over it, heels, her hands adorned with a multitude of rings, and her hair and makeup done to perfection, even though she'd never held a job outside the home. She always reminded Maggie of a Stepford wife. 'Aunt Eilean.'

'You ungrateful bitch. How dare you come here? We took you into our home after your parents were murdered. We were prepared to raise you as our own. Alastaire ran that business for you for years. And for what? This is how you repay us?' She hauled her right hand back and slapped Maggie across the face.

Maggie's left hand flew to her stinging cheek. She stared at Eilean for a moment taking in the hatred in her blue eyes, then turned and walked away, still holding her cheek. Damn, who knew Eilean could hit so hard? When she pulled her hand away, it was red with blood. One of those rings must have caught her cheek. Eilean could lose her damn house for all Maggie cared at that moment.

Maggie walked to Morningside Road and headed north until she found a chemist's. She went in and found the first aid section. A few tissues and a plaster should do the trick. When she had what she needed, she started for the cashier and was stopped by a shop employee. 'You're bleeding.'

Maggie held up the package of plasters and tissues. 'It's fine.'

'We've a nurse in the pharmacy giving flu jabs. She'll take a look at that for you.'

'It's fine,' Maggie said again and started around the woman.

'DC Glass, please. Let us help you.'

Maggie turned back to the woman who looked at her with pleading eyes.

'Please. It's fair bleeding, aye?'

Maggie glanced around the shop, noting several eyes on her now. She nodded and the woman took Maggie by the arm, leading her behind the pharmacy counter.

'Take a seat here. I'll get Lynn.'

She was back a moment later with an older woman, her short blonde hair silvering at the temples. She crouched next to Maggie and said, 'Okay, let's have a look then.'

Maggie removed her hand and winced as the nurse prodded her face.

'It could probably do with a couple of stitches, but I could put some steri-strips on it for you.' She used disinfectant wipes to clean the wound, then applied a couple of steri-strips to hold it closed and placed a small plaster over it. 'There, all set.'

Maggie stood and accepted a wipe from the nurse to clean the blood from her hand. 'How much do I owe you?'

'No charge.'

'Well, I'll need to pay for these.' There was blood on the tissue package and the plaster box. She couldn't very well put them back on the shelf now.

The woman who stopped her in the aisle said, 'Your money is no good here, DC Glass. Margaret Sinclair was my aunt. She went missing fourteen years ago. Earlier this week, they recovered her remains from the bottom of Duddingston Loch. Our family can have a proper funeral, thanks to you.'

Maggie hadn't even been aware they were searching for the bodies. She felt so out of touch. 'I'm happy you've got her back, although I'm sorry for your loss.'

'Thank you. I don't know how anyone could be upset with you for what you did. You're a hero in my family.' She pointed to Maggie's face. 'But, someone clearly slapped you. I can see the handprint. I'm sorry for all of the grief you're taking over this and I hope you get reinstated soon. We need more police officers like you.'

'Thank you. I'm not so sure that's going to happen.' Maggie brushed her fingers over her cheek. She hoped to hell the handprint faded and she didn't end up with a hand-shaped bruise. That would be humiliating.

When she arrived home, she had a flat full of people waiting on her – Sylvan, Iona, Nichola, MacLeod, DCC Drysdale, and a woman Maggie didn't know who was wearing the uniform of Chief Constable.

Drysdale made the introduction. 'DC Glass, this is our new Chief Constable, Kelly Evans.'

Evans held her hand out to Maggie and gave her a firm shake. 'It's a pleasure to meet you, DC Glass.'

'Likewise, Chief Constable.'

'I don't want to take too much of your time, but thought you'd like the news firsthand. All disciplinary action against you has been dismissed. You're officially reinstated, but you don't need to report for duty until Monday morning. Enjoy your weekend, DC.'

DCC Drysdale shook Maggie's hand. 'Welcome back. And thank you for your exemplary service. We're proud of you, DC Glass.'

As soon as Drysdale and Evans were out the door, Iona asked, 'Who the hell slapped you?'

'Shite.' Maggie covered her face with her hand. She looked like a fool in front of the Chief Constable and Deputy Chief. 'I thought I'd check on Aunt Eilean. Turns out she wasn't so pleased to see me.'

There was a loud pop and MacLeod stood with a bottle of

champagne and a wide grin. 'Welcome back, Glass.'

Iona passed around champagne flutes as MacLeod poured. Then he held up his glass and said, 'A toast to the cop with the biggest set of baws.' Everyone laughed. 'Seriously though, it's good to have you back.'

'Thank you.' Maggie raised her glass to her lips and sipped. Two weeks of suffering for nothing. She was glad it was over.

Maggie had a long talk with MacLeod that evening. He apologised for not talking to her earlier, then updated her on the cases against the Lords of Edinburgh. All of the investigations were going full steam ahead, with more and more evidence being collected daily.

It seemed the First Minister had made good on her promise as well. Jack Taggert's accomplices were being identified and dealt with. DCI McTavish was suspected of being in Taggert's pocket and was offered the option between a full investigation into his conduct or early retirement. He took retirement and was replaced by DCI Jane McDonald, an old friend of MacLeod's from his uniform days. Taggert also had contacts in the Fiscal's office, forensics, and just about every corner of the judicial system.

DI Liz Claymore had been able to reopen her investigation into Jack Lord after Maggie's interview as well. It seemed she'd been trying to ascertain Jack Lord's true identity for years. Under that pseudonym, Jack Taggert charged a hefty fee to ensure critical pieces of evidence went missing permanently. Most of his customers were high ranking drug dealers.

'Looks like I'll be coming back to a cleaner police service.'

'Aye,' MacLeod said with a nod. 'You're coming back a hero. A fecking hero, Glass.'

'I'm no hero. I just did what needed to be done.'

'Let me put it this way then, you've earned the respect of

all of your peers.'

Maggie nodded. She would take that.

The following morning, when Sylvan went off to work for her last day before Ghlais shut down for the holidays, Maggie walked across Holyrood Park and up the Royal Mile to the Castle Esplanade. The scorch mark was still visible on the tarmac where Jamie Kenmore had been murdered. Maggie gazed over at the Witches' Well. Nearly three hundred and sixty years had passed since the end of the witch hunts in Scotland and she wondered if they'd made any progress at all.

'Maggie?'

Maggie turned to find Kaleigh Logan walking towards her. 'Hiya.'

'I hear congratulations are in order. I was just about to announce the good news to our viewers. Care to join me?'

Maggie shook her head. 'I think I've had enough exposure, thank you.'

'It's a wonderful thing that you've achieved.'

'I'm sure you had a lot more to do with it than I did.' It was Logan's reports that fired up the nation. 'Thank you. I don't think I would have gotten my job back without you.'

'Oh, I don't know about that. You didn't deserve the suspension, never mind losing your job. Police officers like you should be celebrated, not punished.' She reached her hand out to Maggie. 'Friends?'

Maggie grasped Logan's hand, shook. If you'd told her a few weeks ago, when she first met Kaleigh Logan in this very spot, she'd be making friends with the woman, she wouldn't have believed it. 'Aye, friends.'

Epilogue

Maggie pulled in front of the Fonab Castle Hotel in Pitlochry, bathed in purple lights, and grinned at Sylvan's drop-jawed stare. 'I promised you I'd make up for a crappy weekend away.'

'I'd say this more than makes up for it and I told you it was no bother.'

'It's Christmas. I thought this would be a nice way to celebrate.'

'You didn't want to spend it with Iona?'

'She's with friends in Inverness.' Maggie got out and retrieved their suitcases from the back of the Range Rover. She wheeled them to the front desk with Sylvan by her side. 'Reservation for Glass.'

'Welcome to Fonab, DC Glass. You're booked into the Castle Penthouse for three nights.' The receptionist slid two keycards across the desk to Maggie. 'I'll have your luggage taken up. Is your car out front?'

'Aye. I can move it to the car park myself.' She passed one of the keycards to Sylvan. 'I'll be up in a minute.'

'Penthouse?' Sylvan whispered.

'Aye. And we're booked into the Woodland Spa tomorrow morning for the,' Maggie air quoted with her fingers, 'Fonabulous Spa Day.' That was Sylvan's first Christmas present.

After moving the car, Maggie found Sylvan standing in the middle of their room, gaping at her surroundings – the luxurious king-sized bed, vaulted wooden ceiling, crystal chandelier, and stone fireplace. And she hadn't even seen the views yet. Loch Faskally, Ben Vrackie, and Craigower Hill wouldn't be visible from their windows until morning. 'Will this do?'

Sylvan turned her head to Maggie, mouth still agape. 'Are you joking?'

'No, if you'd rather, I think there's a Premier Inn down the road.'

Sylvan stalked to Maggie and slid her arms around her waist. 'Well, we're here now. May as well tough it out.'

Maggie laughed then brushed her lips over Sylvan's. 'Happy Christmas.'

Smiling with her lips just touching Maggie's, Sylvan whispered, 'That's the first time in years hearing those two words together feels right.' She rested her forehead against Maggie's. 'I don't have anything to give you, except myself. If you're ready.' It wasn't Sylvan's reluctance that had kept them from making love these past couple of weeks. It was Maggie's despair.

Maggie released a quick laugh. 'I was going to say I was ready when we met, but that's not true. A few weeks ago, I wasn't capable of feeling what I feel for you now.'

'And what is it that you feel for me now?'

Maggie couldn't keep the grin from her face. She took Sylvan's hand and pressed it to her heart. 'Do you feel that? My heart is full with love for you. I love you, Sylvan.'

With a certainty she couldn't explain, Sylvan believed Maggie's words. 'I love you, too. So much.'

About Wendy Hewlett

This Scottish-born Canadian writer has returned to her roots. Originally planning to spend a year exploring Scotland, she has moved permanently to her birth city of Edinburgh and is loving life there.

Wendy began writing in earnest in 2011, after being laid off during the economic decline of the big three auto companies in North America. Her first novel, *Saving Grace*, has received a 5-Star Readers Choice Award and set the stage for the Taylor Sinclair Series of novels that have followed to date – *Unfinished Business, Runed, and Trafficked.*

Strong female characters are Wendy's passion and most of her main protagonists have suffered through childhood trauma, coming out the other side as strong, determined women. After *Saving Grace* was published, Wendy was awed and inspired by the women who contacted her to thank her for helping them to heal from their own childhood trauma. As a former Addictions counsellor, Wendy is well aware that there are far too many people, men and women, who have suffered trauma in their youth. The fact that she can help with their healing through her writing is humbling and motivating.

Wendy's other passions include reading, spending time with family and friends, and travelling and exploring Scotland. She hopes to spend more time travelling around Scotland, England, Wales, and Ireland … and possibly beyond.

Witches & Whisky is Wendy's eighth novel

published to date and she looks forward to continuing the Taylor Sinclair Series, the Solstice Coven Series, and the DC Maggie Glass Series.

Books by Wendy Hewlett

Taylor Sinclair Series
1. Saving Grace
2. Unfinished Business
3. Runed
4. Trafficked

Solstice Coven Series
1. High Priestess
2. Guardians of the Sacred Moon

DC Maggie Glass Series
1. Witches & Whisky

Stand Alone
Ailey of Skye

Visit the author's website at: wendyhewlett.com and sign up for her Monthly Newsletter to stay up to date on news, new releases, giveaways, and more.

Follow Wendy on:

Reviews are the bread and butter of an Indie Author's career. Please take a moment to write a quick review where you purchased this book. It is greatly appreciated and allows Wendy to continue writing and publishing page-turning novels with wonderful, strong female protagonists.